The Convict and the Rose

JAN SIKES

RiJan Publishing

The Convict And The Rose Copyright © 2014 by Jan Sikes

Cover Design by Donna Osborn Clark at: creationbydonna.com

Interior Design and Typesetting by: interiorbookdesigns.com

ISBN 978-0692203422

Without the love and support of my two amazing daughters, Deva and Crystal, my sister, Linda Broday and my amazing friend, Kay Perot, these stories would struggle to come into existence. Thank you from the bottom of my heart.

~Reviews~

The Convict and the Rose looks at a number of universal problems we all face and is an inspiring guide to making a better life regardless of our circumstances.

Dr. Bob Rich
Bobswriting.com

Jan shows a mastery for descriptive storytelling...

Sharon Galligar Chance
Sharon's Garden of Book Reviews

The narrative that takes place in this novel is realistic and raw...

Red City Reviews

The story is real life but is so big it seems like the best fiction ever!

George Martin

Jan has managed to make "real life" an exciting and touching experience.

Angela J. Shirley

Author, Jan Sikes has mastered the art of literary climax!

Katandra Jackson
FreedomInk Publishing

 Prologue

Date: March 29, 1981

A shiny Celebrity Coach tour bus pulled to a stop at the front entrance guard tower of Leavenworth Penitentiary.

"Declare your name and state your business," ordered the guard.

"My name is Tommy Overstreet and I'm here with my band, The Nashville Express, to play a show for the inmates."

"Do you have any firearms on your bus, Mr. Overstreet?"

"Yes. I have a 357 Magnum and ammunition."

"Please deposit the gun and all of the ammunition in the dumbwaiter and you can reclaim it on your way out."

Tommy followed the instructions. He couldn't help thinking how the stark place resembled a mausoleum, but with razor wire and guard towers. Cold chills ran down his spine.

The bus driver parked at the front entrance. Tommy and the band climbed out and eyed the long set of stairs leading to the door. They had no choice but to carry all of their instruments and equipment up the steps.

While the band unloaded equipment, Tommy went inside where he met the warden and chief guard. They welcomed him, thanked him for donating his time to entertain the prisoners, and lastly informed him that all inmates had been instructed not to speak to him or any of the band members without permission.

"I don't have any problem speaking to any of the inmates who want to talk to me," Tommy assured them.

One by one, their amplifiers, speakers, cable boxes instruments and cases were thoroughly examined by guards before they were brought through the main door. Each member of the band, along with Tommy had to submit to a search. Then they were allowed to enter the theater where they would perform.

The band began setting up, assisted by a select handful of prisoners. Tommy stood backstage visiting with the chief guard.

"Just out of curiosity, what did that husky blonde-haired guy helping my sound man do to get locked up?"

"Allegedly, he asked his father to loan him $20. When his father refused, he killed him, then drove across the state line so he'd get federal time. Then he turned himself in. He got five years."

Another guard approached with a note, which he handed to Tommy.

The note read, "I don't know if you remember me or not, but I'd like to talk to you," signed Rick Sikes.

Tommy looked up at the guard. "Of course I remember this man and yes, I'd like very much to talk to him."

"They want to know if his bass player, Red, can come back too."

"Of course." Tommy puzzled over this turn of events. He'd known Rick back in the days of the Slim Willett Big State Jamboree in Abilene and had wondered whatever happened to him.

Within a few minutes, two men escorted by a guard, approached.

Rick put out his hand. "Tommy, man it's good to see you. This is my bass player, Red Jenkins."

Tommy shook the men's hands. "My God, Rick what are you doing in here?"

"Well, times got hard. Allegedly, I robbed a bank." Rick chuckled.

"I'd never have recognized you in a million years." Shock washed over him. Rick was tall and thin with slightly stooped shoulders, he wore a white t-shirt, brown khaki pants and handmade moccasins. A silver cross necklace along with Indian beads hung around his neck. He had long hair pulled back into a pony tail and a full beard.

"Yeah, lots of things have changed for sure. I've been reading about you in the Country music magazines. You've made quite a splash. I remember us both just starting out on Slim Willett's jamboree in Abilene. That seems like a million years ago now." Rick replied.

Tommy asked. "Is there some place we can sit and visit, maybe get a cup of coffee?"

"Sure thing."

The men walked out into the hallway, accompanied by a guard. Tommy noted that the wide hallways were polished to a high gloss.

Once they reached the cafeteria, with cups of coffee in hand, the men sat at a long table.

Tommy talked about the places he'd been touring. He was having success with several of his songs making it to number one on the Country Music Charts over the past few years. Then he asked Rick to tell him about prison life.

Rick recounted an incident. "My cell is on the main floor and there are tiers of cells up above me. I was working on a painting in my cell one afternoon when I heard a dripping sound. I looked around, but didn't see anything. I went back to painting and the sound got louder. Finally, I looked out my cell door and saw a puddle of blood forming on the concrete. It was dripping down from the cell above me and I had splatters of blood on my pants leg. I threw down my paints, washed the blood out of my clothes the best I could and hauled ass out to the yard. Of course, they called me into the interrogation room since my cell was directly below where the inmate had been murdered. Thank God I had the good sense to get out of there. I knew who had killed the guy, but I couldn't say a word or I'd be next. That's how it is in here."

After a while, Tommy stood. "I've got to go get ready for the show, but it sure was good seeing you, although I'd much rather it be under different circumstances."

"Me too, hoss. I'd like a picture with you, if that's alright," Rick requested.

"Of course. Come back to the theater with me."

Tommy's view on the show he did that day, was that the prisoners were uninterested, for the most part. They were simply happy to be out of their cells and offered polite applause.

Before Tommy left the prison, he and Rick exchanged addresses. They corresponded over the next few years and in 1983, Tommy Overstreet wrote a letter to the Texas Board of Pardons and Paroles on Rick's behalf, asking that he be considered for parole.

Tommy never got over the stark difference between the five year sentence one man got for murder compared to Rick's seventy five year sentence for two alleged bank robberies in which no one was harmed, much less killed.

Interview with Tommy Overstreet on 1-11-14
(Used with permission.)

"They locked me in a tiny cell, made my life a miserable hell."

Chapter 1

The stone cold gray walls and unforgiving steps leading to Leavenworth Penitentiary spared no welcome to Luke Stone as he descended from the prison bus.

Iron ankle chains chafed his skin and the heavy handcuffs and belly chain bit into his wrists. He hopped from the bottom step to the ground and cast a wary glance at his destination.

The man ahead of him stumbled and fell to his knees. The guard quickly prodded him with his night stick. "Get up, convict. No lagging behind."

Luke gritted his teeth and tightened his jaw but remained in line.

The formidable steps grew as he went. Thirty-seven...thirty-eight...The chains gnawed at the skin around his ankles...number forty-two. The massive doors groaned open, ready to swallow his life as he passed through.

Guards escorted the prisoners through a total of six heavy metal doors leading deeper into the belly of the prison. They slammed shut with a deadly ring that echoed off the stone walls.

Jaw set, eyes as hard as the steel that held him captive, Luke shuffled forward.

Armed guards stood with pointed guns, ready to fire at any sign of aggression as they lined the new prisoners up in military fashion.

Luke glared as a lieutenant removed his chains. "Welcome to Leavenworth Penitentiary, boys. You're in admissions and orientation." A captain walked down the line looking each convict in the eye. "This is gonna be your home for a while, so I suggest you treat it as such."

Luke didn't blink when the man paused in front of him. He'd never think of this prison as home. Thoughts of his family back in Texas crowded his mind, leaving an incurable ache inside his chest.

How could he have let himself get so reckless and uncaring? He'd been a damn fool to get caught in the tangled mess that landed him behind bars.

Standing to the left of Luke, Tommy "Red" Johnson shifted from one foot to the other. The sheriff of Tom Green County had sneered when he announced to them that as rap partners, being sentenced at the same time for the same crime, they would cell together in Leavenworth.

It had been a long trip from Texas to Kansas. Luke hoped this orientation bullshit wouldn't last much longer.

The words from the aging judge still echoed in his brain. "Luther Martin Stone, I hereby sentence you to twenty-five years in the federal penitentiary for armed bank robbery. This sentence is to run concurrently with the fifty year State of Texas sentence you already have."

Shit! That was a lifetime. He longed for freedom and the open sky. His identity now consisted of a number, 87047-132. The last three digits indicated where the arrest and conviction took place. He guessed the first part of the number was simply the next available in line since Red's was 87046-132. At any rate, the number would forever be branded in his DNA.

Red's sentence, identical to his, put him in captivity alongside Luke. Now here they stood, like a herd of cattle at Leavenworth Penitentiary, on December 12, 1971.

The continuing nightmare unfolded one dreadful scene at a time.

Luke's naked skin burned as a blast from the water hose and the chemicals it contained hit him with force. Like the other convicts, he tried to dodge the onslaught. After gritting his teeth through a humiliating cavity search, a guard issued him a set of clothing consisting of khaki pants, a white t-shirt and a button-up khaki shirt. Among too many things to name, he missed the blue jeans, boots and western shirts he'd customarily worn on the outside.

Once dressed, guards ushered the new inmates into a rectangular room where a lieutenant delivered further instructions. "You'll stay in the admissions and orientation unit of this facility until you receive job and cell block assignments. Your personal belongings are being processed and will be returned to you once they are inspected and approved."

Luke and Red followed the rest of the men into another long narrow room where twenty or more metal cots lined the walls. Coarse cotton sheets and a thin wool army blanket lay on each bed. The frigid December air permeated the stone walls, settling deep into their bones.

Luke located his prison number on a card attached to a cot and plopped down.

Red's was the next bed down the line. He sat down, lit a cigarette, passed it to Luke and then lit another for himself.

"Well hoss, this sure ain't no kind of a home and it's damned cold here in this Yankee prison." Luke took a long drag off his cigarette.

Red reached for the blanket lying on his cot and wrapped it around his shoulders. "Fuckin' cold for sure." He lowered his voice glancing around. "I learned when I was locked up in Florida that kitchen duty is the job to ask for. We can get a hustle goin' tradin' shit to moonshiners for cigarettes and coffee."

"At least it'd be warm in the fuckin' kitchen. We'll ask for it. We've gotta stick together." Luke stood and spread the sheets and blanket on the cot.

A captain made his way down the row of beds. He paused to watch Luke haphazardly spreading the sheets. "Stone, that ain't no way to make a bed." His voice cut into Luke like a razor blade.

"What do you mean?" Luke struggled to keep his voice even as he turned to face the uniformed man.

"You're supposed to make your bed military style."

"Is that so?" Luke's eyes narrowed.

"Don't know what military style is?"

"The only military I've ever recognized was the Confederate Army and they didn't have a damn thing except a blanket to sleep on the ground, if they had that much."

The captain snorted. "I'm going to show you once how to do it. You need to bounce a quarter off the sheets."

"No disrespect sir, but quarters ain't allowed in here."

The captain's face flushed. He made the bed and tightened the sheets down, then bounced a quarter off them. "That's the way it's done, smart ass, and that's the way I want to see it from now on."

Luke lay back on the metal cot and the man moved on down the line.

Red attempted to imitate what the captain had done. "Hell, I didn't know we were gonna to be in a military prison."

"We ain't, stud. They can't throw us out of here for not making our bed right, so fuck 'em." The rebel spirit he'd lived with all of his life rose up full force. What could they do to him? He was already in prison, so what else?

"Man, I don't wanna get in trouble and be sent to the hole."

"Shit, Red, we're already in the hole."

"Solitary confinement's different. You're in there all by yourself."

"That sounds damned good to me. Think if I don't make my bed right, they'll take me to the hole?"

"I don't know, man, but I don't wanna go."

The men lay on the hard cots and finished their cigarettes. The smokes would have to last until they could get some goods to trade for more.

Being a survivor, Luke Stone knew he could make it in prison. His size and toughness served him well on the outside and would here too. He'd never taken any shit off anyone and wasn't about to start now, prison be damned!

He wasn't sure about Red, but he'd protect the smaller man with his life. Hell, Red was like a brother to him. They'd been through a lot together.

A few days later, they received their cell assignment and started kitchen duty. The caseworker questioned both of them as to their reasons for wanting that particular job. It was common knowledge that convicts generally hated working in the kitchen.

Sticking to the plan, they proclaimed an interest in going into the restaurant business when they got out of prison. The caseworker bought their story.

It didn't take long to figure out how to smuggle sugar, fruit juice, bread dough from the huge vat, tomato paste and anything else that could be used to make booze. They secured the loot in plastic bags and taped them to their legs inside the baggy khakis they wore.

***

Christmas Eve came and Luke discovered how little the holidays meant inside these walls. Not one bit of Christmas spirit could be found. The small aluminum Christmas tree with a couple of scraggly ornaments did nothing to help.

Luke and Red were invited by one of the Indian moonshiners who they supplied, to come down to his cell after count for a drink.

Having learned quickly the necessity of staying alert, Luke watched over his shoulder at all times. Men who let their guard down didn't survive. In the short time he'd been there, he'd already witnessed one murder and several beatings.

When they reached the moonshiner's cell, Luke shot a glance in both directions down the long tier, before entering.

Inside the cell, a tall Indian guy named Joe dipped a cup of what looked and smelled like throw-up out of a plastic bag he pulled out of his locker. He poured it into their cups.

"Thanks man," Luke said. He wondered what Joe's crime had been but also knew that you never ask. The stench of the homemade tomato hooch almost made him gag.

Red took a big swig and wiped his mouth with the back of his hand. "This ain't Jim Beam, but it'll do."

Luke forced a couple of sips and his stomach began burning as if a fire had been lit in it. He made polite talk, then excused himself and strode back to his cell.

He'd drank a lot of booze in his lifetime but nothing like this and decided that he'd rather do without than drink the haphazardly made hooch.

Two weeks later after their work shift ended for the day, Luke and Red made their way to the recreation room, where inmates could watch TV, play dominoes or cards.

A few older men with dull-eyed stares sat at the front of the room watching a small TV. Some black men sat behind them and farther back were the Indians and Mexicans. A re-run of *Gunsmoke* blared through the room.

The two men sat down in the back and lit smokes, of which they now had an ample supply from trading with the moonshiners.

After a few minutes, a large burly black man sauntered to the front of the room and changed the TV channel.

The older men grumbled loudly, but no one moved. Luke had no tolerance for bullying. He walked up to the TV and switched it back to *Gunsmoke*.

"Hey, motha' fucker! What do you think you're doing?" The black man yelled.

"I'm changin' the TV back to the show these men were watchin', asshole. I didn't hear you ask anyone if you could change it."

The man stood, legs spread. "Nobody pushes me around."

"Show him what happens to whiteys in here that don't mind their fuckin' business, Eugene," a man bellowed.

"If you don't like it, come on and let's do something about it, you sonofabitch." Luke glanced around for anything that would serve as a weapon.

In the back corner of the room, he spotted a mop with a wooden handle in a bucket. He made a beeline for it and turned around as the man raised his fist to hit him.

A resounding crack filled the air as Luke broke the mop handle over the man's head. He fell to his knees, flailing his arms. Luke continued beating him and kicking him until he sprawled on the floor in a puddle of blood.

Within minutes, a swarm of guards surrounded them. They quickly pulled Luke off the man, cuffed him, and requested a gurney for Eugene.

"What in the hell is going on here?" the guard holding Luke growled.

"This sonofabitch came at me. I had no choice."

"We don't tolerate fighting in here. I can send you to the hole for this offense."

"Take my ass to the hole. I don't give a fuck. From what I've seen so far, this entire place is a hole."

The guard motioned to two other officers. "Get this man out of here!"

Inside the small isolated boxlike cell, Luke lay on the hard cot in the semi-dark. It was finally quiet. No noise from the hundreds of other men who shared the cell block with him. No radios, no yelling, no sounds of masturbating or rape. He relaxed for the first time since he'd been escorted through the doors of Leavenworth.

For a brief moment, he allowed himself to think of Darlina Flowers, the sweet lady he'd left behind in Texas. She had captured his heart completely and often invaded his thoughts in the wee hours of morning. The familiar floral smell of her silky auburn hair etched in memory haunted him. He ached for her touch, the taste of her warm lips and her sensuous body.

In anger, he pushed her out of his mind. He couldn't let himself have a weakness for anyone or anything.

He knew the fight with Eugene wasn't over. There would be retaliation.

Animal instincts were all he had to rely on in order to survive in this place and he'd use all of his senses to stay alive. He'd dared to dance with the devil and damned if it didn't look like the devil was winning.

"Trouble has no friends. Winners win from losers..."

Chapter 2

Luke kept a continual furtive watch for the man called Eugene, after being released from the hole. He knew the man would come for him at the first opportunity.

With kitchen duty finished for the day, Luke and Red walked down the long narrow hallways that led back to their cell block.

The muscles in Luke's arms tensed and his jaw clenched when he saw Eugene walking toward them. "This is it, Red."

He put his hand into his right pocket where he now carried a crudely fashioned prison shank honed from a simple butter knife taken from the kitchen.

Eugene continued to walk toward them. He stopped five yards from Luke. "We ain't got no problem, do we brother?"

Luke narrowed his eyes. "First of all, asshole, I ain't your fuckin' brother. You ain't no kin to me. We ain't got no problem as long as you stay the hell away."

"I don't need no problems, man."

"Me either. Just keep the fuck away and we won't have any."

Eugene turned and walked back in the direction he'd come.

"What in the hell do you make of that, Luke?" Red spoke in a hushed voice.

"Shit, I don't know. I was ready for him." Luke relaxed his hand.

Still puzzling over the episode, several days later, Luke questioned a convict he worked with in the kitchen.

"Roy, you're pretty tight with the group Eugene hangs with. What's up with him?"

"Shit man, you don't know? Word's out that you're fuckin' crazy and to stay the hell out of your way."

"Well that's a damned good deal because I am fuckin' crazy like the kind of crazy you can only find in Texas and I'll cut any sonofabitch's throat that messes with me or Red." Luke stabbed a piece of overcooked processed turkey with a large kitchen fork.

"I'm only tellin' you what they're sayin', man. Eugene's one of the biggest and baddest mothas in here and you fucked him up."

Eyes narrowed, Luke replied. "Yeah, well if he ever comes at me again, he won't be fucked up, he'll be dead."

Turning away, Luke felt a sort of strange exhilaration. If being crazy was the way to survive this hell hole, then he'd be the meanest and craziest bastard that ever walked through the doors. It wasn't what he wanted, but then none of this shit was what he wanted.

Luke Stone walked a little taller and swaggered a little more that day. Damned if he'd let this place suck the spirit out of him.

Following the end of another shift, Luke and Red returned to cell block D. The captain in charge called Luke into his office.

"Yeah, what do you want?"

"Stone, I've got my eye on you. I know what the convicts are sayin' about you. I don't want any trouble on my watch."

"Me neither, cap'n. Is that all?"

"You can go, but I'm warning you, I'm watching." The captain dismissed Luke with a wave of his hand.

Back in the cell, Red's curiosity took over. "What did the cap'n want with you? He lit another cigarette off the one that hadn't yet gone out.

"Nothin'. Said he was watchin' me. Now that we have cigarettes to trade, think we could rustle us up a couple of those little transistor radios like some of the men have?"

"That shouldn't be hard to do. I'd like that myself. I wish they had some decent instruments down in the music room. I miss playin'."

"Me too, hoss. Sure would like to strum on my ol' Martin again. Don't reckon there's any way they'd let me have it in here."

"Probably not."

Luke picked up his writing tablet and penned a letter home. Red shuffled cards for a poker game with their other two cellmates.

***

Mail call became a very important part of the day. Letters from anyone on the outside were like a breath of fresh air in a deep dark mine shaft.

Today, he held in his hands a letter from his mom and dad. He read each word slowly. He longed to sit with them at the round oak kitchen table again, drinking coffee and eating homemade chocolate pie.

His mom rattled on about the holidays and how happy they were when Joyce let them take all the kids for a few hours. The backs of his eyelids stung with unshed tears.

He saw the faces of his children: Joseph with his tough boy attitude, Lexxi with her turned up nose and uncanny ability to know things before they happened, Martin with his stubborn ways and Nathan who struggled to keep up with the older boys. His throat constricted when he thought of the hardship he'd placed on his children by being arrogant, reckless and foolish.

Hopeless despair washed over him like a thick heavy fog rolling in off the ocean. He hated the helpless feeling that gripped him.

His kids were having a tough time and he'd give anything if he could change things. They didn't deserve any of this.

"Time to go to chow hall, Luke." Red interrupted his thoughts.

"You go ahead, stud. I'm not hungry." Luke placed the letter back in the envelope.

"You've been skipping a lot of chow lately. You okay?"

"Yeah, I'm all right. Can't quite stomach the slop they're shovin' out. Hell, you've seen the convicts in the kitchen hack and spit in the food. Don't know how you can still eat it."

"Shit, I'm hungry. That's how. I don't think about it."

"Then go on without me. I'm gonna stay here and answer Mom's letter."

"Tell 'em howdy for me." Red joined the other convicts.

Luke placed small plastic ear phones in his ears and turned the dial on the transistor radio to a Kansas City country music station. Red turned out to be a pretty damned good hustler and Luke now had tablets, pencils, coffee, cigars and a radio.

He took a long drag off his King Edward and settled back to answer the letter from home, wishing he could stuff himself in the envelope and magically be back with his loved ones.

A package of peanut butter crackers and a cup of instant coffee fed him another prison supper. Survival came naturally to him.

He thought of Darlina and wished he had her address. How he would love to get sweet perfumed letters from her. He sighed and wrote, "*Dear Mom and Dad.*"

By the time Red returned, Luke had finished the letter and two poems to send along with it.

The other two men who shared their cell came in behind Red with news that there would soon be a new warden in Leavenworth. Luke listened to them talk, not caring one way or the other about the old or new warden.

"They say he's a Harvard man," the one they called Ace reported.

"I don't give a damn if he's from Harvard or a shoeshine boy, he's takin' on a shitty job." Luke turned his back to the others and sprawled onto his bunk.

"Heard that he wants to meet each of us personally," the other cell mate they called Georgie added.

"Really?" Luke sat up suddenly interested. "Talk to each one of us?"

"That's what I heard."

"When is this new warden supposed to be here?"

"Soon's all I know." The men pulled out metal chairs and sat down, shuffling a deck of cards.

Luke pondered this news while the men and Red played poker. If it's true and he will talk to each convict, he'd damn sure be there. He had lots to say.

Time passed slowly behind the forty foot walls of Leavenworth Penitentiary. With Red's expert trading skills, he and Luke began to accumulate a few belongings and an extra pair of long johns was the latest commodity acquired. Finally, they would both be warm for the first time since they'd arrived.

Several weeks later, the prisoners were informed of a mandatory meeting in the auditorium.

Buzz of the new warden's arrival spread up and down the cell blocks.

Luke could only hope that this warden might actually listen to the men's concerns. The threadbare thin mattresses they slept on were filthy and so old they might have come over on Noah's ark. The food was barely more than slop a farmer might feed his hogs. He made a mental list of all the things he would mention when he got a chance, including asking permission to get his guitar shipped in to him.

As the long lines of prisoners filed into the auditorium, Luke wondered how this warden would manage to speak to over 1,800 prisoners individually.

Once seated, the associate warden approached the microphone. "Quiet please! Everyone quiet down. We've got a few announcements to make tonight and you all need to listen."

The noise gradually subsided.

"I want all of you men to respectfully welcome the new warden of Leavenworth Federal Penitentiary." Turning to his left, he motioned to a tall thin man with graying hair, in a double-breasted suit and Italian made shoes.

"Warden Sutton, come say a few words to the residents."

The man took the microphone with a flourish, sporting a diamond ring that flashed in the lights as he shook the associate warden's hand.

Turning to face the prisoners, he spoke with a Boston accent. "I'm George T. Sutton and I'm proud to be the new warden of this fine facility. There are a few things that I want to change here and I expect that each of you will respect and strictly adhere to them."

Luke began to get a sense of foreboding as the man continued.

"First of all, I want to emphasize that violence of any kind will not be tolerated and you will be punished harshly for any provocation. I demand that all of you men clean and maintain your quarters. You are subject to search and seizure without notice. If contraband of any kind is found, you'll be punished accordingly. You will be expected to regularly visit the barber. I will not tolerate your hair touching your collar at any time."

Luke glanced around as some of the men grumbled. Most of the complaints about the short hair came from the Jamaican and Virgin Island prisoners. Once again, he felt the familiar rebel spirit rise up. He sprang to his feet.

In seconds, guards surrounded him. "Sit down! The warden ain't done talking."

"Yeah, well, I'm done listenin', podnah."

"You can't leave." The guards grabbed his arms.

The warden grew silent and all eyes in the auditorium turned to Luke and the scene unfolding.

Finally the warden spoke. "Guards, please remove this prisoner from the auditorium so that I may continue."

The guards pushed him toward the door. Turning, Luke shouted, "I thought you were gonna to talk to us, Warden. This is just more bullshit!"

At that, a guard hit him across the shoulders with his night stick and shoved him through the exit door.

In the hallway, they quickly cuffed him. "What the hell is wrong with you, Stone? You know you can't talk to the warden like that."

"Fuck you. Fuck him. Fuck this whole fuckin' place!"

A captain approached the group. "Take him to the hole, men. I think he needs time to think."

"Yeah, take me to the fuckin' hole. Leave me in the fuckin' hole. See if I give a shit."

"Oh you'll give a shit after you're over there for a while, tough boy." The guards dragged him down the hall.

Once inside the solitary confinement section of the prison, three guards roughly pushed Luke into a cell hardly bigger than a box. They took turns beating him with their sticks, kicking him with their heavy boots when he fell to the floor and slamming his face against the concrete.

Satisfied they'd taught him a lesson, they backed out of the cell and flung the door shut.

Luke lay in a pool of blood, barely moving. The handcuffs bit into his wrists as he tried to raise himself up.

Anger boiled up like steam in a pressure cooker. If only he hadn't been handcuffed, he'd have made them sorry they'd ever been born. Damn this place! Damn it all!

He finally managed to sit up against the wall. With his head back, blood trickled down his face and onto his khakis. He began to plan his escape. He had to find a way out of this hell hole. He vowed to show them that they couldn't beat him down.

He envisioned himself climbing the forty foot walls that surrounded him and dropping down the other side. It wouldn't matter if they shot him or if the fall killed him. Either way, he would find freedom.

And being free was all that mattered.

"Tomorrows are maybes but still I'll hold you tight."

Chapter 3

Darlina Flowers towel-dried her long auburn hair and opened the windows in her apartment. Spring filled the air and bright sunshine filtered through the curtains as a gentle breeze rustled them.

April 30, 1972 was shaping up to be a beautiful spring day. The radio played *"Bye bye Miss American Pie. Drove my chevy to the levy but the levy was dry..."*

She hummed along with the song and looked forward to a long ride in the countryside on the back of William Brocker's Harley Davidson with its long raked front and high chrome handlebars. After Luke's incarceration, Will had turned out to be one person who didn't judge her or Luke.

She loved riding on the motorcycle with him and even though six months had passed since her sister had first introduced them, they'd never kissed or shared more than a brief hug. It provided a comfortable friendship Darlina desperately needed.

Sipping a fresh cup of coffee, she sat at a small kitchen table and let her vision drift out the open window. A fat robin perched on the tree branch and a butterfly floated by.

As they so often did, her thoughts turned to Luke Stone. There was no forgetting their first encounter at the Faded Rose where she worked part-time as a fledgling go-go dancer and waitress. She'd been drawn to him like a moth to an all consuming flame. They couldn't have been more opposite – her, young and naïve, and him a seasoned Texas musician with two marriages under his belt. He took her breath away and captured her heart completely. What a rollercoaster ride he'd taken her on from his first indecent proposal to an unbreakable bond of love that formed between them.

If only he hadn't been sent to prison, things would have been so different. She gazed at the small photograph on a shelf; a memory frozen in time from a trip to Mexico with Luke. He'd made her feel alive, made her feel loved and most of all, made her feel like a woman. How was she supposed to live now without those things?

An idea hit her like a bolt of lightning along with an urge so strong it shook her. Why hadn't she thought of this before?

She needed Luke's address. Letters would be a much better than imaginary conversations. The only sure way of getting that would be through Luke's parents, whom she'd met what now seemed like, a lifetime ago.

Without any hesitation, she picked up the phone. Once Will's voice came on the other end, the words gushed. "I can't go riding with you today, Will. I have to go to Brownwood."

"Okay. Want me to take you. We could ride over there."

"No. This is something I've gotta do by myself."

"I'll miss having you behind me today."

She thought she heard sadness in his voice. "Tell you what. I'll be back by five o'clock and if you're still out and about, come on by."

"Sure you don't need my help?"

"I'm sure. I'll explain everything when I see you." She hung up the phone and rushed to get dressed in bell-bottom jeans and baby blue peasant blouse.

Would she remember the way to Mr. and Mrs. Stone's house at Lake Brownwood? Would they even talk to her? A million butterflies fluttered in her stomach.

If she stood any chance of getting Luke's address, it would be through his parents.

On the road between Abilene and Brownwood, she tuned the radio to a local country music station. Conway Twitty, Jerry Lee Lewis, Tammy Wynette, Loretta Lynn and Merle Haggard crooned one hit after another. They took her back to the happy days when she rode up and down the Texas roads with Luke and his band.

Luke Stone and The Rebel Rousers were undoubtedly the most popular country band in Texas from the 1960s until the federal government took him away for a crime he did not commit.

Darlina determined not to allow herself to cry. She shouldn't look a mess in case she did find Mr. and Mrs. Stone.

Once the Brown County sign came into view, she searched her mind for the route that Luke drove, the day he took her to meet his folks.

Highway 36 passed beside Brownwood Lake, but none of the roads looked familiar.

In the parking lot of the Lakewood Club, she contemplated her next move.

Maybe if she started from the apartment she and Luke had shared, the road would be more familiar.

Her heart raced and her breath caught in her throat. Being back where she'd lived with and loved Luke gave her weary heart a blow.

She turned the car around and drove into Brownwood with trembling hands. Once she turned onto Cottage Street, all the resolve and determination not to cry disappeared in a flash.

The duplex apartment at the end of the street that once glowed with their sweet and tender love sat abandoned. Weeds grew in the yard and boards covered the windows.

She turned into the driveway and killed the engine.

Great sobs wracked her body. How foolish to think she could come back here and not re-live the pain, hurt and sorrow all over again.

Startled by a hand on her shoulder through the open car window she looked up.

"Can I help you, miss?" A gray haired man peered in.

"I...I...I'm looking for somebody," Darlina answered shakily.

"Well, if it's Luke Stone yer lookin' for, he ain't nowhere 'round here."

"I know. I'm looking for his folks, but I can't remember the way to their house." She attempted to wipe her eyes and blew her nose into a tissue.

"Can't help you there. Don't reckon you oughta be here though. Hear tell the law still watches this place in case any of them bank robbers come back around." The old man ran his fingers through his stubble of a beard.

"I'm leavin' now." Darlina started the engine and backed slowly out into the street, then giving the apartment one last longing look, pulled away.

Her clammy hands gripped the steering wheel and she looked ahead with unseeing eyes. The Piggly Wiggly store around the corner seemed like a safe place to park and think.

Luke's words echoed in her mind. *"I'm thirty-five years old with a fifty year prison sentence....promise me you'll forget about me and get on with your life."*

She'd promised Luke that day she would try, knowing full well she could never forget.

She only wanted an address. Was that asking too much? Was she simply being a foolish young girl grasping at a dream that could never be? What to do?

After some time of watching people dressed up for church come and go from the grocery store, she started the engine and headed back toward Abilene.

She searched the roads as she drove, looking for anything that might jog her memory, but saw nothing. Wishing she'd paid more attention that day, she had no choice but to go back to Abilene. She'd failed.

Down in the dumps, sitting outside on the curb, she looked up when Will pulled into the driveway on his rumbling Harley.

She stood as he came to a stop and got off.

"Are you okay, Darlina?" He laid a hand lightly on her shoulder.

"No, I'm not, but I will be. Can we ride?" She put her arm around his waist and they walked to the motorcycle.

By now, she was a pro at hopping on and off the big bike and soon they were roaring down the street and out into the country.

Darlina sucked the spring evening air deep into her lungs as the scooter sped down a two lane road. One by one the cobwebs cleared from her brain.

Luke was locked away for a very long time and that was a cold hard fact. How foolish to hold on to the dream that one day he would get out of prison and come back to her.

Sitting next to the lake on a large boulder, Will finally broke the silence.

"You wanna tell me what's going on?"

Darlina turned to look at him. "I had to work through some things today."

"And did you?"

She slid off the rock and positioned herself between Will's legs, facing him. Then without another word, pulled his face down to hers and kissed him. He didn't kiss her back, but didn't push away.

Pulling back, she replied. "I think I did."

"You know I'll listen if you wanna talk."

"I know but I don't wanna talk." She raised herself up on her tip toes and kissed him again.

This time, he wrapped his arms around her and returned the kiss.

The bright moon shone down on the two as they cautiously held each other and for a moment, Darlina almost believed it smiled at her.

Somehow, bit by bit, she would force the sweet memory of Luke back into the recesses of her mind where it belonged.

Perhaps a new life could begin with Will and although they didn't share deep undying love or passion, what they did have was comfortable.

She'd had the other and suffered the pain of losing it. She never wanted to feel that kind of intense agony ever again.

No, this time she would play it safe and enjoy the ease of having a friend like Will.

After a while, Darlina removed herself from Will's embrace and sat beside him on the boulder.

"That was nice." Will reached into his pocket for a joint and lit it, passing it to Darlina.

"Yes it was."

"Want to tell me what brought that on?" Will took a drag off the joint.

"I think it's time for me to get on with my own life and put past memories in their place." A stray tear trickled down her cheek.

"Some things in life aren't meant to be forgotten. Don't be too hard on yourself."

They sat in silence for a while, sharing the joint and staring at the glassy blue water.

Finally Darlina spoke. "I know I won't ever forget Luke Stone, but I'm ready to put that part of my life away and start over, or at least try."

"Well, if that involves kissing again, I'm all for it." Will chuckled.

Darlina reached for his hand. "I have a feeling it just might."

An easy silence returned and after some time, Will slid off the boulder, helped Darlina down and climbed on the motorcycle.

Riding back to town, Darlina thought about the kisses and tried not to compare them to Luke's. They didn't come close, but she didn't mind settling for a safe comfortable relationship with Will.

By the time they arrived back at her apartment, sadness dissipated, she cautiously dared to think that perhaps life could be good again if she let it.

No, Will wasn't Luke Stone, but the fact remained that no one was.

Luke would forever live in her heart but she needed more than a memory.

With that thought, the future appeared less gloomy.

"I'm a forgotten part in an unwritten play..."

Chapter 4

SEVERAL MONTHS LATER

Luke Stone spent a lot of time in solitary confinement. With each day that passed in Leavenworth Penitentiary, he grew more sullen, withdrawn and bitter.

Red, on the other hand, managed to make a few friends and during the periods of time that Luke was in the hole, he carried on with prison life in the best way he could.

Frigid cold winter morphed into a blazing hot summer and as uncomfortable as the cold had been, the hot days proved to be just as intolerable. The yard turned out to be the only place where temporary relief from the stifled air inside the walls could be found.

The prisoners could take advantage of the basketball courts, play football, jog or any other ways they wanted to get physical exercise.

Luke and Red walked the perimeter of the yard, shirts off soaking up the sunshine. Red stopped to light a cigarette when he was bumped from behind.

He whirled around, coming face-to-face with a man sneering at him. "Got any more of those cigs?"

"What if I do?"

"Then give me some." The man advanced toward him.

Luke stepped between the man and Red. "Hey hoss, I suggest you walk away while you still can."

"What are you gonna do, big man?"

Luke put his right hand in his pocket. "I'll cut your fuckin' throat. That's what I'll do."

"Shit man. I just wanted a cigarette."

"Then you damned well better learn how to ask if you don't wanna' wind up dead." Luke curled his lip back in a snarl.

The man turned away grumbling to himself.

"You didn't have to take up for me, Luke."

"Don't let anybody bully you, stud. If they do, you let me handle it." Luke fell in step beside the smaller man.

"All right, but I'll be okay."

The two men continued their walk around the yard. Red spoke to several of the men as they passed, being much more social than Luke.

One hot summer evening, Luke leaned against the wall on his sweltering bunk, listening to the current country music of the day playing through his transistor radio ear plugs.

The pit of his stomach burned as if it were being eaten away by acid. Something was wrong and he knew it, but he had no faith in the quacks they called prison doctors. The horror stories he'd heard from other convicts gave him plenty of room to doubt their medical abilities. Hell, he heard of a man who went in with a sore throat and came away with one less toe.

He opened a bag of Fritos along with a pint of milk and poured them together. It faintly resembled the cornbread and milk he'd loved to eat on the outside and the milk soothed his burning stomach for a while.

Haggard and growing thinner, he ate very little.

***

What in the hell was Joyce going to pull next? A letter from home informed him that she'd taken a job at the local hospital as a nurse's aide only to be fired for stealing drugs. He knew his kids were suffering. All of it along with the burning acid gnawed away at his gut.

If only he could claw his way out of this hell hole and get to his family.

Early morning found him and Red walking down the familiar hallway to go work in the kitchen as they did every day.

A sharp prod came from behind. Luke whirled around, fists closed and raised only to find a guard grinning at him.

"What the fuck do you want?" Luke barked.

The guard took his night stick and put it under Luke's chin, raising his head. "Looks like you need to visit the barber, Stone. You're hair's touchin' your collar."

Luke brushed the stick away. "It wasn't 'til you pushed my head back, asshole."

"You can't speak to a correctional officer like that, convict."

"I just did. What are you gonna do about it? Throw me back in the hole? Beat me some more? What?" Every muscle in Luke's body tensed.

The guard grinned at him. "Nah, not this time. Get your ass over to the barber shop today, though."

Luke whirled around without a reply and after a few steps turned to his friend. "Red, why do you reckon they want to constantly fuck with me?"

"It's simple, Luke. Because you won't conform. They want to break you."

"And what if I don't break?"

Red's voice was hushed, "Then they'll kill you."

Luke thought over Red's answer, knowing full well he spoke the truth. He couldn't make this penitentiary be different and the stress of the fight had already taken its toll.

"Then maybe I'll take on the Uncle Tom, hat-in-hand attitude. I can grin and call the guards "boss man" but I'll be thinkin' "sonofabitch.""

"Whatever works for you, Luke."

The two men continued on their way to work.

Once he was back in the cell block that evening, Luke knocked on the captain's office door.

"What do you want, Stone?" The captain shuffled papers on his desk.

"Can I come in, boss man?" Luke stood respectfully, hands behind his back.

"I guess so, but I've only got a minute." The captain pushed back his chair as if on guard.

"I've got a problem. My stomach burns all the time like it's being eaten away by acid and I'm throwin' up blood. I need permission to see a doctor."

"Throwing up blood, huh? That sounds pretty serious." The captain picked up his phone. "Pete, I'm sending a man over to see the doc."

He wrote a permission slip and handed it to Luke.

"Thank you, sir."

"You know, Stone, if you'd just try to get along with us, I think you'd find that we'd treat you a whole lot better."

"Yessir, mister boss man." Luke reached out his hand for the slip of paper. "Thanks."

Luke's footsteps echoed off the stone walls as he maneuvered the maze of hallways that led to the prison infirmary. He never let his guard down, ready for anyone or anything that might pop out from the shadows.

He'd witnessed enough already to know these people he shared the penitentiary with were animals.

The aging doctor took Luke's blood pressure, looked in his eyes, ears and throat before speaking. "What are your symptoms, Mr. Stone?"

"My damn stomach burns like fire all the time and I'm throwin' up blood."

"Sounds like you may have stomach ulcers, but I'll need to run some tests. Report back over here first thing in the morning and don't eat or drink anything after midnight tonight."

"I can do that." Luke slipped his shirt on and headed back toward the cell block. After a second thought, he made a detour to the barber.

Later that evening, Luke sat alone in the cell, writing tablet and pencil in hand. Red and the other two cellmates had wandered down to the recreation room for a few rounds of poker.

A knock on the cell door startled him. He looked up to see a white haired man with piercing eyes and high cheekbones waiting for an invitation to come in.

"Yeah?" Luke said looking up from his writing.

"Can I come in?" The old man's quiet demeanor piqued Luke's curiosity.

"Reckon so."

Luke motioned to one of the empty chairs. "Have a seat, old man. What can I do for you?"

"Got any coffee?" The old man's hands trembled slightly as he rolled a cigarette from a tobacco pouch he pulled from his pocket.

"Yeah I got coffee." Luke stood and after letting the water run in the sink until it was finally lukewarm, he made two cups of instant coffee. "Want sugar or cream?"

"Nope, black will do."

"What's on your mind? Do you have a name?"

"My name is Nakos Blackhawk and I have been sent by the spirits to talk to you."

"The spirits, huh? What in the hell do the spirits have to say to me?"

"Son, I watch you struggle and fight something that is bigger than you, something you cannot change. I bring message from spirit world that you need to stop fighting."

"Yeah, well that goes against my grain, old man. If I stop fighting, I grow weak."

"There are many different forms of strength. Do you think I am weak because I am old?"

"Maybe. Are you?"

"When I first came here I was angry much like you and in that anger found weakness."

"What are you in for?"

"The white man came to our reservation." His eyes took on a far-away look. "They shoved us aside. They dishonored our women. I fought back."

Luke gripped his coffee cup. "I too am a red man even though my skin is white. I've always been a damned ol' greasy Indian inside."

"That is why I come. You have many more years behind bars and I want to help you."

"What's your suggestion?" Luke lit a cigarette and leaned back in his chair.

"Find yourself an ol' lady and settle down."

"An ol' lady? He leaned forward. What in the hell are you talking about? Are you crazy? There ain't no ol' ladies in here, in case you haven't noticed."

"There are many young boys who pretend to be women. It's not the same, but it works."

Luke sprang out of his chair. "You are plumb fuckin' crazy! I ain't seen nothing on any of these hairy-legged freaks that even begins to resemble a woman. You can take your spirits and messages and get the fuck out of my cell."

The old man stood. "I was trying to help."

"Yeah, well, you can take your help somewhere else, podnah. I ain't turnin' queer just because I'm locked up. Your ancestors would spit on you."

The old man stood without another word and exited Luke's cell.

Once he'd left, Luke contemplated what the old man had said, except for the turning queer part. He knew he fought a losing battle but to stay true to himself, couldn't quit.

Red and the other men returned from their poker game just as Luke finished his cup of coffee. The burning started again and instantly he regretted drinking it.

"Red Hoss, I've got a problem." Luke washed his cup in the sink.

"Fuck, man, I've known that for a long time," Red showed a toothy grin.

"No seriously. I went to see the doctor today. He thinks I may have stomach ulcers. I've gotta go back tomorrow and he's gonna do some sort of test."

"Oh shit, Luke! I'm sorry. I knew somethin' was eatin' at you but just thought it was this fuckin' place." Red lit a cigarette.

"I hope they can give me some medicine to fix it, but I've been puking up blood for a while now."

Red stretched his long skinny legs out and pushed back in the chair. "If there's anything I can do, you know I will."

"I know and I appreciate it. I'll find out something tomorrow." Luke lay on his back on the hard bunk. "There's a bunch of shit that needs changing around here and it needs to start with these fuckin' hardass filthy mattresses they expect us to sleep on."

"I agree but don't see any way to fix it." Red finished another cigarette.

"We're supposed to be in custody and care of the United States government. Maybe I'll start writin' letters to congressmen and senators and newspapers. Hell, there has to be a way."

Red yawned. "Maybe so, Luke. Guess it couldn't hurt." He crawled into his bunk.

Luke lay still, listening to the strangely familiar sounds around him. He could hear two convicts yelling at each other across the cell tier, radios playing different stations, scuffling sounds, chairs grating on the concrete floor and the sound of the guard's boots echoing off the steel bars as he made his rounds.

What the old man said about fighting a losing battle was true, but damned if he didn't have to try.

Night shadows crept across the cell block like a velvet cloak and finally the depraved world inside the penitentiary fell semi-silent.

Sweet poignant memories of Darlina Flowers floated across Luke's mind. He groaned inwardly as his need for her overtook him. He'd give most anything to have her softness against his skin and feel himself inside her. He turned toward the wall and in the darkness relieved himself.

"As we journey upon life's seas, our days are numbered like falling leaves..."

Chapter 5

L uke Stone had dealt with lots of hardships, sickness and troubles in his life, but this one knocked him to his knees.

Dr. Huston brought news by the end of a full day of testing. "Mr. Stone, you have bleeding ulcers. I'll prescribe some medication for you, but most likely you will need to undergo surgery to remove them."

Luke stared at the doctor. "What are the chances of curing them with medicine?"

The old doctor ran his hand through a shock of white hair. "To be honest, probably none, but it might keep them in check for a little while. You need to avoid spicy or greasy foods and eat a bland diet."

"I can't stomach most of this prison slop, so avoiding it ain't a problem. Sure hope the medicine works 'cause I don't wanna have surgery here in this place. No offense, Doc."

"None taken. If the medicine isn't effective, I'll recommend that you be transferred to the Federal Medical Center in Springfield for surgery."

"Springfield, Missouri?"

"Yes. That's the nearest medical facility."

"Shit! When can I get the medicine and start taking it?"

"I'll write you a prescription. Stop by the pharmacy when you leave here and get started right away. If you have any complications, I want you to see me immediately."

"Okay. Thanks, Doc."

Luke left the infirmary with prescription in hand and a mind full of troubling thoughts. He didn't want to have surgery but it also troubled him to think that he might be separated from his old friend. Red had proven he could take care of himself, but still Luke would prefer that they stay together.

Back in the cell, he broke the news to Red. "I've got bleeding ulcers. The doc gave me a prescription and said he'd watch it, but that I might have to have surgery."

"Shit, man. That's not good."

"You're tellin' me. The prison hospital is in Springfield, Missouri."

"I've been thinkin' about trying to get this left eye worked on. I can't see a damn thing out of it. If you have to go to Springfield, I'll see if they'll let me go too."

Luke breathed a small sigh of relief. "I was worried about goin' off and leavin' you here, stud."

Red chuckled and lit a cigarette. "Hell, I'm doin' okay, Luke. You're locked up in the hole most of the time anyway."

"I know, man. I can't conform to their ways of thinkin' and they damn sure ain't gonna stop tryin' to make me. I gotta find a better way to fight 'em."

"I don't have much hope of any of it changin'. Hell, this new warden's worse than the one that left out."

"There's gotta be something we can do. I've never been one to give up and roll over." Luke opened the bottle of medicine and drank a big swig of the chalky liquid.

Within minutes, his stomach stopped burning for the first time in several months. Ahhhh, relief.

Over the next few weeks, he faithfully took the medicine and it seemed that perhaps this treatment would work.

By July 15, 1972, Luke knew he was in big trouble. He sat doubled over with abdominal pain in the cell that evening after work.

"Hey man, is there anything I can get for you?" Red's concern registered in his voice.

Groaning, Luke replied, "Not unless you've got a shotgun and can get me out of my misery. Dammit to hell, Red. Looks like I'm gonna have to give in and let 'em cut me open."

"Hell, Luke, I sure hate it, but like I told you, I've got it all set up with the doctor to go with you to Springfield."

"I don't think I can go to work tomorrow. I'm too damn sick. If I live through the night, I'll go see the ol' doc in the morning."

"Can you think of anything that might make you feel better other than a two dollar whore?"

"Shit man. I couldn't do anything with a one dollar whore as sick as I am right now." Luke raised himself slowly up off the chair and dove for the bed.

He swallowed the remainder of the chalky liquid in the medicine bottle and hoped for sleep.

After being awake and throwing up most of the night, Luke made his way to the infirmary early the next morning.

The captain did not hesitate to give him the required permission slip and expressed genuine concern. Perhaps some of these people were human after all, Luke conceded.

The doctor took one look at him and dialed the warden's office. "Sir, I've got a man here that's seriously ill and I need to make transfer arrangements to Springfield as soon as possible."

Luke only half heard the conversation. A deep agonizing pain so severe that it took his breath away came in waves.

The doctor returned with a syringe. "Mr. Stone, I'm going to give you something to help ease the pain a little. I've put the transfer to the hospital in motion."

Luke nodded and finally exhaled once the drug began to take effect and the pain dulled to a throb. "Thank you, Doc." He lay back and closed his eyes.

"Why don't you rest here a little while and I'll be back to check on you."

Luke nodded again, already drifting off into unconsciousness.

When the doctor woke him, with the pain lessened, he bargained. "I'm feelin' much better, Doc. Think I might buy a little more time before I go under the knife?"

"Mr. Stone, we've bought as much time as we possibly can. I've already put the wheels in motion to transfer you to Springfield."

"Can you start the wheels for my rap partner too, Thomas Johnson?"

"I'll contact the opthamologist there and make the referral."

"Thank you, doc. You're okay." Luke pushed himself into sitting position. With the movement, the pain intensified.

"It might take up to a week to get all the paperwork necessary to transfer you. I've written a work excuse for you to give to your caseworker. I want you to take it easy until we can get you out of here."

With a new prescription in hand and work release permit, Luke trudged slowly back to the cell block.

The captain sat behind the desk with his door open and Luke walked in. Handing him the paperwork, he turned to leave.

"Mr. Stone, I hope they can get you fixed up. Good luck"

"Thanks."

***

The white prison bus transported Luke, Red and two other prisoners to Springfield, Missouri on a blazing hot July day. With pain medication in his veins, Luke sat drowsily, half seeing as he looked out the window through the bars.

Two guards accompanied the convicts, who were all handcuffed with one hand to the metal frame of their seat.

Sitting across the aisle, Red gazed out the window.

The bus slowed down as it cruised through a small Kansas town.

Red handed a lit cigar across the seats to Luke. "Look at all these folks, Luke. They're starin' at us. Sure would like to be out there walking around with 'em."

"That'd be damn fine. Not sure we'd know how to act around civilized human beings."

"How are you feelin'?"

"Kinda dopey. That shot the doc gave me is keepin' the pain down."

"Maybe we'll get there before it wears off. Hey man, won't it be great if they can fix my eye where I can see out of it?"

"Yep, that'd be great, Red."

"Once we're all patched up maybe we can get back to playin' some music."

"Maybe so. Those guitars down in the music room ain't much to play on. Sure would like to have my ol' Martin." Luke's gaze wandered to a woman and her children walking down the sidewalk. His thoughts immediately turned to his own children back in Texas.

With an aching heart, he watched the youngsters skipping along beside their mother. What he wouldn't give to hug Joseph, Lexxi, Martin and Nathan once more and tell them how much he loved them.

Town faded away and the native sycamore, oak, maple and pecan trees lined the roadway with their green foliage,

Luke dozed most of the trip, awakening as the bus turned a corner or slowed down.

The medication wore off before long and by the time they arrived, Luke sat doubled over in pain. Two male orderlies boarded the bus with a gurney and helped him onto it. He could hear them conversing.

"This one's gonna have to skip a & o and go straight to building two. We'll radio ahead and let the doc know we're bringing him."

The next few days became a blur for Luke. While waiting for a surgeon, they kept him sedated and in a haze. He worried about Red and hoped he was okay. He hated being even more out of control of his own circumstances.

Finally, a caseworker visited the ward to give him the admissions and orientation information he'd missed upon arrival.

Luke only half-listened to the spiel. The caseworker droned on, repeating words he must've said thousands of times. Once he finished, he looked over the top of his black framed plastic glasses. "Mr. Stone, do you have any questions?"

"Yessir, I brought some writing tablets and things with me, but they carried me straight over here off the bus. Do you know where they are?"

"Any personal property you brought with you would have been placed in a locker in admissions and orientation."

"Can you please check on it for me? I've got lots of songs written on those tablets. My rap partner, Thomas Johnson, came in with me. Do you know where he is?"

"I'll let you know about the personal property. Mr. Johnson was processed through a & o and is being housed in building one until his surgery can be scheduled. Is there anything else?"

"I need some way to let my folks know where I am and what's happenin'."

"I can arrange for you to make a phone call, but you'll have to call them collect." The caseworker ran his hand tiredly through his short cropped black hair.

"When can we do that?"

"I'll be back around this way in a few hours and can take you to a phone then."

Luke relaxed slightly on the steel framed hospital bed. "Thank you. I didn't catch your name."

"Norman Holland."

"Thank you, Norman Holland." Luke closed his eyes. Damn! It would be really good to talk to the folks for a minute. Knowing how his mom would worry, he hadn't told them anything about the ulcers or the possibility of surgery. Perhaps he'd hoped the ulcers would simply go away and he wouldn't have to ever mention them.

True to his word, the caseworker returned four hours later. He shook Luke to wake him. "Mr. Stone, I'm here to take you to a telephone."

Luke groggily opened his eyes. "What?"

"Remember me? I'm your caseworker, Norman Holland. I'm here to take you to a phone so you can call your folks."

Awake now, Luke pushed himself up into a sitting position. "My tablets?"

"They've been placed in a holding locker until you can claim them."

Mr. Holland pushed a wheelchair next to the bed.

Luke gingerly transferred from the bed to the chair, hopes now high about speaking to his folks.

He placed the call and drummed his fingers on the ledge beside the phone as it rang once, then twice.

He heard his mom's voice. "Hello."

"Would you accept a collect call from Luke Stone?" the operator's voice asked.

"Well, yes," Mrs. Stone replied. Luke knew her well and immediately detected worry in her voice.

"Mom, it's Luke."

"Oh son! What's wrong? Are you okay?"

Luke could hear his dad's voice in the background. "Luke? Is it Luke on the phone?"

"Yes, daddy it's Luke," Mrs. Stone reported.

The next instant, his dad's voice boomed into the phone. "Luke? Is that you?"

"It's me, Dad. I can't talk long and hated like hell to call collect, but I need to tell you both something."

"Don't worry about the collect call. What is it, son?"

"I've been transferred to the federal medical center in Springfield, Missouri with bleeding ulcers. They're gonna do surgery to remove them."

Luke heard his mother gasp.

"Please tell mom not to worry. I'll be alright. I had to let you know where I was."

"Son, you take care of yourself. What about Red? Is he there with you? Can you give me a number where we can call and check on you and get the address and all?"

"Red Hoss is here. He's having surgery on his eye. I'll hand the phone to my caseworker and he can give you all the information. I've gotta go. I love you, Dad and you too, Mom. Please tell the kids I love 'em."

Tears stung his eyes as he handed the phone to Mr. Holland.

Hearing the voices of his folks left him shaken and refueled the intense desire to be back home where he belonged.

He listened to the caseworker give his father the details and turned his head so that tears could escape undetected.

Dammit, none of this was right. He knew the strain all of it placed on his loved ones. Anger replaced the longing and he vowed once again to try to figure a way out if he survived the surgery.

"A spin of the wheel, turn of the card, can change one's destiny..."

Chapter 6

As he recovered from the surgery, Luke did a lot of thinking about his life and the many mistakes he'd made, some of which cost him dearly. He knew it could all have very easily ended on the operating table. He'd heard stories about the many convicts who never emerged from a prison operating room. To these people who held guard over him, he would mean nothing more than one less convict to feed.

His life had been spared for a reason.

He took a drink of milk and watched as it snaked its way through the stomach tube protruding from his side, clabbered and green.

Hell, he reckoned he'd never done anything worth a shit except write a few songs, and protect Darlina Flowers from getting caught up in the mess that'd sent him to prison. Even though she might never understand, he'd done what he could to look out for her.

The recovery ward consisted of twenty hospital beds, which were all filled. The blended smell of antiseptic and bleach burned his nostrils.

The pungent odor transported him back in time when he'd been hospitalized in the small Santa Anna, Texas hospital, as a young child with rheumatic fever.

Luke passed the many days, weeks and hours filling his writing tablets and visiting with some of the other men around him. He immediately hit it off with an older Italian man who already had a ten year stint behind him.

Luke could easily picture the short stocky man, in a pinstriped suit, with a Borsalino hat and two-tone wingtips.

Nico Romano now sat in his wheelchair beside Luke's bed, his Italian accent so thick you could cut it with a knife. "What in'a da hell do you keep'a writing on dos'a tablets of yours?" He handed Luke an expensive Cuban cigar.

"Thanks for the smoke, man. I write songs, Nico. Songs and poems and I do little drawings."

"You play'a da music?"

"I did...Had a band for a lot of years and played all over the Southwest. Hell, I had a number one record in Denmark once upon a time."

Nico laughed. "Denmark not'a so big as'a dis whole damn state."

Luke chuckled, "I always figured it was the smallest country in the world, but they liked my song."

"I'm a so sad'a today, Stone. My granddaughter is'a...what'a ya say? My'a English not'a so good...she's a bella, bella..."

"Beautiful?" Luke prompted.

"Ah yes, beautiful'a young lady, announcing her'a engagement. Big a' party! I should'a be dere."

"Shit Nico, at least your family's got money and don't have to worry about how they're gonna make it with you gone."

"Aye, dios mio, does not'a make'a being in'a here easier. I still'a handle da famiglia business. I gotta people to'a do what'a I say."

"See what I'm talkin' about. I've got nobody 'cept my mom and dad to try to help look after my kids. They've got it rough."

"I donn'a know what'a I do if'a mi famiglia was hungry. I only wanna do'a my time and getta da fuck outta here."

"Me too, hoss. Once I get this belly healed up, I've gotta figure it out. Hell, maybe I can find something over in that law library to get me free."

"Mind'a me asking what'a ya in'a for?"

"Nope. Bank robbery. You?"

"Racketeering, they'a call it. Was'a simply workin' da famiglia business. Da feds'a take offense."

Luke chuckled. "Yeah, they'll do that sometimes. I can honestly say I never went in a bank with a gun and robbed it."

"Then why'a ya here?"

"Because I wouldn't turn rat and tell them what I knew."

"Ah, dat'a da reason Nico like'a you."

The doctor making his rounds interrupted the men. "Mr. Romano, why don't you go back to your bed and I'll be around to check on you in a few minutes."

"Arrivederci!" Nico shook Luke's hand, then wheeled himself down the row of beds, puffing on his cigar as he went.

"Let's see how you're doing, Mr. Stone." The doctor took Luke's temperature, checked the drain tube and the incisions. "I think we might be able to take this tube out in a few days. Looks like you're healing up nicely."

"I'm ready to get it out, doc. Don't care much for layin' up in the bed."

"Don't rush things. It's not like you have somewhere to go."

Luke's eyes narrowed. "What's that supposed to mean?"

The doctor apologetically replied, "I'm sorry. I didn't mean for it to sound that way. I want you to be healed up good before you go back into population."

"Yeah, well I'd like to go back to real people population and not this damned prison, but that don't look too promising."

"I expect within a couple of weeks you'll be moved off this ward. I've set up an appointment for you to see a staff psychologist when you feel up to it."

"I ain't crazy," Luke snapped.

"It's simply routine, Mr. Stone. Every inmate is required to have one evaluation session. Whether or not you have any more is up to you."

"I can tell you right now there won't be any more, hoss. I don't need a shrink. I need my freedom."

"Nevertheless, it is required. As soon as you are up and around, I'll set it up with Dr. Cunningham."

"Whatever you say."

More bullshit to go through, Luke thought. He didn't have any control over much of anything right now other than his own mind.

Red had been over to visit him a couple of times. He sported a big patch over his eye, and brought stories about the prison they were now in. He'd laughed when he told Luke that they didn't care about the length of your hair here and that lots of convicts had long hair.

Having been confined to the bed for a while, Luke's hair had grown down past his ears and curled up on the ends. Maybe he'd just let it keep growing for the hell of it.

He picked up the tablet he'd been writing on before Nico's visit. Heartfelt words flowed from his stubby yellow pencil.

> I wonder if there is ever a blue sky
> Or if there's a tear in anyone's eye
> As all the sad songs I've ever sung
> Gather around to see me cry
> Who'll carry on the concerts and shows
> Sing ballads of love? No one knows...

***

Ten days later, Luke sat across the desk from the prison psychologist, Dr. Cunningham, sizing him up. He'd always been able to read people and formed immediate first impressions. He guessed this doctor to be in his mid to late thirties and had to wonder why he wasn't in a private practice instead of working in this shit hole. The man shuffled through stacks of papers on his desk, eyes darting around the room landing now and then on Luke.

"You been here long, doc?" Luke scooted forward on the chair placing his elbows on the desk.

"I've been in this position for two months, Mr. Stone. It is noted in your file that you don't associate much with the other inmates." He peered over his glasses.

"Well, I don't."

"Are you anti-social?"

"No, but do you realize that ninety percent of these guys in here are felons? You wouldn't want me hangin' out with felons, would you? I'm not allowed to fraternize with the guards, so who would you recommend I hang out with?"

"You have a point." He scribbled some notes on the paper. "You'll be required to work once you are fully recovered from your surgery. What sort of work did you do on the outside?"

"I was a musician and had a band." Luke drummed his fingers on the desk.

"I see. What other interests do you have?"

"I'm interested in gettin' out of here.

"I understand, but that's not what I meant."

"I've always liked drawing."

"I'm going to recommend you be given some light custodial duties until the doctor releases you."

"It don't matter much to me as long as I don't have to clean out shitty toilets."

"Okay, Mr. Stone. I wish you well. If you ever need to talk with me about anything, I'm here." The doctor stood, signaling the end of the session.

"I won't, but thanks anyway." Luke pulled himself into standing position, holding onto the desk.

Back out in the hallway, Luke noticed the number of convicts who shuffled along, never looking up. When he'd asked about them, he learned they were doing what was referred to as the Thorazine shuffle.

Mental patients with a "P" (psychiatric) number never did a day of their time until they were determined to be competent. Luke heard of a man, a member of the old Purple Gang, who'd been in Springfield for over thirty years and never stood trial because he had a "P" number. Nothing could be worse, in Luke's opinion.

As he passed by the prison craft shop, he couldn't resist peeking in. A gray haired lady, body twisted with rheumatoid arthritis, laboriously moved around the rectangular room with rows of wooden tables and benches.

On instinct, Luke opened the door. "Ma'am, do you need some help?"

"Always, sir," she replied in a warm voice. "Come on in."

Luke entered the room with drab brown walls that smelled of paint and leather. "What can I do?"

"This gentleman here is making a keychain and having difficulty getting the ring through the leather fob. Perhaps you could assist."

Luke pulled up a chair next to the white-haired man shakily struggling with the keychain. "Let me see what I can do with that, old timer." He expertly threaded the metal ring through the leather.

The elderly lady stood beside him. "What is your name, sir?"

"Luke Stone. And yours?"

"I'm Mrs. Yarbrough. Have you done craftwork before?"

"Nah, not really. I did a lot of artwork decorating stages and night clubs, but nothin' like this."

"Are you interested in learning?"

"I've always loved the smell of leather. It makes me think of Mexico." Luke grinned at the woman.

She returned his smile with one of her own. "If you're free to come down here, I'd love to have you join us."

"As far as I know, I'm free to go pretty much anywhere inside these walls. At least if I ain't, I don't know it yet. I don't have any money to buy materials with."

"I've got plenty of scraps lying around."

"Then you've got a deal. Hey, mind if I bring my rap partner with me?"

"Not at all. I work with prisoners in here from eleven to three each day."

Luke stood, careful not to pull the sore muscles in his stomach. "Then I'll see you tomorrow, Mrs. Yarbrough."

Luke walked the rest of the way back to the occupational therapy ward, where he and Red now lived, thinking about the lady in the craft room and her spirit. Hell, most folks he knew all crippled up like her would be hiding at home, not out in public working, especially not with a bunch of sorry-assed convicts.

He knew without a doubt he and Red would be there tomorrow and looked forward to creating something. Maybe he'd even be good at it.

His mind drifted back to a happier day when he sat at his kitchen table with Darlina Flowers, cutting and sewing soft supple deerskin leather, to make a new go-go costume for her.

That day now seemed like another lifetime or perhaps just a dream far removed from the stark reality of prison. A sigh escaped his lips as an old familiar ache overtook him. He cursed fate for not allowing him to meet Darlina before he'd screwed up.

His shoulders drooped and he felt much older than his thirty-seven years. Two years of his life had been wasted locked behind bars. Two years he'd never get back and what had he accomplished? Nothing as far as he could see.

Something stirred deep down inside of him; a warrior spirit from ancient times began to emerge. He straightened his shoulders and held his head up.

"Fuck 'em! They're not going to break me," he said out loud.

"My dreams of you come so easy. Wish these dreams could come true..."

Chapter 7

"**B**aby, I've missed you so much." Whispered words along with soft kisses on her eyelids, face then down to her throat. Her breath came in ragged gasps and she arched her back rising to meet every touch. Luke Stone took his time, expertly caressing the soft curves of Darlina's body.

She responded with her own whispers and touches. "Oh Luke, I thought I'd never be in your arms again."

Suddenly, they were floating up, up, up into the clouds. Cool mist drizzled on her face in stark contrast to the sizzling heat that radiated from her body. They floated, joined together, arms and legs wrapped tightly around each other. Luke's mouth found hers and the intensity of wanting rose along with the ascension.

As quickly as they had gone up into the clouds, they floated back down onto the familiar black and gold antique iron bed they'd lain upon so many times. Luke moved on top of her and she felt his hardness enter her. The crescendo that followed resembled a Fourth of July fireworks finale.

Darlina Flowers opened her eyes into the blackness of night, heart pounding wildly inside her chest. With her breath caught in her throat, she re-lived the scene she'd awakened from. It was more than a simple dream. She'd been in Luke Stone's arms and they'd made sweet passionate love. Even now, fully awake, she could still feel his strong hands touching her, his breath on her neck.

She looked over at Will Brocker, sound asleep beside her and quietly slid her long legs from under the damp sheet. With a thin robe wrapped tightly around her, she stepped out into the sultry Texas night air. Leaning against the porch railing, she let her imagination take her back into the dream. Tears rolled from under her closed eyelids. She'd never missed Luke more than she did right now. Just when she thought she was moving on with her life, here he came stampeding back in with soft kisses and warm touches.

Resigned to the fact that no one would ever be the lover Luke was to her, she accepted Will's fumbled attempts. At least he didn't ask much of her and their relationship continued to be comfortable.

She looked up at the stars and wished with all her might for Luke's return.

A sigh escaped her lips. Sadly, she brushed her tears away and moved back inside the house. Will had not moved and sleep now eluded her.

Finding a piece of paper on the kitchen counter, she wrote a quick note and fifteen minutes later, entered her own apartment.

The small clock on the shelf showed it to be four a.m. Darlina brewed a pot of coffee and after a second thought, went into the bedroom for writing paper and pen.

With a steaming cup beside her, she penned a letter to Luke.

My Dearest Luke,
God, how I've missed you. It seems like a lifetime ago since you left. Even though I have no way to mail this letter to you, there are some things I need to say anyway. I've tried to pick up the pieces of my life and go on, but it's so hard when your memory comes so fresh and strong over and over again. We made love tonight in a dream. It was so real and powerful, I have to wonder if you were dreaming the same dream too. I know you told me to forget about you, but that's totally impossible, honey...

By the time the sun peeped over the horizon, with the coffee pot emptied, she had filled six pages. Somehow, it felt better, even if she couldn't mail them to Luke.

The phone rang as she stepped out of the shower, towel drying her wet hair.

"Hello."

"Hey, Darlina. How come you left last night?" Will sounded a little contrite.

"I couldn't sleep and didn't want to bother you, so I came on home."

"Everything all right?"

"Yes. Getting ready to go to work. I'll see you this evening. How about I cook for you at my place tonight?"

"That sounds great."

"Okay. Gotta run."

"Bye. See you later."

As she put the phone back on the cradle, she glanced over at the neatly written pages still lying on the table. She folded them and placed them inside her dresser drawer with an aching heart.

Once again, Luke Stone had to be put away so that her life could go on. That's the way it had to be.

Darlina's sister, Norma, whom she worked with at the boiler factory, questioned her. "What's wrong, Darlina? You're a million miles away today. Did you find the contracts I left for you to type?"

"Sorry, Norma. I had a vivid dream about Luke last night and it brought it all back again. Don't worry. I'll get the contracts done."

"Let's go get a drink after work. How does that sound?"

"It sounds good except I'm cooking dinner for Will tonight."

"Are you getting serious about him?"

"I don't know. He's easy to be with, but there is definitely no passion between us."

"Sometimes passion's not all it's cracked up to be."

"True. I do love riding the motorcycle with him."

"Then don't worry about it. Enjoy whatever you can. At least it seems to help you forget about Luke."

"Sometimes. But it always returns."

"Give it time, sweetie. I've got to go get some orders out. If you won't go for a drink, then at least have lunch with me."

"Okay, let me know when you're ready."

Darlina turned to the stack of contracts awaiting her attention. No one could understand what she felt and how much she struggled to let go of Luke. She appreciated Norma and Will and the rest of her family and friends who attempted to help, but the truth was she didn't want to be helped. She wanted Luke. That would never change.

Later that evening, sitting in the same chair where she'd sat earlier sharing her deepest thoughts with Luke, Will expertly rolled a joint while Darlina added the finishing touches to their dinner. She couldn't help but notice that Will's blonde hair and red goatee had grown longer and he'd started braiding the goatee, giving him the look of a viking.

"Darlina, I've been thinkin' about somethin' today."

"What's that?"

"I think we should move in together. You're either at my place, or I'm here most all the time anyway."

"I don't know, Will. Pup stays at your place a lot and your biker friends are always coming and going."

"Pup's just a kid and his folks give him a hard time about riding so he hangs out at my place. I can tell him he'll have to go home, or he could go stay with Rabbit, if it would convince you to move in."

Will handed Darlina the lit joint.

"I'll think about it."

"I wanna be initiated into the Banditos Motorcycle Club in Dallas. Rabbit and Square John say they can sponsor me."

"Isn't that a little dangerous?"

"Naw...they get a bad rap, but they're like family to each other and really look out for their brothers."

Darlina placed food on the table and sat across from Will. "Like I said, I'll think about moving in."

She pondered this latest proposal. Her family certainly wouldn't like the idea, but Will was right. They were spending most of their time outside of work together.

"This smothered steak is delicious." Will woofed down bites of the meat and potatoes.

"Thanks." Darlina cut small pieces and chewed slowly.

"Let's go for a ride when we get done."

"Okay. Hey, I've been working on something I wanted to surprise you with." Darlina ran into the bedroom and returned with a denim vest she'd decorated with Harley patches, Indian beads and silver chains. "Look."

Will stood. "Very cool. Try it on."

Darlina slipped the vest on. "What do you think?"

"I think you're lookin' more and more like a biker's ol' lady. I like it." He embraced her and she turned her face up to accept his kiss.

"Let's get the dishes cleaned up and go for that ride."

As the wind ripped around her face a short time later, she let her thoughts wonder where they may in the way she'd become accustomed to when they rode.

Luke Stone's memory came parading through her mind and she allowed the dream of their lovemaking to return. How could she move in with Will and still hold on to these dreams and wishes? It didn't seem fair to either Will or Luke. But, Luke was gone and even though she always hoped for his return, the odds of that were slim.

After an hour of riding, Will pulled into the parking lot of a biker bar on the outskirts of Abilene.

"Look, there's Rabbit's scooter. Let's go in for a few minutes."

ZZ Top's smash hit, *Tush*, blasted them as Will opened the door. Darlina followed him in.

"Hey, Will. Over here." Rabbit stood waving from a table in the back corner. He slapped Will on the back and embraced Darlina, letting his hand slip down to her bottom. "Hey man, I want you to meet someone."

He turned to the grizzled man sitting at the table with him. "BoJack, this is the dude I've been tellin' you about."

BoJack stood eye-to-eye with Will. "So you wanna join up with the Banditos?"

"I sure do." Will shook hands with the biker.

"Is this your ol' lady?" He ogled Darlina.

"This is Darlina," Will placed his hand on her back.

"Gotcha' a purdy one there. Where's your scooter?"

"Outside. Come on out and I'll show her to you."

The three men and Darlina walked back outside.

She stood behind Will as the bikers lit smokes and admired each other's motorcycles. BoJack cast a leering look her way now and then.

Finally he slapped Will on the back. "Come on back in and buy us some fuckin' drinks, man."

Will glanced at Darlina. "Sure."

She made certain she sat between Will and Rabbit at the table. This man from Dallas made her more than a little nervous.

She remained quiet as they discussed everything from carburetors and valves to the tits on the woman who had just walked through the door.

After buying three rounds of drinks, Will stood. "BoJack, it was cool meetin' you, man."

BoJack remained seated. "You too. Hey, why don't you ride up to Dallas on the twenty-third? We're having a helluva party. You'd be welcome and bring your ol' lady."

"Thanks man, I'll do that." Will slapped Rabbit on the back and waved as he and Darlina went out the door.

Once outside, Darlina turned to Will. "That man gave me the creeps."

"Awww, he didn't mean no harm. He just knows a pretty girl when he sees one."

"It was more than that, Will. I'm not sure about this whole Bandito thing. I'm afraid it's gonna be dangerous."

"You worry too much. Hop on and let's ride some more before we go home."

She climbed on behind him, still troubled. No matter what Will said, she didn't trust this man. A cloud of apprehension settled over her.

Less than twenty-four hours ago, she was lying in Luke Stone's arms making sweet love. She filed the dream away with reverence in the recesses of her mind to be recalled when she needed it the most.

For now, her reality was on the back of the motorcycle with Will and the crazy idea he had about being a Bandito.

Chapter 8

"Will, you've been wearing that damn chicken foot pinned to your vest for several days now and it's starting to stink," Darlina complained.

Will laughed out loud. "Hell, I know it. I love havin' people stare at me when I walk in a room. It's my new image."

He and Darlina had ridden the Harley for several hours and stopped at the local Whataburger for food.

"I don't like the stares so much." Darlina took a sip of her coke.

"You didn't mind being stared at when you were up on stage go-go dancing," Will argued.

"That was totally different. For one thing it was dark in the club and I didn't stink." Darlina chewed her bottom lip.

"Well, this new look is gonna help get me into the Banditos motorcycle club. Just you wait and see."

"Maybe so, Will. You want it bad enough, that's for sure."

"You have no idea what an honor it is to be invited to party with the club. Not many people get that invitation but I did and so did you. You don't seem too excited about it." Will reached for Darlina's fries and she slapped his hand.

"I'm excited." Darlina looked away to hide the lie.

She remembered a similar time with Luke, when she'd pretended everything was fine even though she'd been petrified as they deliberately hit a deer with the band car, slit its throat, and tossed it into the trunk. She couldn't forget the acrid smell of blood when she'd forced herself to package the meat because Luke asked her to.

Now, just as she'd done then, she smiled and pretended to be excited along with Will at the prospect of partying with the Banditos. Rabbit and Square John were riding with them to Dallas and somehow Darlina found that slightly comforting.

***

They met at a truck stop outside of Abilene early on the morning of the twenty-third. Rabbit had a female rider with him and Square John rode alone.

Standing beside their choppers, Will took a coffee can out of his saddlebag. "I got some shit to take to the party. Ya'll want some?" He offered a handful of black capsules to Rabbit, Square John and the woman riding with Rabbit.

"Hell yeah. Thanks for the mollies, man."

Will swallowed two with a swig of coffee, and then turned to Darlina. "Want some speed?"

"Sure." She swallowed the capsule as Will stuffed the can back into the saddlebag.

Rabbit cranked up his scooter. "Let's ride," he shouted above the roar.

The three motorcycles sped down the highway, Rabbit taking the lead.

The men made a game out of getting close enough to each other on the highway, at breakneck speed, to pass joints back and forth. In less than three hours, Rabbit led them into a Dallas neighborhood that he appeared to know well.

Darlina buzzed and tingled from the combination of pot, speed and the ride. She curiously surveyed a large rundown wood-frame house on a corner lot with a tall chain link fence surrounding it. The open gate had a brass padlock hanging on one side. Two big Rottweiler dogs on heavy chains lunged toward them barking and snarling.

A row of shiny Harleys lined one side of the driveway where the riders from Abilene parked their own motorcycles.

Loud music came from inside the house and even though it was a hot day, all of the windows were open. Beer cans and various motorcycle parts littered the yard. The sweet smell of marijuana drifted through the air.

BoJack along with two fellow Banditos, Jocko and Speedy, greeted the guests.

"Shit man! Didn't think you'd really come." BoJack slapped Will on the back.

"Hell, I told you I would."

"Shut the fuck up!" A half empty beer can sailed through an open window toward the dogs, hitting one on the head. The dog yelped, and they both settled down, still eyeing the strangers.

Square John shook hands with the three Banditos as did Rabbit. The woman who'd ridden with Rabbit joined Darlina.

"Whew, that was some ride, huh?" She tossed her short black hair, after removing a bandana.

Darlina smiled at her. "Yep, it was. I don't think we were ever introduced. I'm Darlina."

"I'm Cassidy. You Will's ol' lady?" She batted her long eyelashes, thick with mascara and eyeliner, and fished a cigarette out of her jeans pocket.

"Sort of. We've been together for a while." Darlina couldn't help but notice Cassidy's short cropped tank top and heavy purple eye shadow.

BoJack interrupted the two girls. "Well, well...lookie who came to join the party."

Darlina positioned herself behind Will.

Cassidy boldly wrapped her arms around his neck and rubbed her tits against his chest. "We sure as hell did, honey. Where could a thirsty lady find a cold beer?"

"Shit man, ya'll come on in the house."

Darlina walked a step behind everyone, thankful Cassidy had taken the attention off her.

Inside, a round of introductions began. With nicknames like Stumpy, Mojo, Cutoff, Bull, Skully and a variety of others, Darlina knew she wouldn't remember any of them. Two of the Banditos' women whisked her off into the kitchen with them. They chatted, made small talk in between taking hits off a joint and offered Darlina a beer.

"No thanks, but I would love a drink of water." She drew on the joint passed her way. "What are ya'll cookin'? Can I do anything to help?"

The older woman of the group everyone called Mom seemed to be in charge. She stood graceful, tall and slender with dark brown eyes and tinges of gray through her hair. She had obviously been a beautiful woman in her day. Darlina quickly learned she was Lenny's wife and he was the respected president of the club.

Mom smiled at her. "You're green, aren't you sweetie?"

Forcing a smile, Darlina answered. "It's my first time in Dallas, but I've been ridin' with Will for a good while now."

"Well don't let these big bad bikers scare you. Their bark's worse than their bite most of the time." Mom stirred a large bowl of cornbread mix.

A couple of hours later, a commotion from outside the house drew their attention. Peering out a window, the women could see a small group of bikers at the gate.

Lenny led the welcoming committee. "What do you wetbacks want? Can't you see we're busy?"

"I came to take my little sister home. Speedy brought her over here yesterday and she didn't come home all night."

Lenny yelled over his shoulder, "Speedy, you got this wetback's sister with you?"

Speedy stepped forward. "She wants to be here, man."

"You heard him. She don't wanna come home."

"She's only sixteen, assholes. I can get the law out here."

"Speedy, go get this meskin's sister."

He returned with a young girl. "Do you wanna go home with your brother, Elena?"

"No, Speedy. I wanna stay here with you." She turned to her brother. "Vaya en casa, Raul. Vete."

"Vamos, Elena! Papa esta enojada. Vamanos, puta!"

"No, Raul. Chinga usted!" She put her hands on her shapely hips.

"You heard her, meskin. You and your wetbacks need to get the fuck out of here."

"We'll leave, Lenny, but we'll be back. We're gonna get my sister."

The intruders sped away, shooting them the finger. Jocko closed the gate and fastened the padlock in place.

Back inside the house, Lenny strode into the kitchen. Taking a key off a large chain, he unlocked a hidden pantry and removed rifles and handguns. "They'll be back and when they do, we're gonna blow their shit away." He handed Mom four guns. "Make these cunts useful." With an arsenal in hand, he went back into the living room and Darlina could hear him barking out orders.

Mom quickly assigned each of the girls to a post and put a gun in their hands.

Darlina sat on a hard back wooden chair in front of an open window, holding a loaded forty-five revolver in her shaking hand. She knew beyond a doubt she could never shoot anyone and swallowed back the bile that rose up in her throat. Sweat covered the palms of her hands and her heart raced from the speed she'd swallowed earlier and adrenaline. She gripped the handle of the heavy revolver and clenched her teeth to keep them from chattering.

She jumped when Mom placed a hand on her shoulder. "You ever shot a gun before?"

"No."

Kneeling beside Darlina, she took the hand that gripped the gun and raised it to rest on the window sill. "Just put your wrist here and you damn well better shoot, if we tell you to."

"I'll try," Darlina stammered.

She had no idea where Will had gone, but assumed he'd been posted as a guard too. This wasn't where she wanted to die at the age of 20 and began to pray for their safety.

Maybe this would end Will's desire to wear the Bandito patch.

After an uneventful hour of the vigil, Lenny posted a couple of men at the gate along with the dogs, and resumed partying.

Darlina happily surrendered the revolver to Mom and went searching for Will. She found him sitting with a group of bikers, laughing, drinking beer and passing a joint.

Rabbit disappeared into a bedroom with Cassidy, Bull and Mojo. Square John was nowhere in sight. She sat down beside Will and placed her hand on his arm.

He turned toward her. "Darlina, you havin' a good time?"

"Sure, Will. You?"

"You bet." He turned back to the men he'd been conversing with.

She sat quietly, wishing for the day to be over when suddenly, large hairy hands cupped her breasts from behind causing her to jump. Turning, she found BoJack's face two inches from her own. She struggled to break his grip. He grinned and held on tighter.

"Hey Will. You wanna be a fuckin' Bandito, why don't you loan me your ol' lady for a couple of hours?"

Darlina twisted and kicked, trying to escape.

Will turned around glassy eyed. "Hell, BoJack. That'd be up to her, not me."

"You wanna go spend a little time with ol' BoJack, sweetheart?" The grizzled man nuzzled the back of her neck with his thick scraggly beard.

Darlina finally wrenched herself free and sprang to her feet. "I'd rather lay down with a snake and I'd appreciate you keepin' your hands off me."

BoJack laughed raucously. "You got yourself a little tiger there, Will. Sure you're man enough to handle her?"

Square John spared Will a reply by making a quick entrance into the scene. He moved directly to Darlina, put his arm around her waist and moved her toward the door to the next room. "You don't get a turn before I do, BoJack!"

Darlina leaned against Square John, knees shaking. She gave Will a pleading look before she disappeared through the door.

"Just relax, Darlina. I'm not going to do anything. Sit here on the couch with me and BoJack will leave you alone."

"Thanks, Square. I owe you one."

"Nah, don't think nothin' of it. You'll be okay. Will oughta have his fuckin' ass kicked though."

Darlina stayed close to Square John or Mom the rest of the day and breathed a sigh of relief when it finally came time to go.

As they said their farewells, Darlina noticed Cassidy wasn't with Rabbit.

Her curiosity got the best of her. "Rabbit, aren't you forgetting something?" she asked.

"Like what, sweetheart?"

"Cassidy." Darlina tied a red bandana around her head.

"Shit! The bitch decided to stay here for a while. I'll pick her up sometime next week, if at all." Rabbit kickstarted his big Harley.

All the way back to Abilene, the wind ripped one thought and then another from Darlina's mind. The one troubling fact remained, that Will had done nothing to protect her.

Luke would never have tolerated that kind of treatment toward her from anyone, not even his own brother. She thought about her first meeting with Luke's brother, Bobby. He'd arrived at the night-club drunk and had been disrespectful toward her. A fist-fight between the two brothers ended with bloody noses and torn clothing.

As they neared Abilene, she'd made up her mind. "I want to go home, Will."

"Let's go to my place. We won't sleep tonight."

"I know. I just need to go home."

"Alright. I'll take you, but I don't know what you're so bowed up about?"

"Really? You don't know?"

"No, but I have a feelin' you're gonna tell me."

"Not tonight, Will. Not tonight."

She slid off the motorcycle and went straight to her door without saying goodbye. She had some thinking to do.

The roar of the Harley rang in her ears as she sank onto the sofa.

She wished for sleep so that the day could disappear into oblivion, but with the speed in her belly, she wouldn't close her eyes for many hours.

Why had Will turned so cold toward her? She thought they had a true friendship, but now it only felt like a foolish game she'd played to try and forget about Luke.

Mindlessly, she turned on the TV, hoping the noise would drown out her thoughts. She busied herself in the kitchen cleaning, sorting and rearranging until the sun slowly peeked over the horizon.

Drawn back to the TV by a flashing news bulletin, she gasped in horror. At a house in Dallas, belonging to the president of the Banditos motorcycle club, a shooting had occurred, leaving three people dead. The reporter stated it was believed to be an altercation between two rival gangs and no other details were known at this time.

Darlina crumbled to the floor. Apparently, the Mexicans had come back to get Raul's sister. Instinctively, she whispered a prayer, thanking God for letting her escape the bloody scene she saw on TV.

Oh, Luke, why did you have to go away? Turning the TV off, she walked slowly toward the bedroom. Her shoulders drooped and sadness penetrated her weary bones.

"Sometimes I take me to yesterday, rainy November and a rose I knew..."

Chapter 9

"**Y**ou're all fuckin' crazy if you think you can escape from here." Luke sat in his cell with four other convicts and Red.

"I'm tellin' you, we've got ourselves a foolproof plan. Come on and join with us, Luke. Don't you want out of here?" The convict crushed out his cigarette with the heel of his shoe.

"I probably want out of here worse than any of you, but I'm not stupid enough to think it can be done, Grady. Hell, let's just say you do make it over the walls, then what? You'd be on the run the rest of your life. You couldn't go near your family and you'd have to be willing to kill anyone that got in your way. Nope, it's not for me. I'm gonna get out of here legit." Luke leaned back in his chair and stretched his legs.

"Shit man, you just watch us. We're gonna make it out." Grady looked at the other men who nodded in agreement.

"Yeah, well me and Red ain't rats so we sure as hell ain't gonna tell anybody what you're plannin', but we ain't in it with you. Got that straight?"

"Suit yourself. You'll be wishin' you was with us when we're over those walls and livin' the good life down in Mexico."

Luke snorted. "Sure thing, man. You be sure and send us a post-card. Come on, Red Hoss. Let's go tool some leather."

Although it had been two months since the surgery, Luke was still sore and groaned as he stood. He and Red sauntered toward the craft room.

"You gonna be okay, Luke?" Concern registered in Red's voice.

"I hope so. My belly's still sore, but my left leg is throbbin' like a robin's ass. Now how do you figure that?"

"Maybe you better have the doc look at it."

"Nah, it's probably just a charley horse or some shit. It'll straighten out."

"That leather handbag you're workin' on sure is gonna be purdy when you get done." Red slapped his old friend on the back.

"Who the hell knew we could do this shit. If I'd known I could tool leather, I would've made me a bang-up pair of cowboy boots instead of buyin' 'em in Mexico all those years."

Luke had quickly gone from helping Mrs. Yarbrough to working on his own projects. He particularly loved working with leather and found he had a knack for it. Red piddled with it, but didn't really have his heart in it.

Another convict stopped them as they continued down the long hallway. "Hey, Red. Would you take a look at my watch? Damned thing just quit tickin' and I have no idea what's wrong with it."

"Sure thing, Pete. Bring it by this evening and I'll take a look." Red lit a cigarette and they continued on their way.

"And who would've ever guessed you'd have a knack for workin' on watches? Hell, with that bad eye, I don't know how you see those tiny little parts." Luke stopped to rest against the wall.

"I guess we're findin' out a lot of shit about ourselves we never knew. You think those guys'll make it over the wall?"

"Hell no! They're crazy for thinkin' they can. When we first came in, I probably would've joined them, but from what I've seen, they don't stand a Chinaman's chance in hell. For one thing, they talk too damn much."

Red chuckled. "Yeah, they don't seem to care who hears 'em."

"Mark my words. The guards will get wind of it and shut 'em down pretty quick." Luke began to walk again, wincing with each step.

Luke and Red had grown accustomed to spending most of their free time in the craft shop. Luke's first impression of Mrs. Yarbrough proved to be accurate. She maintained her sunny disposition in spite of her disability. Luke wouldn't stand for any of the convicts being disrespectful to her and had intervened on her behalf several times, putting some asshole in his place.

She brought out natural talents in Luke that he'd never realized he had. Not only had she taught him how to tool leather and make things with it, but she also encouraged him to try his hand at painting and to take a graphic arts design course offered by the prison, which he excelled at.

Today, she seemed particularly anxious to see Luke and Red. The craft shop was practically deserted with only a handful of convicts working on various projects.

"Mr. Stone. So glad to see you." She flashed a genuine smile.

"It's always a pleasure, Mrs. Yarbrough. I'm hoping to finish that handbag I've been workin' on today." Luke proceeded to take his project out of the bin assigned to him.

"That's wonderful, Mr. Stone, but what I want to talk to you about today has nothing to do with your project. I wonder if you and Mr. Johnson would consider playing music for our annual Christmas party this year?"

"Oh, I don't know. It's been a good while since we've played and the instruments they have in here leave a lot to be desired."

"That's not a problem we can't fix. Do you still have instruments on the outside?"

"Yes, ma'am." She now had Luke's full attention.

"Then let me help you put together a request to submit to Dr. Ciccone and get them shipped in to you." A triumphant smile crossed her face.

"I tried getting approval for my guitar back in Leavenworth and my request supposedly got lost."

"If you'll allow me, I'll personally deliver the request to Dr. Ciccone's office. I can promise it won't get lost here."

"Me and Red sure would enjoy playing, wouldn't we, stud?"

"Not only yes, but hell yes! It's been way too long." Red's eyes lit up.

"Perhaps you'd be inclined to put together a band and provide some entertainment for these poor folks."

"Well, that's what I did for a livin' for many years. I have no doubt we could do it in here too." Luke slapped his knee. "Alright, let's write that request."

By the time the men left the craft shop that day, a request was being hand-delivered to the administrative office.

"By damn, Red Hoss, maybe this time the request will get seen. I know I can get mom and dad to ship our guitars in."

"Shit, man, it'd be great to play again for sure. We need to think of a good name for a prison band." Red ran his fingers through his now shoulder length hair.

"That's easy, hoss. We'll call it Luke Stone and the Survivors." Luke lit a cigar and chuckled.

When they arrived back at their quarters, Luke grabbed a tablet and sketched a long-haired hippie cowboy holding a guitar. "What do you think?" He held it up for Red to approve.

"Looks good to me, Luke. I especially like the hair. Hell, you can draw damn near anything, can't you?"

"Guess by God I can. I just never knew it. Had to get locked up to find out what I can do. When we get our guitars in here, I'm gonna figure out some way to record a bunch of these ol' songs I've been writin'."

"Don't reckon you've found anything over in the law library to help get our asses out of here yet?"

"Nope. But I ain't givin' up. Mom always said, where there's a will, there's a way and I damned sure got the will." Luke removed the rubber band that was holding his hair in a short pony tail and shook it out.

"Mail call." A voice boomed out from down the hallway. Luke rose and stood in the doorway, hopeful he would have letters from home. He treasured each one he received.

"Here you go, Mr. Stone." The mail clerk handed him three letters.

"I've got one for you too, Mr. Johnson." He passed the letter to Red.

"Thanks, Charlie." Luke peered down at the envelopes in his hand. One letter was from his mom and dad, one from his grandmother and one from his old friends, Louise and Johnny Monroe.

He chose to read the one from Louise and Johnny first. She caught him up on all the latest news from the honky-tonk world he'd ruled for such a long time. He chuckled out loud when she recounted a confrontation between Bill Pierce and Johnny. He'd never liked Bill and even though he'd bought a gun from him once, he didn't trust him. Sure enough, after Luke's arrest, Bill came forward and ratted about the gun transaction.

The last paragraph caused his breath to catch in his throat and he didn't exhale until he'd read it over twice.

"Luke, I ran into Darlina the other day in the grocery store. She seemed so very sad and we talked for a while. She's taken up with a biker dude named Will and said she's been riding a lot. She cried when I told her I'd been writing to you. She asked me if I would give her your address and I said I would but I didn't have it with me. She invited me over to visit soon. I want you to have her address just in case you'd like to write her. She lives at 1412B North 12th Street, Abilene, Texas 79604. If it's okay with you, I'll give her your address as well, or hell, you can just write to her and she'll have it. She still loves you, Luke. There's no doubt about that..."

Tears rushed to Luke's eyes and he quickly blinked them away. A convict can't let anyone see him cry. He slowly read the words over again and stared into nothingness, thinking about Darlina. Riding a motorcycle with some dude sounded dangerous to him and he hoped she wasn't being careless.

Louise said she seemed very sad. That wasn't what he wanted for her. He wanted her to be happy and enjoy good things in life. Should he write and encourage her or would it be best to just leave her alone and let her find her way?

"Everything okay, Luke?" Red broke into his thoughts.

"Louise wrote and told me she ran into Darlina in the grocery store the other day. Said I should write to her and gave me the address. What do you think, Red hoss? Should I write to her?"

"Hell man, what could it hurt?" Red folded the letter he'd been reading and stuffed it back in the envelope. "My mom and dad say they are doing okay, but having some health problems. I know they're disappointed in me."

"There's a lot of people disappointed in me, so join the club. Maybe you're right. What could one letter hurt?" Luke opened his locker, took out pen and paper and sat on the edge of his bunk.

As he waited for the words to flow from the pen, he drew a single red rose at the top of the blank page.

"My dearest Darlina, I hope you won't mind me writing to you. I heard through the grapevine that you are sad and still not enjoying life. Sweetheart, you have to find something that brings you happiness. I wish with all my heart and soul I could stand beside you all the days of our lives and make sure you are happy, but fate had other plans...I'm sorta' doin' okay here. Had to have surgery for ulcers and Red Hoss had surgery on his bad eye. I hear regularly from Mom and Dad and they're trying to help take care of the kids...Mom said they are thinking about moving back to Coleman...I also hear from Bobby now and then. He's living in Alaska and is working as a tour guide. He seems to like it. I'm told you are hanging around with some biker dude and I only hope you aren't putting yourself in any danger. Please remember what you promised me about taking drugs you don't know anything about...It is important to me that you take care of yourself. Honey, I don't have any idea if you'll welcome a letter from me or not. If you don't want to hear from me, simply don't answer and I promise I won't bother you again..."

Two hours later, Luke finally folded the sheets of paper and stuffed them in an envelope. Would she answer him? His heart raced at the thought of opening a letter from her and smelling her sweet fragrance on the pages.

"Don't count on it, fool," he admonished himself. There was a distinct possibility that she might not answer back and he should be prepared for that outcome.

Well, he'd done his part and tried to encourage her in the best way he knew. If she chose not to respond, that was her right.

That night as he lay in the darkness, he offered up a prayer for Darlina. He selfishly wanted to pray that she would answer his letter, but instead just prayed for her safety and happiness.

For now, that was all he had the right to ask for.

He closed his eyes and a restless sleep came. He dreamed about Darlina and a motorcycle gang and she was in danger. He struggled to protect her but she was always just out of his grasp.

He awoke in the early hours of morning, a thin bead of sweat on his brow.

Something was amiss. He could feel it. He only hoped that Darlina would be smart enough not to put herself in any compromising situations. He'd been around lots of bikers in his many years of playing music and for the most part, they showed no respect for women.

"You have to answer my letter, my sweet Darlina," he whispered. "I have to know you are all right."

"Stars we wished on still shine. I guess they always will."

Chapter 10

Finally, Darlina knew someone who had Luke's address. Only she'd blown it and now she mentally kicked herself for letting it slip through her fingers.

A week ago, when she'd bumped into her old friend Louise Monroe, in an Abilene grocery store, their conversation quickly turned to Luke. Darlina's heart skipped a long beat when Louise told her she regularly wrote to him.

Now, as Darlina drove home from work, she couldn't stop thinking about it. What a dumbass! Her mind had obviously taken a vacation at the shock of Louise's statement. She'd simply invited Louise to visit her soon. How stupid could she have been? She should've followed Louise home right then and there and gotten the address she so desperately wanted. To make things worse, she didn't know where Louise and Johnny lived.

Frustration formed a knot in her stomach. Just when she seemed to make progress, fate sent her tumbling all the way back to the moment the judge had sent Luke away. It reminded her of the carrot dangling in front of the horse's nose, always just out of reach.

Two months had passed since the party in Dallas with the Banditos motorcycle gang and she'd barely spoken two words to Will. He failed to see anything wrong with the gang in spite of the bloody shooting that occurred after they'd left the party.

She missed riding with him and the easy friendship she thought she'd found. He'd changed and she wasn't willing to change with him or to accept it.

The familiar roar of a Harley made her turn and look. She saw Rabbit riding at breakneck speed down Mockingbird. Maybe she should go to Will's house and try to talk to him. It was obvious to her, if the friendship could be saved, she would have to make the first step. From the way he'd acted when she confronted him about his behavior toward her in Dallas, she doubted that he had much interest in salvaging it.

Sighing, she pulled into her driveway and as was her normal routine, gathered the mail from the box before going inside.

She tossed the small pile on the kitchen table. Seeing the familiar electric bill on top, felt sure there wasn't anything important under it.

After slipping into comfortable jeans and her favorite tie-dyed shirt, she opened a coke, then picked up the phone and dialed a familiar number.

"Hello." Will's voice responded.

"Hi, Will. It's Darlina. Remember me?"

"Of course I remember you, Darlina. What's up?"

"I want to talk to you. Are you gonna be home for a little while?"

"Sure. Come on over. I'll be here."

"Then I'll see you in about thirty minutes."

"Hey, dress for riding, ok?"

"Okay. See ya." She put the phone receiver back.

Absentmindedly, she thumbed through the stack of mail. When she uncovered the last piece, her heart stopped dead in its tracks. The return address read, "Luke Stone 87047-132, Springfield Federal Medical Center, PO Box 4000, Springfield, Mo. 65801."

With trembling hands she carefully opened the envelope. The image of the rose Luke had drawn at the top of the page immediately caught her gaze. Impatiently, she brushed away the tears that formed and carefully read each line.

Luke still loved her. He wanted her to be happy and safe.

For the longest time she sat, not recognizing the sound of her own sobs. She clutched the letter to her heart and the faint smell of tobacco wafted up to her nostrils.

The ringing of the telephone startled her back to reality. She had no idea how much time had passed. She held Luke's precious letter, longing beyond words to put her arms around him and hold him as tightly as she did the letter.

After several rings, she blew her nose, wiped her eyes and answered.

"Hey, I thought you were coming over. What kind of fuckin' game are you playin'?" Will yelled in her ear.

"I'm not playin' any game. Somethin' came up," she muttered. "I can't make it."

"Are you high? What's wrong? I'm coming over."

Before she could object, the telephone went dead.

She reverently folded the letter and placed it back in the envelope. She resolved to face Will and end whatever it was they'd started.

Luke was back! Not physically, but at least now, she could talk to him. Will wouldn't be happy about that, but it was none of his business. After the way he'd treated her in Dallas, she owed him nothing.

Gently tucking the letter under her pillow, she made an attempt to wash away the traces of her tears.

A loud knock on the front door caused her to jump.

"Open the door, Darlina." Will's voice penetrated the door.

"I'm coming."

She unlocked the door and swung it wide. Will stomped into the apartment.

"I wanna know what's goin' on and I wanna know now." Will faced her squarely.

Closing the door, Darlina took a step backward. "I think we need to call it quits, Will. This is not workin' anymore."

"Why? I thought we were friends."

"So did I. But apparently I was wrong. A friend would never have fed me to the wolves the way you did in Dallas."

"Oh hell! You're still hangin' on to somethin' that's over. You seem to have that problem." Will pulled out a kitchen chair and sat.

"You're right. I do have that problem. I don't like being treated like a piece of ass and never expected that from you."

"You don't understand, do you?"

"No, I don't."

"I had to act that way in front of those guys. If they thought I was weak in any way, I'd never get in the club."

"Gettin' into that gang is more important than anything else to you and I don't fit into the picture. You need an ol' lady like Cassidy that will sleep with them all."

Will replied quietly, "That hurt, Darlina."

"Then you know how I felt in Dallas. That hurt, Will." She pulled out a chair and joined him at the table. "You've turned into someone I don't know anymore."

Will faced her. "I'm sorry. I thought you understood what I had to do."

"I didn't and I still don't. Your obsession with the Banditos has taken over everything, including our friendship."

"That's not fair. I care about you. Hell, I asked you to move in with me."

"And thank goodness I didn't. I'd be in a helluva mess right now, if I had. Look, I'm not tellin' you what to do or not do, I'm just tellin' you what I'm not going to do and that is be a piece of meat to be passed around to your biker friends." Darlina leaned forward in her chair. She hoped he would leave soon so that she could return to her letter from Luke.

Will put his head in his hands. "Please don't do this, Darlina."

She touched his shoulder. "I can't fit in that world. I love riding with you but all these people you're hanging around with and all the drugs...it's not me."

He raised his head to meet her gaze. "Come with me. Let's ride."

"Not tonight, Will. Haven't you heard anything I've said?"

"Yeah, I've heard. I don't wanna believe you really mean it. Somethin's different about you."

"Maybe. I just know what I'm willing to accept and I've told you as plain as I know how."

"Are you blowin' me off for someone else?"

"There's no one new." Her heart wanted to sing out that Luke was back, but didn't dare share that precious news.

"I don't know what's changed, but something has," he grumbled. "Wanna smoke a joint with me?"

"Thanks, but I don't wanna get high." Darlina tried to think of a way to end the conversation and the visit. The letter called to her, tugging on her heartstrings.

Will stood. "Okay, I'll be goin', but don't think for a minute, I'm givin' up on us. I'll check in on you in a day or two."

"You don't have to." Darlina walked to the door and opened it.

"I know I don't have to, but I want to." Will leaned over and kissed her cheek. "I'll earn your trust back."

"Take care of yourself, Will." She held the door for him.

Once he left she closed and locked the door then ran to the bedroom and retrieved her letter.

Her heart raced when her fingers touched the envelope. She stretched out on the bed and held it as if it were gold. Once again, she opened it and unfolded the sheets of paper. She read every word over twice more before she gathered pretty flowered stationery for her reply.

"My dearest Luke, I cannot tell you how happy it made me to get your letter. Thank you for writing to me. I've longed to have a way to talk to you ever since you went away and even drove to Brownwood once to try and find your folks and ask for your address. I couldn't remember the way to their house and came back defeated. Next time I see Louise, I am going to kiss her for giving you my address. She is truly a friend..."

She continued writing for the longest time, telling Luke how she'd met Will and that he'd been a friend. She also told him how she rode the Harley in protest to what had been done to him by the so-called justice system. She talked about her job and how glad she was to be back at the boiler factory. The words flowed on and on much like a geyser that had freed itself and spewed high into the air. After she'd caught Luke up on her life, she let loose a barrage of her deepest feelings on the paper.

"Luke, I've missed you so much. I know you told me to go on living, and I swear I've tried, but nothing takes your place. I dreamed about you one night. We made such sweet love and it seemed so real. I even felt you explode inside of me. How can something that strong not be real? I wonder if you dream about me or even think of me much...I cannot begin to imagine what it's like where you are. I'm so sorry you're forced to endure such hardships. I wish with all my heart I was there to take care of you in every way...I'll never forget you. I'll never stop loving you. You put a mojo on me that won't go away and there is nothing I can or want to do to change that...I can't wait to hear from you again. Please tell Red I said hello and answer back when you can. I love you, Luke Stone....FOREVER!!"

When she finished writing, she had filled eight pages front and back. There was so much to say; so much to catch up on. She rummaged through a picture box and found a recent photo of herself to include in her letter. She wrote on the back of it, "To Luke with all my love, Darlina."

Once she'd sealed the envelope and addressed it, she wandered back to the kitchen. Her stomach growled and she realized she'd not eaten a bite of supper.

Halfway through a sandwich, the phone rang again. She hesitated before answering. "Hello."

"Darlina, are you still up?" Her sister Leann's voice sounded troubled.

"Yes, I'm still up. Are you okay? Is the baby okay?"

"Yes, he's doin' good. Can you talk for a little bit?"

"Of course. I have some news to tell you, but was going to share it with you at lunch tomorrow."

Leann sighed. "Sounds like you might have good news, so you go first."

"I got a letter from Luke today."

"Oh my God. What did he have to say? How did he get your address? Is he all right?"

"Louise sent him my address. Oh Leann, it was so wonderful hearing from him. He still loves me!"

"I know how much it means to you to hear from him and I'm sure he does still love you."

After a few minutes of chatting, Darlina remembered her sister's tone of voice when she'd picked up the phone.

"What's going on with you, Leann?"

"I hate to even say anything but I'm worried about Mama."

"Why?" Darlina toyed with the phone cord.

"I don't think she is well. You should see the picture she sent of her and Daddy. She looks awful."

"Have you talked to her?"

"When I ask, she says everything is as all right as it can be. Even though it's been almost three years, she still hasn't gotten over us leaving home."

"I haven't talked to her in probably six months or more. I hate to call because it seems like she doesn't ever want to talk and there isn't much about my life I can tell her."

"Well, I think you ought to reach out. I know she can be hateful sometimes, but she is still our mother."

"You're right. I'll call this weekend. I keep hoping things will finally be different with her."

"I know. It literally broke her heart when we both moved out like we did and then when you moved in with Luke, it only made things worse."

"She never accepted Luke or the fact that I love him with all my heart."

"She can't help being the way she is. Poor Daddy does his best, but she gives him what for too."

"I'll never forget going to Hobbs for my birthday when you and Wayne lived there and getting to see them. That was a special time and it felt like she softened a little then."

"Well, when the baby was born and she came, I thought so too. That is what makes me think she might really be sick. I'll show you the picture when you come over tomorrow."

"Okay. Surely if anything was wrong, Daddy would tell us, don't you think?"

"Maybe. You know he ain't much of a talker and he never really learned to use the phone very well."

Darlina chuckled. "No he didn't. Okay, I'll see you around noon tomorrow. Want me to pick anything up?"

"No, I'll cook. See you then. I love you."

"I love you too. Goodnight."

Darlina hung up the phone, thinking about her family. She wished so many things could be different. If Luke hadn't been taken away, eventually her mother would have accepted him, especially once he'd divorced Joyce and married her.

She kissed the letter from Luke, breathed in the manly smell of it, then placed it under her pillow and laid her head down to sleep.

She prayed for dreams of Luke tightly holding and loving each other until they became one, no longer distinguishing where she ended and he began.

For the first time in a long time, she felt his presence near and found it warm and comforting.

Yes, Luke was back. Maybe not in body, but in spirit and that was good enough for the moment.

She'd never give up hope for his release and not in a million years would she give away the love she held in her heart for him.

"Goodnight sweetheart," she whispered as she clutched the precious letter under her pillow.

"Somebody write a love song, Someone package a dream..."

Chapter 11

Lightning flashed in the sky and huge raindrops pelted the barred windows as Luke sat in the Unit Manager's office.

The uniformed officer scrawled his signature across a permission slip. "Mr. Stone, the Recreation Supervisor has requested that you come to the rec. room as soon as possible."

Luke's heart soared. It could only mean one thing. His long awaited guitar had arrived!

The booming thunder, dark skies and cold dampness could not touch him and he hurried as fast as his ailing leg would allow.

His hands trembled slightly when he signed the stack of paperwork necessary to gain possession of the guitar. The last form stated he was receiving a "personally owned musical instrument" and would be expected to keep it in his possession or cell at all times.

After a thorough inspection of the guitar and case with the supervisor, Luke closed and fastened the lid. He could hardly wait to get back to the cell and play it.

Red jumped to his feet when Luke burst through the door. He slapped his friend on the back. "Hell man, you got your ol' guitar."

Luke laid the case on his bunk, opened it and took the guitar out. He ran his hands lovingly over the mahogany, rosewood and spruce body and then lightly touched the strings. Tears welled up in his eyes and he blinked them quickly away.

When he could trust himself to speak, he glanced at Red. "Look, Red Hoss. It's got brand new strings on it. Mom and Dad must have splurged for them. Needs tuning, but it's here."

"Why don't we go on down to the music room so I can play along on one of those cheap ass little Jap guitars in there?" Red's eyes shone with excitement.

Luke placed the guitar gently back in the case and closed the lid. "Let's go."

The two men left the cell and a short time later sat in wooden chairs across from each other, playing the familiar tunes they'd played night after night in the Texas honky-tonks. Luke's smooth baritone voice rang out and echoed off the stone walls.

Other inmates gathered around. One played a squeaky worn-out violin. Another played the bottom of a chair as a drum and others joined in with a harmonica, maracas, and more guitars.

Luke grinned. "We're playin' fuckin' music, Red."

Red grinned back, cigarette hanging from his mouth. "Damn sure are, man. Damn sure are."

Luke spoke to the men gathered around them. "If any of ya'll wanna join up with a prison band, me and Red are gonna be playin' for the Christmas party. I need a drummer, a fiddler and a lead guitar player. Meet me here tomorrow if you're interested."

The men talked among themselves and a buzz of excitement filled the air.

One of the men called out. "This band got a name?"

"Yep. Luke Stone and The Survivors."

"I like it. I'll be here for sure."

Some of the other men nodded in agreement and Luke shook hands with them as they left.

That night after being forced out of the music room to return to their cell for head count, the two men sat smoking.

"You know, Red, we might survive this shit after all."

"Reckon we don't have a whole lot of choice. Sure enjoyed playing music again. Hell, I've missed it."

Luke's voice became gravelly with emotion. "I was sick and tired of the honky-tonk scene, but never lost the love for the music. If hard times and deprivation make for good songs, I oughta be able to write some doozeys in here."

"That Mrs. Yarbrough is a remarkable lady. Wish I could've got my bass shipped in, but I wasn't surprised that it had disappeared."

"Yeah. That lady is one tough gal and has my respect. I'm gonna go out of my way tomorrow to thank her, and we will by God play her Christmas party." Luke stretched out on the hard mattress covering the iron frame bunk.

"Hey Luke." Red settled into his bed.

"Yeah, Red."

"I don't know a whole lot and I ain't educated or nothin' but I do know it felt damn good to play again tonight."

"Yes it did, hoss."

He reached out and caressed the guitar case sitting beside his bunk one last time, as darkness overtook the cell. Luke slept more soundly that night than he had in a very long time.

***

The men played the music they loved every day as the next few weeks rolled around. Christmas wasn't far away and Luke wanted to sound his best if for no other reason than to repay Mrs. Yarbrough for her kindness.

"Kiss me another farewell. We'll put it off tonight. Let me hold you, you hold me tight. We'll pretend though we can't break the spell and we both know...every kiss is another farewell."

Luke Stone held the last note while he played a rift of chords. "What do you think?"

"It's good, Luke. Says a lot."

"I think I've got it down good enough to try and record it. Let's see if that kid, Larry, that played drums for us yesterday, will come and hold point so you can sing some harmony."

Luke fished a small tape recorder out from under his bunk, along with a cassette tape titled *God's Greatest Gift*. He placed small pieces of scotch tape over the corners. In a few short minutes, Red returned to the cell accompanied by a tall skinny young convict.

"Red said you guys need me to hold point so you can record a song." Larry lit a cigarette as he stepped inside the cell.

"I'll give you a pack of cigs if you'll watch out for the guards. If you see 'em comin', just start whistlin'." Luke popped the tape into the player. "Ready, Red Hoss?"

"Ready."

Luke pressed the record button and the two men sang the freshly written song while Luke played his guitar.

When they finished, he rewound the tape and they listened back.

"Not bad for recording over a Jesus tape." Luke hit the rewind button again.

"The chaplain thinks we've gotten awful religious lately, asking for all these tapes." Red chuckled.

"It's the only way I can figure to get the new songs recorded. When I mail out the next box of crafts to Mom, I'll sneak a couple of them in with the stuff so at least they'll make it to the outside."

"You better warn her so she don't accidentally rat you out."

Luke laughed. "She sure as hell don't understand how any of this works. She thinks we oughta' be able to do whatever we want."

"It was mighty good of 'em to ship your guitar in. I know it cost a pretty penny."

"I'm gonna get their money back as soon as I sell some more purses and wallets."

"Luke Stone." Nico Romano's voice boomed out.

"Hey, Nico. Come on in. How're you doing, man? Finally got sprung from the recovery ward?"

"Hella' yes. It'sa good ta see ya." Nico took Luke's face in his hands and kissed him on both cheeks.

"Shit, Nico. Don't be gettin' too fresh now." Luke chuckled.

"It'sa famiglia tradition."

"Sit down and talk, man. You remember Red Hoss? And this is Larry. We were just finishing up recording a new song I wrote. Wanna hear it?"

"Recording? How're ya recording?" Nico passed out expensive cigars to all three men.

"We sucked up to the chaplain and told him we needed some religious tapes to listen to, so he loaned us a little recorder and gave us some tapes. Now, those religious tapes are gettin' recorded over with brand new Luke Stone music."

Nico slapped his knee. "Now'a that's 'a smart'a man. Ya know 'a how 'a ta use 'a ya head. Let 'a me hear 'a some."

"Larry?"

"Yeah, I've got it, man." Larry stood in the doorway casually looking up and down the hallway puffing on the newly lit cigar.

Luke pressed the play button on the recorder and watched Nico's face while he listened.

"That's 'a some damn 'a good 'a music." Nico waited until the last note faded away.

"Thank you, Nico. It sure as hell helped to get my guitar shipped in. It strapped my mom and dad, but they did it anyway. Hey, we're playin' for the Christmas party here in a few weeks. Bring your friends and come hear us."

"I'll 'a be dere. I have 'a some 'a colleagues I wanna ya ta meet."

"Sounds good, friend. I'll look forward to it. Hell, things are lookin' up for us ol' cons."

"It will 'a look uppa for 'a me when I getta outta this joint."

"Well, me too hoss, but in the meantime, at least I can play music. I'm making tooled leather purses and sellin' 'em in the visiting room so makin' a little cash for commissary."

"That's 'a good 'a, Stone. I'll tell 'a my people ta buy 'a some 'a your work."

"I appreciate that, Nico. It's sure good to see you." Luke stood and extended his hand.

Nico ignored the handshake and kissed him on both cheeks again. "That's 'a the way'a we do it in'a Italy."

Luke chuckled. "Bring your friends to the Christmas party. I look forward to meeting them."

"Arrivederci, Stone." Nico took leave, waving over his shoulder.

***

A makeshift wooden stage sat at the end of the long chow hall on Christmas Eve, 1972. Luke, Red and six other convicts gathered on the stage to start the show.

Luke had visited the barber and wore his hair in the traditional style he'd worn on the outside. He and Red wore neck scarves they'd ordered from a catalog along with the mandatory white prison attire issued to every inmate in the medical facility.

Luke had found two pretty good electric guitar players, two more acoustic players, a bass guitar for Red, a drummer and a percussionist.

A glittering gold and red Merry Christmas banner hung above the stage.

The men played one song after the other, moving from traditional country music to rock and roll. The inmates cheered, danced around and enjoyed the music.

A few of the "P" number inmates gathered in front of the stage, mouths gaping open, some drooling. Luke thought he saw a little spark in their eyes for a brief moment, then it faded back into the recesses of the drugs that sedated and dulled them.

He poured his heart and soul out, and for a short time, it seemed as if he was back on the outside, playing the music he loved.

He thought about the many nights he kept a watchful eye on Darlina Flowers from the stage and winked or blew a kiss whenever she looked his way. His eyes misted as he remembered one special night that he stepped off the stage and asked her to dance with him. She hadn't complained when he clumsily stepped on her toe. Now, that seemed like a lifetime ago.

He spotted Nico Romano standing to the left of the stage with a group of older distinguished looking men. He grinned and waved to him and Nico returned the wave with a flourish of his cigar.

Mrs. Yarbrough sat at a table with other employees of the facility and nodded her head to the beat of the music.

For a brief moment in time, no one was a prisoner. No one suffered from deprivation, heartache, sickness or grief.

In the magic of the music, everything, even the forty foot walls surrounding them, could be forgotten.

Luke Stone knew, as he had for many years of his life, that he could entertain folks and make them feel what he felt with the music that came through of his hands and out of his heart.

He looked over at Red and nodded, then stepped up to the microphone and gave a rousing rendition of *"Pusher Man"* with the two electric guitars twanging every note.

When the last echoes of the chords died away and the room began to empty, Luke carefully wiped each string and placed his guitar in its case.

He accepted praise from fellow inmates, Mrs. Yarbrough and some of the guards. Making his way to Nico's group, he held his head high and even though he limped, he almost swaggered as he'd done in the outside world.

This wasn't living, but it was a damn sight closer than anything he'd done since he landed behind the iron bars.

He knew sleep would elude him this night. He had a long letter planned to Darlina and would relish sharing every detail with her. Smiling, he reached Nico and his group.

THE CONVICT'S GUITAR

Hear these stories of times, places far away and near
Tales of bad times, good times, loneliness and love so dear
Where living was reality, not untouchable tomorrows afar
Songs from the soul, played on a Convict's guitar.

Behind these walls, the lost and saddened heart wails
Ballads mourning for life come from deep within the cells
Today lasted forever, and well, left its scar
Unnoticed, another tear falls on a Convict's guitar.

Pitiful realization that yesterday and hopes are gone
A dead mind buried in memories, the bodies live on
Reality screams you are here, does humanity know you are?
No one hears the sad refrain of a Convict's guitar.

Play upon those golden strings, my friend, a few of us care
And though the world has turned cold and unaware,
Your song echoes truth from a bright and distant star
The melodies ring eternally, from your Convict's guitar.

"There is peace, joy, goodwill and themes of love; melodies of the holiday horn..."

 Chapter 12

Darlina awoke on Christmas Eve, 1972 with a smile on her face and a song in her heart. She bounded out of bed and made short work of a bowl of Cheerios and cup of coffee. She couldn't wait to get to Leann's house.

The beautiful hand-tooled leather purse she'd received from Luke in the mail two days ago sat beside the stack of presents she had wrapped to take with her.

She parked in front of her sister's house by nine o'clock and with her arms full, knocked on the door.

Leann opened the door, immediately taking some of the presents from Darlina's arms. "Come on in, sister. Lordy, it's cold out here today."

"Is it?" Darlina laughed. "I didn't even notice."

"I don't know who is more excited about Christmas, J.J. or you." Leann added the packages to an already overflowing mountain under the tree.

"I can't help it. I'm so happy to have Luke back and now getting to spend Christmas with my family makes me even happier. Look what he sent me." She proudly held the purse up for Leann to see.

"That is really beautiful, Darlina. Luke made this?"

"Yep. He's making all kinds of crafts. Said he's learning to do Indian beadwork too. The best part of the package was a cassette tape stuck in a pocket of the purse. It's Luke and Red singing some new songs Luke's written."

"Oh, I'd love to hear that. After Christmas is over, you'll have to let me listen."

The girls turned around at the sounds of a young child. The small boy ran to the Christmas tree, squealing with delight.

"J.J., don't you get any of those presents out from under the tree yet. We have to wait for Granny and Papa and Grandma and Grandad. Wayne, come get J.J. or he's gonna have every one of these packages torn open."

Wayne switched on the TV. "You get him. I'm busy."

"Let's get started in the kitchen." Leann sighed and led the way. She plopped J.J. in his highchair with some crayons and coloring book.

"What's with Wayne?"

"Oh, he's just being a horse's ass." She tied an apron around her waist.

"So what are we cooking?" Darlina accepted the apron her sister passed to her.

"Wayne's mom is baking the turkey, but I'm making the dressing because she don't do it right. Norma's bringing a fruit salad and pumpkin pie and we're doing the rest. I'm letting Mama fix the sweet potatoes after she gets here. No one can cook like her."

Darlina pushed up her sleeves and the two girls soon had holiday smells coming from the kitchen.

One by one, family gathered in, shedding coats and gloves. Warm hugs and genuine smiles filled the house. Even though the cold wind howled outside and a flurry or two of snow floated around, the roaring fire in the Dearborn heater and love of family melted them away.

Laughter echoed around the room, as they watched the antics of Leann's little boy, J.J., trying to stand up and balance on the seat of his new tricycle.

A warm glow spread through Darlina and settled into every crevice of her heart. The only thing missing was Luke. She couldn't deny the happiness she felt that he was back, even though it was only through letters.

She walked across the room and sat beside her mother, placing her arm around her shoulders. "Mama, this is a good Christmas, don't you think?"

"The best one I've had in a few years. It's good to be here with you girls."

"Are you feeling okay?"

"I feel all right. I've been going to Weight Watchers up in New Mexico and that's how I lost all this weight. Everyone says I look sick, but I'm not. I sure do get tired of tuna fish though."

Darlina laughed. "I never liked tuna fish, and can't imagine eating it every day. Glad we have some turkey and dressing. You better eat up."

"Oh, I'll get enough. You're the one that needs to eat up. You're skinny as a rail."

"I eat. Leann makes sure I do. I love livin' so close to her and seein' J.J. a lot. I have lunch with her at least a couple of times a week."

"Yes, I'm glad you girls are close by each other. I know you had to go your own way, but I was so afraid you weren't ready and that you'd get hurt and sure enough you did. If you'd only had enough sense to listen to me."

"Guess that's how we learn." Darlina wanted so badly to tell her mother that she was writing to Luke in prison, but knew it would only upset her and today wasn't the day for that. In time, there would be opportunity to share the joy she got every time she opened the mailbox to find a letter.

"I'm happy you finally got over that no good outlaw musician. When are you going to settle down with a good man and get married?"

Darlina ignored the jab at Luke. "Oh I don't know. Maybe never." She laughed. "Who wants to play Aggravation?"

The day passed with good feelings, food, games and football on TV. Over and over again, Darlina thought of Luke and pictured him sitting forlornly in his prison cell longing for his children and family. It wasn't fair. A small twinge of guilt seeped into her soul.

She asked Leann to take a picture of her in front of the Christmas tree so that she could send it to him.

Too quickly, Christmas Eve was over and one by one, the family left to go their separate ways.

Darlina cleaned the kitchen while Leann put a very tired J.J. to bed. Humming to herself, she reflected on the Christmas Eve she'd spent with Luke, watching him sink deep into the abyss of a night-mare. She'd never felt more helpless, as she kept vigil beside the bed while he tossed and turned and screamed out in pain. For days, he remained lost in unconsciousness and relived over and over the agony of having his leg amputated on a long ago battlefield during the Civil War.

Darlina's heart caught in her throat as she remembered the anguish he'd suffered. She made a mental note to ask him, in her next letter, if he'd experienced that again since he'd been locked away in prison. She knew, if he did, that Red would stay beside him.

Her thoughts and musings were interrupted when Leann came into the kitchen. "He's fast asleep. He was one tired little boy. Wow, you've been busy in here. Why don't we get a cup of hot chocolate and go sit by the fire and rest."

"That sounds like a good idea. This was a very good day, Leann."

"Yes, it was."

The two girls walked back into the living room a few minutes later to find Wayne sound asleep in his recliner.

"I'll wake him up when I go to bed. I'm glad he's asleep because there's something I want to tell you."

"Okay."

The sisters sat down on the sofa. Leann kicked her shoes off and reached for a throw at the end of the couch.

"I think I'm pregnant." She ran her finger around the rim of her cup.

"And that's a good thing, right?"

"I don't know. I just wish things were better before we have another baby."

"Well, I guess if we waited until everything in life was perfect to do things, we'd never do them. When will you know?"

"I made an appointment with the doctor the first week of January and I'll know then, but I can tell."

"Then I'm happy for you. Another baby will be good for our family."

"Wayne's folks are moving to Henrietta next month and I have a feeling that we'll soon be following them. Wayne doesn't get very far away from them."

"Oh no. I don't want you to leave again. I hated it when you moved back to Hobbs."

"I know. I'm not crazy about the idea, but I do think things will be better for us out of Abilene."

"You have to do what is best for you and your family. With another baby, maybe it would be good to start over again somewhere else, but I'll miss you terribly."

"I'm glad you have Luke to talk to again. I really do want to hear his new songs."

"I'm glad too, and I'll bring the tape over soon. We can listen to it over lunch. I've been thinking about Will today. I haven't seen or talked to him in several months. I do hope he's doing okay."

"Whatever happened between you two? You never told me."

"I'll tell you sometime, but I don't wanna talk about it tonight. He just didn't act the way he should have."

"Well, it wouldn't hurt to wish him a merry Christmas. You know how Mama always said that we shouldn't burn our bridges."

"Yeah, maybe I will." Darlina yawned. "Guess I better be gettin' home. It's late and you need to get in bed. Santa has to come in the morning."

Leann laughed. "Yes he does and J.J. will probably be up at the crack of dawn."

Darlina hugged her sister. "I'll drop by sometime tomorrow. We can eat leftovers. I'm happy that you're going to have another baby. Hope it's a girl."

"A girl would be nice. The way I figured the months, it will be due in August."

"Hey, maybe she'll be born on my birthday."

"Who knows. Maybe. Goodnight, Darlina. See you tomorrow."

"Goodnight. I love you, sister."

"Love you too."

Darlina shivered as she walked out into the frigid night air. She should have started her car and let it warm up, but thankfully she only had a few blocks to drive.

Once inside her apartment, she turned up the heat, found her stationery and a pen. Wrapped in a blanket on her bed, she began her letter to Luke.

"My Dearest Luke,

I have had the most wonderful Christmas Eve with my family. I wish you'd been here with us. Mama and Daddy came and she seems to finally be lightening up some. All I could think about all day was you, honey.

I remembered the Christmas Eve you had the fever and I sat by your bedside feeling so helpless to do anything for you. Have you had any of the fevers since you've been locked up? I truly hope not. I know Red would help you, just as he did back then, but no one else would understand.

I loved showing off my new purse to my sisters today. They both told me how beautiful it is, but I already knew that...As I lay my head down tonight, I am going to pray for dreams of you. I'm also going to pray for the miracle that frees you from prison and puts you back in my arms...Merry Christmas, sweetheart. I love you..."

As she folded the perfumed pages she'd written, she imagined Luke sitting in his small cell with his own pen and paper, writing a new song, poem or letter to his loved ones; maybe even a letter to her.

With a heart bursting with love, and a smile on her face, she slept.

***

Luke Stone sat in the quiet darkness of his prison cell. His leg throbbed and sleep evaded him. He let the night's events replay in his mind.

The joy of having his guitar and entertaining again was unmistakable. He'd known at a very young age that it was what he was born to do. Thinking about the grins on the faces of the convicts and prison staff, he understood on a deep level that music is therapeutic for everyone involved. It didn't seem to matter if they were the audience or the performers. Music carried magic.

The group of Italian men Nico introduced him to had been warm and accepting. He knew they were Mafia, but compared to the run-of-the-mill convicts, they were decent God-fearing men. He didn't mind being a part of their group. At least they weren't homosexuals and didn't mess with dope. They were about business and continuing to conduct the family business from inside prison. They, like him, simply wanted to do their time and get the hell out.

He reached for the switch on a small lamp attached to the wall. From the snores vibrating off the walls, he knew Red was sound asleep.

Pulling a box from under his bunk, he retrieved his writing tablet and a pen. After drawing a unicorn sitting on top of a fluffy white cloud, he began his letter to Darlina.

"My Dearest Princess,
Words can't begin to tell you how happy it makes me when I get a sweet letter from you at mail call. I live for those days and moments and relish every word you write.
Merry Christmas, darling. I wish with all of my heart I was there beside you, watching you be excited about Christmas and loving you. There is nothing I'd like better...
I played music tonight for the convicts and prison staff and it was amazing to watch the sad depressed faces turn into smiles...
I've met some Italian men that seem to be taking me into their fold. In here, there is so much dope and homosexual shit and lots of killings behind both of those things. It is refreshing to meet men like myself who are only interested in doing their time and getting back to the business of living...
Sweetheart, I love you with all my heart and soul and that will never change. Of course, if you find someone you want to spend your life with, I'd quickly and happily give my blessings. I want you to be happy and have babies around your feet. It is what you deserve in life...I can't give you that and even though I selfishly want to keep you to myself, I know that isn't right or fair. Please go on living, baby, and be happy...most of all be happy..."

With the long letter written, folded neatly and put in the standard white prison envelope, Luke switched off the lamp and stretched out on his bunk.

He let his mind drift back to warm happy times with Darlina by his side and in his bed. He groaned with want and need and pictured her lying with her head on his shoulder, her long auburn hair spread out on the pillow and shapely legs intertwined with his.

Desperately yearning for and thinking only of her and her warm touch and kisses, he gave into the need.

Thankful for the darkness, he let pent up emotions flow onto his hard flat pillow. Finally, brushing the tears away, he gave a ragged sigh and prayed for sleep.

Only in dreams could he escape, scale the forty foot walls, and be with those he loved.

"Look up, the light shines. You are not alone..."

Chapter 13

L uke Stone had adapted to the routine of prison life in the medical center but expected to be shipped back to Leavenworth any day. Even though his leg stayed swollen, he'd recovered from the ulcer surgery.

He'd come to appreciate small things. Even the most ordinary ones that he'd overlooked or taken for granted on the outside suddenly mattered. On this early February 1973 day, he sat huddled on a bench in the yard.

A dazzling red bird flew down and landed a few feet away. He had an instant flash of his childhood, living in the country, hunting with his faithful border collie, Fireball. Even though a chill hung in the air, the sun's rays warmed him through.

The sound of someone's lame attempt to play a trombone pulled his attention away. He turned to see a convict marching around the yard, blowing on the horn.

With amusement, he watched the guards approach the man.

"Columbo, give us that horn," one of the guards bellowed.

Columbo marched faster, tooting his horn, ignoring the guards. They followed behind, continuing to negotiate. It resembled some sort of crazy parade and made Luke think of Benny Hill.

Columbo broke into a trot and the guards trotted with him.

Luke began to chuckle.

Finally, Columbo stopped, threw the horn on the ground and moved into a karate stance. "Ha yah! I'll kill all of you with my bare hands."

"Come on Columbo. You don't know karate." One of the guards advanced closer.

"Don't come any closer, I'm warning you." Columbo jumped and threw his hands at them in chopping motions.

"Come on, man. It's time to go take your medicine."

"Oh okay." Columbo put his hands to his sides and stood as the guards led him back into the building.

Red had joined Luke for the show. "Man, you see some funny shit in here, don't you?"

"Sure do, hoss. Look at that one over there. Every time he comes to a crack in the sidewalk, he stops and jumps over it. Makes you wonder what goes on in their minds."

"I don't think I wanna know." Red lit a cigarette and handed it to Luke.

The men were soon joined by Nico and two of his Italian friends.

"Beautiful day, gentleman. You just missed the show." Luke pointed in the direction of the disappearing Colombo.

Nico, Giovanni and Stefano each kissed Luke and Red on the cheek and sat down with them.

"Luke, ya know 'a that 'a fancy handbag 'a ya gotta in 'a the visiting room 'a for 'a sale?" Nico lit his big cigar.

"Sure, Nico. What about it?"

"When 'a my sister come 'a next 'a week, she 'a going ta buy it."

"That's great, man. I can sure use the money. I'm still tryin' to pay my folks back for gettin' my guitar shipped in here."

"It's 'a beautiful 'a piece 'a work, Nico proclaimed. Giovanni and Stefano both nodded in agreement.

"Well stud, I've got lots of time to work on that shit."

"Ah, but 'a ya gotta the talent." Giovanni waved his hands in the air as he spoke.

"Nah, man, anybody could do it."

Red tapped Luke on the shoulder. "Looks like we've got company, Luke."

Luke turned to see four guards stalking toward them, their nightsticks slapping against their legs. His gut told him they weren't coming to talk about guitars or music.

"What the hell you reckon they want?"

"I think we're about to find out." Red crushed out his smoke.

"Can we help you, Officers?" Luke stood.

"Luke Stone and Thomas Johnson, you need to come with us." The guard braced his feet apart, hand on his nightstick as if expecting trouble.

"What's going on?" Luke stepped back.

The guard waved to Nico and his friends. "You guys move along now." Turning back to Luke, he continued, "We were told to come get you both." He put his hand on Luke's elbow.

Luke pulled away, narrowing his eyes. "I wanna know what the hell is going on?"

"You'll find out when you go before the IDC Committee. The guard again, put his hand on Luke's arm.

"What the fuck are you talking about, man?" Luke snarled and jerked his arm away.

"We're taking you and Mr. Johnson to segregation while you wait for a hearing." The guard motioned to the other three standing behind him.

Luke kicked at the first guard that reached him and drew back to throw a punch.

"I wouldn't do that if I were you, Stone. You'll only make it harder on yourself."

"What are we being charged with?" Red yelled.

"Cuff 'em." The guards stepped forward, and in no time had Luke and Red cuffed.

Luke looked at Red. "What the hell, hoss?"

"I don't have any idea, Luke."

Nico, Giovanni and Stefano watched from a distance, as their friends, escorted by the guards, disappeared into the building. They shook their heads in confusion.

When the guards reached the solitary confinement unit, they shoved Red and Luke into separate tiny box-like cells with only a small metal window on the door that could be raised from the outside.

The guard that Luke had kicked at and threatened to punch followed him into his cell.

Luke looked up at him. "Aren't you gonna take these handcuffs off so it will be a fair fight?"

The guard smirked. "Now why would I wanna do that, Stone?" With that, he hit Luke and knocked him into the back of the cell. When Luke slid to the floor, the guard kicked him in the stomach with his heavy steel toed boot. Luke doubled over in an attempt to protect the delicate area. The guard kicked him in the back, then slammed his head on the concrete.

"Next time you think about throwin' a punch at me, maybe you'll reconsider."

"Fuck you!" Luke growled, still doubled over on the floor.

After four days in solitary confinement, a sullen Luke sat before the IDC (Incident Disciplinary Committee), jaw set, eyes flashing.

"Stone, stand up," the captain ordered.

Luke struggled to stand. His leg had swollen until he could no longer move it. "What am I charged with?"

"You are charged with planning and attempting escape."

Luke scoffed. "Sir, have you taken a look at me? I just got over a belly operation and my ol' leg is all swelled up. Hell, I'd have to hijack an ambulance to escape from here."

"Don't get smart with me, Mr. Stone."

"I wasn't, sir, just stating the facts."

"Some of the people you've been seen associating with were found with gear that would indicate they are planning to escape. What do you know about it?" The captain continued.

"I don't know anything about an escape plan." Luke squared his shoulders.

"We're gonna find out and it sure would go easier on you if you'd tell us what you know."

"I'm tellin' you that I don't know anything."

"Then you will be held in solitary confinement until we sort this all out. If you decide you want to talk, you let a guard know."

"Cap'n, if I knew anything about an escape, I'd sure tell you, but I swear to you I know nothing." Luke looked directly into the man's eyes.

Luke crouched in the tiny cell that evening with nothing but thoughts and bruises. He clutched his stomach, hoping the beating hadn't hampered the still healing stitches.

He remembered the visit he'd received from a representative of the Irish Republican Army in the Eastland County jail, before he'd ever been convicted or sentenced. If he'd known then what he knew now, he'd have taken their offer to bust him and Red out of jail and take them to Ireland.

He reflected on his folks and his children and how they were his reason for refusing the help from the IRA after being told he could never contact his family again.

That was a one-time offer and he'd refused it, believing he'd never be convicted.

What was he to do now? Mrs. Yarbrough crossed his mind. Her patience with the inmates in the craft shop went far beyond what most of them deserved. She inspired him to be a better man.

Then there was Darlina. How he loved getting letters from her and having the chance to share his feelings, hopes and dreams with her.

Had he ever done anything worth a shit in his life? All night, in the darkness of the tiny cell, Luke Stone contemplated who he was, who he'd become and who and what he wanted to be.

It seemed that the only chance he had of surviving prison lay in creating something positive. How in the hell was he going to do that with negativity surrounding him?

When the guard came to do nightly rounds and slid the small metal window open, Luke took the opportunity to make a request. "Hey man, my leg is hurtin' really bad. Can I have an aspirin or something? And is there any way I could have a pencil and some writing paper?"

"I don't see why not. I'll bring you some next time I come around."

"Thank you." Luke stretched out on the tiny metal cot to wait.

Luke felt the presence of someone or something with him in the restricted space in the cell. But, clearly, he was alone.

For a moment, he wondered if he'd gone as crazy as some of the lunatics that resided here.

When he finally slept in the early morning hours, he dreamed that he walked through fields of lush green grass with sweet smelling flowers all around. The sun shone and birds chirped. A brilliant rainbow of breathtaking color decorated the sky. As he walked, he became aware of someone walking beside him.

"Who are you?" Luke asked

"I am you. We are the same," the Being replied.

Puzzled, Luke tried to see who had answered but when he looked, all he saw was a reflection of himself.

The grating of the metal window sliding open awakened him. He slowly sat up.

"Breakfast is here, Stone. Oh and I got you a tablet and a pencil. Here's a couple of aspirin." The guard shoved a styrofoam plate through the opening along with paper, a pencil and two white tablets.

"Thank you." Luke groaned as he managed to stand on one leg.

Once the guard slid the window shut, he sat back on his cot, leg stretched out in front of him, and opened the container. Cold scrambled eggs and soggy toast didn't appeal to him. He closed the lid and scooted it across the floor. He swallowed the two aspirin with a sip of water.

After staring at the blank page for the longest time, he began to write.

Discovery

Through life's wilderness I wandered aimlessly seeking my way.
Seldom looking up to see the light of day
Stumbling blindly till so weary, I could go no more
In total exhaustion I fell to the earthen floor
My eyes focused upon a wounded but lovely thing
Seemingly an Angel felled with broken wing
Said I, "Stranger, what will be your name?"
A voice spoke softly, "Yours for our names are the same."
I replied angrily, "That cannot be."
In understanding the voice spoke again, "Look and you shall see."
"What song do you sing?" I asked as I drew nearer.
"Your song, my friend. Listen and you shall hear."
"You know me?" said I, as the sweet melody began to flow.
"From the very first," the voice whispered. "Yes, you I know."
"You are fantasy, you are imagination, you are not real."
Patiently, the voice said in soft tone, "Satisfy your doubt, touch and feel."

I shouted, "You are the Death Angel come to take me away."
"No, I am faith and compassion left behind yesterday."
I replied, "When others are worthy, why did a wretch like me you select?"
The gentle voice asked, "Who is the being my eyes reflect?"
In kind loving eyes sparkled an image of me
Not the hopeless, cast-out soul I thought myself to be.
The spirit smiled and said, "I saw your need and I came."
Respectfully, I asked, "How can you help me when you yourself are lame?
"Truth, but my wound does not exceed your own.
My friend, together we shall mend and then travel on.
Walking slowly and cautiously, gradually regaining our strength.
In confidence and with patience, our stride will soon reach full length.
For in peace, love and understanding you shall stay.
In your heart I will dwell no matter how hard the way."
Leaving behind the dark wilderness, where lost I had been
To tread upon a sure path that is lighted from within.

Luke read the words that had poured out through the end of the pencil. Tears came to his eyes and it began to dawn on him that this was his truth. He'd left behind compassion and faith many years ago. He was wounded and yet, felt strongly he had a spirit companion that traveled with him, perhaps with wounds of his own.

He put the tablet down and bowed his head. He sat like that, talking to the Great Spirit for an hour or more.

"I'm gonna find a way to turn all of this shit into something positive and good or else I'm gonna find a way over these damned ol' forty foot walls."

As he mulled it over, he felt a sense of obligation toward his family and friends, the few real friends he had in the world, and knew he couldn't simply disappear on them.

"I'm gonna crawl my way up from the bottom an inch at a time. I don't care what it is, any little bitty tiny thing I can do in here to better myself. I want to make people feel glad to have known me and not think I am a total waste."

That was a final decision. Luke knew something big had happened, a turning point.

He looked up and continued talking out loud with conviction. "My body is captured, but my mind and soul are not."

"Hands full of nothing, hearts full of dreams; living on hope today for whatever tomorrow brings..."

Chapter 14

L uke faced each painful day after another in the confines of the tiny cell. He wrote with a passion, as he waited for the bogus charges to be cleared. Soon he had a tablet filled with words that flowed out of him like molten lava from a volcano.

The metal window grated open and a guard peered in. "Stone, come on, it's time to go out on the yard."

"I've told all of you dipshits that I can't, man." Luke snapped.

"It's your choice, but I'd damn sure take the opportunity to get out of this box, if I was you."

"I can't fuckin' walk." Luke attempted to stand. "Hey, I sure could use some more pencils and another tablet, though."

"Shit, what's the matter with you?"

"I keep telling you I can't walk. I guess that damned rheumatic fever I had when I was a kid has come back on me."

"Okay. I'll get the doctor to come check on you."

"Thanks." Luke propped himself against the wall, his leg extended. "Hey, don't forget another tablet and pencils. Oh, and can I have a few more envelopes?"

"Okay, I'll bring them next time I come around, but I'm gonna put in a request for a doctor."

The metal window grated shut.

Luke read back over the many pages he'd written. Perhaps if he died in this cell, someone would send all of them to his folks. He thought about his guitar and Red and wondered how his partner was faring. He made a mental note to ask about them both when the guard came back around.

He'd flooded Darlina's mailbox with letters, poems, songs and musings. He hadn't told her of the latest struggle with the leg or the bogus charges. He figured she didn't need any extra worries.

Several hours later, the window grated open again. This time, the Chief Medical Officer peered in. "Stone, they tell me you're refusing to go out on the yard. What's wrong with you?"

"It's my leg, sir. It's all swollen and I can't walk."

The doctor turned to the guard. "Unlock the door. I need to examine this man."

Once inside, the doctor instructed, "Drop your pants, Stone. Let me see that leg."

Luke unbuttoned his loose pants that were now two sizes too big for him.

"Oh my God," the doctor exclaimed. "Guard, get a gurney over here now. This man's got Phlebitis in a bad way. I don't want that leg moved one iota." He turned to Luke. "Lie back on your cot and don't move."

"What in the hell is Phlebitis?" Luke questioned.

"Blood clots in your leg and if they break loose and go to your heart or brain, you'll die instantly."

"Holy shit." Luke lay back on his cot.

"I'll get you moved into the critical care unit immediately. We need to get blood thinners started right away."

Luke looked at the guard. "Can you tell me how my partner, Mr. Johnson is doing and where my guitar is?"

"Mr. Johnson went before the committee today and he's been released back into population. You were scheduled for tomorrow. Your personal belongings have been secured in a locker until you can claim them."

"Thanks." Luke clutched his tablets as he lay on the cot.

"Give me those, Stone," The guard insisted.

"Hell no. I ain't lettin' go of 'em. They go with me or else I'll refuse to go."

"Don't upset this patient." The doctor faced the guard, then turned to Luke. "Mr. Stone, you can bring your tablets with you. Just don't move that leg."

In no time, the gurney arrived. Monitored by the eagle-eyed doctor, orderlies lifted Luke onto a stretcher, then wheeled him through the hallways to the critical care unit.

Once they transferred him to a hospital bed, the doctor began barking out orders for a Heparin drip, a strap to keep the leg from moving and an injection.

"Mr. Stone, I am serious about you not moving. This is a very critical situation. I'm going to order something to help keep you relaxed and calm."

Luke simply nodded and placed his tablets on the small table beside his bed.

The nurses moved swiftly and soon Luke drifted off to sleep.

Every four hours, they brought more medicine. He fell into a lethargic state and lost all track of time, days and weeks.

***

Darlina hurried to the mailbox after her workday only to find bills again. A sense of foreboding settled over her. Even though she continued to send letters to Luke, she got no reply. Now, here it was, the middle March and there had been no letter from Luke since January. Something was wrong.

What if he'd died? How would she ever know?

Shoulders drooping and eyes full of unshed tears, she turned to walk into the apartment.

The roar of a Harley caused her to look up. Will Brocker wheeled the shiny chopper into the driveway and came to a stop.

"How about a ride in the country?" He hopped off the chopper.

"It's kinda chilly, ain't it? Have I remembered to tell you how nice you look with your hair and beard trimmed?" She accepted his embrace.

"Yes, about a dozen times. It's not too cold to ride if you bundle up. Why the sad face? Hope it wasn't anything I did this time."

"No, Will, nothing you did. I'll go change. It's nice to have the old Will back." They walked into the apartment.

"I never really left, just got sidetracked. It took a while to sink in that the Banditos were just using me. They never intended to offer me a prospect patch."

"Guess you had to figure it out on your own. Nothing I said made a difference."

"Sorry...And if I haven't told you enough, I'm sorry about what I let happen to you in Dallas. I should've had my ass kicked for that."

"It's water under the bridge. Want a coke or something while change?"

"I don't need anything. Just hurry. I'm itchin' to ride." Will made himself comfortable on the sofa.

Darlina returned with her thermals, jeans, boots and vest on, bandana tied around her head and ready to ride.

"I've really missed this." She sat on the sofa beside Will. "My sister, Leann, moved to Henrietta, and now my other sister, Norma, is moving to Houston to take a new job. I'm feelin' pretty much alone."

"I'm here. There's somethin' I wanna tell you, but let's ride first." Will stood and pulled Darlina to her feet. "Get your jacket."

With the cool Texas wind whipping around their faces, they roared down the highway. Soon, Will turned off onto the country road that led to Lake Fort Phantom.

After a while, he pulled the motorcycle into the familiar place they'd stopped at, such a long time ago, on their first ride together. They climbed to the top of the boulders and sat side by side, looking out at the sun sinking low behind the scrub oaks.

Will lit a joint and passed it to Darlina. She sucked on it, then passed it back. "What did you want to tell me?"

"My parents have bought a ranch outside of Austin and they're moving. They're gonna build a house and retire there. They've asked me oversee the construction of it."

"That's great for them and you're a good carpenter." Darlina had never felt more alone. Now Will was leaving too.

"There's an old farmhouse on the property that's still livable, but they're buying a mobile home to live in until the house is finished. You don't have to answer me right now, but Darlina, I'm askin' you to move with me to Austin and live in the farmhouse."

Darlina sat silent. She turned to look at Will. "I don't know. That's a big decision. I'll have to think about it."

"I promise you I'll look out for you and believe me when I tell you there will never be a repeat of what happened in Dallas."

She took Will's hand. "I know, Will, and I do believe you. Just give me a few days to think about it."

"What has you so troubled besides your sisters leaving?"

Will's hand felt warm and comfortable in hers. "I haven't mentioned this because it didn't seem like I needed to, but I've been writing to Luke in prison."

"Shit, now I know why you ditched me."

"That wasn't the only reason, Will. You deserved to be ditched." Darlina laughed.

"True. I did. So, what is it about writing to Luke that has you so worried? Do you feel like you're betraying me?"

"No. It's just that I haven't heard from him in over six weeks and I was getting letters every other day or so. Something is wrong. I can feel it."

"I know you don't want to hear this and I certainly don't want to upset you, but Luke is locked away for a very long time and you need to move on. I'm sure that's why he quit writing. He knows that too."

She sighed. "He tells me that in every letter, but I can't imagine why the letters suddenly stopped. You know how I feel about him."

"Yes, and I have to admit I'm a little jealous. I have to wonder if you can ever feel that way about me, but I'm willing to try. Please move with me to Austin. It's a chance for you and me both to start a new life."

The fading sunset shadowed his face, softening his sharp features.

Darlina's mind reeled. "I'm not saying yes and I'm not saying no. I need to think about it."

Could she leave her job again, just as she had done to be with Luke, and take off into the unknown with Will? Could she totally trust him not to throw her to the wolves again? Words were cheap, as she'd found out the hard way. All of it left her numb.

"Okay. I won't mention it again until you're ready."

The two sat in silence, getting high and watching the brilliant red and gold sunset painting the sky above them.

Riding back to town, cloaked in darkness, Darlina let her mind wander. The haunting feeling lingered that Luke was in trouble, or dead. Her breath caught in her throat and her heart constricted.

How would she ever know? What if she never heard from him again? Tears quickly came into her eyes with that thought. It had been so sweet, exchanging letters and proclaiming their love for each other. In a way, it was almost like having him with her again except she couldn't touch him, feel his body against hers, or smell his fragrance.

And now, Will was asking her to move away with him.

If only she could talk to Luke about it. He would encourage her to move on and that was a fact. He always advised her to live life to the fullest and be happy.

Would she be happy living with Will? So much to ponder.

Stopping at a red light, Will turned around. "You wanna get something to eat?"

"I'm not really hungry, but I'd like a cup of coffee."

"You know my favorite place."

Darlina nodded.

Sitting across the table from him at Whataburger, Darlina sipped on her coffee and watched him consume his burger. "I promise I'll have an answer about moving to Austin by the end of the week."

"Fair enough." Will wiped his mouth. "Sure you don't want anything to eat?"

"No. This coffee is good."

"Would you spend the night with me tonight?" he asked.

"I've got to be at work early in the morning. We've got some big whigs coming in to tour the factory. Maybe soon."

He couldn't hide the disappointment on his face. "Give me a chance, Darlina. That's all I'm asking."

"I know. I always give people chances until they don't deserve it." She laughed. "Don't be so serious."

"This is serious to me. I really care about you and I want us to be like we were before I got obsessed with the Banditos."

"I care about you too and I'm not saying no to you. I'm only asking for a little time."

"Take all the time you need. I'm not going to push you."

"Thank you. Let's ride a little more before I have to go home."

They tossed their paper and cups into the trash can by the door and walked out into the cold night air. Will straddled the motorcycle and held it while Darlina got on.

Before she swung her legs over the seat behind Will, she leaned in and kissed him on the cheek.

"Thanks for that." He smiled.

That night in her apartment, lying in her bed, she tossed and turned with her troubling thoughts. How could she find out what was going on with Luke? Should she move to Austin? What if she moved and Luke reached out to her? How would he find her again?

She finally fell asleep only to be awakened by a terrifying dream. An icy chill enveloped her and she couldn't stop trembling.

She saw Luke lying in a casket in her dream and no one was there to mourn for him. He lay there alone, cold and stiff, a permanent grimace on his face.

She sat up sobbing into her hands. "God, please don't let Luke be dead. Please..."

"In the most secretive hiding places, truth finds me there..."

Chapter 15

L uke drifted in and out of sleep with little awareness of his surroundings. When he did awaken, he could hear moans and groans of men in various stages of dying.

Troubling dreams filled his head and always included someone in trouble whom he could not help. Sometimes it was one of his children. Sometimes his father would be falling off a roof or at times, it was Darlina in jeopardy and he couldn't reach her.

On a bright spring day, Luke awoke to find a nurse at his bedside with another pill for him to take.

"What is this shit you're givin' me? I can't seem to do anything but sleep." Luke threw the sheet back.

"It's the Valium Dr. Ciccone ordered for you." Scowling, she handed Luke a cup of water and the pill.

"Well, no offense to the doctor, but I ain't gonna take any more of it. How long have I been here?"

"You've been on this ward six weeks."

"Six weeks? Shit, I've lost all track of time. I need to see the doctor."

"Sir, if you'll just take this pill, I'll make sure Dr. Ciccone knows you need to see him." The nurse again offered the water and pill.

"I ain't gonna stay doped up all the fuckin' time. You can tell Dr. Ciccone I said so and take that shit yourself." He pushed her hand away.

"I'll tell him, but he's not going to like it." The nurse wrote on his chart then walked away.

***

Mrs. Stone, Luke's mother, paced the floor and fretted, waiting for Mr. Stone to return from town. In one hand she held a letter and the other, a Kleenex.

It had been weeks since she'd had any word from Luke and now this letter arrived.

It brought distressing news and added to the worry.

She read the letter through again, with sentences jumping out at her. "Right after your visit to Luke, he and Red and five others were placed in the segregation unit of the hospital on a phony charge of attempted escape and they were locked up for about two weeks. I have not seen Luke since that time, for he went from segregation (the hole) to the hospital section on account of his leg got swollen and full of blood clots and I could not visit him."

She wiped her eyes and read on. "Luke, Red, myself and a few others had the courage to speak out and write out about the horrible conditions of that madhouse where life is cheap and good men die for no other reason than the fact that no one cares about them."

Looking up, she sighed and whispered a prayer for Luke. She couldn't wait for Mr. Stone to get home so they could decide what to do. More than anything, she prayed for him not to die.

She read the words of warning twice before folding the letter and placing it back in its envelope. "Please do not believe Dr. Ciccone on anything he tells you for he is the top man there and he is a lying treacherous killing man."

The letter was signed by Charlie Grillo, a friend of Luke's she and Mr. Stone had met when they visited the prison after Luke's surgery. The postmark was from Massachusetts.

Mr. Stone strode through the door and she ran toward him waiving the letter. "Daddy, we've got to do something. Luke is in a bad way." He took the letter and she continued to pace while he read it.

Finally, he looked up. "Mama, find a phone number for this doctor. We need to talk to him."

***

As the effects of the drug wore off, Luke became more aware of his surroundings. He'd heard about this place. It was referred to by the convicts as the Dead Dick Ward. It was where they brought men to die. From every corner of the room came agonizing sounds of men suffering. He observed a nurse covering a man's face with a sheet, a common daily occurrence.

Four hours later, when a new nurse brought more medication, Luke repeated himself. "I told the other nurse, I'm not taking any more of this shit. I asked to speak to the doctor."

She frowned. "Mr. Stone, this is the medicine Dr. Ciccone prescribed for you. It's very important that you stay calm and not move that leg."

"I understand all of that, but I'm tellin' you that I'm not takin' any more of it. I need to talk to Dr. Ciccone."

"All right. I'll make sure he knows."

Luke narrowed his eyes. "You be sure and do that."

Screams came from the end of the room as some poor soul shrieked in pain. All Luke knew was that he had to get off this ward and back where he could communicate with people on the outside.

Later that evening, Dr. Ciccone stopped at Luke's bedside. "Mr. Stone, your chart indicates that you are refusing the medication I prescribed for you."

"Doc, that damn Valium is keeping me all messed up and I don't know if it's day or night."

"So you're refusing medication."

"You can take those blue Valium and stick 'em up your ass. I ain't takin' any more of them."

"Then we'll have to move you off this ward."

"Hell, move me. I don't give a shit. I just know I'm not takin' any more of 'em."

"I'll put in a transfer order to another unit tomorrow." The doctor pursed his lips. "You have a very critical situation with these blood clots."

"I understand that, but I also know I ain't takin' any more dope. I'm tired of being soggy." Luke glared.

The doctor did not respond, but wrote on the chart, then walked on to the next bed.

They moved Luke to the Occupational Therapy Unit the following day. He remained bedfast, but at least he was out of the death ward.

Luke immediately liked Dr. Menare, the chief medical officer for the unit. He made customary rounds once a week to check on each patient and made eye contact when he spoke.

The physician directly under Dr. Menare looked to be no more than twenty years old. He'd commented to Luke that he'd been assigned to this medical facility for his internship.

Luke nicknamed him Twinkle Toes because he wore patent leather shoes shined to a high gloss.

Twinkle Toes, an ambitious young doctor, took it upon himself to initiate an aspirin regimen for Luke, in addition to the Coumadin and Heparin he already received. After several days, with the aspirin dose being increased every eight hours, Luke's stomach began to burn much like it had with the ulcers.

A kindly civilian contract nurse, Mrs. Goode, administered Luke's medicine. "Mr. Stone, if you say I told you this, I'll probably get fired, but you're not supposed to be taking aspirin with Coumadin and Heparin. That is not good medical procedure. The next time Dr. Menare comes around, you should mention it to him."

Luke winked at her. "Thank you, ma'am and I won't rat. I appreciate you tellin' me."

On Friday, Dr. Menare accompanied the young intern on his usual rounds. When they stopped at Luke's bed to examine him, Luke casually broached the subject. "Doc, these aspirin are killing me."

Dr. Menare raised his eyebrows. "Aspirin? What are you doing taking aspirin?"

He took the medical chart from Twinkle Toes and opened it. After a minute, he looked up. "What in the hell are you thinking giving this man aspirin and why are you giving him this dosage for godsake?"

The young doctor replied. "I was testing his tolerance to aspirin."

Dr. Menare set his jaw. "We need to talk."

The two doctors walked into the hallway and Luke couldn't hear their words, but could tell from the tone of Dr. Menare's voice, Twinkle Toes received a reprimand.

When they returned, the young doctor addressed Luke red-faced. "We won't be giving you any more aspirin, Mr. Stone."

"Well that's good, because my ears are ringin' and my stomach is burnin' like fire."

Dr. Menare tapped his pen on the chart. "Those symptoms should start to go away within a day or two."

"Thanks, Doc."

Red came to visit the very next day. "Man, you gave me a scare. I don't know if they've bothered to tell you, but we've been cleared of the attempted escape charges. I knew they didn't have anything that would stick. How are you feelin', brother?"

Luke clasped his hand. "I told ol' Pete to let you know I was over here. I saw him mopping the floor in here yesterday. I'm not out of the woods by a long shot, hoss. They won't even let me get up to go to the pisser. Said if I move around, the blood clots could go to my heart or brain. They're pumpin' me full of blood thinners."

"Guess you're damned lucky to be alive. I've been gettin' letters from your folks. They're worried as hell about you. Said they'd got a letter from Charlie and he'd opened their eyes about this place. They've called Dr. Ciccone several times and wrote him letters, trying to find out how you were."

"Hell, man, I haven't been able to do a fuckin' thing but lay on this damn bed and not move. Now that I'm off the dead dick ward, I can start writing to everyone again."

"When I come back, I'll bring some things."

"They said they'd put all of my personal belongings in a locker until I can claim them. Sure hope they didn't mess with my ol' guitar or my tablets full of songs."

"Yeah, that'd be the shits. Can we smoke in here?"

"Yeah and I'd sure like a cigarette. Think you might be able to get into my things and bring me my address book? I need to write a lot of folks, especially Mom and Dad and Darlina. I'm sure they wonder what happened to me."

"I'll ask the cap'n what all I can bring you including your mail." Red lit two cigarettes and handed one to Luke. He pulled a wooden chair next to Luke's bed and sat.

"Red Hoss, I've had a lot of time to think and I've made up my mind, if I live through this, I'm gonna do something that's worthwhile."

"Aw, Luke. You've always done all right."

"No, I mean it, Red. I'm gonna prove that you can be positive in a negative place. Hey, reckon they'd let you bring me some books from the library? At least while I'm laid up on my ass, I could read."

"I'm sure that won't be a problem. What kind of books do you want?"

"I'd love to have some American Indian medicine books, or books about the power of the mind. You know, anything along that line."

"I don't know anything about shit like that, but I can ask the librarian. I'll be back in a day or two." He reached for Luke's hand and shook it.

"Thank you, stud. Tell Nico and the boys to come see me."

"Will do." Red stood and scooted the chair back to the wall.

"Hey, Red. Would you mind dropping Charlie a line and let him know I'm still kickin'?"

"I already have. See ya Luke." He waved over his shoulder as he walked out.

Luke dozed off and on out of shear boredom, hoping Red would come back soon with reading material. He felt a burning desire for some answers.

Two days later, Red returned with an arm full of books, a new tablet and a stack of mail he'd managed to convince the captain to retrieve.

Once Red left, Luke quickly opened the letters. The ones from his folks expressed their worry and concern. They told him they'd been writing to and calling Dr. Ciccone about his condition. There was a stack of letters from Darlina. The last ones expressed how worried she was because she hadn't heard from him.

Luke felt a twinge of guilt. He hadn't intentionally made any of them worry. It had all been out of his control. He would have to figure out how to write lying down. They deserved to hear from him.

He curiously thumbed through the books Red brought. He was happy to see a book about Native American healing and Spirit communication, a Kahlil Gibran book, an Edgar Cayce book and one by Herman Hesse.

Spirit Healing – Native American Magic & Medicine tugged at him and sounded exactly like what he wanted to study. He especially liked the words, "*Magic & Medicine*". He'd always felt he had special

Indian medicine and for reasons not known to him, had grown up with a strong affinity to the owl.

The chapter title, *Talking to your Guardian Angel*, on page twenty-four jumped out at him. He reflected on the dream of the Angel or Being walking beside him, and the poem that flowed following the dream. He felt excited as he continued to scan the book. A chapter on finding and communicating with your Spirit animal also grabbed him. Maybe he'd finally know what the owl meant.

Next, he thumbed through "The Prophet" by Kahlil Gibran. These words went straight to his heart like an arrow:

"Out of suffering have emerged the strongest souls; the most massive characters are seared with scars..."

Again he considered the words of his poem, *Discovery*.

He read the description on the back of the Herman Hesse book..."*Explores an individual's search for authenticity, self-knowledge and spirituality.*"

He let the book fall open where it may and scanned the page.

"I have always believed, and I still believe, that whatever good or bad fortune may come our way we can always give it meaning and transform it into something of value."

It was as if this man had read his thoughts. He pondered for a while on things he'd done in the past that caused others pain. He'd hurt Darlina clean down to the core when he brought DeeDee, another go-go dancer, home with them. He knew at the time she would be crushed, but told himself it was for her own good, hoping it would drive her away. What an ignorant ass he'd been.

The picture crossed his mind, as clear yesterday. Darlina lay curled in a ball in front of the Dearborn heater, wrapped in a blanket, sobbing her heart out. It didn't matter that he hadn't been able to have sex with DeeDee or that he didn't even particularly like her. What mattered most was that he'd scarred Darlina in a way that should have made her hate him. Yet, she continued to love, even after he dove into the bottle in an effort to lessen the pain and guilt he felt for all of it.

Devising another plan to keep her from being dragged into the shit he knew was coming, he'd said cruel and hateful things while taking her back to her sister's house in Abilene. He left her standing on the curb, bags beside her, staring after the car that carried him away. He could still hear her anguished cries. He hadn't deserved her then and sure didn't now.

The memories caused his heart to constrict with guilt. It was clear that there would be some reckoning. It was time to do the right thing and stop being a selfish jerk.

He finally stacked all of the books on the small table beside his bed, reached for a blank tablet and laboriously managed to write two very short letters before his arms gave out.

He closed his eyes and rested. He hadn't realized how weak he'd grown from lying in the bed for so long.

When he opened his eyes again, he reached for the *Spirit Healing* book and slowly absorbed each word.

When he shifted to prop his arms up, a book mark fell from the pages. His eyes misted as he read.

"O' Great Spirit, whose voice I hear in the winds, and whose breath gives life to all the world, hear me! I am small and weak. I need your strength and wisdom. Let me walk in beauty, and make my eyes ever behold the red and purple sunset. Make my hands respect the things you have made and my ears sharp to hear your voice. Make me wise so that I may understand the things you have taught my people. Let me learn the lessons you have hidden in every leaf and rock. I seek strength, not to be greater than my brother, but to fight my greatest enemy---myself. Make me always ready to come to you with clean hands and straight eyes. So when life fades, as the fading sunset, my spirit may come to you without shame."

Exactly what he hungered for!

"She'll take what he's giving. That's her way of living.."

Chapter 16

Near the middle of March, shortly after Will's twenty-second birthday, Darlina made preparations to move to Austin. She packed boxes and notified her landlord she would be vacating the apartment. When she'd turned in her two week notice at work, she had a déjà vu experience from the time she'd done the same thing to move in with Luke.

Now, she stood at the counter inside the post office, filling out a card to have her mail forwarded to the new address.

She approached the clerk at the window. "Can you tell me how long this forwarding request stays in effect?"

The lady looked over the top of her glasses. "It's good for six months. I'd advise you to notify everyone of your new address."

"Thank you." Darlina left the post office.

If she hadn't heard from Luke within six months, she'd feel sure he had died. Nothing made sense. He'd always encouraged her to have a happy and good life, but never failed to proclaim his love. He wouldn't just stop writing out of the clear blue.

She opened the passenger door to the gold Oldsmobile Toronado, where Will waited for her.

"Get it done?" He reached over and squeezed her hand.

"Yep. The lady said the forwarding order would be good for six months."

"You okay?"

"Yes. So, tomorrow, we load everything up and head out?"

"Uh Huh. I've already had the utilities turned on at the farm-house. You're gonna love, it, Darlina. It's a rustic two-story house built in the late 1800s."

"I can't wait to see it."

Will pulled her across the seat beside him. "Thank you."

"For what?"

"For saying yes and coming with me to Austin."

Darlina turned her face away from Will. "I want to come. With my sisters both gone and you leaving, I don't want to be in Abilene by myself. Besides, it will be an adventure."

He put his hand on her cheek and turned her toward him. "I promise everything will be all right. My family already loves you and it'll be like beginning a whole new life."

She blinked back tears. "I know."

"Have you talked to your mom and dad?"

"Yes, I talked to them last night. I told them we were going to be roommates and that your sister would be living with us too. They weren't too thrilled, but then nothing I do ever meets with their approval."

"Don't worry. It'll all work out."

***

Two days later, Darlina settled into the farmhouse. She loved that it had oak floors and even though it was old, everything was functional.

She took on the role of cooking and cleaning. Will helped break ground on the new construction for his mom and dad while Tessa, Will's younger sister, spent a lot of time with her new boyfriend.

Every day, Darlina walked to the end of the dirt road where the mailbox sat, hoping to find a letter from Luke.

Finally, after almost four weeks, it came. Her heart fluttered inside her chest and she raced back to the house.

Luke was alive!

In the solitude of the kitchen, she ripped open the envelope. Her eyes quickly scanned the short letter. When she'd finished reading, she folded it and put it away.

Only then did she realize tears streamed down her face. Relief, mixed with heartbreak for all Luke had to endure, overwhelmed her.

She couldn't wait to write him back and explain everything about her new life in the country with Will and his family. Glancing at the clock, she groaned. There wouldn't be time today. She had to get supper started.

Tessa joined her in the kitchen. "Have you been crying, Darlina?"

"Oh no. I'm just having some allergy stuff today. My eyes are watery and itching." She stuffed Luke's letter in her pocket.

Tessa munched on a handful of carrots while she watched Darling prepare the meal. "I think this house is haunted."

"Why do you think that?"

"Because the light in my room came on all by itself last night."

"Maybe the switch has a short in it." She stirred the potatoes.

"Maybe. I'll ask Will to take a look at it. What if someone died in here?"

Darlina laughed. "You're letting your imagination run away. It's just a house."

"You wanna smoke a joint?" Tessa fidgeted with her bright red curly hair.

"Sure. That'd make supper more fun."

Tessa left the kitchen and returned a minute later, joint in hand. She struck a match to light it, drew on it and passed it to Darlina.

"Is this out of Will's stash?"

"Yeah. He told me I could though."

The two girls were soon giggling over everything and nothing at the same time.

Will ambled through the kitchen door, dusty, dirty and sweaty. "What are you two laughing about?"

Darlina looked up. "Nothing."

"You can tell me."

"No really. Nothing." She and Tessa burst into giggles again.

"You two are high. I'm jealous. I'm gonna go get a quick shower, then I'll catch up with you. Supper smells good." He patted Darlina on the butt.

"Hurry if you don't want to eat cold food," she warned.

With supper over, dishes put away and Tessa in her bedroom, Will sat at the kitchen table rolling joints and laying them in neat rows. "Let's go riding, Darlina. Want to?"

"Sounds good, but I have something to tell you first."

"Okay. What?"

"I got a letter from Luke today. He's been bedfast with blood clots in his leg for months."

"Really?" Will's lips formed a thin line and he looked down. "Are you gonna write him back?"

"Of course. I said that I won't keep secrets. That's why I'm tellin' you."

"Well, I'd be lying if I said I was happy about it, but I can't tell you what to do. Thank you for being honest. Let's ride. This sure is beautiful country in the spring."

"I'll go braid my hair. Be right back."

Darlina ran up the stairs to their bedroom. She put Luke's letter in her dresser drawer. She'd write to him first thing tomorrow. At least she knew he was still alive and that made her heart sing.

After the exhilarating ride, they found a forlorn Tessa wrapped in a shawl sitting on the front porch steps of the farmhouse.

"What's the matter, sis?" Will asked as he put the kickstand down and killed the engine.

"This damn house is haunted. I'm scared to be in there by myself."

"I think you're imagining things."

"Oh yeah? Come in here and let me show you."

Will and Darlina followed Tessa into her bedroom and she flipped on the light switch.

"So?" Will asked

"Just wait."

The three stood in the middle of the room waiting for something to happen.

Finally, Will said, "You need to stop letting your imagination run away with you. What kind of dope did you do today?"

Tessa pouted. "Just smoked some pot. Nothing else. I'm tellin' you the light goes off and on by itself."

Will wiggled the switch. "Look. I can't even make it go off by wiggling it. There's nothing to be afraid of. Come upstairs and let's listen to some music."

Tessa followed them up.

Will selected Led Zeppelin's *Houses of the Holy* and placed it on the turntable.

After lighting another joint, he stretched out on the bed, his back propped against the wall. The two girls sat in bean bag chairs beside the bed.

They passed around the joint as the music blared. When *The Rain Song* started playing, the stereo suddenly went off.

"What the hell?" Will got up from the bed and flipped the switch turning it back on.

"I told you this house is haunted," Tessa said.

"It's probably just this old wiring. Maybe a surge went through." He stretched back out and the music continued.

In less than thirty seconds, the stereo went silent again.

"Shit." Will got up. He checked the connections to the stereo and turned it back on. Before he could reach the bed, it went off again.

"Oh no. Maybe Tessa's right. Maybe this house is haunted. Let's talk to the ghost." Darlina reached for Tessa's hand.

"Are you crazy? Both of you, there is no such thing as ghosts. There's just something screwy with the electricity," he insisted.

"Put on a different record. Maybe the ghost doesn't like Led Zeppelin," Darlina suggested.

"I've never heard anything so ridiculous in my life!"

"Try it." She got up from the bean bag and thumbed through the record albums. "Here. Put this one on." She handed him a Carly Simon record.

"I think you've both lost your minds." Will slipped the record out of the sleeve and placed it on the turntable.

He sat down on the side of the bed and waited. The record played perfectly with no more interruptions.

"See. The ghost likes Carly Simon. He didn't like Led Zeppelin." Darlina chuckled.

"I don't know about you guys, but I'm sleepin' on the couch at Mom and Dad's tonight." Tessa bit her lower lip.

"I'll say it again. There's nothin' to be afraid of in this house. I'm not going anywhere and neither is Darlina."

"Yeah, well you two have each other. I'm downstairs by myself."

"Suit yourself." Will yawned. "I'm beat. It's time to get some shut-eye."

Tessa stood to leave. "I'll see you tomorrow. Don't let the ghost get you while you're asleep." She threw a pillow at her brother.

"If we're not here in the morning, you'll know it got us." Will playfully tossed the pillow back at her.

Darlina lay awake long after Will's snores reverberated off the walls.

He didn't ask much of her and seemed to genuinely care about her. What was missing? The moment she had the thought, she knew the answer. There was no passion between them. They were simply good friends.

As she thought about the multitude of differences between Will and Luke, she tried to imagine living with Luke there in the farmhouse.

That thought excited her. She looked over at Will. Without any hesitation, she began to touch him and kiss his closed eyelids. She closed her own eyes and pictured Luke.

She kissed and caressed him until he stirred awake, fully hard.

"What are you doing, Darlina?" Will asked.

She opened her eyes. "I couldn't sleep."

Will braced himself on top of her and exploded almost the instant he entered. "I'm sorry. I don't seem to be able to control it."

She didn't reply and lay still until he was asleep and snoring again.

Darlina blinked back tears and sighed. Lovemaking with Will would never be like it was with Luke. That was a fact she'd have to accept.

She got up from the bed and went into the bathroom. In the darkness, she relieved herself as tears coursed down her face.

The final words in Luke's letter reverberated in her heart. He'd signed it, "*All of my love forever and always, Luke.*"

"I miss you so much, Luke," she whispered.

"Thinking of you warmly, while nightfall is new, and hoping that Angels bring happiness to you..."

Chapter 17

L uke sat in a wheelchair, facing a narrow barred window, savoring the April midday sun on his face. In his hands, he held Darlina's last letter.

He knew he should be happy for her and be thankful she was finally doing what he'd always encouraged her to do, but in spite of himself, he felt only immense emptiness and loss.

Even though she promised to continue writing, he knew men and their egos and if Will Brocker was any kind of a man, he would eventually insist that Darlina break all contact with him.

Dammit to hell! There was nothing to do but answer her letter and pretend to be happy for her, even though it would be a lie.

He had no right to do anything else. Holding the letter up to his face, he inhaled the perfumed fragrance. He ached for her touch, her sweet voice and her gentle ways. Will Brocker was a very lucky man and Luke hoped he knew it. He vowed that if Will ever did anything to hurt Darlina, he would claw his way out of this fuckin' prison and make him pay. He clenched his jaw.

Luke wheeled himself down the corridor to his bed and penned a letter back to her. He didn't draw roses or unicorns on the paper, and when he read back over it, the words sounded stiff. With a deep sigh, he folded it and stuffed in the envelope. It was the best he could muster.

***

Luke sat on the edge of his hospital bed while Dr. Menare examined him. "Mr. Stone, you've come along quite nicely. I think we can release you back into population. Are you ready?"

"Sir, I've never been more ready. I think four months of this shit is about enough. Hell, it's already July and I've been down since early spring."

"I have to warn you that if you see any signs of swelling in that leg, you come see me immediately. For the time being, the blood clots seem to have worked their way out. I'll keep you on a blood thinner for a while longer for safe measure." Dr. Menare listened to Luke's heart and lungs.

"I'm about as weak as a cat, Doc, but I'll build my strength back up."

"Don't overdo it. I'm issuing a cane to help you keep your balance walking until you get the muscles built back up in your legs."

"A cane? Hell, I'm like some ol' geezer." Luke chuckled.

"It's not permanent." Dr. Menare completed his examination and handed Luke a stack of papers to sign.

Luke scrawled his name at the bottom of each page, then handed them back. "Is that it, Doc?"

"Yes, that's it. You'll be in your old ward. Go report to the captain. He's expecting you." Dr. Menare extended his hand and Luke shook it.

"Thanks again for everything."

By the time Luke reached his old cell block, clouds hid the bright spring sun. He rapped on the captain's open door with the cane.

"Yes?" The captain didn't look up.

"Sir, it's Luke Stone. I've been released from the hospital and was told to report to you."

"Oh yeah, Stone. I got a call saying you'd be coming. Let me finish up here and I'll take you to the locker your personal belongings are stored in."

Luke leaned against the door frame catching his breath. It would take some time to gain his strength back.

After a few minutes, the captain shuffled the papers on his desk into a stack and stood. "Let's go."

Luke followed the captain down a narrow hallway and through two sets of doors, thankful for the support of the cane.

They entered a large room with rows of lockers the size of small closets. The captain unhooked the keys off his belt and opened number four, which held Luke's possessions.

"Cap'n, I've gotta sit down." Luke's arms and legs trembled. "Will you help me carry this back to the cell?"

"There's a cart over in the corner we can use." He pulled a metal chair from across the room and Luke sank into it.

He chose the guitar to inspect first. He let out an audible sigh when he found no sign of damage. He fell in love with it all over again. The depth of the wood and vibrancy that it carried never ceased to amaze him.

He quickly found his tablets, personal pictures, and a carton of cigarettes.

"Looks like it's all here. Thank you, Cap'n."

Back in his cell, with Red looking on, he organized and put away his things, taking time to tape a picture of his children on the wall behind his bunk.

"My ol' Martin looks just like it did. Shit man, it's good to be out of the bed." Luke ran his hand through his brown hair. "I need a fuckin' hair cut."

Red chuckled. "You are startin' to look like a damned ol' hippie."

"Maybe a skinny ol' hippie. I'm gonna need to go to the damn clothing room and ask for smaller clothes tomorrow." Luke settled in a chair and tuned his guitar.

He touched the strings with reverence and felt the surge of energy flow through him and into his hands.

"Shit, Luke, tune 'er up and let's have some music." Red lit smokes for the two of them.

Luke tuned the strings, then strummed a C chord.

"Tonight I hear the falling rain.

Tripped on a dream and I'm comin' down. Can't sleep at all just feel the pain. Pieces of memories lie around.

Talkin' is just words what more can I say, Except I missed you tomorrow yesterday..."

"When did you write that one?" Red asked as the last chords of the song faded.

"While I was in the hole. Got a bunch more too. I don't know how long I can hang, but let's go to the music room and pick a while." He laid the guitar in its case.

The two men spent the next two hours playing and singing new and old songs.

"Stud, I never get tired of this, but I'm wore plumb out." Luke stretched and lit a fresh cigarette.

"I know what you mean. It makes a person forget where they are for a little bit."

"Yes it does. You know, they've got our bodies captured, but not our minds. That's our freedom."

***

When he reported for his work assignment, Luke discovered that Mrs. Yarbrough had requested that he be assigned to clean the craft shop after it closed each day.

For the first time since landing behind bars, he had a gig that he enjoyed. Once he finish cleaning, with the door locked, he'd keep working on his pieces until time to report for head count.

Luke sat at a bench pounding designs into the leather when a stranger entered. He looked up with mild curiosity.

Mrs. Yarbrough, in her usual friendly manner, greeted the man. "Hello, sir. Are you here to participate in our craft program?"

"I come to see." The tall graying man with slightly stooped shoulders spared no words. A rubber band held a long pony tail and his gaunt frame failed to fill out the prison garb he wore.

"Mr. Stone, could you possibly show this gentleman around?"

"Of course." Luke stood and approached. The leather pouch the man wore around his neck aroused his curiosity and the high cheekbones and brown skin left no doubt that he was an Indian.

Turning to the stranger, she continued. "What is your name, sir?"

"Walter Little Crow." His dark eyes darted around the room.

Luke extended his hand. "Mr. Little Crow, I'm Luke Stone."

The man eyed Luke, then shook his hand. "Nice to meet you."

"What kind of crafts do you like to do?" Luke pursued.

"I do beadwork as shown to me by my father and his father before him."

"I've dabbled a little at beadwork, but don't have a solid technique down. Think you could teach me?"

The man hesitated. "Why you want to learn?"

"I find good medicine in making things with my hands. I'm fixin' to start makin' a guitar strap. I'd love to make a beaded one. I'm a greasy ol' Indian too, just have white skin."

"I show you." Walter Little Crow offered. "I come tomorrow and bring my loom."

During a quick tour of the small shop, they were pleased to find a good supply of seed beads.

"These are perfect for beading with a loom." Walter ran his long fingers through the bin.

A surge of new excitement washed over Luke. He liked the quiet matter-of-fact manner of this man and looked forward to learning the ancient art.

By this time, he'd read a shelf full of American Indian books and had absorbed the rituals and beliefs of his ancestors.

Studying owl medicine and the meanings of the Indian symbols brought an understanding of the power they held. He placed them strategically on everything he made as his way of sharing the magic with whoever received it.

And now, he had a teacher who would show him the old way of Indian beading.

When Walter Little Crow left the craft shop that day, Luke warmly shook his hand. "I look forward to learning from you."

The man nodded and left.

As time continued to pass, Luke became even more outspoken about conditions in the prison, writing letters to congressmen, senators, radio stations, newspapers; anyone who he could find an address for.

Not much changed, but at least he felt better for having tried.

His relations with Nico and the Italians solidified and he learned important legal information from them. He'd taken their advice and dug into the law books in the prison library. He now worked to put together yet another appeal for his and Red's cases. It might not accomplish anything, but at least he'd feel better knowing he'd tried.

Today, nearing the middle of May, he received a welcome letter from Darlina. He digested the words she wrote and then read between the lines. She wasn't telling him everything and it left a sour taste in his mouth. Smoking pot and taking pills once in a while was all she admitted, but Luke's gut feeling told him there was more to it than occasional use. The deep sadness and loneliness that lay beneath the false claim that everything was good shattered his heart. More than anything, he wanted her to be happy. As much as he hoped she would find that with Will Brocker, it didn't look too promising.

As always, she ended the letter with *"I love you Luke, forever and ever."*

He would continue to encourage her to give Will a chance, even though he wanted to beg her to leave the drug-headed biker and have nothing else to do with him.

If she ever found someone she could truly love and be happy with, then he could let her go. Until that happened he could never totally let her slip through his fingers. When he raised the letter to inhale its sweetness, all he smelled was the faint smell of marijuana. He frowned. A lecture about too much drug use was in order.

He had just finished the letter and placed it in an envelope when Red rushed in. He held a paper in his hand.

"Look here, Luke. Springfield's got a new little weekly paper with poems and artwork and articles contributed by convicts."

"Really? Let me see it." He scanned the mimeographed paper. "The Weekly Echo, huh?"

"There's an article in there by the Italians. Looks like they're organizing a club of some sort. Talk to Nico and see what's up. Reckon they'd let us join even if we ain't dagos?"

Luke chuckled. "Don't know if I wanna join any club. You know how that shit goes. Next thing you know, they're wantin' you to do somethin' for the cause."

"True. But, I do think you oughtta submit some of your artwork and poems. Couldn't hurt anything." Red pulled out a chair and plopped down.

"That's a good idea, stud. I'll look into it." Luke read each page of the small paper before he handed it back to Red. "Ol' Walter told me that the American Indian Brotherhood is tryin' to get something goin' in here. Now that one, I'd join. He said they wanted to get permission for a pow wow and bring in folks from the outside and maybe some buffalo meat. Damn, that'd be good."

"Sure as hell would."

As his hands and mind stayed busy creating and learning, he realized a healing inside and out started to occur. The changes, although subtle, were real.

He'd never stop loving Darlina, but also understood that for now he had to let go and hope that she'd find her guiding star. He silently prayed to Wankan Tanka to watch over and keep her safe.

> "We must take the lessons of life that are written upon the whispers of the wind, and learn from them so that we may walk and grow in harmony with the Great One."
> Chief Dan George

Luke reflected on the words of the great chief. He could almost smell the campfires and see his ancestors gathered around. This is the way he would choose to walk. This would be his path, even locked in a cage.

"After dreams are shattered and lie scattered all around, among the ruins, treasures of memories are found."

Chapter 18

D ays passed in a quiet haze on the farm outside of Austin. Darlina missed the frequent love-filled letters from Luke. They'd become occasional and less personal. She understood what he was doing, but longed for words of endearment. He hadn't sent a poem, song or artwork since she'd moved in with Will. He kept his distance without losing touch.

Nevertheless, she continued to write her own words of love to him. She did her best to explain that she didn't feel that kind of love for Will. He told her to let it grow. She puzzled over that. How could something grow that wasn't there?

In his last letter, he'd admonished her about too much drug use. She knew he was right, but getting high was her ticket to escape the stark reality of being imprisoned behind invisible bars of loss and loneliness.

Besides, it was all she and Will had in common except for riding the Harley.

A restless yearning for more from life stirred beneath the surface. She had too much time on her hands. Cooking and cleaning didn't challenge her mind or fill her days. That evening, on the front porch, watching the dazzling sunset paint the sky, she approached the subject.

"I think I want to get a job in town, Will. I need more to do than cooking and cleaning."

"I don't think that's a good idea at all. Do you need money for something?"

"No, I'm bored. It doesn't take much time every day to do my chores and I've read every book on the place." She bit her bottom lip.

"I'd really rather have you here. Why don't you give it a couple of months and we'll talk about it again."

"Okay. Fair enough." She twirled her hair around her finger. "I do like being in the country. There's a certain freedom out here. I don't think we could sit on the porch in town and smoke a joint."

"I can assure you that we couldn't. I love not being in the city. I planted some pot down by the creek when I first started coming out here with the folks. I checked on it yesterday and looks like it'll be ready for harvest soon."

"What if your dad finds out?"

Will scoffed. "Hell, the old man wouldn't know a marijuana plant from a bunch of weeds."

"You think they know we smoke over here?"

"Nah. If they do, they figure at least we're not getting into trouble."

Tessa drove up in her 1970 Chevy Chevette. The engine sputtered when she turned it off. Running up the steps, she threw a baggie in Will's lap. "Lookie what I scored today."

"Where the hell did you get these?" Will held up a quart bag of assorted pills.

"Paul got 'em for me. Said there's a little bit of everything in there." She plopped down on the top step.

"You gonna share?"

"Hell yes. You always share with me. Pick out some for you and Darlina."

Will went inside the house with the baggie and the girls followed. They watched as he separated them out.

"What are those black and yellow ones?" Darlina asked.

"Those are called yellow jackets. It's speed." He held up a red one. "Now this one will put you to sleep. It's a Seconal."

"I read about those in "*The Valley of The Dolls*." She perched on a kitchen chair. "I see pink hearts. Those were always my favorite. What are the blue ones?"

"Those are Valium and they relax you. Here take one." He dropped the pill in Darlina's hand.

She hesitated, remembering Luke's warning. "This ain't gonna mess me all up is it?"

"No, it'll mellow you out."

She swallowed the blue pill with a sip of water.

By the time Will sorted out all the pills there were over a hundred. He kept thirty of them and handed the rest back to Tessa. "You better go easy on these. We don't want Mom and Dad down our throats."

She pouted. "You can trust me. I'm not stupid."

"I just don't want a big scene. You know how Dad can get."

"Don't worry." She popped a yellow capsule in her mouth and washed it down with a Dr. Pepper. "I'm gonna go wait for Paul out on the porch. He'll be here in a few minutes."

Will downed a red and green capsule and put the rest in an empty aspirin bottle. "Let's go hang out." He took Darlina's hand.

Once upstairs, he stashed the aspirin bottle in the stereo cabinet with the pot and put on a James Taylor record. "Come here." He patted the bed.

Darlina kicked off her sandals and stretched out beside him. "Hope our friendly ghost likes James Taylor."

"I'm still not buying into the whole ghost theory. Are you happy, Darlina?" He stroked her hair.

"I suppose so." She played with the hem on her shirt. "I'd like to be working, but other than that, I guess I'm happy."

"I wish I could make you smile more. The only time I hear you laugh is when you're high."

Darlina chuckled. "Well then that's pretty much every day."

"Yeah, guess that's true. Hey, wanna come with me tomorrow to look at the plants?"

"Sure."

"Too bad your ghost can't flip the record over." He moved off the bed to the stereo.

"If he gets that brave, I'm gonna be scared." She swung her legs over the side of the bed and watched.

She thought about Luke's words of advice to let the love grow for Will. As much as she might want to make it happen, she knew there would never be the intensity of what she felt for Luke, even now in his absence.

Maybe she wasn't being fair, but she was being honest.

***

Spring exploded into full bloom with Bluebonnets and Indian Paintbrush everywhere. Without a phone at the farmhouse, Darlina hadn't been able to stay in touch with Leann and Norma. She wrote letters to Leann, but seldom received more than a short answer. Darlina knew how busy she must be with two active toddlers. She longed to sit across the table from her sister and spill her deepest thoughts like they'd so often done.

She hated going to Will's parents' house to use their phone as someone was always listening.

With the windows open and birds singing, they sat at the kitchen table while Will rolled joints.

He lit one and passed it to her. "Wanna have sex? We can do a couple of poppers."

She took a long draw before she replied. "Sure."

Upstairs in their bedroom she shivered as she got undressed. She braced herself for more fumbled attempts at lovemaking.

As had become her habit, she closed her eyes under the covers and pretended it was Luke instead of Will.

He nibbled on her breasts, never fully taking the nipple in his mouth the way Luke did. She'd learned not to touch him before he entered, or he'd never make it inside of her. She wondered if someday he would get better at controlling himself.

It always left her longing for Luke with his slow hand and steady touch. She remembered how he took her to heights of ecstasy that she never knew existed, and how he taught her to be bold and take what she wanted from him. He'd been a good teacher and she an eager student.

Even though she tried to hold back tears, inevitably they came and she turned her head away so that Will wouldn't see.

He groaned and rolled over on his back. "Dammit! I don't know why I cum so quick. I can't help it."

Not trusting her voice, she whispered. "It's alright. You did just fine," she lied.

A loud insistent knock on the front door startled them both.

Will grumbled. "Who in the hell could that be?" He pulled on his jeans.

Darlina pulled the covers up under her chin. "I don't know, but it sounds serious."

A minute later, she heard Will open the door and there was no mistaking the voice.

Will's father stomped into the house yelling. "What in the hell are you thinking planting dope on my property?"

She heard Will's defensive response. "I don't know what you're talkin' about."

She slipped into her clothes and moved to the top of the stairs where she could see them. Will's father waved a handful of plants around.

"I know damn well this is marijuana, Will. I won't tolerate it. I won't have you putting me and your mother in jeopardy with shit like this. I've seen Tessa walkin' around here with glassy eyes and I know she's doin' dope too. I ain't gonna put up with it from either of you."

Darlina's breath caught in her throat. Mr. Brocker was more than mad. His face turned beet red and the veins bulged in his neck.

Will took a step back. "I'm an adult, Dad. I don't think you can tell me what I can and can't do."

Mr. Brocker exploded. "I damn sure can tell you what you can and can't do on my property and I'm tellin' you that I ain't gonna put up with you growing pot on my land. You got that?"

"Yeah, I got it." Will growled. "Maybe I'll just move off your damn property and you can get a new construction foreman."

"I can damned sure do that. I want all those plants pulled up and burned and if you don't, I will."

"I'll pull 'em and I'll be off your property as soon as I can find a job and apartment in town."

Mr. Brocker didn't reply, but turned on his heel and stomped out the door, slamming it behind him.

Darlina slipped down the stairs, joining Will. "Wow! He was mad."

Will paced back and forth in the living room. "He thinks he can still tell me what to do and how to do it. Well, he's got another think comin'. I'll go into Austin tomorrow and I bet I come back with a job. We'll get a fuckin' apartment in town."

"I can work, too. Soon as we get moved and settled, I'll find a job. We'll be fine. I think you knew this would eventually happen."

Will continued to fume. "No I didn't. I never imagined he'd find it or even know what it was. This sucks. I'll go pull all the plants but I ain't gonna burn 'em, except one leaf at a time rolled in paper. Will you go with me to get 'em?"

"Sure. In the morning?"

"Nope. Now. If we wait until morning, they won't be there. Let's go."

Darlina had no words to ease Will's mood. She knew Mr. Brocker was right. Will had no business growing pot on his land.

Maybe it'd be best to move into town and get real jobs.

She hadn't told Will, but Tessa had already made plans to move to Austin with Paul. Darlina guessed this incident would speed up her plans.

Together, they drove down a dirt road along the property line to the back corner. They pulled twelve large marijuana plants out of the ground and threw them into the trunk of the car.

Then Will gathered a small bundle of twigs and branches and lit them with his lighter. Once it'd burned down, he scattered the ashes.

"There. He'll think I burned 'em."

She felt a little sorry for Will. His father had humiliated him. On the other hand, he'd deserved it.

The next day, they found a small affordable studio apartment on the south side of Austin and Will landed a job building cabinets and doing finish work on new houses. Darlina picked up applications from three different temp agencies and planned to return them completed soon as they got moved.

For now, she had another letter to write Luke. Every thought and every action always came back around to him.

Darlina had always been a dreamer and spent a good deal of her life living through the books she read. That was until she'd met Luke. He'd been bigger than life itself and never left her with the need to dream or escape. She loved every minute she'd spent with him, whether it was in his arms, or simply riding beside him in the car.

Yes, it had been the one time in life she'd had no need to wish for anything different. But, he'd been taken away along with her happiness.

That life was gone and perhaps gone for good. It was up to her to make the best of what she now had.

No matter what happened, no matter how much time and distance separated them, she'd always hold the memories of Luke close to her heart. Nothing or no one could ever destroy them.

Those memories were as precious to her as the next breath she took and would last forever on through eternity.

In the meantime, she would make an effort to be a companion to Will and perhaps eventually the friendship would grow into some sort of love. Or maybe not, but at least she would give it a chance.

After all, wasn't that what Luke was pushing her to do?

"I've traveled a hard road, but those times are gone. It don't matter now, if I was right or wrong..."

Chapter 19

S ummer 1973 waited right around the corner and time stretched endlessly for the convicts trapped in an unforgiving world with each other.

Luke mastered the art of tooling leather and adorning it with silver, turquoise and now beads. For the first time since he'd been locked away, two and a half years ago, he could contribute and help his family back home by selling his handiwork.

Learning the intricate art of beadwork from Walter proved to be therapeutic. The patience it took to pick up one tiny bead after another and loop the string in and around it taught him a very important lesson in how littles can makes bigs.

He'd gone through all of his adult life like a bull thrashing around in a china closet. He knew he'd blown some big music deals because of his attitude and in all honesty, destroyed a couple of marriages the same way. Taking on the role of a rebel and outlaw had only landed him here in this godforsaken place.

He'd never taken the time to stop and look at any of it. He took the "fuck 'em" attitude and barreled ahead playing the tough guy all the way. Being tough was expected of him growing up, and it came easy. He'd never been accused of being weak and never would, but he was learning there was more than one way to be strong.

Now, he patiently picked up one small bead at a time and after a while, an intricate pattern appeared and if he kept going, soon he'd have a beautiful piece of art.

With warmer days, Luke and Red frequented the yard at every opportunity. The sun's warmth soaked through the skin and deep into their bones.

He observed an inmate standing directly across from them on this particular day. The man faced the center of the yard and made casting motions with his arms, then reeled the line back in over and over.

Luke thought aloud. "Wonder what's going on in Fisherman's crazy head. It's like he's stuck in some segment of time that involved fishing. Maybe he let a memory make him crazy."

"Who the hell knows. He's squirrely for sure."

"I can think of a few segments of time I wouldn't mind being stuck in. Maybe he's not the crazy one. Shit, maybe he's the sane one and the rest of us are fuckin' loony."

"Bet he's got a helluva muscle in that casting arm." Red chuckled.

"Probably so." Luke stood to go inside. The convict stopped casting and stared dead into his eyes. For a minute, Luke was certain he saw a spark of life, then the eyes dulled and the man returned to fishing.

"Catching anything today?" Luke asked.

"Nope. Not biting," Fisherman mumbled.

***

On a hot mid-July morning, Luke was summoned to a caseworker's office who handled crisis situations. He marched through the hallway, having discarded the cane long ago, back rigid and staring straight ahead. Any time a convict got called into this office, he was sure to receive bad news.

The spit dried in his mouth and he could not swallow past the lump in his throat. His steps slowed as he neared the open door.

The caseworker looked up with cold gray eyes, when Luke knocked. "Mr. Stone?"

"Yes sir." Luke entered the small office.

"I have some bad news for you and I hope you aren't going to make this difficult." The caseworker tapped his pencil on the desk.

"Just give it to me straight." Luke struggled to keep his hands from shaking.

"Your father passed away yesterday."

The air suddenly left Luke's lungs and he gripped the edge of the desk to steady himself. "Dad?"

"Now, I hope you're not going to set up a howl to go to the funeral. You can go, but you'll have to pay for two Federal Marshalls to accompany you. You'll also have to wear chains and cufs to the service and stay in jail overnight there." He continued to stare with cold unfeeling eyes.

"Do you honestly think I would wear chains to my Dad's funeral and disgrace my family?" Luke's eyes narrowed.

"I don't know or care. That would be a requirement. Besides that, there's really no point in you going. You can't help him. He's already dead anyway."

Luke felt the vein in his neck pop out and clenched his jaw. "That's right, you sonofabitch. We all die someday."

"Are you threatening me, Mr. Stone?"

"No sir, I'm making a statement that you're gonna die one of these days."

The caseworker pushed his chair back and pointed his finger. "Get out of my office."

Luke turned on his heel and despite the trembling in his legs and hands, managed to walk out into the hallway. Once out of sight, he collapsed against the wall and great heaving sobs shook his body. A few convicts passing by spared a blank stare, but mostly no one noticed or cared.

Memories of the closeness he'd enjoyed throughout life with his father danced before his eyes. And now Dad was gone. He'd never experienced a grief so intense and painful, not even when his little baby boy died at one week old. His poor mother. He couldn't imagine her without Daddy. What would she do?

He longed to talk to her and cursed the bars that held him. Anger replaced the grief and he pounded his fists against the wall. Damn prison and the people who put him here! And damn these forty foot walls around him!

With anguished heart, he stumbled back to the cell.

Red looked up when he came in the door. "Luke, what the hell?"

Luke sank down on the side of his bunk. "Dad died yesterday." He stared ahead, unseeing.

Red gasped. "Oh no. I'm so sorry."

"Yeah, me too. If I go to the funeral, I'll have to wear chains and pay for two Marshalls to go with me. Hell, I'd rather die than do that to Mom." He put his face in his hands and his voice trembled. "Dad was the best friend I had on this earth."

Red stood and touched Luke's shoulder. "He was always good to me. Is there anything I can do for you?"

With eyes full of unshed tears, Luke mumbled. "No, hoss, there's nothing."

"I'm gonna go down the hall and leave you alone, but I'll check on you in a bit."

"Thanks, man." Luke lay back on his bunk.

More than anything right now, he needed solitude. He made a mental note of the date, July 16, 1973. That meant Albert Stone died on the fifteenth.

Damn it all! Once again, the stark reality of helplessness gripped his heart. He hated that his father died knowing his son remained locked away in a cage like an animal. The hardship he'd placed on his family weighed heavy on his heart. He'd never intended for any of it to turn out this way.

He remembered the last time he'd seen Albert Stone. He and Mrs. Stone had driven all the way from Texas to visit him after his ulcer surgery. He'd been shocked and moved when his father told him that he admired him and held no judgment toward him for the choices he'd made.

His father had taught him the importance of being an honest good man, and by damn, he wasn't going to let him down! Even locked in a cage, a man can choose how he thinks and acts.

Luke resolved to be the man his father believed him to be.

Over the next few days, grief lay heavy on his shoulders as he went through the motions of existing. The only solace he found was through quiet repetition of beading and the words and music that came to him daily.

Sitting in his cell late one evening, he reached for his guitar. Minutes later, the words flowed along with the melody.

"I awoke in the early hours of mourning. Heard a song riding on the wind. Felt the chill of a cold day dawning. Saw the world coming to an end. The sun is setting at daybreak. Loneliness comes once more, bringing hurt and tears and heartaches. Love just walked out the door..."

Luke continued writing until the song was complete and at the bottom of the page, printed, *"A loving tribute to the finest man I ever knew, Albert Stone."*

How much could a man lose before he lost his mind? He'd lost his father and best friend, the woman he loved with all of his heart, not to mention his children. What else would he be robbed of before he got out of this godforsaken place? He thought about Fisherman. He couldn't let it destroy him.

***

Things back in Texas went from bad to worse, after Albert Stone passed away. Luke's mother moved back to Coleman from Lake Brownwood, then two of Luke's children came to stay with her. She struggled to make ends meet working at a local sewing factory.

She didn't tell Luke everything but he could read clearly between the lines. He knew the details she was leaving out. She didn't want to worry him, but he knew.

For once, Luke felt proud that he was able to contribute by selling things he made with his hands. Even though it wasn't much, he knew every little bit helped.

He took great pains to make each piece as near to perfect as he could and swelled with pride when one handbag sold for $425 in the visiting room. It gave him a sense of satisfaction to have the money sent home.

He regretted that he'd not been able to make it clear to her how the money exchange worked. She wrote details in letters about who sent it and how much.

Twice Luke got called in and reprimanded for what they called "doing business." Luke assured them he wasn't blackmailing or pressuring anyone to buy his pieces.

He encouraged his mother to come visit and they finally arranged a date when she would travel with Lexi, Luke's daughter, to Springfield. Luke doubled his efforts to get money to her for the long trip. He couldn't wait to see them.

Early in the day on August 25th, Luke was called to the visiting room for the second time in almost three years for a visit other than more interrogation by the FBI. He'd told the agents over and over that he didn't know where any bank money was buried. Hell, if he had money, didn't they know he wouldn't be rotting here in prison?

His breath caught in his throat as he burst through the door and Lexi bounded toward him, arms outstretched.

He picked her up and hugged her so tight she objected. "Daddy, you're squishing me."

Luke laughed, wiped his tears away and sat her down. "Mom!"

Both he and his mother wept as they embraced. All of the grief, the sorrow, and immense loss manifested in that moment.

"Oh son, it's so good to see you. I wish Daddy could have visited one more time." Mrs. Stone wiped her eyes and blew her nose loudly.

"Me too, Mom. I know you miss him something awful." He pointed to three empty chairs against a long wall. He didn't miss the sadness in her eyes, or the age showing in the lines on her face. She'd always been a short heavyset woman, but somehow she seemed smaller than he remembered, and Lexi had grown as tall as her grandmother. With her dark hair, brown eyes and delicate facial features, she was without a doubt going to be a beauty.

As soon as Luke took a seat, Lexi crawled up in his lap. "Daddy, I sure have missed you."

"I've missed you too, Princess. Look at you. You're almost grown up." Luke smoothed her dark hair, and hugged her again, then moved her to the chair beside him. "Sweetheart, you can't sit on my lap in here. The guards won't allow it, but you can sit right up close to me." He put his arm around her shoulders.

She grinned up at him, batting her big brown eyes. "Daddy, I'm almost twelve. Pretty soon I'll be old enough to date boys."

"Whoa there." He looked over her head and winked at his mother. "I don't know about that, Sissy. You're still a mite young."

Mrs. Stone patted Lexi on the arm. "No need to rush things, or give your daddy a heart attack. I don't want to have to keep my shotgun by the front door just yet."

"But Nanny, you already do." Lexi wiggled on her chair.

Luke chuckled. "If I remember right, you always kept a loaded gun somewhere in the house. Are you still a crack shot with that little 410?"

"I haven't shot it in a while, but I did threaten to use it the other day when I had to run Joyce's girlfriend, Big Evie, off. She came to the house looking for Joseph and I let her know she wasn't gonna get to him without going through me."

"What was she all in a tizzy about?"

"I don't know, son. Joseph said he found a ditto and cut it up and that made her mad. I don't for the life of me know what it was that he cut up."

Luke laughed out loud. "Mom that was a dildo. It's a sex toy."

Her face turned bright pink. "All I knew was she wasn't going to lay a hand on Joseph. I swear Joyce has really messed up this time with that big ol' woman. Everybody in town knows she's a lesbian. My God, son, you're even skinnier than you were when me and Daddy came to visit last year." She rushed her words as if she were afraid the visit would end before she said all she had on her mind.

"I don't know what to tell you about Big E. I'm glad Joseph and Lexi are with you though. Tell me about Martin and Nathan. And before I forget, there's something I need to explain while you're here about the money coming in the mail to you."

"Oh my Lord, Luke. You have no idea how much that helps me." Mrs. Stone fished a cigarette out of her purse and Luke lit it. "The little boys are doing good, as far as I know. I don't get to see them very often, but Joseph goes over and checks on them and so does Lexi. What about the money?"

"Well, you can't tell me in your letters who you get money from. They read all of our mail coming in and going out. They've called me in twice and harassed me about doing business. We're not allowed to do that."

"I don't understand. Do you buy the materials to make the hand-bags and things?"

"Yes."

"And you put all the hours into making them?"

"Yes, Mom."

"But, you can't sell 'em to people you don't know?"

"Right."

"That makes no sense to me. Looks like they would encourage you to try to do better for yourself. Maybe I need to talk to the warden while I'm here."

"Oh no, Mom. You'd sure make things hard on me if you did that. It's the way it is, so when you need to tell me you got money, just say it's from Uncle Fred, or Aunt Dorothy or another family member. I'll know who you're talking about, but when they read my mail, the guards won't know. Okay?"

"Well, I don't see the sense of it, but okay."

Lexi tugged on her father's arm. "Daddy, how come you have long hair?"

Luke chuckled. "Well, honey, you see in here there are so many rules you have to go by and when they said I didn't have to cut my hair anymore, I let it grow."

His little girl was growing up fast and he ached deep inside because he wouldn't there to protect her as she turned into a young woman.

He paid a heavy price for his carelessness and so did his loved ones.

Too soon the visit ended with a promise of one more the following day before they headed back to Texas. Luke knew what a sacrifice his mother made to drive the long distance and bring Lexi. He renewed his resolve to help ease her burden. He'd work even harder to make pretty leather and beaded things that people on the outside would pay money for.

***

Determined to stay positive and productive, he'd begun practicing rituals he read about in his study of sacred American Indian ways. He gave thanks to Great Spirit with a tobacco ritual, blowing smoke in the four directions. He carried an Apache Tear in his pocket to help repel negativity. He learned to chant affirmations and do meaningful ceremonies daily.

He loved the feel of tapping into the ancient energy of his ancestors. Almost as if by magic, negative thoughts began to fall away. He had to struggle to pull back the feeling of anger and hatred for the guard who beat him and kicked him or remember people's names that he'd carried a grudge for.

Things were changing inside of Luke Stone...Big things.

"Can't see the forest for the trees. Can't stand upright down on my knees. Does it ever end? When will it stop?"

Chapter 20

Within one week, Darlina found a temporary job placement through Kelly Girls in Austin. Ecstatic to be employed again she dressed in her best work attire, grabbed a cinnamon roll and cup of coffee and headed out the door.

Driving on the one-way streets in Austin proved to be a challenge. The building in downtown Austin that she looked for on this bright August morning sat directly across from the Capitol. The sun glared off the tops of the tall structures and she reached for her sunglasses.

The receptionist job sounded perfect for her experience and it would be nice to be productive again. It had been too long since she'd used her mind for anything other than simple housework and she looked forward to being around other people.

As she drove, she thought about the last letter she'd received from Luke and her heart broke for him when she read that Albert Stone had passed away. She remembered an early winter morning, when Mr. Stone had dropped by her and Luke's apartment unannounced. He'd always shown her warmth and kindness and offered to play devil's advocate with Mrs. Stone for her. He was a good man and no doubt his passing left Luke devastated.

She looked at the numbers on the buildings. There it was. Pulling into the shadows of the parking garage, she removed her sunglasses and tucked them away. The parking attendant directed her to park on level two and placed a sticker on her windshield.

She'd resisted the urge to smoke a joint before she left the apartment that morning. She needed to be straight for her job. Luke's words of warning about too much drug use echoed in her brain, but it had become a way of life with her and Will.

The day flew by and Darlina soaked up the opportunity to converse and socialize with people. Even though it had only been a few months, it seemed as if years had passed since she'd been around anyone other than Will and his family.

When she drove her rundown Chevy back to the apartment that evening, she passed a Volkswagen car dealership. She stared at the shiny new cars and made a decision. Once she had a couple of paychecks under her belt, she would buy a new car. The sign on the window of a baby blue Volkswagen Bug read, "$2,500." In that instant, she knew it was the car for her.

The minute she put her purse down inside the tiny apartment, she opened a drawer in the kitchen and took out her stationery and pen. She wrote a happy letter to Luke, relating the events of the day on her new job. When she finished, it was time to start supper.

By the time Will returned from work that evening, she had food on the stove and a joint lying on a napkin beside his plate. She hummed along with Janis Joplin on the stereo as she moved about the small kitchen.

He strode in, sweaty and dirty from work, went straight to the shower and returned a few minutes later, his blonde hair hanging wet on his shoulders. He walked up to Darlina from behind and put his arms around her waist. "Something sure smells good in here."

"Oh you mean besides me?" she teased.

"You're in a good mood."

"I loved going to work today. I met some really nice folks and it felt good to be around regular people again."

"What do you mean regular? Am I not a regular person?"

She laughed. "You know what I mean. I've been cooped up at the farmhouse for months. All I'm sayin' is that it was a good day. I rolled us a joint. Wanna smoke before or after supper?"

"I'm starving. Let's eat first." Will sat at the table big enough for two chairs and Darlina filled their plates.

"I made a decision today."

"What's that?" He filled his mouth.

"Soon as I get a couple of paychecks, I'm going to buy a new car. I looked at a Volkswagen bug and that's what I want."

"You might wanna wait until you land a steady job. A car payment comes around every month."

"I know, but I think I'll be working somewhere permanent soon. A lady I met today told me about a position coming open in an office on the floor above us and said she'd put in a good word. I'm going to apply for it tomorrow." She sipped her glass of iced tea.

"Okay. It's good to see you excited about something for a change."

"I know it'll make for strained relations with your folks for a while, but I'm almost glad your Dad found the pot and made us move."

"I don't know about being glad, but it happened."

"How was your day?"

"All right. I'm workin' with a bunch of nice guys. One of 'em rides a Harley. He told me about a new subdivision they're fixin' to start on the east side of Austin. I'm gonna try to get on there. It would be steady work for a long while."

"Sounds like a good idea. Things are looking up for us."

"Yeah, I suppose they are." Will pushed his chair back, put his plate in the sink and covered the short distance to the living room.

They'd moved their small couch and brightly colored bean bag chairs with them from the farm house and Will chose to stretch out on the sofa. Darlina pulled one of the bean bags close.

"Do you think we might get a telephone soon, Will?" She took the lit joint he offered.

"Maybe after we see how much money we're gonna bring in."

"I'd like to call my folks sometime soon and let them know we've moved."

"There's a pay phone on the next street over. You could walk over there and call them."

"Okay. Maybe tomorrow."

They smoked the rest of the joint in silence.

"Wanna g go for a ride?" Will asked.

"I'd love that. We haven't explored much of Austin yet. One of the younger ladies I met today said there are some cool bars down by the university with lots of live music. Think we could go check it out this weekend?"

"Maybe so." Will stood and pulled on his motorcycle boots.

Soon they were flying down the streets of Austin, as the sun sank behind the horizon. Darlina smiled as they rode. She hadn't even realized the empty shell she'd become but working again and being around other people seemed to be the get out of jail free card for her.

Friday came and Darlina received her first paycheck. She beamed as she held it in her hands. She'd earned almost one hundred dollars! She stopped at a local bank and cashed it.

As soon as she reached the apartment, she changed out of her work clothes, rolled a joint, lit it and picked out Jethro Tull to put on the turntable.

Looking through the freezer, she found nothing that appealed to her for supper. She'd wait until Will came home and suggest they eat out tonight. It would be her treat.

As she inhaled the smoke, she began to relax. She thought about a conversation she'd overheard between two of the women at the office. When an older lady complained that her husband never felt like having sex, the younger one told her she should get a vibrator, then she wouldn't need her husband. She didn't have a clue where she might find one but decided to ask the girl on Monday.

Will arrived home excited about an invitation.

"We're going to a party tonight, Darlina. The guy I told you about that rides a Harley invited us out to his place."

She jumped up. "That sounds fun. I'll get my boots on and my hair braided, and I'm buying us supper tonight."

"Get the bottle out of the stereo cabinet and let's drop something that will make this more fun. It's the weekend!"

She retrieved the aspirin bottle and Will chose black mollies for them. He opened one capsule and shook out half of the powder, then put it back together and handed it to her. While she swallowed it, he licked the powder off his hand and downed two others.

While he showered, she dressed for the party, taking time to re-apply her makeup. She wanted to make a good impression on Will's new friends.

By the time they left the apartment, the top of her head tingled and she no longer had any want or need for food.

"You still want to get some supper?" Will asked as he lifted the kickstand and jumped to start the Harley.

"Nope. Not a bit hungry now. Let's go." She climbed on behind him.

"We'll get something to eat after the party." He kicked the motorcycle into gear and they roared away.

The party turned out to be at a house on Lake Travis. Darlina counted ten people altogether and for the first time since she'd met Will, it seemed to her that he was proud to introduce her.

A beer keg sat on the back deck overlooking the lake. People passed joints back and forth and the men visited the keg often.

A petite girl with long straight blonde hair attached herself to Darlina. "Hi, I'm Meredith. Want a drink of my Strawberry Hill?"

"No thanks. I don't drink much." Darlina observed Will out of the corner of her eye. He passed money to a man, then put something in his pocket. She was curious, but didn't have to wait long.

"Darlina." Will called out. "Come over here."

"Excuse me," she said to Meredith. "I'll be back."

Will took her arm and guided her off the deck and under a large oak tree. He pulled her close, and eagerly kissed her.

"What's that all about Will?"

"I've been watching you and I don't tell you often enough that I'm proud to have you with me."

She laughed. "It's true you don't. It's nice to hear you say it. What did you buy from that man?"

"That's really why I wanted to get you out here. I bought a couple of hits of Orange Sunshine."

"What's that?"

"Acid." He pulled the small package out of his pocket and opened the foil. He tore one small corner off a square piece of paper and handed it to her. "Put this under your tongue and let it dissolve."

She hesitated for a brief moment, then threw caution to the wind and did as he instructed. He put the rest of the contents of the package under his tongue.

"What's it gonna do?"

"It's gonna make everything orange and sunshiny!" He laughed. "Let's go back to the party."

She followed him and re-joined Meredith.

Darlina didn't know what happened over the next hour, but the room began to glow and the walls vibrated. Panic gripped her like bands of steel as reality slipped away.

She didn't have any specific thought pattern. As soon as one entered her head, another replaced it. Her breath quickened and the artery in her neck throbbed with each beat of her heart. Everything became magnified. The voices and laughter of the people at the party took on shrill and unearthly sounds.

Frantically, she looked for Will. When she found him and tried to focus on his face, it melted and ran down his shirt. She put her hands over her eyes and with concentration fought to control her breath and the violent pounding of her heart.

She looked at the people around her. They were all tripping, everyone lost in their own minds. Her blonde friend stood facing a wall, placing her hands one in front of the other as if they were walking up the wall.

Darlina dashed into the bathroom with the intention of washing her face, but when she looked in the mirror, she became lost in the reflection of her own image. Her hair took on an orange glow and her eyes grew to half the size of her face. Her mouth shrunk until it was hardly visible. She didn't have any idea how long she stood there. Maybe hours, maybe minutes. She turned on the faucet and watched the water run over the tops of her hands forming a brilliantly hued waterfall with blended orange, red, yellow and green colors.

Did she need to pee? Was she peeing? She managed to look down only to see that her blue jeans were dry. She pulled down her pants and sat on the toilet. Again she didn't know if she sat there for hours or simply minutes.

Someone knocked on the door, startling her. Fighting with all of her might, she pulled herself back into reality enough to use the bathroom, pull up her pants and leave. When she opened the door, whoever knocked had moved on.

Back in the living room, she sat on a sofa. As the drug intensified, convinced she was on an island surrounded by orange water, she pulled her legs up under her to keep them dry. Even though she could see other people, she couldn't reach them and they couldn't reach her. She was totally alone on her island. Panic began to be replaced by tranquility and she threw her head back and laughed.

When she did, the ceiling moved in orange ripples above her. She stopped laughing and stared at the show taking place on the ceiling.

***

By Sunday evening, Darlina managed to force a few bites of food into her mouth. She vaguely remembered the ride home on the motorcycle, the trailing lights that seemed to follow them and the wind on her face.

She didn't like being so out of control and remembered one other time in her young life that she'd been trapped in the clutches of a drug that separated her from reality.

The scene flashed back as if it were only yesterday. She'd taken Psilocybin when her friend, Sherry, had promised it would make the hurt of losing Luke stop.

Powerless to pull herself back into reality, she'd insisted that Sherry take her to the club where Luke and the Rebel Rousers played that night. She recalled the cutout gingerbread men that danced across her line of vision over and over again for hours and how she'd sob one minute and laugh hysterically the next. Luke had been angry and disappointed in her and made her promise that she would never take a drug like that again.

She'd broken her promise and hated herself for it, but she couldn't undo it.

She'd never tell Luke about the Orange Sunshine and was glad that no one but Will and a house full of strangers knew. Even now, she could see signs that Will hadn't fully returned to reality, but unlike her, he appeared to enjoy tripping.

Never again would she partake of any psychedelic drug, and she would make that very clear to Will.

Even though she was physically free, her heart remained imprisoned in the cell with Luke Stone, leaving her broken and incomplete. But, drugs weren't the answer.

"Burning flesh tingles for our hungry lips. No bars shall prohibit our needs..."

Chapter 21

With winter fast approaching, Luke braced himself for another dismal holiday season behind bars. Having been in prison for three long years, he'd witnessed numerous suicides between Thanksgiving and Christmas.

He understood. Men got drove up, especially if they didn't hear from home. He'd watched hardened criminals break down and sob when they received a "Dear John" letter or even worse, no letter at all.

Everyone, even the cruel, evil, demented and twisted souls who resided behind prison walls, longed for someone to give a shit about them.

Luke spent every waking hour of the day creating with his hands and mind, determined to stay so busy that depression couldn't edge its way in.

On this dreary winter day, he sat beside Red in the craft shop, stamping designs into a piece of brown leather that would eventually be a handbag.

He received occasional letters from his older children and their words melted his heart. They always said how much they loved and missed him and wished he wasn't in prison. He answered each letter and sent drawings and poems. For his daughter Lexi, he wrote a poem called

Little Girls And Roses
Roses are like pretty little girls
Petals swirling, lovely curls

Sweetly blush the morning roses
Angel cheeks, buds like little noses
Tender, fragile blooming at random
Prettiest ones are where you find them
Dew kissed angels from above
Rare beauties, symbols of love
Delicate and soft, seem they fantasy
Charming warmth assures reality
Thankful am I that each one grows
Pretty little girls and the beautiful rose

She was growing up way too fast and turning into a stunning young woman. How he wished he could be around to protect her from the wolves.

Joseph, his oldest son, on the brink of becoming a man, told his dad in a letter that he wanted to ride bulls in the rodeo. Next year he'd be old enough. Luke had started tooling a pair of leather chaps to send to him for Christmas.

The two younger boys still lived with their mother and Luke didn't hear much from them. He'd written to Joyce a few times and hoped they could be civil to one another. He offered to give her a divorce if she wanted to marry someone else. He knew she faced a hard struggle, but was beginning to understand that the most difficult battle she faced was within her own self. He wrote words of encouragement, but could never get past the wall of hateful bitterness she had toward him.

Then there was Darlina. As much as he selfishly wanted to keep her all to himself, he knew he couldn't. He had to live with the thought of her lying in someone else's bed. Dammit, he couldn't expect a young girl with her whole life ahead of her, not to find someone to spend it with. He always stressed that to her, even though it killed him to do so.

She'd told him she wasn't happy with Will, but maybe it could grow into what she needed. He'd been thrilled to read her happy letter about going back to work. At least she was trying. The last thing in the world he wanted for her was to sit around waiting for a broken down convict to get out of prison.

Learning to accept things he couldn't change turned out to be a very big lesson for Luke Stone.

These thoughts filled his head as he worked with his hands.

"Chow time." Red put his tools away and stood.

"Wonder what brand of slop they're feedin' us today? Did you hear what Freddie told me yesterday about gettin' in a shipment of army rations dated 1947?"

"Yeah, I heard him. Guess they figure they're feedin' the bottom of the barrel."

"I'm sure they do, but I'll be firing off some letters tomorrow to bring a little attention to it. We may be convicts, but we don't have to eat shit like that."

Red and Luke reached the chow hall, filled their plates, then joined Nico and a group of Italian men at a long table.

The men stood and as Luke had learned, their tradition of kissing on the cheek, was not to be ignored.

Once they were all seated, Luke turned to Nico. "Man, I sure do appreciate you giving my address to your sister to pass around. I got three letters this week from ol' gals that want to correspond with me."

"She 'a tell 'a me there 'a lotsa women that will 'a write a con. You 'a know 'a Italiana women 'a beautiful." He kissed the fingers on his right hand and raised them in expression.

"Yeah man, Sophia Loren's about as pretty as they come. Hope they don't mind writin' sex letters. It ain't like the real thing, but better than nothin' at all." He scooped up a bite of mashed potatoes.

Nico and the others laughed and nodded in agreement.

"You 'a okay, Stone. You 'a having some 'a luck over inna the law library?"

"Nah, none to speak of. I'll keep diggin' though. Shit!" Luke spat into his hand. "My fuckin' tooth just broke in half."

"Oh thatsa not 'a good."

"That's the third damn one. Guess I'll have to go see that quack of a dentist they have in here and let him take a look."

The men turned at the sounds of a scuffle and loud cursing. At the next table over, two men tangled in a fight.

The guards came running to separate them.

"What do you reckon that was over?" Red asked.

"You know how it gets in here this time of year. Tempers are on short fuses so who the hell knows?"

"Thatsa the truth. Two 'a days ago, I saw 'a con threaten ta cut a man'sa throat 'a over a piece a fuckin' meat."

"It can get crazy. I just don't want any of 'em messin' with any of us." Luke shoved his plate away. "I'm out of here. See you guys later."

"I'll be along in a bit. I'm gonna finish my chow." Red reached for Luke's abandoned plate.

"Suit yourself, hoss." Luke bid the men farewell and headed to the dentist's office inside the prison.

***

Three weeks later, a few days before Christmas, Luke sat in the cracked and worn dentist chair while the dentist pulled the last remaining teeth out of his mouth.

"Okay, Mr. Stone," the young dentist washed his hands. "Once your gums heal up, I'll get you fitted for dentures. Like I told you before, your teeth crumbled due to all of the blood thinners they pumped into you in a short period of time."

Luke mumbled. "I'm turnin' into a fuckin' old man."

"Oh it isn't so bad. Once you get your dentures, you'll look like you always did, only your teeth won't ever hurt again."

"Whatever, man. Are you done?"

"Almost. I need to pack the extraction area and you'll be free to go."

Luke opened his mouth while the dentist finished, then without another word, left the dentist office.

Even though he fought it, depression lapped at Luke's heels. Hell, now he didn't have any teeth. How could any woman ever want a toothless old man? He laughed out loud, what the fuck was he worried about? He wouldn't be seein' a woman for a long time and by the then, he'd be eligible to be a toothless old man and not give a shit.

Once he reached the cell, he stood looking in the mirror at his reflection. His jaw was swollen and his left eye had turned black from the tugging the dentist had done to get some of the roots out.

He narrowed his eyes at the reflection and took off the rubber band holding his ponytail. He shook his head and let his brown hair fall around his face.

He looked old beyond his thirty-eight years and still had lots more time to be locked behind these bars.

With a sigh, he lay down on his bunk and closed his eyes. If he thought real hard, he could recall the scenes in life that had meant the most to him, but little by little, they were slipping away, being replaced by the reality of now.

He drifted off to sleep and when he awoke, found his mouth caked with dried blood.

He washed it out and with a renewed will, left the cell for the craft shop. There he didn't have to think at all and could lose himself in the art he created.

This was his sanity.

***

Luke sat on a straight-back wooden chair quietly strumming his guitar. It was New Year's Eve and in a few minutes, would be 1974. The small lamp glowed in an almost mocking way, reflecting his gaunt frame on the wall behind him.

In the stillness of the night, his thoughts turned to Darlina and he wondered where she'd be spending New Year's Eve. He thumbed through the tablet and found a blank page. He had to put his thoughts on paper. He didn't know if she'd ever see the words he wrote, but if she did, she'd know instantly they were for and about her.

He absentmindedly strummed chords while looking at the empty page waiting to be turned into a song.

He felt the familiar surge pass through his fingers to the guitar and in that moment, everything connected. The dots all fit together. He wrote with vigor, stopping to strum and write down chords.

> I'm losing you and Lord knows
> I've lost enough to know
> There's nothing I can do but let you go
> I just want you to know
> What's in this heart of mine

I love you more this moment
Than he will in a lifetime
I can't stand to think of tomorrow
It will be so hard to bear
I'll need you more in times of sorrow
These tender words I share
True love is what I feel
And I love you more this moment
Than he ever will
There is more to you, woman
Than just loving charms
It would thrill anyone
To hold you in their arms
But they don't really know you
There's much of you to understand
I love you more this moment
More than he ever can.

Luke sat for the longest time letting the words he'd written echo through his lonely soul. How was it possible that one man and one woman could love each other so deeply that nothing, not time nor distance or even death could destroy it?

Needing solace, he reached for his ceremonial feathers and tobacco. A peace washed over him that came with this new way of worshipping the Great Spirit. He wished for a window that he could gaze out at the stars, but had none, so created stars in his mind to see through closed eyes.

After tying a strip of leather around his head and slipping feathers into it, he sat cross-legged on his hard bunk. He lit the tobacco in a pipe and began sacred ceremony to celebrate the gift of a new year of life.

He slowly turned over in his mind everything he could think of to give thanks for. Funny, how a man could find thankfulness even in this desolate God-forsaken place.

The smoke from the campfires of his ancestors swirled about his head. In the midst of it, he heard the chants of the Medicine Man, calling in magic and protection for his people.

In Luke's soul, he was a part of this.

His vision took on personal proportions and he saw Darlina dressed in a simple leather dress, feathers and flowers in her hair, watching him with pure love in her eyes. In his imagination, he moved toward her and took her into his outstretched arms.

The feel of her moving against him was as real as the beating of his heart. He let the scene unfold before him and like an intruder, watched as he slipped the dress over her head leaving her naked body glistening in the firelight.

Laying her gently down on a soft buffalo robe, he reverently touched every part of her warm waiting body. His breath came in ragged gasps as the want and need for her grew.

Slowly he moved over her and when he entered, the whole world stopped turning. That powerful moment, frozen in time, held a magic that transcended the physical.

In the swirling haze of smoke, the vision began to fade. It seemed to Luke as if he had truly been allowed to be with Darlina. He wondered if she'd felt it too.

Edgar Cayce wrote about the power of the mind and connecting to others. This fascinated Luke. It gave him a way to be with the ones he loved, even from behind bars.

The vision tonight was the most he'd ever experimented with the theory and left little doubt about its validity.

He had time, lots of time, to do more experiments and learn everything he could about the power of both mind and spirit.

So, he forced the vision to return and savored the sweetness of making love to Darlina. He lay on the buffalo robe with her wrapped tightly in his arms.

"I'll never be able to completely let you go, Darlina." He spoke the words in an anguished whisper. "It's not within my power, sweetheart. You're as much a part of me as the blood that flows through my veins."

"Leaving behind the dark wilderness, where lost I had been, to tread upon a sure path that is lighted from within."

Chapter 22

With a fulltime job and a new Volkswagen Bug to drive, things were finally on the right track for Darlina. Christmas loomed right around the corner and on this first day of December, she hummed while she put Christmas decorations around the house she and Will now lived in.

It had been an easy decision to move out of the apartment when Will found a small house for rent through a friend of a co-worker.

She looked up as he came through the kitchen door. "Hi, how was your day?"

"Okay. How about yours?"

"It was all right. What do you think of the Christmas decorations?"

"Looks good. Hey, I've gotta take a shower and go meet a man in an hour. Why don't you go with me and we'll grab a burger on the way?"

"Sounds good. I'll be ready."

In less than half an hour, the two sat in Will's gold Oldsmobile Toronado, munching burgers and fries.

"Who's the man you've gotta meet?" Darlina sipped on her Coke.

"Just somebody John introduced me to. With work slowing down for the winter, I've gotta do something to make a little extra money. I'm buying five pounds of pot."

Darlina cleared her throat. "Is that safe?" She hated the sense of foreboding crawling up her spine.

"Sure. I'm meeting him on a deserted country road. No problems. Once we get home with it, I'll stash it under the floor in the closet and we'll start bagging it up. I know I won't have any trouble selling it."

"I'm sure you won't, but that's a lot of pot to have at the house. What if we get busted?" She chewed her bottom lip.

"We won't get busted, Darlina. You're just bein' paranoid."

"Maybe, but it would screw up my job at Texas Oil Marketers if we did and I'd never be able to face my family again."

"We won't. I don't wanna talk about it anymore." He tapped his fingers on the steering wheel. "You done eating?"

"Yeah." She could never get used to Will's lack of concern about how his actions might affect her.

Darlina couldn't help looking around in all directions as they rode in silence on the way to the rendezvous.

Will turned off the highway onto a dirt road leading to a cemetery. Halfway down, he pulled over and turned off the engine and headlights.

Darlina bit her fingernails. "I'm scared."

"Nothin' to be scared of, I promise. He'll be here in a minute and we'll be on our way back to the house."

No sooner than Will said the words, a car flashed its headlights, then stopped in front of the Oldsmobile. "Stay here. I'll be right back."

Darlina watched as a tall thin man got out of the blue Chevrolet Impala and walked toward Will. She couldn't hear what they said, but saw Will hand the man cash. The man walked to the trunk of his car, opened it, then he and Will carried large packages to the Oldsmobile.

As soon as Will slammed the trunk shut, he shook the man's hand and jumped back into the driver's seat. "See. I told you. All done."

He turned the car around on the narrow dirt road and drove back to town. They didn't speak again until Will pulled into the driveway at their house.

"If you do that again, I don't want to go with you. I'll wait at home. I don't like the way that felt." Darlina twisted her hair around her finger.

"All right. Don't make a big deal out of it. If I sell all this pot, I'll triple my money. Plus, we get all we want to smoke for free. You can't tell me you don't like that idea."

"Sure. That part's great. Sorry I overreacted. But, I don't want to go with you again to make a buy like that."

"I won't ask you." Will pulled under their carport and unlocked the kitchen door. "Will you help me carry it in?"

"Of course."

Together, they made short work of getting the packages into the house and on the kitchen table.

After locking the door, he said, "Let's see what quality of stuff we've got here. He told me it was Columbian." He took a knife out of his pocket and slit one of the packages open.

He sifted through the marijuana with his hands and then held a bud up to his nose and sniffed it. His eyes lit up. "This is some good shit."

Darlina sat at the table and touched the fresh moist pot with her fingertips. "Roll us up one and let's try it."

***

A few weeks later, Darlina and Will spent an awkward Christmas day with his folks on the farm and she was relieved when it ended.

She made a point to call her own mom and dad to wish them a Merry Christmas, then a short conversation with Leann completed her holiday.

A Christmas package she'd mailed to Luke had been returned. Apparently it hadn't been sent through proper channels. Discouraged by the attempt, she'd written him an immediate letter with a card in hopes that it would arrive before the holidays were over.

Now, it was New Year's Eve and Will stood at the kitchen door. "You sure you don't wanna come with me? You don't have to drop acid just because everyone else'll be trippin'." She'd been disappointed when Will continued to use the drug on a regular basis.

Maybe it was time for her to think about moving out and getting her own apartment.

"Yeah, I'm sure I don't wanna go. I really wish you wouldn't do so much acid. Obviously, it doesn't affect you like it does me. I won't ever do it again."

Will snorted. "You never gave it a chance. Just because you had one bad experience, you think it's like that all the time."

"That's enough tryin' for me. Go ahead and have fun but I'm stayin' here."

"Suit yourself. Happy New Year." With that, Will was gone.

When the car backed out of the driveway, she almost ran to stop him. She didn't want to spend New Year's Eve by herself, but she also didn't care to spend it with a bunch of people trippin' out of their heads. Will's use of psychedelic drugs had gotten out of hand, in her opinion.

With a sigh, she locked the back door and walked through the empty house.

Maybe she should go somewhere. But where?

It had been a warm day for December, but as the night settled in, a chill hung in the air. Darlina reached for a sweater and wrapped it around her shoulders.

She pictured Luke sitting in his cell alone, separated from everyone and everything he held dear. In that moment her loneliness seemed comparable to his.

Pacing the house, with a restlessness that couldn't find a cure, she finally rolled a joint, curled up on the sofa, and turned on the TV.

Sometime near midnight, she awoke with a start. The only sound in the house came from the TV. She shivered uncontrollably and pulled her sweater tighter around her.

Had it been a dream? Her body reacted in a way that made her wonder. She'd been with Luke, only it had been in another time and place. The smell of smoke from the Indian campfires and the distinct odor of deerskin leather lingered still.

Disoriented, she walked to the bedroom in a fog and threw herself across the bed. "Don't go away, Luke. Finish what you started."

She closed her eyes and traveled back to the place she'd been with Luke. Almost instantly, she was there again. Luke laid her gently on a soft buffalo robe and made sweet slow tender love to her. She let the experience take her completely and once Luke exploded inside her, he was gone.

She turned into her pillow and sobbed. "Come back, Luke. Come back."

Darlina knew at some point, she would have to make a decision to either be with Will and give him one hundred percent, or abandon him for a lover that she could only interact with in her mind and on paper.

For now, tonight, she preferred her spirit lover and wished with all her might he would return. Maybe if she closed her eyes tight enough and wished hard enough, he would make another appearance.

***

January 10, 1974 turned bitterly cold with a north wind blowing strong across the Texas Hill Country. Darlina stood at the kitchen stove, stirring a pot of vegetable beef soup when Will came through the kitchen door, letting a blast of cold air in with him.

"Somethin' smells delicious in here." He covered the short distance from the door to the stove.

"It's soup and cornbread. Hungry?"

"As a bear! I met the strangest man on the job today. His name is David and he had a light in his eyes and on his face like I've never seen. I thought he was high, but when I asked him, he said he didn't do drugs."

"That's odd."

"Yeah, well anyway, he invited us to come to a meeting with him on Saturday and I told him I'd ask you first, but I think I wanna go."

"What kind of meeting?"

"He said it was a bunch of people who get together to have what he called satsang. He said it was kinda' like testimony or something and that they practice meditation and follow a guru from India. He said this guru is the new Messiah, but I don't know about that."

"A guru? What is his name?"

"Guru Maharaj Ji. I really think we should go check it out. You know I love gettin' high, but if there is a way to feel like that without drugs, I wanna know about it."

"Me too. I'm game." She handed him a joint ready to be lit. She couldn't help having a glimmer of hope that there might be a different way of life for them other than staying stoned.

Two days later, in the living room of a large two story house in an old Austin neighborhood, Darlina sat in awe as she and Will heard person after person proclaim the peace and love they'd found in their lives through Guru Maharaj Ji.

They'd gotten high before they went, but by the time the meeting was over, the high had escalated to a whole different level.

Everyone made them feel welcome and were more than willing to stay around after the meeting and visit. They smiled and their eyes shone as they shared how the knowledge imparted by the guru changed their lives.

They rode in silence most of the way home. Finally, Will put his thoughts into words. "That was pretty amazing. What do you think?"

"I don't know exactly, but I loved the way it felt there. Everyone seems so happy and peaceful, like they've found what's been missing from their lives."

"I want to know more. Let's go to more meetings and learn all we can."

"I'd like that. What was it they kept referring to themselves as?"

"Premies, I think. Maybe we should be a part of this group."

"Maybe so." Darlina smiled openly at Will. "Maybe so."

In less than a month, Will and Darlina became devoted followers of the guru. On February 3rd, they both received what was referred to as Knowledge imparted directly to them by a Mahatma (holy man).

As Darlina sat in the circle of ten people waiting to receive the mysterious Knowledge she couldn't help but think about Luke and how this step she was taking would put her farther away from him. She couldn't see him ever accepting anything like an Eastern guru or way of life.

She'd written and told him about the new discovery and he'd advised her to be cautious and referred to the guru as a cult leader. He obviously didn't understand how real this experience was.

"Clear your mind," the Mahatma said.

Darlina closed her eyes and willed Luke to go away.

"Listen only to the breath moving in and out of your body," he continued.

She struggled to control her thoughts and focus only on her breathing.

The Mahatma went on in his broken English. "The gift you are about to receive is directly from Guru Maharaj Ji and is more precious than anything else in life. Nurture it and allow it to grow and you will find everlasting peace."

At some point, she stopped listening and began to focus on the wave of peace and contentment that engulfed her. By the time the Mahatma came to her in the circle, she openly received his instruction, then the holy breath was blown into her ear.

After the instruction, dialogue and ceremony, which lasted four hours, the older Premies prepared a celebration for the newbies.

Darlina had learned that there were two Premie houses in Austin where devotees of the guru all lived together communally. This particular house they'd come to for the Knowledge imparting ceremony was one of them.

Will had already talked to the House Father of this one about moving in and Darlina had no argument against it. They embarked on this new journey wholeheartedly, embracing all of it from the austere lifestyle to the daily practice of meditation and being vegetarian.

Darlina couldn't help comparing the stringent lifestyle to the one she'd grown up in. She could see similarities between the strictness of the Holy-Roller church and the simple austere way the followers of the guru lived. None of the women wore makeup and that was something she'd enjoyed since she left home. She wasn't quite sure she could give up that again or let the hair grow on her legs or wear long dresses.

She had to wonder exactly how all of that affected the well-being of your soul, but the leaders seemed to know things she didn't. Perhaps in time, she could become enlightened enough to see the correlation.

At the end of the day, back in their home, they sat in silence contemplating the amazing turn their lives had taken.

Darlina penned a glowing letter to Luke telling him how wonderful this young guru was and how she'd decided to devote her life to him. She stressed how no drugs were used by this group and how they lived in communes and last of all that she and Will had decided they would move into one of them.

Not caring what anyone else thought, she believed she'd found something that would bring lasting peace. At the very least, it had to be better than staying high. Surely Luke couldn't argue with that.

~Photos~

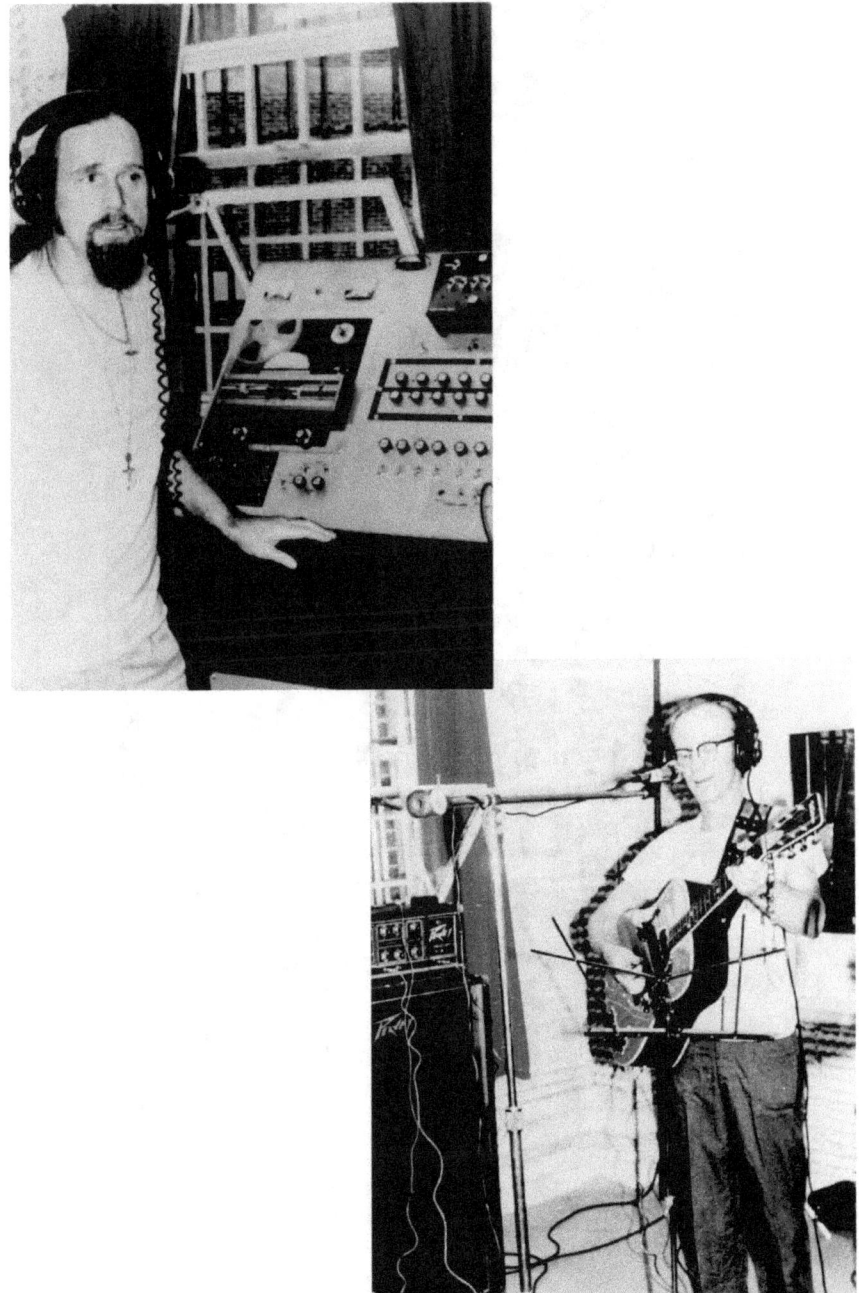

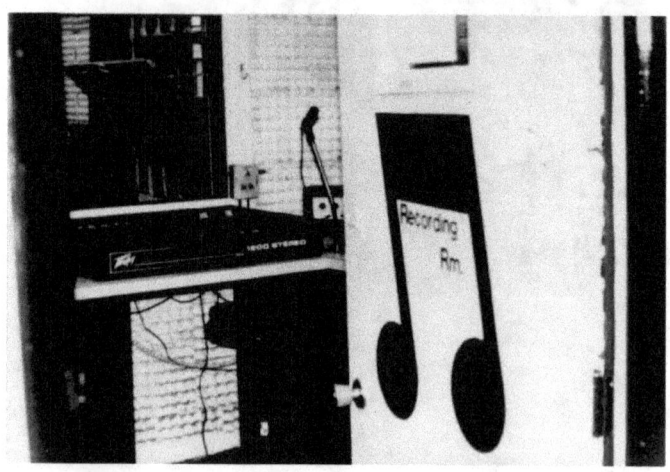

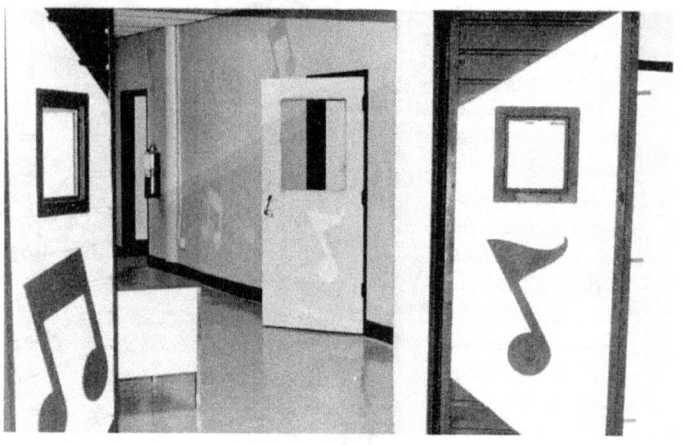

"I'll not wait on bad times to pass, for I am master of my own way."

Chapter 23

As was the nature of a federal medical center, residents came and went. During Walter Little Crow's short stay, Luke became proficient at Indian beading and under his supervision, designed and built a custom bead loom.

Most of Luke's daylight hours were spent working on projects in the craft shop. He always kept a tablet close at hand to capture any song or poem inspirations that might come out of the blue, as they often did.

On this March morning, he finished putting the last few beads on a guitar strap. He figured he had about fifty hours of time invested, but what was time to a convict?

Only he and one other man occupied the craft shop at this early hour. Mrs. Yarbrough entrusted him with the key and the freedom to come and go as he pleased.

She approached Luke as he unstrung the bead loom. "Mr. Stone, that is a beautiful piece of work. I don't believe I've ever seen anything nicer."

"Thank you, ma'am. Ol' Walter sure didn't lie when he said he could teach me the old way of beading. Now, I've gotta put this onto the leather and I'll have a new strap." He held the piece at arm's length.

They both looked up when the door opened. An elderly black man hobbled in, back bent, hair graying.

"Good morning, sir." Mrs. Yarbrough greeted him.

"Mahnin'," the man replied with a deep Southern accent.

"What can I do for you?" Mrs. Yarbrough laboriously moved toward him.

"Well, ma'am, I'se a painter. I likes to paint. Do you have any canvas in here?"

"Yes, I do. Come with me and I'll show you what I have. By the way, what's your name, sir?"

"I be Henry Taylor, ma'am."

"Nice to meet you, Henry Taylor. Here are some easels, paints and brushes. You are welcome to use what we have until you can purchase your own."

The black man followed her and Luke couldn't help observing the similarities in the difficulty they both had walking.

Mr. Taylor picked up the brushes, held them up the light and felt the bristles. "These ain't the best, but they'll sho 'nuf do. When can I start?"

"Now, if you want."

"I do wants to get started."

Luke watched the old man set up an easel with the grace of a pro. Henry opened the oil paints and poured small amounts onto a well-used palette.

The man hummed to himself as he spread Periwinkle blue paint on the canvas with long strokes.

Luke ambled across the room. "Looks like you know what you're doin', pahdnah."

Mr. Taylor looked up. "I does know. I be paintin' all my life."

"My name is Luke Stone. I heard you tell Mrs. Yarbrough that you're Henry Taylor. Mind if I watch you for a minute?"

"Nah sir, I don't mind a bit. I seen that beadwork you was holdin' up over there. Mighty fine work."

"Thank you. I had a good teacher. Reckon if I wanted to learn to paint real good, you could teach me?"

"Ah don't know. Never did try to teach nobody befoh."

"Then we'd be even, because I never tried to learn. I've dabbled a little bit in watercolors and I draw, but I know working with oil is completely different." Luke dragged a chair beside Henry and sat down. "I'll just watch you first and you think about teaching me."

"Yah sir. Yous welcome to watch."

Luke spent well over a week, sitting beside Mr. Taylor, concentrating and watching each brush stroke. He enjoyed conversing with the old man and learned that he was in prison because of "a no-good low-down cheatin' woman", as he so directly put it.

One morning, when Henry Taylor arrived at the craft shop, Luke had an easel, blank canvas, paints and brushes set up beside the old man's.

"I'm ready to learn, Mr. Taylor."

"Son, I does believe you sho might be ready." He sat down in front of his own canvas before he continued. "Fuhst thing you gots to learn is to sees something when you looks at it."

"Okay," Luke replied. "Give me an example."

"You sees that doh knob ova dere?"

"Yes."

"Tell me, what does you see?"

"Well, it's round and it's metal and it's attached to a piece of wood."

"Nah sir, yous ain't lookin'. You sees the shadow on the left side? You sees all dem diff'rent shades of metal in that doh knob? Look again and this time, really look with moh than yoh eyes."

Luke stared at the door knob and began to see what the old man said. He could see the shadows around it and the different hues of bronze and brass in the metal. "Mr. Taylor, I see what you are saying. Now, how do I put that on canvas?"

The old man reached for a blank canvas and sat it on his easel. Luke matched his moves, brush stroke for brush stroke, imitating everything Henry did.

After three hours of working, Mr. Taylor laid down his brushes and pushed his chair back. "Look at dem from back heah now."

Luke pushed his chair back even with Mr. Taylor's and grinned when he saw what he'd created. "Mine looks almost as good as yours."

"Yah sir, it do. I believes you can be a painter, son."

"Maybe, if you'll keep teaching me."

"For so long as I be heah. Don't know rightly when dey gonna ship me back to Pollack, but I shows you all I knows."

That evening, back in the cell Luke shared with Red, he related what the old man had shown him about the door knob.

"That don't make a lick of sense to me, Luke, but I ain't no artist. Hey, did you see this week's edition of "The Weekly Echo?"

"Not yet. Why?"

"Your artwork is on the front cover plus they printed one of your poems."

"Well, I'll be damned. I'll have to pick up a copy tomorrow."

"Saw the eye doctor today and he told me I'm healing up good in that left eye, but now they wanna work on the right one. Guess I'll let 'em. I can see better than I could before, so figure it can't hurt."

"I reckon you're right. Don't think I'll ever get used to these fuckin' teeth. Hell, they look like horse teeth. I'm gonna go back over there and make 'em fix me some that fit my mouth. I never was buck tooth in my life."

"Hey, did you see the stack of letters we both got today?" Red pointed to the envelopes sitting on a small table.

"Yeah, haven't opened 'em yet, have you?"

"Yep."

"It ain't half bad gettin' letters from women that don't mind talkin' dirty or listen to an ol' con ramble on. We've got Nico's sister to thank." Luke pulled a chair up to the small table.

"Shit, I got one yesterday from some little ol' gal in New Jersey and she sent me a picture. Not bad lookin' at all. Said she had a couple of kids, but that don't bother me none. It's somebody to write to."

Thumbing through the envelopes, Luke noticed postmarks from New York, Massachusetts, New Jersey and Pennsylvania. The last one in the stack was from Darlina.

He hesitated to read it. As of late, all of her letters were filled with praise and adoration for the guru. It gave Luke a bad taste in his mouth. He didn't want to say or do anything to offend her, but he couldn't condone the blind worship of another human being. No matter what they claimed, he knew this kid from India was not the new Jesus Christ and savior of the world.

He'd held his tongue when she described how she and the others in this commune slept on two inch foam mats on the floor and how they all worked and turned their earnings over to one person who paid the household bills, then sent the rest to the guru. How frustrating that he couldn't seem to say anything to make her see the blind trust she had and how wrong it all was.

One thing about being in prison, you never had to tear open an envelope. They all arrived opened, stamped and censored.

He slid the letter out and unfolded it. He remembered when she used to send letters written on scented stationery and now they arrived on plain white ruled paper. He guessed stationery wasn't considered a necessity in the commune.

"*My Dearest Luke,*" she wrote. At least that stayed the same. "*I wish I could really explain to you the peace and joy I've found in my life.*" Luke muttered under his breath, "Yeah, at the price of your freedom."

As usual, the letter went on and on about the wonders of the guru and his divine mission.

She ended the letter thanking him for the beautiful hair pipe choker he'd sent to her and promised a picture with it around her neck.

Luke slowly folded the letter and put it aside. He didn't feel the need to rush an answer back. He was very happy that the heavy use of drugs had stopped, but it seemed to him that she'd simply replaced them with another crutch. He could only hope that she'd eventually find her way.

He read the other letters and even though he enjoyed the banter with the other women, it occurred to him how shallow the words were. Nevertheless, he'd play the game because it was better than nothing at all.

He reached for his guitar and let his fingers glide across the strings. After a few minutes, he found words flowing in a lyrical melody.

> I always knew you'd be going
> I knew some day you'd be gone
> When I hear the wind a blowing
> I can't stand being alone.
> Woman you came to me knowing
> That I sang a different song
> My love kept on growing
> Till it was much too strong
> Connected we were mirrored by the sea

For together we did belong
The only reflection now is me
And I can't stand being alone...

Luke leaned on his guitar and stared at the stack of letters. He realized he hadn't put Darlina's letter in the same stack as the others. As he looked at it now, lying alone he knew she'd always be separate.

You couldn't mix love with bullshit.

"We are the determiners of our own destiny. We make the choices..."

Chapter 24

In the meditation room lit only by a single flickering candle, just after ten o'clock, Darlina sat under her meditation cloth of India Batik. She concentrated on her breath and watched the bright light ever pulsing in the middle of her forehead. She could hear the sounds of people leaving the room, but tonight, she wasn't interested in sleep.

She continued breathing, in and out, slow and deliberate until her mind became crystal clear.

Tomorrow she would quit her job and sell her car. The position of house mother for this commune, had recently been vacated and she would announce in the morning that she would fill it. That's what her heart told her to do.

A slight twinge of remorse gnawed at her when she thought about turning in her resignation. She'd thoroughly enjoyed working, but now it didn't seem so important. Devoting her life to serving Guru Maharaj Ji was all that mattered.

She'd watched Will turn into a glowing beacon of love and light and showed no surprise when he traded his Harley for a blue and white Volkswagen Van. He'd been thrilled to trade straight across. Then, he proceeded to sell his gold Oldsmobile Toronado and donate all of the money to Guru Maharaji Ji's Divine Light Mission.

With his hair cut short and clean-shaven, he was a far cry from the long haired biker she'd first met at her sister's house in Abilene, Texas.

They served the guru together, alongside the other Premies (interpreted in English means lover of God), but shared no intimacy.

Darlina let out a long slow sigh. She'd finally found the one thing that could fill the emptiness losing Luke had left.

The guru taught that everything around her was an illusion and that the only reality was the life force inside.

In her new life, she learned how to prepare and enjoy vegetarian food. She practiced Yoga and gave massages.

Patchouli and Sandalwood oils replaced Evening In Paris and she wore only cotton clothing.

Letting go of wearing makeup was a huge stumbling block, but eventually she realized it was her ego and as the Mahatmas (holy men) taught, ego was bad.

Now, as house mother, she would have time to study herbs and their medicinal purposes. She would use this knowledge to take care of her housemates if they took sick.

She embraced this organic lifestyle. In her long letters to Luke, she shared her experiences of meditation and discovering who she really was. The answers to everything lay inside and through meditation, all problems could be solved. She wanted him to understand what she was trying to say because it would help him endure prison.

News came in April that set the entire Premie house abuzz. Guru Maharaj Ji announced a festival in Florida. Everyone would go and Darlina couldn't contain her excitement. To see Guru Maharaj Ji in person and listen to his teachings would be amazing. But most important of all would be the opportunity to kiss his feet and receive the holy breath that she'd heard so much about.

Early on the morning of May 9, 1974, Darlina, Will and three other residents of the Premie house left in Will's van. They'd loaded it with tents and camping supplies. They joked about writing "Florida or Bust" on the back window.

Darlina had prepared homemade granola, yogurt and an assortment of fruits, nuts and raw vegetables to sustain them on the trip. She'd tackled her new job of house mother with enthusiasm and loved learning all the new things she could prepare.

Halfway through the trip, Will pulled the van into a gas station and everyone climbed out to stretch their legs.

He caught Darlina's arm as she bounded out of the van. "When we load back in, ride up front with me so we can talk. We've barely said more than a few words to each other in months."

She smiled and patted his hand. "Sure. I'd like that."

Soon they were riding down the road again and the countryside began to turn into swampland. Darlina curiously watched out the window. "I've never seen this part of the country. Look at all that swamp. Bet there's gators out there as long as this van."

Will chuckled. "I bet you're right." He reached over and took Darlina's hand. "You do know that you're glowing and have been ever since you received Knowledge."

"I know. I finally feel complete, Will. All the emptiness and ache I tried to cover up with drugs is gone."

"Yeah, for me too. I didn't even realize I was trying to cover anything up with all the drugs, but I was. I just didn't talk about it."

"I love Guru Maharaj Ji and I'm so excited to get to see him."

"I've heard so many stories about how amazing it is to kiss his feet and receive the holy breath. I can't wait to find out for myself."

"I just know it's going to be something I'll always remember." She puzzled over the warmth in Will's hand and the way he squeezed hers.

"Do you think you might share my tent at the festival?"

"I had planned to stay with three of the other girls, but I can easily change my plans. Don't you already have someone staying with you?"

"No. I was daring to hope that you might consider it."

"Are you talking about having sex, Will?"

"No. I'm simply suggesting you share my tent and we can go to all of the festival events together."

"Well then, I'd be happy to. I can't wait to get there. I heard there was going to be over ten thousand people. That's a lotta folks in one spot."

"It's going to be an experience for sure."

They traveled on in comfortable silence and Darlina pondered Will's proposal. He hadn't shown any interest in her or any affection toward her since they'd joined this group and moved into the big house. She supposed he simply wanted to share this experience with her and she had no objection to that.

***

Saturday morning, May 12, 1974 in Miami, Florida dawned warm and sunny.

Darlina had slept on her mat and Will on his in the tent he'd brought. Now, they prepared for an early morning group meditation.

It seemed to Darlina that she could feel the ground vibrating beneath her feet as she carried her meditation pillow and cloth to the giant pavilion. Excitement rippled through her. A far as the eye could see, rows of tents with a few campers scattered amongst them dotted the landscape. A line of vehicles turning into the festival grounds stretched for two miles.

Darlina and Will managed to squeeze in for the group meditation. It was already crowded even at this early hour. She covered her head with the cloth and almost instantly, the energy fairly leaped out of her body. The brilliant light pulsated and danced in her forehead and peace washed over her in waves.

They moved together, she and Will, throughout the day, attending various satsangs (company of truth), workshops and music events. The level of excitement continued to build and soon it was time to prepare for Guru Maharaj Ji's appearance.

"I want to take a shower before we go, Will." Darlina said as they arrived back at the tent.

"Me too. The bath houses are on the other side of the road. I'll walk with you."

"Let's hurry though because I want to get down to the stage area and get a good seat."

"Yep, me too."

They hurriedly showered, donned clean clothes and walked briskly back to the main stage area.

The sun was beginning to melt into the horizon when Guru Maharaj Ji walked out onto the stage. He wore a garland of flowers around his neck, a long flowing royal blue robe and a jewel-studded gold crown on his head.

Darlina stood beside Will, arms outstretched to the heavens, chanting in her loudest voice along with the rest of the crowd. "Bolie Shri Satgurdev Marahaj Ki Jai (All praise and honor to the perfect master)."

She glanced at Will to see tears streaming down his face as he chanted.

Looking back at Guru Maharaj Ji, she believed he was, without any doubt, the Messiah. No one else could have that much power.

The energy rose to a crescendo and the guru finally motioned for everyone to sit then took his place on the throne prepared for him.

He spoke in a heavy eastern accent. "We have all assembled here, or at least supposed to be assembled here, to listen and to talk about this strange thing. Supposedly a phenomena to the world called this peace. Everybody is looking for this, in different ways, of course. Some people think it's in money, some people think it's in the external pleasures, some people think it's in the Himalayas, some people think it's in nature. People are looking for it in different, different ways, but really it is in one place -- right within our hearts."

He continued speaking for over an hour and the followers attentively absorbed each word.

Once he finished speaking, a band played two songs of devotion to him. Then he stood, waved to the crowd and exited the stage.

The crowd rose to their feet, chanting again. Then came the announcement. Guru Maharaj Ji would be giving darshan (coming into the presence of the perfect master) tomorrow starting at 9 am.

Without thinking, Darlina reached for Will's hand, as they strolled back to the tent. There was no need for words.

The next morning, they were in line by 6 am and surprisingly it already stretched around the stage and down a side road.

They stood quietly and reverently for the six hours it took for them to have the opportunity to pass in front of Guru Maharaj Ji, kneel and kiss his feet, then stand and cup their right hand behind their ear to receive the holy breath.

Once Darlina passed through the line, she waited for Will at the bottom of the stage. He approached with a smile on his face and a light in his eyes. He embraced Darlina. "That was the most wonderful experience of my life. It was way beyond anything any drug can provide. I feel dizzy."

"I do too. My head is spinning and my feet aren't touching the ground."

They walked side by side through the campground. "Let's build a fire, Will and I'll cook some rice and vegetables for us."

"Okay. Darlina?"

"Yes?"

"Darlina, would you marry me?"

She stopped dead in her tracks and looked at him. "I don't know, Will. I feel like we're just getting settled into this new life."

"We are, but when I kissed Guru Maharaj Ji's feet, I felt like he told me that we needed to get married."

"I can't give you an answer today. I'm totally and completely wrapped up in what has happened over the past two days. Let's talk about it when we get back home."

"Fair enough, but I won't let you forget."

***

Back in Austin, daily routine resumed and Darlina didn't think again about Will's proposal until a week later.

The Premies sat in a circle in the living room of the big house after supper sharing satsang. Will gave his testimony. When he finished, he turned to Darlina in front of everyone and asked her again. "Darlina, I asked you in Florida and you said to wait until we got back home, so we're back home and I'm asking you again, would you marry me?"

Darlina blushed and the people in the circle applauded. "We'll talk about it later, Will. This doesn't seem the right place or time to discuss it."

He grinned. "Seemed like it to me. I'm serious, Darlina."

"Okay. Just let me think about it."

That night during meditation, the only thing she could think about was Will's proposal. Could she really marry Will when she still loved Luke?

She tried concentrating on her breath as she'd been taught, but the thoughts kept coming in. Finally, she knew the answer. She couldn't say yes to Will's proposal until she saw Luke.

Without a car and no money, she decided that she would hitch-hike to Springfield to see him. She had to talk this over with Luke before she said yes to Will.

The next morning, before Will left for work, she explained to him what she had to do. She didn't miss the disappointed look on his face, but nevertheless, it was something she had to do. She would leave the next day.

The house father expressed his concern for her traveling alone and instructed another Premie, Chad, who was unemployed at the time, to accompany her. Ironically, he had an aunt who lived in Springfield. Together, they were given a ride to the outskirts of town.

Darlina knew she was protected by God's divine light, but was happy to have company.

They caught a ride with a trucker right away and he took them all the way to Tulsa, Oklahoma. Then after only thirty minutes, another trucker picked them up and took them the rest of the way to Springfield, making the trip uneventful.

As she drew close to her destination, Darlina felt her heart beat a little faster. It had been more than three years since she'd seen Luke. What would he look like? What would he think of her with no makeup? What would he say? The thoughts raced through her head one after the other.

She tried desperately to remember what she'd been taught, to control her breathing and thoughts. Somehow, away from her life in Austin, it seemed more difficult.

The idea of seeing Luke outshone everything else. The old familiar ache set in and she trembled with excitement. She couldn't wait until tomorrow when she would go straight to the Federal Medical Center.

Luke would be so surprised!

"I'd do things different if I could. I'd change the way wishes fall on reality unheeded and deaf..."

Chapter 25

Darlina awoke early the next morning to sunlight streaming through the window of the motel room in Springfield, Missouri. They'd been lucky enough to find a place a few blocks away from the Federal Medical Center on Sunshine Street. She was grateful that the house father had allowed them fifty dollars for the trip and the motel room with two beds had cost less than twenty.

Chad had been easy to travel with. He didn't pry or ask questions, but listened when she felt like talking. She'd shared a tiny bit of her and Luke's story, but it was enough for him to understand the importance of the trip.

After a quick shower, Darlina tried to sit still and do meditation. She found that with Luke just down the street, she could not find the concentration needed to focus on her breath and the light between her eyes.

After a while, she gave up trying, nibbled on some granola and prepared to walk to the prison. She wished she had some makeup to put on so she could look nice for Luke. What if he didn't want her anymore?

"Chad, I hope you can find your aunt today and that you have a good visit. I'll see you later this evening. Wish me luck."

"Thanks and good luck, Darlina."

Seeing it in daylight, the facility seemed daunting with the tall fence, razor wire around the top and a guard tower. She choked back a sob and willed her pounding heart to be still. Luke was just inside.

The front steps were open access to the main building, with a fence on either side. Darlina made the short climb and struggled to keep tears from forming, at 8:30 a.m. on Friday, May 17, 1974. It occurred to her that it was her sister, Leann's birthday today. She felt a twinge of guilt that she hadn't remembered to send a card.

Once inside the big double door, a woman sitting behind a barred window with a nameplate displaying "Laurie Shoemaker" greeted Darlina. "May I help you?"

"Yes ma'am, I'm here to visit an inmate." She shifted her purse from one arm to the other.

"Are you on his visiting list?"

"No, ma'am. I didn't know I had to be. I've traveled from Texas to see Luke Stone." She held her head high.

"Well, I'm very sorry you've come all this way, but unless you are an approved visitor, you won't be allowed to see him."

Darlina fought back tears and her voice trembled. "What do I have to do to get approval? Can that be done today?"

"Let me talk to my supervisor. I'll be right back. Are you a relative?"

"I'm a friend."

Ms. Shoemaker frowned. "I'll see what I can do."

Darlina shifted from one foot to the other as she waited for Laurie Shoemaker to return. How could she be this close and not be allowed to see Luke?

She wasn't sure her heart could stand that kind of disappointment.

After thirty minutes or more, Ms. Shoemaker returned with an official looking paper. "My supervisor said you can fill this out and we'll need a copy of your driver's license and social security card. But, even if you get approval, visiting doesn't start at this facility until tomorrow morning. We only have visiting on Saturday and Sunday."

"Oh." Darlina didn't attempt to hide the discouragement in her voice. "I didn't know."

Her demeanor softened. "Look, I understand you've come a long way, but you should have gotten approval first. Fill out this form and we'll see if we can make an exception."

"Thank you." Darlina took a seat and completed the long form. They sure did ask a lot of questions. She had to list her entire family history and then give an explanation of how she knew Luke. As an afterthought, she noted that she was a member of the Divine Light Mission, hoping that might help. After all, wasn't it common to do ministry in prison? She'd play that card if she had to.

Once she completed the form and signed it, she returned to the window with her driver's license and social security card in hand.

"I'll make a copy of these and give them back to you." Ms. Shoemaker took the cards.

"How soon will I know if I've been approved?"

"Just have a seat and I'll call you. I don't know how long it will take."

Darlina returned to her seat and took a moment to examine her surroundings. The facility seemed clean enough and it was very quiet. She wondered where all the prisoners were. The slate gray walls only displayed official posters warning of the penalty for bringing contraband into the prison. She tried to imagine life inside but couldn't.

With nothing to do but wait, Darlina turned all of her thoughts to Luke. She recalled every poignant moment she'd spent with him from their first meeting at The Faded Rose to the last visit they'd had in the Eastland County jail, after his sentencing.

He'd been happy to see her then. She hoped this time would be the same. She remembered the way he smiled his crooked grin and blew her a kiss as the guard led him through the door back to his cell.

Tears burned her eyes and she blinked them away. This wasn't the time or place to get emotional. She began to pray that God would allow her to see him. She needed desperately to talk with him, to see his face and piercing blue eyes that could twinkle at the drop of a hat.

Her heart remained caught in a vise of emotion as minutes ticked away turning into hours. She didn't move.

Finally, after two and a half hours, Ms. Shoemaker called her name. "Ms. Flowers, you've been approved to visit Mr. Stone. Visiting hours are tomorrow from 8:15 to 3 pm." She handed her a stack of papers. "Read these over carefully. Heed them. Any violation of even one rule will terminate the visit."

"Thank you so much." Darlina struggled to stop them, but a tear escaped and rolled down her cheek.

"We need to take your picture and get your fingerprints, then you are free to go."

"Okay."

By noon, Darlina walked out the front door and down the steps to the street, relief and joy heightened with each step. Tomorrow she would see Luke.

Her stomach growled as she skipped back to the motel.

While she recounted everything to Chad, she opened a bag of dried fruit and nuts and munched on them.

"I talked to my aunt on the phone and she is going to come pick me up in the morning. Wonder if we could possibly find a place to get a meal anywhere around here?" Chad asked.

"I have no idea. I'd be willing to bet that vegetarian food is hard to find in Springfield, Missouri. Maybe we could get a grilled cheese sandwich or something though. That's great that you're going to get to see your aunt."

***

Darlina awoke all during the night from dreams of being denied the visit once she arrived back at the prison. She wondered if Luke could sense that she was nearby.

Before dawn, she was up and sitting under her meditation cloth. She forced the thoughts to take a rest and focused only on her breath and the light.

By 7 a.m., she was dressed in a pair of bell bottom jeans, and cotton tie-dyed shirt. As an afterthought, she placed the hair pipe choker that Luke had made for her around her neck. She thought about walking to the prison, but decided to sit tight.

She passed a little more time eating a few bites of food. If she got to see Luke, it would be mid-afternoon before she would have food again and she didn't want her stomach growl during the visit.

She glanced in a mirror and wondered what Luke would think of her plain looks. Her straight auburn hair pulled back in a pony tail and no makeup was a far cry from the days of go-go dancing on stage with her poofed hair, heavy eyeliner, shadow and mascara. Would he turn away from her now?

As the clock ticked and the time grew closer, a knot formed in her stomach and her jaw tightened. Questions raced through her head but there were no answers to them. Only endless waiting.

At 7:45 a.m., she left the motel room and walked to the prison. It didn't matter if she was early, she just needed to get there and know for sure that she could see Luke.

***

Luke walked to the craft shop, as he did most every day. As he neared the hallway that led to that wing of the building, a guard caught up with him.

"Hey, Luke Stone, stop. You have a visitor." The guard announced with a raspy voice.

"If it's the FBI tell 'em I've already talked to 'em as much as I'm going to." Luke growled.

"It ain't. It's a woman."

Luke looked up in surprise. "A woman?" His mind churned. He wasn't expecting anyone.

Luke smoothed his hair back as he followed the guard.

Maybe the FBI decided to trick him and send a woman to question him. Surely if his Mom had made trip, she would have told him she was coming. Who could be here to see him?

What Luke Stone was not prepared for was to see Darlina once the guard opened the door and ushered him into the visiting room. A million thoughts flooded his head all at once, and he let out an audible gasp.

As soon as Darlina saw him, she stood, her knees weak. She brought a shaky hand to her forehead, tears forming behind her eyelids. She wanted nothing more than to rush into his arms, but had read the visiting rules and knew only a quick embrace would be tolerated.

Luke walked toward her wearing his white prison garb. It was a far cry from the fancy designer suits and cowboy boots he'd worn on stage when he sang.

She in turn moved toward him on unsteady legs, their eyes locked.

Once they were within touching distance, Luke extended his hand. She came into his embrace, then quickly pulled back. She didn't want to do anything that would cut this visit short.

"Darlina, what in the hell are you doing here? You didn't tell me you were coming. How did you even get in?"

"I didn't know myself that I was coming until three days ago. There wasn't time to get a letter to you. I pretty much talked my way in. I had no idea I had to be on an approved list."

"My God, honey, I've missed you. What brought you here? It must be something big."

"It is, Luke, and I've missed you something terrible. I want to stay in your arms, but I sure don't want to get thrown out of here before we have a chance to talk."

Luke chuckled. "Darlin', I'd like nothing more than to hold you and never let you go, but you're right. We have to be careful not to do anything out of line, 'cause they'll grab me and take me back to the cell in a heartbeat."

His voice became hoarse. "You're my first thought in the morning and my last thought at night. You don't know how many times I've turned over and for a moment felt you beside me.

Are you okay? Why are you here? Did you drive? You told me you sold your car. You're not wearing any makeup."

Darlina smiled and twisted her hands. "I hitchhiked here to see you, but the house father sent someone with me so I wouldn't be traveling alone. Can we sit somewhere that's quiet?"

"That'll be a hard bill to fill, but come over here." Luke took her by the elbow and led her to the last two chairs on a long row against the wall. His voice grew stern. "Darlina, do you know how dangerous it is to hitchhike?"

She looked up at him, unshed tears glistening in her eyes. "I didn't know how else to get here," she whispered. I've missed you so much, Luke. Seeing you now, I hardly remember why I'm here. My God, you've gotten skinny."

"Prison chow ain't the best and after the stomach surgery, well I don't eat much. You're mighty skinny your own self."

"Luke, I didn't come all this way to talk about how we look. There's something serious I have to discuss with you."

"I'm all ears." Luke reached for her hand and held it in his, dropping his arm down beside them so as not to be visible to the guards.

With his strong warm hand holding hers, she had difficulty making the words come. All she wanted was to be in his arms. But, she forced herself to talk, starting with the events of the festival in Florida up to Will's proposal.

Luke leaned back, stretched his legs out and lit a cigarette. "Sweetheart, you know I can't tell you what to do. It's ultimately your choice. I know you haven't been happy with Will in the past, but sounds like both of you have gone through a lot of changes."

"We have, Luke. I am totally drug-free and so is he and we've found a peace that's better than any high. But, how I can marry him when I still love you so much?"

Luke sighed. "Princess, you can't wait around forever for me to get out of prison. It may be many years, if ever, and you're still young. You need to have babies and enjoy life. I'd be lying if I told you that I'd be happy about you marrying, but I have no right to tell you not to. The most important thing is your own happiness."

"I never really told you in the letters, but I'm sure you read between the lines. It wasn't fair, but anytime I had sex with Will, in my mind, I was making love to you. Remember the garlic ritual and how you told me that no other man would ever be able to satisfy me?"

Luke chuckled. "I didn't mean it literally. It was just a fun thing to do."

"Well, I believed it then and still do. Will doesn't satisfy me. So, how can that make for a good marriage?"

"You've just gotta give it a chance, honey. You do know that I'd like nothing more than to lay you down right here, right now and make love to you?"

"Yes. I want it too, more than you can imagine. That's what you do to me. Will doesn't have that effect on me." She squeezed his hand. "I'm so confused."

"Oh believe me, I can imagine." Luke grinned his crooked grin. "You turn me on just like you always did even if you do look like a little California hippie girl."

Darlina laughed. "I didn't know what you'd think about me not wearing makeup."

"Sweetheart, you could be dressed in a toe sack and you'd still turn me on. You have the magic."

Darlina squeeze Luke's hand. Sitting beside him seemed the most natural thing on earth to her.

"You know the FBI still harasses me now and then, pressuring me to tell them where the money from the bank robberies is. Don't be surprised if you get a visit from them since you came here."

"I know nothing to tell them, so they can ask me all they want."

"That was my plan. When I took you back to Abilene, all I could think about was getting you away from the shit that was coming down. You didn't deserve to be dragged into it."

They talked on and on while the hours flew by. Twice Luke put his arm around her shoulders and twice the guard monitoring the room reminded him to remove it. The second time, he threatened to end the visit if he had to tell Luke again.

Luke showed her the leather pieces he had for sale in the visiting room display case. Darlina praised the quality of his work.

Before they knew it, the clock chimed 3 p.m. The guard announced that visiting hours would end in fifteen minutes.

"Luke, I'll be back tomorrow, then I have to go back to Austin. Please think about all that I've said and tomorrow, let's try to figure things out."

"Honey, there really isn't anything to figure out, but I'll be very happy to see you again tomorrow."

They stood and embraced and then Luke exited through the doors leading back into the prison.

Darlina stood until he was out of sight, then retrieved her personal belongings from the guard behind the desk and left.

She walked slowly back to the motel, mulling over each word spoken, each look, each touch and the sound of his voice. She knew now more than ever that Luke Stone was the keeper of her heart, even though he was locked behind bars. But what did that get her? She had a decision to make.

Until she reached the door of the motel room, she didn't realize that tears streamed down her face.

Luke still loved her and she still loved him. Yet, the fact remained that he was locked behind bars for a very long time. She tossed and turned on the motel bed that night unable to sleep.

She sat under her meditation cloth and managed to focus on her breathing until the forceful emotions strangling her passed and complete calm took their place.

Tomorrow, she'd see Luke once again. She would treasure every minute of the visit, but she already knew that when she got back to Austin, she'd agree to marry Will.

She thought about the age showing in Luke's face. Maybe he was right when he told her that he'd most likely grow old and die in prison. An ache pressed around her heart so powerful that she couldn't breathe. She turned into the pillow to smother a sob.

Beyond any doubt she'd hold the memory of this weekend close for the rest of her life. When she thought about it, she could still feel his hand warmly nestled in hers.

The love they shared, Luke and Darlina, would never die nor could it be destroyed.

How on earth would she be able to wait for 8:15 a.m.?

"Every now and then I try to find someone new. Baby, they're just not you..."

Chapter 26

Luke Stone sat in his cell that evening, thinking about the way his heart had lurched inside his chest when he'd seen Darlina in the visiting room that day. What a surprise!

He worried about her hitchhiking but was glad she had someone with her. If she could see the evil demented people he was forced to live with, she'd hightail it to her house and never come out. Her fresh way of looking at the world was one of the things that had attracted him to her in the beginning. He only wished she wasn't still so naïve.

He thought about her plain looks and austere lifestyle. He predicted it would run its course, but for now she seemed totally engrossed in it. At least she was off the drugs.

It was time to let her go. He couldn't deny it. He also knew that even though she'd be back for another visit tomorrow, she would marry Will. He'd have to somehow make his peace with that.

After lighting a cigar, he leaned back on his bunk. Life sure takes some funny twists and turns. He'd give anything to be the one marrying her, but it wasn't possible. Oh, he'd heard of jailhouse marriages, but that didn't seem fair to anyone. He'd never ask her to make that sacrifice. No, it was time to back away. He'd always love her and had no doubt she'd always love him.

Who knows? Maybe fate would eventually turn in their favor. For now, he had no hope of getting free from these bars anytime soon and she needed to live her own life. Tomorrow he'd make that perfectly clear.

Out of habit, he sat up and reached for his guitar. He strummed a few familiar chords, then let his fingers wander over the strings.

After a while, he found words coming with a new melody and reached for his tablet to capture the song.

> I guess it's over for you and me
> Seems that way, far as I can see
> I guess nothing could bring you back to me.
> I know wishing won't bring it around
> But a dreamer I am
> My dreams of you come so easy
> Wish these dreams would come true.
> Woke up, had a don't care feeling
> Emptiness within. Then your memory
> Came softly stealing
> And the easy dreams started again.

***

Back in Austin, Darlina sat in the backyard with Will after supper.

"I know you're waiting for my answer, Will. Thank you for understanding about my need to see Luke. I've never tried to hide the way I feel about him."

"I know and I appreciate that. Tell me everything." Will ran his fingers through his short blond hair and faced her.

Darlina talked for an hour without stopping, telling Will every detail of the visit, how Luke appeared to her and their conversation.

When she stopped, silence prevailed.

"So, will you marry me, Darlina?"

She looked into his eyes. "Yes. I'll marry you."

Will jumped up from the chair he was sitting in and kneeled in front of her, taking her hands in his own. "Thank you for saying yes. I won't be so bold as to promise you happiness because we've both learned that comes from inside of us. But, I can promise you I'll always be faithful and provide for you and for our children."

Darlina smiled. "Children? Aren't you getting a little ahead of yourself?"

"Just dreaming out loud. You're gonna make a wonderful mother."

"Should we continue to live here, or look for a place of our own?"

"I think we should have a place of our own. There's not much privacy here. While you were gone, I went out to the farm and had a
heart-to-heart talk with Mom and Dad. I'm going back to work for
them until their new house is finished. I apologized to them for the
disrespect I showed and told them there would never be a repeat of
that."

"Oh that's wonderful, Will. No need to leave karma undone when
you can fix it. Let's go tell the others there's gonna be a wedding."

***

On June 24, 1974, Will Brocker and Darlina Flowers said their wedding vows surrounded by family and friends. The backyard of the
Premie house had been decorated with white lilies and freesia. The
fragrance of incense floated through the air.

Darlina wore a long white dress dotted with pink, yellow and
blue flowers that she'd made. Will wore a suit and tie with two large
Guru Maharaj Ji buttons pinned to the lapel and tie. The couple stood
in front of an altar with Guru Maharaj Ji's picture prominently placed,
to cite the vows.

Darlina's parents, her brother and his family along with two of
her sisters and families attended the wedding.

The strained relationship between Darlina and her Mother seemed
to relax. Perhaps the relief of Darlina marrying someone, anyone
besides Luke helped ease the tension.

It made Darlina happy to see her mother smiling and enjoying the
festivities. Darlina's brother made jokes about having to take their
shoes off at the door and everyone joined in with their own.

Will and Darlina moved into a small duplex apartment and began
their life together as husband and wife.

***

Luke threw himself into perfecting the craft of oil painting. People
began to commission him to paint portraits of loved ones. What he

enjoyed most were the American Indian scenes he painted. This, along with the leather, beadwork and songwriting kept him busy. Busy was good. He'd watched too many men become despondent and wind up committing suicide. He was determined to keep depression away by creating with his hands and mind.

Most every evening, he and Red played and sang the songs Luke wrote. The chaplain seemed impressed with their frequent requests for more Jesus tapes, not knowing they were using them to record over.

Luke often thought of Darlina. She still wrote regularly, but now when he answered, he always addressed his letter to Will and Darlina. He wanted this marriage to work and for her to be happy.

Months passed and another gloomy Christmas approached. The scrawny metal Christmas trees made their appearance and the feeble attempt to conjure up the spirit of the season fell short. By now, Luke didn't expect anything different.

It gave him great pleasure to send out a Christmas package to his children while money from his artistic endeavors flowed regularly to his mother, easing her struggles.

The caseworker had told both Luke and Red they would receive a transfer back to Leavenworth any time. It didn't much matter. One prison was about the same as another.

Luke awoke on the morning of January 5, 1975 with chills and fever.

"Man you better get over to see the doc, Luke." Red advised his friend.

Luke coughed a deep rasping cough. "I think you're right. Can you walk with me? I'm not so sure I can make it all the way over there."

"Wait here, Luke. I'll go get the lieutenant."

Lieutenant Harlow entered Luke's cell. "What's the matter, Stone?"

"I'm sick as a dog, Lieutenant."

Lieutenant Harlow took one look at him and wheeled around. "I'll call for a wheelchair."

Luke's eyes glazed over as the wracking cough produced spots of blood on his handkerchief. "Red, watch after my shit until I get back."

"Sure thing, Luke. Don't worry."

***

After a quick examination, Dr. Menare ordered Luke to be placed in quarantine.

"It might be pneumonia, but it also might be tuberculosis and we can't take any chances," Dr. Menare explained.

"I need some antibiotics, Doc."

"I can't order anything for you until we rule out tuberculosis. I'm sorry."

"I'm fuckin' miserable, man. You're tellin' me you can't give me anything?"

"I can't prescribe anything more than aspirin until I complete the testing. I'll check on you later today. Drink plenty of fluids."

Luke grumbled under his breath. He knew he had pneumonia, but all he could do was go along with what the doctor ordered.

Two weeks passed and Luke was very sure he was going to die. He asked a nurse for a pen and paper and wrote Darlina what he thought might be his last letter. He explained to her that he was very sick and near death's door. He wanted her to know that he'd always loved her and begged her to be happy and live life to the fullest. Then he penned a letter to his mother. He didn't want to worry her, but she needed to be informed.

If they didn't give him some medicine soon, he'd be checking out. Dammit! Seemed like every step he took forward, something pushed him back two.

After eighteen days, Dr. Menare came into Luke's quarantined room. "Mr. Stone, we finally have the tests results and you do not have tuberculosis. You have pneumonia and I'm starting antibiotics immediately."

"It's about fuckin' time, man. I'm almost dead." Luke's voice trembled.

"I'm sorry, but we had to be sure about the TB."

"I told you what it was."

Dr. Menare didn't answer him, but barked orders to the nurses on duty.

Luke had no argument left in him. In his weakened state, he barely had enough energy to breathe, much less argue. At least he'd finally get medication and maybe he wouldn't die after all.

Without any doubt, this turn of events delayed his transfer back to Leavenworth.

The end of March neared before Luke obtained his release back into prison population. It had been a touch and go struggle, but apparently the Great Spirit wasn't through with him in this lifetime yet.

**

As Luke regained his strength, he returned to his projects in the craft shop with vigor. Not only did he dive back into painting, but started new beading projects and continued making leather pieces, which he sold in the visiting room.

By Mid-April, Mrs. Yarbrough announced that she would be leaving the facility. She assured Luke that the gentleman taking her place would let him continue to be the caretaker of the shop and that he'd be easy to work with.

Luke hated to see her go, but understood. She'd been a true supporter and promised her that he would continue to turn out the same quality of work after she was gone.

Red brought news that evening. "Hey Luke, I ran into a guy today over in the small engine repair class who says he knows how to make jewelry. He's a meskin dude but he was wearing some pretty silver and turquoise jewelry. I told him you'd wanna meet him."

"Sounds good, hoss. What was his name?"

"Hell, I don't remember. His last name was Carrasco, but don't remember the first name. I invited him to come by after chow this evening."

"I've always loved silver and turquoise. I'm gonna go tomorrow and get a haircut. I'm tired of this fuckin' hair."

"Yeah, I've been thinking the same thing. Wonder when they're gonna ship us back to Leavenworth."

"Hell, reckon it don't make much difference. One prison's about the same as another. I'm gonna put together a baseball team this year. Want to play?"

"Of course. I know at least five other guys that'll wanna play too. I'm sure glad you're back in the land of the living, hoss."

Luke chuckled. "This ain't living, it's existing, but I'm damned sure glad I ain't dead. Did you hear that Mrs. Yarbrough's leaving?"

"No, shit? That's too bad. She's one fine lady."

"That's for sure. She's been more than good to me. Hell, Red, look at all the shit I've learned to do since we hit Springfield. I never had any idea I could do any of it, but she always encouraged me. She gave me supplies before I had money to buy my own. A man don't forget that."

The men were interrupted by a knock on their cell door. They both looked up to see a short Mexican man standing at the door.

Red stood. "Hey Carrasco! Come on in, man. I told Luke you'd be stopping by. Luke, this is the man I told you about."

The Mexican man extended his hand to Luke. "I'm Ramon Carrasco. Nice to meet you."

Luke towered over the man who was barely over five feet tall and shook his hand. "Red tells me you make jewelry, Ramon."

"Aw si, back in San Antonio, that is what I did for a living." He held his hands out to Luke, with several fingers displaying silver and turquoise rings.

"Those are nice. Reckon you could show me how to do that kind of work?"

"Si, senor. You get supplies, I show you."

"I'll get supplies. Can you come to the craft shop tomorrow? We can go through the catalogs and order whatever it takes to make this quality of jewelry."

"Si. I come tomorrow.

"Want a smoke, Ramon Carrasco?" Luke held out a cigar.

"Gracias." He accepted the cigar. "You play guitar?" He spotted the guitar case beside Luke's bunk.

"I sure do. Wanna hear some music?"

Luke took the guitar out of its case and began to play "Rancho Grande" with a crooked grin on his face. He looked over at Red and winked. Red chimed in singing the words in Spanish and Ramon joined him.

After Ramon left, Luke found a new excitement at the prospect of making jewelry. He would have no trouble selling pieces like Ramon wore.

In some odd way, he felt like a lucky man. Even though a judge had taken his freedom away, he'd received some things in return that would last him a lifetime.

He could never be happy about being locked in a cage, but could damn sure make the best of it. With creative projects he kept going, songwriting and answering a growing correspondence list, he never had an idle minute.

Through a friend he'd known all of his life, he now corresponded with a lady in San Angelo named Sue. He hoped that perhaps she could fill the empty place Darlina's marriage left. At any rate, it was nice to have someone to write romantic poems to again. Truth being told, each time he wrote one, it was Darlina's face he saw, not Sue's.

He had to give Darlina the space she needed to build a life with Will. She came to him often in dreams and many times he awoke feeling her presence. He never told her this, but wrote poems and songs about it.

It seemed they were joined by something bigger and more power-ful than human; something divine. But for now, they didn't talk about it. Their letters were superficial and stiff but neither of them wanted to let the contact fade away, so they kept writing.

Luke wrote a poem and tucked it away, hoping someday he could give it to Darlina. Someday when she was back in his arms where she belonged.

Angel of Night

Few are awake but guards in towers
In solitude of early morning hours
You come every night without fail
To lie beside me in my cell
Answering a lonely man's prayer
Making life's burdens easier to bear
Sharing loving moments until dawn
The sweetest by far this day has known
Tenderness, peace and joy you give
Loving encouragement, desire to live
Bringing hope, rhyme and reason
Dissipating gloom and doom of prison

Tasting your lips, feeling your hand
Every need you understand
The world revolves around you
The compassionate things you do
You cuddle me into slumber tight
To return tomorrow, my Angel of night!

"Thoughts wander through my mind like an endless summer dream..."

# Chapter 27

L uke learned the art of jewelry making quickly from Ramon Carrasco. Using raw gemstones he ordered, he cut and polished them until they glowed with perfection. He particularly liked working with turquoise, coral and tiger's eye stones. It seemed the craft shop had most every kind of equipment necessary for all types of handiwork.

The bright June sunshine reflected off the barred window as the new director of the craft shop made his way around each table observing. Luke held a sterling silver thunderbird with a large turquoise stone set in the center. "What do you think, Mr. Thompson?"

"I think it's a fine piece of lapidary work. Well done." Mr. Thompson slapped Luke on the back. Mr. Thompson, with his six foot frame and shock of unruly brown hair, seemed more suited to working with rough male convicts than the disabled woman, Mrs. Yarbrough, who'd recently left.

"The head of the recreation department asked me to put together a band for the Fourth of July picnic. I've been here since 1972 and it's mid-way through '75. I figure they'll transfer me and Red back to Leavenworth any day now. This might be the last time I play music here. You should come out." Luke stopped polishing and held the piece up to the light.

"Oh, I'm coming to the picnic. I think these events are good for the inmates."

"I always enjoy playin'. Of course I never know who my band's gonna be. There's a lot of guys in here that say they can play music. Talkin' it and playin' it's two different things." He liked Mr. Thompson and so far, they had an amicable working relationship.

Mr. Thompson laughed. "I'm sure that's true. If you don't mind me asking, when are you up for parole, Mr. Stone?"

"It don't much matter. When I'm eligible for parole from the feds, I've got a fifty year sentence hangin' over my head from Texas." Luke shrugged his shoulders.

Mr. Thompson shook his head. "That's a damn shame. You seem like a good man."

"Reckon I got what I had comin' even if I didn't do what they convicted me of. I've done plenty of other shit I never got caught for."

"I don't think I could feel that way if I was in your shoes."

"It's taken me a while, but I finally got it through my thick head I wasn't gonna change prison by rebelling. In fact, I can't change prison at all. I can only work on me, although I've been known to file a writ in a heartbeat when somethin's way out of whack."

"Wish more inmates could have your attitude. It sure would make all this go easier."

"Oh believe me, I still have times when I get mad as hell all over again, but it don't get me nowhere. I figure I'm better off puttin' my energy into makin' something."

The craft shop seemed crowded to Luke that day. He looked out the window, longing to feel the sunshine soaking through his skin.

His baseball team, "The Georgia Boys" had played some pretty good games since April and he loved getting outdoors and moving. For the first time, perhaps since he'd hit prison, he felt healthy and well.

He finally had a set of dentures that fit his mouth instead of the ones that made him look buck-toothed. All the ailments that had plagued him appeared to have passed, although he remained on a maintenance dose of blood thinners.

He lifted weights and rode a bicycle every chance he got and as a result began to build lean muscle. The prison owned six bicycles and you considered yourself lucky if you managed to snag one. He rode around and around the yard until he began to picture himself as a hamster on an endless wheel.

***

The Fourth of July picnic came off without a hitch. Luke and four other inmates, including Red, stood in the glaring hot sun and played music for close to four hours. The prison had gone all out providing hot dogs, hamburgers and ice cream for the inmates. They were allowed to have as much as they wanted, which rarely happened in prison.

Luke wiped the sweat from his brow and took a sip of water. He stepped up to the microphone. "We sure hope ya'll have enjoyed this music but we're sweatin' up here like sons of bitches. And besides that, a damned pigeon just flew over and shit on my guitar, so I do believe that is a direct sign from heaven that it's time to quit."

The inmates responded with clapping and laughter.

Luke wiped down his guitar. Damn that pigeon! Why couldn't he have shit on one of those cheap-ass prison issued guitars instead of his Martin?

"Hey Luke, can I use one of these cases to take some hamburgers and hot dogs back to the cell?" Red grinned.

"Hell I don't care, Red. Just use one of the pieces of shit that belongs to the prison."

"It's not often we can have all we wanna eat even it is fuckin' hot dogs."

"That's for damned sure."

***

Two weeks later, as Luke entered the music room, he noticed a poster tacked beside the door. It announced the production of a training film to be made inside prison called "Detour." Inmates were invited to participate in the project.

Being right up Luke's alley, he promptly added his name to the list.

The supervisor of Education, Mr. T.L. McFerren, would be in touch with each inmate who signed up.

A few days later, Luke attended a meeting in the recreation room about the movie.

Mr. McFerren introduced two men standing beside him. "This is John Miller. He works part-time in the education department. You already know Mr. James, the associate warden. Mr. Miller has written the script for the movie and I'll let him tell you more."

Mr. Miller moved forward "I'm making this film as my college thesis and it's my hope that it will become an educational film used in training new officers. It's about assertive behavior behind bars. We'll have several different vignettes showing some common behavior by both inmates and guards. That's where you all come in. We need actors for the vignettes."

Luke raised his hand. "I've never done any acting but I've played music on many a stage."

"That experience makes you a perfect candidate to be an actor. Besides that, I'll instruct you all the way. We figure it might take six months or more to complete this project. What is your name, sir?"

"Luke Stone. I'm not sure I'll be here that long. I'm due to be shipped back to Leavenworth any time, but I'm interested in working on it for as long as I'm here."

"Oh, you're the one Mr. Thompson told me about. I hear you're a damned good artist. Would you consider being my graphics artist for the movie?"

"Sure. When do we start?"

"It might be another couple of weeks before we get together again." Mr. Miller passed out papers. "Read these over and I'll be in touch."

Once the other convicts filed out, Luke shook Mr. Miller's hand. "I'm not hard to find, so give me a holler."

Luke thrived on staying busy. He'd been disappointed when he couldn't interest Red in the movie, but to each his own.

***

Bobby Stone, Luke's brother, lived in Alaska. He'd moved his family there shortly after Luke's arrest and conviction. They corresponded regularly.

Luke loved hearing about the hunting guide business and the vivid descriptions of Alaska.

When he and Bobby were youngsters, they'd made plans to run away to Alaska and live in the wild like mountain men, hunting and fishing. It made Luke happy that his brother was living some version of that dream.

But, the letter that came today from Brother Bobby stunned Luke and tore at his heart.

Bobby had cancer. He would undergo surgeries to remove tumors from his throat. The doctors warned that he most likely would lose his vocal chords. Luke couldn't imagine his brother, who loved to talk incessantly, without a voice.

He would conjure up some Indian medicine for Bobby and pray. It was the most he could offer up, along with words of encouragement through letters.

***

The letters between Luke and Darlina had slowed to barely one or two a month. She assured him that she was doing her best to make the marriage to Will work.

He was glad to hear they'd moved out of the commune into an apartment. He couldn't imagine a new marriage making it in a house full of people with no privacy.

She continued to write accolades of the guru. She'd been completely sucked into that world. Luke supposed there could be worse things for her.

Nevertheless, he always answered her letters and made an effort to keep his judgment to himself. Mostly, he wrote about the things he did to stay busy and shared with her the experiences he'd had through ancient American Indian practices and ceremonies. She responded ecstatically when he'd mailed her a blue beaded necklace with her name imbedded in the pattern. He longed to send her more things he made, but his intuition told him to hold back.

He focused his romantic interests on Sue and showered her with poems and gifts. He tried envisioning Sue's face when he wrote the poems, but inevitably, it was Darlina's that came into view. Such was the case when he wrote this poem late one evening.

Empty Dawn

I dreamed I awoke and found you gone
I felt lost and so alone
Somehow, something was all wrong
Uneasy feelings like a sad, sad song
Sometimes love just can't grow
It withers and dies painfully slow
When there is nothing left inside
No one can revive love that's died
If you're bound for leaving, tell me so
Don't slip away when you go
Look into my eyes, then I will know
For sadly the truth will show
I feel happiness has flown
For sorrow rides the empty dawn

Frequently, he awoke from sleep in the early morning hours, feeling Darlina with him. Was it wrong for a man to hold on to something that was gone? He didn't know, but the need for her remained as strong as ever although she was now married to another man.

He had difficulty getting that concept through to his heart. His mind understood it, but his heart refused.

She deserved a chance and by damn, he was going to give it to her.

"I cannot express happiness in a line, for you are roses in wintertime. The rainbow, moon and stars that shine, Princess of perfection divine..."

Chapter 28

Darlina watched with curiosity as Will constructed a pyramid above their bed. The pleasant early May weather prompted her to open the windows, and the curtains ruffled in the breeze. She found it hard to believe that in one month, she and Will would already have been married for a year.

As it turned out, the neighbor in the first duplex they rented practiced primal scream therapy. It didn't take long for them to tire of the incessant blood-curdling screams and they found another apartment across town.

Will hammered two boards together. "I've been reading about pyramid power. It's amazing the things it can do. The books say that if you sleep under a pyramid, you don't age and that meditation under one is indescribable. They claim you can preserve food by placing it under a pyramid. They also say that sex under one is greatly enhanced."

"I love that. What are you going to put over the boards?"

"A blue silk cloth. Once I have the perfect pyramid dimensions, I'll attach it. Can you hold this board for me?"

"Sure. I found a book today at the health food store that I think has some really good information about exercises we can do when we have sex. It's called tantric yoga and it has solutions for all sorts of sexual problems."

"I'm willing to try anything. You do know that I'd like nothing better than to satisfy you."

"You do all right, Will. I'm not complaining."

"I know. You don't have to. I can see the disappointment on your face when we try. Hand me the tape measure behind you, please."

Darlina reached for the tape measure. "Something else I've been thinking about too. The one thing in life that I've always known I wanted to be is a mother. I'm disappointed that I haven't gotten pregnant yet and I want to do some research on herbs that can help."

"Soon as I get this pyramid up, and we start sleeping and having sex under it, I bet we'll have no trouble getting pregnant."

"Do you think so?"

"Yep. I sure do. There. It's ready for the cloth and then you can help me erect it. It has to face exactly east and west, so I've attached a compass in the top."

She held the structure while Will raised the pyramid just over their bed and secured the legs into the floor.

As soon as the structure was secured, both Darlina and Will sat on the bed under it. She had to admit it felt amazing. "Let's do a meditation."

"That wasn't exactly what I had in mind." Will settled next to her, then pulled her down beside him. "Look up. It's pretty cool, isn't it?"

"Yes it is."

"Where is this book you were talking about?"

Darlina got up and retrieved the book from the living room. She sat cross-legged on the bed and opened it. "Look there's even pictures that show you what to do."

Will looked at the book with her, all the while rubbing her back. "Keep the book open and come over here close to me."

She laid the book on the side of the bed and scooted beside him.

Darlina would never in a million years tell Will that she still thought about Luke when they had sex. It was a secret not meant to be shared. In many ways, she truly wished she could forget Luke and have a good happy life with Will, but Luke was always there.

He stayed in her heart and on her mind. No matter how hard she tried, she'd never forget him and the powerful love that bonded them together.

She closed her eyes as Will began to kiss and caress her. Suddenly he stopped and rolled onto his back. "Why do you always close your eyes when we have sex? Can you make love to me just one time with them open?"

"Okay," she said hesitantly. Her heart raced. How could she imagine Luke with her eyes open? She made herself look at Will and kiss him.

"That's better. Now get that book and let's see what they recommend."

Darlina had to admit that it felt more like a medical procedure or class than making love, but if the exercises worked, it would be worth it.

***

By mid-July, Darlina knew something wasn't right. She lay still early one morning taking deep breaths and waiting for the nausea to pass. Maybe she had a stomach virus.

"I don't think I can get up and fix you breakfast this morning, Will. I feel like if I move, I'm gonna throw up."

"Don't worry about it. You've probably picked up a bug. I can fix my own breakfast. Can I bring you anything?"

"Maybe some crackers and water."

She closed her eyes, not daring to move. Whatever it was, she hoped it was gone soon.

After the fourth morning of the same symptoms, Darlina finally realized what was wrong. She hadn't had a period since May. She was pregnant!

She didn't say anything to Will and waited until he left for work to try and get off the bed. As soon as she sat up, she had to run for the bathroom.

So this was what morning sickness felt like. But, she was going to have a baby. The joy overwhelmed her and as soon as the nausea passed, she danced around the kitchen in between taking care of her chores.

Will walked into the house that evening to the sound of Darlina singing in the kitchen. "You're feeling better, I see."

Darlina ran to Will and threw her arms around his neck. "Oh I couldn't wait for you to get home. I'm busting at the seams to tell you what's going on and why I've been sick."

"Okay. Why?"

"I'm pregnant, Will. I'm having morning sickness."

"Are you sure?"

"Yes, I'm sure. I haven't had a period since May. I just know that's what it is. We're going to have a baby."

Will's face lit up. "Oh wow! We're going to be parents." He grinned wide and hugged Darlina. "So, what do we do?"

"Well, I looked through all my herb books today and found some things that will help with the morning sickness. I need to do some shopping."

"I'll go with you after supper and we can get whatever you need."

"Oh Will, this is going to be the best thing that ever happened. Wonder if it will be a boy or girl? Not that it matters. This baby will be loved beyond words." She twirled around. "Let's eat. So far, I feel fine by around eleven or so in the morning and then I'm okay for the rest of the day. I'd hate to be sick all day. That'd be awful."

"You're right. It doesn't matter if it's a boy or girl. This will be a child of Guru Maharaj Ji."

They ate a quick supper of yellow squash stuffed with rice and vegetables, then drove to the health food store.

Darlina left the store with three books and a bag full of herbs including red raspberry tea and prenatal vitamins. She would make sure that she and the baby were healthy.

She couldn't wait to call her mom and sisters to tell them the news. But most of all, she wanted to write Luke.

She knew the baby had been conceived with her imagining making love to Luke. In some odd way, it was his child too. She wondered if the two would ever meet.

The next day, she made an appointment at a hair salon and had her long auburn trusses cut to a short, easier to maintain, hair style.

That same afternoon, Darlina took out pen and paper and sat at the kitchen table.

My Dearest Luke, I have the most wonderful news to share with you. I am pregnant! I'm going to be a mommy and I'm so happy...I know I shouldn't tell you this, but I feel this child is a part of you also. I can't help but thinking about you every time I have sex with Will. Is that crazy? To most, I know it would be, but somehow, you understand...I always dreamed of having your baby and many times, wished I'd not taken the birth control pills when we were together. If I'd had your child, we would be forever tied together. Guess it doesn't matter because we are bonded together through eternity anyway with or without a child...Love always, Darlina.

***

Ten days later, Darlina received a reply from Luke. Her hands trembled as she opened it, remembering the conversation she'd had with Will three days ago.

"I insist that you quit writing to Luke Stone. We're going to be parents. Don't you think it's time you let him go?" Will had slammed the door on his way out.

She hadn't seen Will angry in a long time, but could feel him tightening his control over her. She'd agreed, but deep in her heart knew she couldn't sever the ties between her and Luke. She'd just have to make sure she made it to the mailbox before he did.

Dear Darlina, I am so happy for you. I know how much you've always wanted to be a mother and you'll be a great one. Sweetheart, you need to stop pretending that I'm there with you. The reality is that I'm not and you need to face that fact. Put all of your energy into being a good wife and a good mother and let this ol' convict slide on away. Don't you know I would like nothing better than to be with you every day of your life? But, it can't be, so holding on to something that is not real is foolish and you'll waste your life in doing that. I won't stop answering your letters, but I plead with you to stop pretending. It's not fair to anyone...Love always, Luke.

Tears fell down her cheeks and dripped onto the letter, smearing the ink. Luke was right, but how could she just let go? It would be as impossible as stopping her heart from beating.

***

On February 29, 1976, a beautiful baby girl was born to Will and Darlina.

Although they'd planned to have the baby naturally at home with a midwife, much to their dismay, Darlina had to go to the hospital. Because the baby was breech, it caused complications.

Fearful of the hospital and outcome, Darlina cried big tears as Will navigated the busy streets of Austin. She turned to him. "I've never been inside a hospital. I'm scared."

"Don't worry. I'll be right with you and everything is going to be fine. We have to do what is best for our baby." He reached for her hand.

"Thank you, Will." For a moment, she almost followed that with "I love you", but stopped, realizing they never said those words to each other.

The midwife who accompanied them patted her on the shoulder. "I'll be there with you too, honey, and I won't let them do anything you don't want them to."

"Thank you, Sharon." Darlina put her hand over her swollen abdomen and groaned through another contraction.

All through the labor, Will and the midwife stayed by her side and coached her breathing. They prayed and gave praise to Guru Maharaj Ji.

Darlina found a spot on the ceiling to focus on and kept that in her line of vision as she labored throughout the night. For once, a thought of Luke never entered her mind. Her full concentration was on getting this baby out.

Because of their odd behavior and prayers, the hospital staff eyed them with a bit of curiosity, but treated Darlina kindly and stayed out of the way.

The doctor assigned to deliver the baby gave the couple an ultimatum. If the baby wasn't born by morning, he would do a C-section. Just minutes before 8 a.m., baby girl made her appearance feet first.

By 2 o'clock that same day, Darlina and Will signed themselves out of the hospital and took their precious bundle home.

Exhausted and sore, Darlina gazed at the tiny red-faced little girl she held in her arms. Her heart, full to the bursting point with love, beat softly inside her chest. She was a mother.

What she'd always wanted and dreamed of now lay sleeping in her arms.

As soon as she was rested, she'd write to Luke and tell him of baby girl's entrance into the world.

"What are we going to call her?" Will peered over her shoulder.

"I don't have a clue. We haven't been able to agree on any names and I thought when we saw her, we'd know." Darlina softly caressed the sleeping baby's face.

"I want to name her Grace."

"Grace sounds like an old lady. I wouldn't mind it for a middle name, but not her first name."

"Well, for now, I guess we'll just call her Baby Girl until we come up with a name." Will draped his arm across Darlina's shoulders. "I haven't had a chance to tell you how proud I am of the way you worked to get her here. I was afraid the doctor was going to insist on a C section."

Tears shone in Darlina's eyes. "Me too, Will. I was determined to do it. I called Mama and she's going to come and stay with me for a few days. I could sure use her help."

"Good. I have to go back to work and I'd feel better knowing someone was here with you."

The next few days Darlina spent with her mother turned out to be wonderful. All the tension seemed to have melted between them with the birth of Baby Girl.

Six weeks later, Lily Grace Brocker finally had a name.

"My Dearest Luke." Darlina sat holding the pen staring off into the distance. Finally she put the pen on the paper and wrote. Six pages later, she folded the letter and included a snapshot of Lily.

She smiled as she licked the envelope. She'd enjoyed introducing Lily to Luke. A familiar pang tugged at her heart. She'd always dreamed of having Luke's baby. Maybe in some crazy unexplained way, Lily partly belonged to him.

***

In mid-June of 1976, they moved back to the Brocker farm at Manor. Lily was only four months old and already sitting up by herself. The trailer that Will's parents had lived in while their house was being built now sat on the west five acres of the land. This became a new home for Darlina, Lily and Will.

Relations with the Brockers improved greatly with the birth of Lily and the fact that Darlina and Will continued to be drug-free.

Darlina threw herself completely into being a stay-at-home mother and loved all that came along with it. Will purchased a roto-tiller and made a small garden plot. Darlina took Lily out with her daily to tend the delicate young vegetables that grew.

One early July evening, Darlina sat on the large porch watching Lily play and waiting for Will to come home from work. When the van drove in, Lily clapped her hands and crawled to the steps.

Will jumped out of the van and a large black Doberman bounded out with him. He waved. "Hi, Darlina. I've got somebody for you and Lily to meet." He reached down and patted the dog's head.

Darlina picked up Lily. "Will, what are you thinking bringing a strange dog home?"

"I found her at the jobsite and she took up with me. I think someone must have dumped her out. I've already named her. Come on, Penny." He took the steps two at a time, the dog close at his heels.

"She's really big. What if she hurts Lily?"

"She won't." He took Lily from Darlina's arms and knelt beside the dog. "Lily, this is Penny. You're gonna love playin' with her."

Lily jabbered and touched the dog's head. The dog sniffed the baby, then lay down.

"I'm not sure this is a good idea." Darlina watched from the other side of the porch. "How do we know she won't bite us?"

Will laughed. "I swear you're a worry wart. She's not going to hurt any of us. Take Lily and I'll get the sack of food I bought for her. I'm sure she's hungry."

Darlina took Lily from Will's arms. "I'll go find a couple of bowls." She tossed a look back over her shoulder at the dog before opening the door to the house.

***

By the time Penny had lived with the family for a month, she took over the job of guarding Lily.

Darlina smiled as she watched the dog move along the edge of the porch to prevent Lily from falling off, as she learned to crawl. Will was right. Penny turned out to be a good dog.

Darlina embraced the natural organic lifestyle and easy country living. Both she and Will continued to practice meditation, follow Guru Maharaj Ji and be an integral part of the Premie community in Austin.

Before long, Will obtained a colony of bees and soon had several boxes of bee hives placed at the edge of the tree line. On weekends, they bottled honey to sell at a local flea market and health food stores.

Darlina continued to write occasional letters to Luke, sharing her peace and contentment about life in general. She loved telling him how Lily was trying to pull herself up to stand and could say several words.

It seemed to her that as time went by, she was able to separate more and more from him. She never mentioned to Will that she still wrote and received letters. She always made sure she got to the mailbox first.

Lily got her full attention and filled her heart with pure joy. For once, her love for Luke took a back seat.

Perhaps, with time and practice, she could truly learn to live without him.

"Rather than to break, reluctantly they bend...so it is with men."

Chapter 29

A cold March wind blew around the Federal Medical Center at Springfield, Missouri. Even through the thick walls, it crept in icy and relentless.

Luke sat on his bunk with a blanket wrapped tightly around his shoulders. He held a pink birth announcement in his left hand and a letter from Darlina in the other. She had a baby girl.

How he wished it was his baby girl that she held in her arms and nurtured.

He sighed. She was finally happy. Although he shared her happiness, it came with a bit of sadness. The cord was cut. Now she could get on with her life while he continued to exist in his.

He folded the letter and placed the announcement back in the envelope. He'd answer later, but for now, his mind was occupied with a new song that he'd dreamed two nights ago. He knew it would continue to haunt him until he wrote it. He reached for his guitar and tuned the strings.

Humming the melody that filled his head, he found the chords that matched.

It's a matter of time until we will be past history.
We keep holding on anyway.
Trying to believe for us it'll be different.
And still we can tell
Every kiss is another farewell
Kiss me another farewell

We'll put it off tonight
Let me hold you, you hold me tight
We'll pretend though we can't break the spell
And we both know every kiss is another farewell
We fight reality like flowers in autumn praying
For one more day of summer
Though it's no use our back's to the wall
Knowing we will fail
Every kiss is another farewell.

After singing it through several times, he closed his tablet and let his fingers drift on the strings to familiar songs he'd played hundreds of times on the stages of Texas honky-tonks.

If he closed his eyes tight enough, he could almost remember the sounds, the smells, the applause...

The freedom.

***

Luke doubled his efforts to provide more financial help to his mother. She traveled to Seattle, Washington to be with Bobby and his family as he endured surgery after surgery to remove the cancer. As always, he wished he could do more, but in his confines, this was his best.

He offered up prayers daily for his brother.

***

Over the next many months, Luke involved himself in the production of "Detour." He hand-lettered the movie credits and played a part in two separate vignettes.

In one scene, he played the part of a religious hypocrite and in another, the part of a man attempting to bribe an officer.

They were close to wrapping up the filming of the movie in May 1976 when a convict working in the officer's mess managed to steal a prime rib roast and some loaves of bread. He brought them to the craft shop, where they were gathered working on props for the last scene.

Luke sniffed the air. "Damn man, that smells good. Get that sonofabitch out here so we can eat it."

Willie Crump unwrapped the roast and opened a loaf of bread. "Dig in. We can't leave any evidence."

The five men ate like starved animals. They put slabs of the succulent meat between the slices of bread and devoured it.

The door to the craft shop opened, causing all of them to scramble and hide the food. John Miller strode in sniffing the air. "What are ya'll eating in here?"

"Nothing, Mr. Miller." Willie wiped his hands on his pant leg.

"Shit, that smells like roast. Don't you guys think I might want some of it too?"

The men laughed and brought out the roast. Mr. Miller joined them in the feast.

"You ain't gonna tell on us, are you Mr. Miller?"

"Hell no. A man's gotta eat. Stone, let's go over the rest of the graphics we need to wind this project up."

Luke wiped his mouth with the back of his hand. "Sure thing, Mr. Miller."

They put their heads together and Luke sketched on a large drawing pad.

A few weeks later, Mr. Miller announced that he'd been successful in selling the film to the Bureau of Federal Prisons as a training film for officers.

Luke received a personal letter from Mr. Miller, as did all of the convicts who participated in the project, along with thirty days extra good time.

Near the end of July 1976, Luke and Red received notice of their transfer back to Leavenworth Penitentiary in August. Luke began to take inventory of the belongings he'd accumulated in the past three years, amazed at how much one can accumulate even with prison restrictions. However, most of his belongings consisted of art supplies.

He sorted through the oil paints and decided to build an art box to store them in. He also made plans to build a bead box for the tiny seed beads he'd accumulated.

All projects set aside, he thoughtfully built these boxes, using scraps of wood Mr. Thompson had in the craft shop. He made small compartments and trays to go inside the bead box so he could keep the different colors and sizes of beads separated and easy to access.

For the paint box, he cut a strip of wood and bored holes into it to hold the various sized paint brushes, then attached it to the lid of the box. He built dividers for his art tools.

When he'd finished them both, he painted Indian symbols on the outside along with his name and prison number in large letters. There wasn't a chance these would get lost in the transfer.

He then did the same on his guitar case. He painted what looked like a strip of wood about twelve inches long on the front side of the case and then lettered his name and prison number inside the strip.

He made a point to visit with each of the men he'd befriended during his stay.

Nico Romano was quick to write down the names of people Luke would need to connect with once he arrived back at Leavenworth.

He packed up everything he wasn't using daily and prepared to move. Letters were in order to everyone he corresponded with to let them know of the transfer.

On August 1, 1976, Luke and Red boarded a white bus with bars on the windows for the trip back to Kansas.

They both sat quietly as the guard latched the chain around their ankles and secured it to the metal bar at the bottom of the seat.

"Do we have to be handcuffed, Lieutenant?" Luke questioned.

"Nah. These ankle chains will make damn sure you don't go any-where."

Luke looked over at Red. "This is a far cry from the bus trip up here, ain't it, hoss?"

"Sure is. Wasn't too sure you were going to make that trip."

"Me either. I was mighty sick. I felt a little sad sayin' goodbye to Nico and the boys this morning. They're good men."

"Yeah I know. We made some pretty damned good friends here in Springfield."

The bus began to roll and Luke glued his eyes to the window and the outside world. He didn't remember the trees and grass being such a vibrant hue of green. The azure blue sky stretched forever decorated by an occasional fluffy white cloud.

How he longed to roam the earth again and feel a breeze on his face.

Because of the hot temperature, the windows were lowered halfway and although the wind coming through was like a furnace, he inhaled deep gulps of fresh air.

He and Red both peered out of the windows at people walking down the streets in each town they passed through. No words needed to be spoken. Each man knew the other longed for this kind of freedom in a way that didn't require expression.

The bus ride lasted five hours and the men reached Leavenworth by 4:00 that afternoon.

The long flight of steps to the front door, the thick stone walls and guard towers remained unchanged and as unwelcoming as Luke remembered.

They sat waiting for the guard to unchain them from their seats.

He was relieved that he wouldn't have to maneuver the steps again in leg chains.

"Home sweet home, Red." Luke grinned.

"Shit, man. It ain't no home to me."

"Reckon it might as well be. We've got a long time to be here."

Guards boarded the bus. "Welcome home, Sisters." One with a gap between his front teeth grinned at Luke and Red.

"Fuck you, man." Luke narrowed his eyes.

"Don't get bent outta shape, convict. Just tryin' to keep it light."

"You can take your humor somewhere else, podhah. I ain't interested." Luke stood and followed the guard and other men off the bus.

By 9:00 that evening, Luke and Red were placed in a two man unit in cell block D, referred to by convicts as "The Dog House."

Cell block D, one of the original sections built in the 1800s, had housed the famed Birdman of Alcatraz for six years from 1910 to 1916. It consisted of red bricks stacked five tiers high. No modern heating or cooling had been added and brick walls separated the cells.

As the guard closed the cell door, he sneered. "Don't know if you pussies remember the rules, but I'll be watchin' you."

"Go right ahead and watch, asshole. It won't do you a bit of good." Luke clenched his jaw.

He desperately tried to hang on to his resolve to think and act positive. He couldn't let negativity get to him.

Once the guard left, the men collapsed on their bunks lighting cigarettes.

Red broke the silence. "Guess we had it pretty good in Springfield, all things considered."

"Reckon we did, Red. I'm not gonna let these assholes discourage me. I've gotta keep writing and makin' things. Once all of my stuff gets processed in, I'm going to get back to beadwork and painting."

"I know you're right, but sometimes I just get the feeling I'm gonna die in here."

Luke stood and walked to the bars. He could see men lined up along the bars all down the tier. Some yelled across the tier to others. Most all of them smoked cigarettes, and listened to radios. Some played cards and some engaged in sexual activity.

A bad taste rose up in his mouth. Prison...Fuck it all! He shouldn't be here. He should be back home looking after his children and helping his poor mother and brother who struggled to make ends meet.

No matter what, he couldn't let negativity creep in. If he did, he might as well lay down and die like Red said.

He thought about the sweet picture Darlina had sent him of baby Lily and herself. How he ached to hold them both.

Often, he had to remind himself that she was now married and tried to rein in his thoughts when longing overtook him.

In his mind's eye, he replaced the vision of her with Sue and tried to focus on her instead of Darlina.

Suddenly he had an idea. He would write Sue and ask her to visit Darlina. He could tell her that he needed someone he trusted to check on her and the baby.

He wondered if Sue would go along with such a crazy idea. As soon as he had his paper and pens, he'd ask.

The worst she could do was refuse, but trusting his power of persuasion, had no doubt she'd agree.

The thought excited him. It wouldn't be the same as getting to see her himself, but at least he could know through Sue's eyes how things really were.

Knowing full well that he needed to let Darlina go and let her move ahead in her life with Will, still he held on. He told himself that he simply needed to be sure she was doing as well as her letters indicated.

"Lights out," the guard shouted.

Luke could hear grumbling from the other men, but within fifteen minutes, all was quiet in cell block D.

Lying in the sweltering heat with nothing on but his briefs, he couldn't keep his thoughts from turning to Darlina and her soft yielding body that he loved so much. The need came on strong and he could do nothing but relieve himself.

He'd give anything if he could go back and undo all the wrong that landed him here. It was too late. There was no chance of him getting out of prison anytime soon and Darlina had moved on. He had to let her go. At least that's what he told himself over and over again.

Perhaps if he said it enough, he would start to believe it.

"She's barefoot and looking hungry while others wear finery upon their backs..."

Chapter 30

E ven with all the windows open and fans blowing, Darlina guessed the temperature inside the trailer house to be in the 90s on this late August day. She picked Lily up from the floor and wet a cool rag to wipe her flushed face. The baby's reddish blonde hair lay plastered to her head with sweat.

Will had made it clear that they couldn't afford to run the central air unit. She looked longingly at the thermostat, tempted to turn it on for a little while. She sighed and turned her attention back to the baby. She'd better to leave it alone.

At the sound of a car coming up the driveway, Darlina wiped the sweat from her own face and looked up. Who could be coming? She wasn't expecting anyone. Penny's ears perked up and she ran to the door barking.

Moving the stack of diapers waiting to be folded off the table, she attempted to smooth her hair. She sat Lily in the middle of the living room floor with her toys, then walked to the door in time to see a dark haired woman step out of a small red sports car.

"Can I help you?" Darlina called from the doorway, holding Penny by the collar.

"I'm looking for Darlina Flowers." The woman wore red cowboy boots, jeans, a white fringed western shirt and carried a beautiful leather purse over her shoulder with beaded leather fringe that hung below her knees.

Darlina suddenly felt plain and drab in comparison to this woman with her fancy clothes, hair piled high and heavy makeup.

"I'm Darlina Flowers." Her voice wavered.

The woman walked onto the porch. "Hi, Darlina. I'm Sue Potts. Luke Stone sent me to see you. Does your dog bite?"

Her heart lurched. "Luke? No, I don't think she'll bite, but I'll lock her up." Darlina tugged Penny's collar, guided her into a back room of the house, then quickly returned to the porch.

Sue waited patiently. "Yes, Luke's a friend. He wrote and asked me to come and check on you and the baby."

"Okay." Darlina offered her hand and Sue shook it. "It's awful hot inside. Why don't we sit out here on the porch? Can I get you something to drink?"

"Sure. Do you have any Vodka?" Sue sat in one of the two chairs on the front porch. Her manicured fingernails matched the shade of red in her boots.

"I'm sorry I don't. I can offer you water or herbal tea."

"Water would be fine."

Darlina went into the house, picked Lily up off the floor and returned to the porch with a glass of water. "So you're a friend of Luke's?" She sat in the empty chair and held Lily on her lap.

"Yes. We've become quite good friends over the past year or so. This is a purse he made for me." Sue held the fringed purse out for Darlina to see.

A twinge of jealousy arose and Darlina clenched her teeth. Why hadn't Luke made her a fancy purse like that?

"And he made this necklace and bracelet." She pointed to her neck and wrist.

"They are beautiful," Darlina managed. Why had Luke sent this woman? "I don't understand why Luke asked you to come see me."

"He just said he'd been worried about you and the baby and thought it would be a good idea for me to check on you. I drove from San Angelo. This farm was a little hard to find."

"You drove all the way from San Angelo because Luke wanted you to check on me?" She knew she was repeating herself, but it didn't make sense.

"Yes. This must be Lily." She reached out and touched the baby's arm.

Lily hid her face in her mother's bosom. "Yes it is. Lily, can you say hello to the nice lady?"

The six-month-old baby glanced at Sue and hid her face again.

"She's a little shy. We don't get many visitors out here."

Sue glanced around. "Do you and your husband farm?"

"No. We have a garden and he raises bees, but we don't farm. Tell me again how you know Luke."

Sue fanned her face with her right hand. "A mutual friend introduced us and I started writing to him. He's quite a man."

Again, Darlina couldn't stop the twinge of green jealousy. How did this woman know about the kind of man Luke was? She forced a smile. "Yes he is. I've known Luke for a very long time. Sorry you had to drive all this way for nothing, but you can report back that me and the baby are doing okay."

"Are you sure? Don't you have air conditioning in your house?"

Darlina shrugged. "Yes, but it costs too much to run. We have fans." She squirmed uncomfortably, hoping this fancy lady would be on her way soon.

They made an attempt at more small talk then Sue asked if she could take a picture of Darlina and Lily to send to Luke.

Darlina agreed, wishing with all her heart, she had makeup to put on and could fix her hair first.

After Sue left, Darlina sat on the porch with Lily on her lap for the longest time.

Her thoughts and emotions ran amuck. She hated her drab appearance next to the bright colorful woman.

Darlina recalled a time when she'd dressed herself in scanty sequined costumes, wore makeup, curled her auburn hair and danced on stage in go-go boots. That was a lifetime ago, when she was known as Luke Stone's woman.

Obviously, Luke and Sue had some sort of romance going on through their letters. Why was she jealous? She had married another man. She had no right to feel that way.

Maybe that was what Luke wanted her to see.

Lily finally squirmed out of Darlina's arms and crawled to the door. Darlina picked up the baby, went back inside and quietly finished her chores.

She made two decisions. One, she would not tell Will of Sue's visit. Two, she would purchase some makeup.

Once she'd cleared away supper dishes, she took a deep breath. "Will, can you watch Lily for me so that I can run into town and do a little shopping?"

"What do you need? Can't I pick it up for you tomorrow?"

"You wouldn't have a clue what to get. She lifted her chin. I want to buy some makeup. I'm tired of looking like a plain Jane."

"That's your ego talking." Will picked at his teeth, leaned back in the chair and let out a loud fart.

"I don't care if it's my ego. It's something I need for me, not for anyone else but me. Please, Will. I don't ask for much and I'll be really quick, I promise."

"I'm tired, Darlina. I don't see why it's so all-fired important all of a sudden." He pulled his sweaty t-shirt over his head.

Tears formed behind her eyelids. "It's important. That should be enough. I'll go to Gibson's on 290 and be back in thirty minutes. Lily won't be any trouble."

Will stood, face flushed from a combination of the heat and irritation. "No, Darlina. I'll stop there when we go to satsang on Saturday, but I'm not keeping Lily for you to go tonight."

Darlina sighed and turned her face away. Will seemed dead set on keeping her totally dependent on him. "All right, but I won't forget. I don't need much money. Ten dollars should be enough."

Will didn't reply. Instead he went outside to the porch where a slight breeze blew.

Darlina watched him through the window, puzzled as to why her request irritated him so. She didn't care. She was tired of looking washed out and ragged. It was up to her to change it.

The next time she had a visitor, she would have on makeup.

She waited until the following day to write to Luke and tell him of Sue's visit. She thanked him for his concern and assured him that she and Lily were doing fine. She told him that Sue was a beautiful woman and he was lucky to have her for a friend. She kept the letter short and to the point. Luke wanted romance and she understood that he needed it desperately. As much as she would love to be the one to satisfy that need, she'd made her choice when she married Will. She knew the letters would come fewer and farther between and yet neither of them seemed to be able to stop writing. That's the way it was.

They couldn't have each other and yet, couldn't break the bond that held them.

***

The next Saturday felt like Christmas to Darlina, as she hurried into Gibson's while Will waited impatiently in the van with Lily. She wished she had time to look at all the pretty eye shadow colors, but knew she had to choose quickly. She left with blue eye shadow, black eyeliner, a tube of mascara along with a bottle of Cover Girl base and powder. She handed Will $1.79 cents in change when she got back to the car. Maybe it was her ego, but it felt good and she couldn't wait to put on the makeup.

***

In mid-October of 1976, Darlina sat visiting with one of the Premies after satsang, while keeping an eye on Lily.

The girl excitedly told her of an astrology class that was being offered through a local health food store and invited Darlina to attend with her.

Darlina shot a glance at Will who talked with another Premie across the room. "I don't know. I'll have to ask Will. He would have to keep Lily for me, but I'd love to go."

"It starts next week and it's only two nights a week for six weeks. Let me know right away and I'll put your name down."

On the way back to the farm, Darlina shared the exciting possibility. She finished her pitch by offering to ask Will's parents to watch Lily.

He sat silent and for a minute, Darlina was afraid he wasn't going to answer. "I guess it's something that would be cool to learn. You could do all of our charts."

"It costs thirty five dollars and only lasts for six weeks. Surely, we can manage for me to go. I would love it."

"Okay, you can go. I'll talk to the folks and see if they want to keep Lily some of the nights. They love having her around."

"I could feed her right before I leave and she should be fine until I get back from class. Thank you, Will."

"I want you coming right straight home when class is over. No hanging around visiting." Will raised his eyebrows and tapped on the steering wheel with his fingers.

"Of course." Darlina turned to look out the window. She could feel the noose tightening around her neck. "How come we never talk like we used to before we got married?"

She didn't understand his growing need to control everything she did.

"Don't guess we have anything to talk about. Maybe we've said it all."

They rode in strained silence the remainder of the way back to the farm.

Lily slept peacefully in Darlina's arms. She was the one bright spot in her world. She loved this baby girl with all her heart and soul and would lay down and die for her.

The tiny girl adored Darlina and seldom let anyone else pick her up without screeching. Darlina hoped Lily wouldn't cry the entire time she was gone to class. Somehow it would all work out.

She loved the idea of using her mind again to learn something new.

Several weeks later, with a cool late fall breeze blowing through the open windows, Darlina sat at the kitchen table laboring over Luke's astrological chart. As soon as she heard Will's van, she folded the paper and slipped it inside her book.

She took supper from the oven and set it on the table. Will pulled off his work boots before coming into the kitchen. He picked up Lily and whirled around. Although Will kept his hair cut short, he'd grown his red goatee back. Lily grabbed his beard with both hands and giggled.

"Ouch." He extracted the child's hands and sat her in the high-chair. He put his arm around Darlina's waist. "How are my two favorite girls?"

"Okay. Did you have a good day?"

"Yep it was good. After you get Lily in bed, I have a surprise for you."

Darlina raised her eyebrows, but he'd already left the kitchen to wash up.

That evening, as they sat on the front porch, Will reached into his pocket and brought out two joints.

"One of the guys I work with gave me these today. It's been a long time, Darlina."

"Will, we don't smoke pot anymore."

"What could smokin' one joint hurt? Come on."

"It can't hurt you, but I'm still breastfeeding Lily, remember?"

Will looked away. "Oh yeah. I forgot about that. Well, then I'll smoke by myself." He stood, walked off the porch and out into the pasture. In a few minutes, Darlina smelled the sweet familiar scent of marijuana.

A cloud of apprehension settled around her. Neither she nor Will had touched any drugs since they'd started following the guru. She hoped this wasn't the beginning of Will partaking of them again.

When he returned to the porch, she reached for his hand. "How did that feel?"

"Good. It's been a long time. Don't think I can do meditation stoned, though."

"Probably not. You aren't gonna start smokin' all the time again, are you?"

"Nah. Let's turn in."

Darlina switched out the lights and walked with Will to their bedroom. He'd hardly tried to make love to her since Lily had been born and she didn't miss the attempts.

She picked up her meditation cloth, pillow and the t-shaped stick Will had made for her to rest her arms on while holding the arm and hand position. "I'm going to meditate for a while."

Will put his hand on her arm. "I need you, Darlina."

"You have me, Will."

"I've never really had you, but that's beside the point. Skip meditation. Make love to me tonight."

She emptied her arms and pulled her dress over her head. "Okay."

Once again, she tried with all her might to keep her mind from turning to Luke, but it was pointless.

As Will touched her and kissed her neck, she pictured Luke as clearly as if he were in front of her. A sob escaped her throat.

He made his way down to her swollen breasts. She gasped in surprise as he kissed them. He seemed to be in no hurry and it was out of character for him. Most of the time, it was if she was nothing more to him than a common whore, except that she received nothing in return.

She whispered softly. "Take me." She stopped herself. She was within seconds of finishing that sentence with Luke's name.

A few minutes later, Will rolled off her sighing contentedly. "We really should do that more often."

Tears escaped from under Darlina's closed lids. She couldn't reply.

Sometimes it seemed to her that she was trapped in a prison of her own, much like the one Luke occupied. She moved from one day to the next waiting for something to change, but it didn't.

Thank God, she had Lily. That was her saving grace. The bright blue eyes of the little girl made everything worthwhile.

At least for now.

"Folks been saying ever since I've been around, "look up," so I lifted my eyes from the ground."

Chapter 31

Three weeks after his transfer back to Leavenworth, Luke Stone sat in the sweltering cell on a mid-August day. On the other side of the cell, Red concentrated on tiny watch parts he had spread out on a small table.

Luke had been ready for the same contentions he'd faced three years ago in Leavenworth. No matter what came at him, he was determined to handle it in a more positive way. He couldn't appear weak, but he could choose how he reacted. Thankfully, there had been no confrontations so far.

"Things are a little different than when we left here three years ago, hoss." Luke picked up a new issue of Country Music Magazine.

Red looked up. "How's that, Luke?"

"Well for one thing, I thought for sure our first stop the day we got back here would be at the barber shop."

"I hadn't even thought about us coming back here with long hair, but you're right. Guess the new warden don't care what we look like as long as we keep our shit together."

"I do believe the food is a little better too. I heard that the warden was down in the chow hall two days ago asking the men in line if they were happy with the food. The old warden would've never done that. He didn't give a shit if we ate or not."

"Yeah, I guess things have changed a little. But, it's still fuckin' prison." Red lit a new cigarette off the one he was smoking.

"And it always will be. I've got lots to keep me busy and I'm gonna go out of my way to meet the recreation supervisor and let him know we're available to play music. I went to the craft shop when my shit got here and put it in a locker. The supervisor told me I could keep the paint and beads here in the cell with me. He seemed like a fairly decent dude. We gotta keep goin', Red."

"I don't know how you do it, Luke."

"How I do what, stud?"

"Keep goin'."

"I don't see it as a choice. I owe it to the people who have stuck with me to try. I've gotta keep money flowing to Mom. The only way I know to do that is to make stuff and sell it. If my ol' guitar, and the craft boxes hadn't made here in one piece, I don't know what I would've done."

"I s'pose you're right. It just feels like we're gonna rot away and die in here."

"You might, hoss, but I ain't. I'm gonna keep trying to find a way out of this shit hole and you'd be better off if you'd do the same thing."

Red grumbled under his breath. "Sometimes I think maybe you've lost your mind, Luke, with all the chanting and sitting with your eyes closed and shit you do."

Luke chuckled. "I probably have, Red."

The magazine that Luke held caught his attention with an article about Willie Nelson. His latest accomplishments and recordings in the world of country music were getting a lot of attention. An address for Willie's fan club was listed at the end of the article.

Laying the publication aside, he stared out through the open bars. He remembered the year that he and his band, "The Rebel Rousers," backed Willie and his second wife, Shirley, on a tour through Texas because they didn't have a band at the time.

He couldn't recall the exact year, but knew it was around 1962. Willie had been a nice guy to work with and they'd formed a friendship by the end of the tour. Luke wondered if Willie still remembered him.

With some huge hits under his belt, Willie was doing good for himself. Luke thought about the tablets filled with own songs. He would love to send some of them to Willie. If he sent them through the fan club, they'd surely be tossed into the nearest trash can.

Thoughts continued to run through his mind all through the night. There had to be a sure fire way to get Willie's attention. By morning, he had a plan. He couldn't wait for daylight so he could go to work. He'd make a beaded guitar strap for Willie and maybe even a fancy leather wallet. Surely, they wouldn't toss those in the trash.

It was a long shot, but one he was willing to take. A burning desire to get his music outside the forty foot walls spurred him on.

Within two weeks, he had the guitar strap and wallet made and ready to be mailed. Because of prison rules, he couldn't send them directly to the fan club address, but his mom could.

He wrapped them carefully, tucked a short note inside to Willie and one to his mom, giving her the address where they needed to be sent.

Now he would wait.

Luke made it a point the next day to meet the Recreation Supervisor, Larry Nelms.

He found him sitting in a worn out leather chair behind a small beat-up desk.

"Mr. Nelms, I'm Luke Stone and I want to volunteer my services to you as a musician. If you ever need a band, I can put one together."

Larry Nelms weighed close to three hundred pounds and the chair groaned under his weight. But he had a genuine smile.

"Nice to meet you Mr. Stone." He offered his hand and Luke shook it. "I like being the Recreation Supervisor partly because I love good music. I work hard to get outside music acts in here as often as I can to entertain the inmates. Would you like to be on the set-up crew?"

"Sure. Before I got locked up I played music for a living. While I was in Springfield, I put together a makeshift band for some shows and I can do the same here."

Mr. Nelms struggled to get to his feet. "That's good to know. We have several musical talent shows throughout the year and I could use your help."

"I have my own guitar and my cell mate plays a mean bass. He was my bass man on the outside too."

"We've got a show coming up that I think you'll enjoy being involved in. Mr. B.B. King will be coming at the end of September and I'll make sure you're on the crew."

"That'd be great."

After a few minutes, Luke went on his way. He felt good about the connection with Mr. Nelms and hoped it would be an opportunity to keep playing music.

His next stop was to locate the men that Nico Romano had encouraged him to seek out. To his surprise, they were waiting for him, having already received word about his transfer. They accepted him into their circle with no hesitation. Luke surmised that Nico Romano's recommendation of a man carried a lot of weight in the Sicilian community.

***

On September 24, 1976, Luke received an excited short letter from his mom along with a Xeroxed copy of one she'd received from Willie's wife, Connie Nelson. It read:

> The guitar strap and billfold that Luke made for Willie are beautiful! Willie was honestly overwhelmed that anyone would go to the trouble and all the work Luke did for him. He will treasure it always and I'll find time to get his picture made wearing the guitar strap. We wanted to know if there was any way to write to him and send press clippings, magazines, etc. Please tell him I'll keep a bunch of mail and info coming – Thank you for mailing them, Connie Nelson.

Luke slapped his knee. Willie's personal address was written at the end of the letter.

He couldn't get to his writing tablet quick enough. He knew for sure he wanted to send *Soap Creek Saloon* to Willie along with *The Loner, Trouble Is* and *Dreams With You*. He didn't want to impose, but couldn't pass up this opportunity. He explained in his letter to Willie and Connie that his mom would have to mail a cassette tape with the songs crudely recorded as prison rules didn't allow him to send it directly to them.

He hoped he'd put enough information in the letter to jog Willie's memory.

The minute he'd completed the letters, he reached for his bead loom. He would make beaded necklaces for Willie and his wife to show his appreciation.

A new hope came alive and he worked with fervor. Maybe something worthwhile would finally get over the forty foot walls of prison to the outside world.

He'd always told Red that if they could write something good enough, Nashville would break through the walls to get them out.

That was an exaggeration, but still anything was worth trying.

***

That October, Luke received a short letter from Darlina. His heart ached for her and he often looked at the picture Sue had mailed to him after her visit. Darlina looked sad and tired in the picture. He hardly recognized the beautiful girl he'd fallen in love with so long ago. He'd often regretted asking Sue to go and hoped that her visit hadn't caused Darlina even more heartaches than she already had. At the time, he simply wanted someone he trusted to tell him the truth.

He called it the damned ol' greasy Indian "knowing," but at times Darlina didn't have to tell him anything. The reality behind her forced words came through loud and clear.

In the letter that had just arrived, she informed him that Will had a good job opportunity in Houston and they were moving. He sensed that she didn't mind leaving the farm, but dammit, Houston was a big town. For the millionth time, he cursed the walls and bars that held him.

Darlina occasionally mentioned that they barely had enough money to get by, and yet they always found enough to travel to Florida or Colorado to see the guru. He also suspected they gave money regularly to him as well. It angered him to think that Will would let his family do without and yet support the chubby little kid from India who claimed to be some sort of savior of the world.

Maybe someday, she'd get a belly full and wake up.

Letting go of situations he couldn't change was one of the hardest things he'd learned from behind the bars and walls. He'd come to understand that everything in life had its own season and reason. So many things he had no control over.

Where Darlina was concerned, all he could do was let go and trust that she would find her way.

As the months rolled by and a new year came, Luke made a decision to remedy something that he'd always regretted.

At the age of seventeen, he'd insisted on quitting school and going to work in the oilfield. He thought he didn't need schooling, he needed to make money. So, in spite of his parents' pleas, he'd quit school just two short months before graduation and never earned a high school diploma.

The education department at Leavenworth offered a GED program and on January 3, 1977, he enrolled in the class.

By February, he received his GED and promptly mailed it to his mother, knowing how proud it would make her.

***

April 1977 brought an opportunity beyond what Luke could ever have imagined.

A long letter from Connie Nelson included a proposal for him to consider. She and Willie had been overwhelmed with the beaded necklaces he'd made for them. She told Luke that Willie would throw one out to the audience at the end of a show and it was going over big.

Luke had made a fancy leather purse for Connie with turquoise, beads and fringe on it. He sent poems and artwork along with more songs. He always drew something on the outside of the envelopes.

The letter Luke received in April sent his mind spinning.

...The part we wanted to find out from you is this! Your drawings are so good – remember the stagecoach and the one of Willie playing a guitar leaning back on the tree you sent on a letter?? We wondered if you might be interested in drawing an album cover – Willie would pay you top price or whatever you thought it would be worth to you. The main thing I thought was it would be you doing something in there that would be recognized out here by a lot of people. Your name and where you are, where you draw the pictures from could be used or not used (entirely up to you). Please know that this is not an idea to capitalize on "The Convict

And The Rose" album by having a convict help work on the album. I promise the idea is to help you possibly too, because Willie
will still do the album if you don't do the cover (without any mention of you at all). It was just so ironic how "The Convict And The
Rose" song was already cut by Willie and I heard it 4 or 5 times in
with the other songs before I realized the similarity of you sending
the poem to the girls. Maybe the money for the cover could also
help your family or be enough to help you some way. It could be a
standard album size or be a fold-out double sided picture cover,
but only one record. If you like the idea or even want to think
about it, I could send all the words to the songs that would be included or even a tape, maybe. And you could see what you might
come up with for the cover. Maybe different little pictures telling
the story as each song does. Anyway, it's for you to think about
and whatever you decide is fine because your feelings are more
important than the album idea. I thought that maybe selling your
pictures for an album might be as good as songs in one way (and
Willie still hasn't been home to look at them yet, but still will).
Please let me know what you think and there's no hurry. Until
then, we're still thinking of you and tell Red Hoss hi. Love Connie...P.S. It might show a lot of people that there aren't just bad
guys with no feelings or talent in prison too."
Excerpt taken from actual letter

Luke's heart raced with excitement. Maybe this would finally be the
break he'd imagined, hoped and prayed for. It didn't take him long to
answer the letter and tell Connie that he would be thrilled to do the
artwork for the album and expressed how much their faith in him
meant.

As he moved around the prison that day, he held his head a little
higher and walked a little straighter.

The Great Spirit had honored him with this opportunity and even
though it wasn't his song Willie was recording, the chance to do the
artwork on a major album with a major artist was beyond anything
he'd imagined.

Within a few weeks, true to her word, Connie Nelson mailed all of
the song lyrics that were to be on this album and Luke set to work
sketching the images that came into his head as he read the words.

The Intro to the album formed a vivid picture in his mind. Even though the words had been written by Willie Nelson, they rang as true as if he'd written them himself.

> Was it something I did, Lord
> A lifetime ago?
> Am I just now paying
> A debt that I owe?
> Justice, sweet justice
> You travel so slow,
> But you can't change
> My love for the rose.

For the next several weeks, Luke spent every free minute studying the song lyrics and sketching. *I'm Ragged But I'm Right, The Hungry Years, Till I Can Gain Control Again, A Hundred Years From Now, Solitaire, She Is Gone, The Convict And The Rose* and *The Prisoner's Song* completed the album.

Amazed, he thanked God for his good fortune to be able to make this solid connection with Willie and his sweet wife, Connie.

He couldn't help but believe that his determination to do and be something worthwhile had been noticed by the Great Spirit and he was being rewarded.

Of course, it would have been a greater reward to be freed from prison, but he had faith that would come too. Everything in its own time.

"Sometimes love just can't grow, it withers and dies painfully slow. When there is nothing left inside, no one can revive love that's died."

Chapter 32

O ne morning in March 1978, in the Houston smog, Darlina sat across the breakfast table from Will, watching him chew his food. She knew if she put one bite in her mouth, she'd hurl, so she fed Lily and waited for Will to leave for work.

As she watched him mindlessly chomp one bite after another she felt nothing but disgust. She turned her full attention to Lily, but could still hear the smacking sounds he made. Funny that she'd never noticed them before.

That morning's attempt at love making left her cold and empty. She no longer had any connection to Will other than the sweet two-year-old sitting in the high chair and the baby forming in her belly.

She thought about how they used to talk and how things she said mattered, but it had been a long time since any words out of her mouth had reached Will.

He withdrew farther into the belief that he was a special angel sent from God and the mundane things in life were only annoyances. He worked sporadically and from Darlina's perspective, he gave much more of himself and his time to the Houston Ashram than he did to his family.

Yes, she was pregnant and maybe that explained the nausea, but it went deeper than that.

She knew in her heart it was time to make a break. With resolve, she waited until Will left, then picked up the phone and dialed the number of a woman who'd become her friend.

"Charlotte, this is Darlina. I hate to ask this, but can me and Lily come stay at your house for a while?"

Without hesitation, Charlotte cheerfully responded, "Of course. Are you two all right? Where is Will?"

"Yes, we're okay and Will is at work. I just need to get out of here but I have no place to go. I promise it'll only be until I can figure out what to do."

"Get your things together and I'll come pick you up in a couple of hours."

"Thank you, Charlotte. You're a true friend."

Darlina hadn't known who else to call. She'd thought about calling her parents, but didn't want to involve them, although she knew they'd drop everything to come.

Her easiest way out was through the Premie community as they didn't ask questions and went with the flow of the moment.

She pulled the biggest suitcase from the top shelf in the closet, and packed their clothes, Lily's beloved books and toys. She would take nothing else except for the high chair. It wouldn't be the first time she slept on a mat on the floor.

Relief flooded over her. She'd known for a long time that she needed to leave, and today seemed to be the right day. She would give Will the freedom of living without the burden of a family.

As she closed the suitcase, she turned her thoughts to Luke.

Maybe it was being pregnant, but emotions washed over her like a silken cloak. Tears ran unchecked down her face. Why couldn't she just stop loving Luke? Why did he have to invade every thought, every feeling, every wish and desire? She'd tried to make things work with Will, but had never been able to completely give herself to him.

How could she, when she belonged eternally to another?

Lily brought her stuffed animals to Darlina. "Are we goin' on a twip, Mommy?"

"Yes, sweetie, we are, but we aren't going very far. We're going to stay with Charlotte and Mike and Aaron for a while. You like playing with Aaron, don't you?"

"Uh huh." Lily scampered off then came right back. "Puzzles go too?"

"Of course." She reached down and hugged the little girl. She never stopped being amazed at how intelligent this tiny creature was.

Lily had every one of her books memorized and only allowed Darlina to turn the pages while she said the words. She was barely two years old. Darlina didn't know about other children and their development, but thought this was pretty incredible.

***

Two days later, Darlina sat on the front porch of Charlotte's house with Will. Lily played inside with Charlotte's three-year-old son.

"I don't understand, Darlina. If you were unhappy, why didn't you tell me?"

"I did tell you, Will, many times. You didn't hear me. You were never really present with me or with Lily."

Will ran his right hand over his beard. "I don't know what you're talkin' about. I always came home to you and Lily."

"Your body did, but you didn't. Here's a good example. Remember last month when we traveled all the way to Italy to see Guru Maharaji Ji?"

"Of course I remember. It was incredible."

"For you it was. I had a baby to take care of. Where were you when she got her head stuck through the railing on the steps leading up to the coliseum? You weren't anywhere around. Thank God there were other Premies around who helped me."

"That's not fair, Darlina. I was inside praying and meditating."

"I understand, but where did that leave us? Outside with your baby girl's head stuck, that's where. I tried to love you, Will. I really did."

"Maybe, but you never let go of Luke. How's a man supposed to deal with that?"

She looked down at her hands. "I know. It wasn't fair to you, but you have to believe I really tried. You knew my feelings for Luke when you asked me to marry you. I've lived my whole life going with my feelings. That hasn't changed."

"I'm not sure you really ever tried." His eyes narrowed. "Don't you understand that everything in this life is simply an illusion?"

"I hear the words, but to me, it's reality. The baby growing inside me is reality. My two-year-old daughter inside the house is reality. If I cut my finger, the blood that comes out is reality, so no, I don't understand what those words mean."

"Well, I do." He sucked in his breath and cocked his head to the side. "You just haven't reached enlightenment yet."

"And you have?" She didn't try to hide the sharpness in her voice.

"Yes, I have. You do what you have to, but I'm not giving you any money."

"I don't want your money, but would you please give Charlotte and Mike a little for us to stay here and for food?"

"Yeah, I'll give 'em some, but I've got nothing to give to you. My extra money all goes to Guru Maharaj Ji. I am his servant." Will stood and gazed across the yard. Finally he turned to look down at Darlina. "I have to ask. Is there someone else?"

She looked up surprised. "Oh good Lord, Will. I'm four months pregnant with your baby. Of course there's no one else. How could you even ask?"

"I just needed to know." He walked off the porch to his van and drove away without a backward glance.

He didn't even tell Lily goodbye. Darlina searched her heart for any feelings, but all she could find was relief.

The next day, she penned a long thought-filled letter to Luke.

***

On July 6, 1978, around 4 a.m., Nicole Gayle Brocker made her entrance into the world in the front bedroom of a Premie house. Tears of joy flowed down Darlina's face.

What a beautiful perfect little girl. She lay in Darlina's arms and gazed around with the most crystal clear blue eyes at her new world. She didn't cry. She lay perfectly still, turning only her tiny head.

Darlina gazed in amazement at this miracle of life cradled in her arms.

She was very thankful that she'd been able to give birth to this child in a peaceful environment surrounded by Premies with love and light in their eyes.

Will sat beside the bed through the last part of the labor, then shortly after Nicole was born, he left.

They'd been able to maintain an amicable friendship, seeing each other at satsang and other functions involving the guru. Lily always ran to him when she saw him and Will would pick her up and swing her around.

Maybe in some odd way, Will had been as relieved as Darlina when she'd left.

Her world felt complete now with two little girls to care for.

The only thing missing was Luke. Darlina had enjoyed writing openly to him again and letting her letters be her outlet for sexuality. Luke responded eagerly, happy to have that freedom with her again.

She couldn't wait to tell him about Nicole.

Now that she had two children, she had to figure out a way to make a living for them. Will had reluctantly helped take care of them up to now, but made it clear he didn't have any plans to continue.

Once she got on her feet, she would find work. Her friend, Charlotte, had started a house-cleaning service. Darlina felt sure she could go to work with her.

Maybe she and Charlotte could take turns caring for each other's children.

Within a month, she was working with Charlotte, making a little money.

She'd moved herself and the girls into a spare bedroom of a house that belonged to a Premie couple without children shortly after Nicole's birth.

This room had, at one time, been a garage and without insulation, the stifling hot Houston summer was less than bearable. Big water-bug roaches came in through the cracks around the windows and Darlina spent many sleepless nights keeping watch over the girls to make sure the bugs didn't crawl on them.

Exhausted, she made a decision. She called her mother.

"Hi, Mama, it's Darlina. I need to ask a big favor."

"How are the babies, Darlina? What do you girls need?" Her mother's warm voice brought immediate tears to Darlina's eyes.

"Mama, I need to get out of Houston. I don't have a car or any money, but I don't want to live here anymore. There are big bugs in the room we live in and I'm worn out from staying awake to make sure they don't get on the girls. Can you and Daddy come and get us?"

"Of course we can, honey. Get your things together. We can be there Saturday."

"Mama, I love you and thank you. I know I haven't always done things the way you thought I should, and I'm sorry I've caused you grief." Tears spilled from Darlina's eyes.

"Well, you certainly have done your share of that, but me and your daddy will help you and the girls. You can stay with us until you can figure things out."

"Thank you. I love you and I'll see you Saturday. Please tell Daddy thank you for me." Her voice cracked.

"I will. Don't cry. Everything will be all right. Just get packed and we'll come in the pickup."

"Okay."

Darlina hung up the phone and collapsed in a heap of sobs. Another Premie who lived in the house stuck her head in the door.

"Are you okay, Darlina?"

Darlina looked up, wiping her face with her hands. "No, I'm not. I've called my mom and asked her and Daddy to come and get us. I want out of Houston."

"Where will you go?"

"I don't know yet. Mama and Daddy live in East Texas. Maybe I can find a job in Tyler or somewhere nearby."

"Honey, you need to go where there is a Premie house. I have a friend who lives in Shreveport. She is a follower and as far as I know, she lives alone. I bet she'd open her home to you."

"Do you think so?"

"Why don't I call her and find out? At least you'd have a plan."

"Thank you so much. Yes, I do need a plan." Darlina managed a weak smile.

"Come on. Let's go call her." The woman picked Lily up.

Darlina carried Nicole and followed her into the living room.

A few short minutes later, Darlina had an open invitation to move in with Nancy Davis in Shreveport. She sounded excited at the idea of having two little girls in the house and told Darlina the only other occupant of the house was an English Sheep dog.

Relief flooded over her and excitement began to flow. She was getting out of Houston.

Once she had both of the girls napping that day, she sat with pen and paper and told Luke everything. She knew he would be happy that she was getting out of the big city.

Before she sealed the envelope, she wrote a poem and enclosed it.

> My little girls are sleeping
> The clock keeps on ticking
> Where will we go?
> No one really knows.
> Will we find a home?
> Are we destined to be alone?
> The urge to move is strong
> To find some place that we belong
> To Houston town, I bid adieu
> New adventures to pursue
> As I bravely make for us a new start,
> You, my love, are always in my heart

She knew her writing ability didn't equal his, but he always praised any attempts she made.

Besides the two little girls, Luke Stone remained the one constant star in her dark of night.

Was she a fool to keep loving a man who couldn't lie beside her at night...who couldn't help her with the daily struggles of life?

Maybe she was, but the strength of their love kept her believing that some way, some day, they would be together again.

For now, all she had was paper with loving words written on it to sustain and give her comfort. And for now, that was enough, loving her paper man. She remembered the last poem Luke had sent.

PAPER MAN

> I sit alone with pen in hand
> Visualizing your many needs and feelings
> Knowing it must be lonely loving a paper man
> No one could love you as much as I do
> My very soul craves and needs you
> As you read these lines please understand

I realize that your world is reality
Mine is exiled existence in no man's land
Secluded with self-sought fantasy
You in my arms is my dream, my plan
With love, on paper I send my heart
Sincere expressions of devotion I impart
Time will bring us together with the shifting of the sand
Have faith, look up, continue loving your paper man.

"Someday, baby, I'll see you again, yes you again, don't know where or I don't know when, but I will see you again."

Chapter 33

L uke spent every spare minute working on the album cover for Willie Nelson over the next many months. Winter faded and springtime green replaced the drab brown.

He'd been assigned to work in the clothing room upon his return to Leavenworth. Now that spring had arrived, he spent daily time in the yard after work, soaking up sunshine.

The regular correspondence between him and the Nelsons continued. Every letter encouraged him to try harder and reach farther. He enjoyed making the beaded necklaces that Willie now used at every show.

Letters reporting his brother's struggle with cancer left him feeling more helpless than ever. Bobby had now suffered a stroke and on top of having no voice, he would also be paralyzed on his left side. Luke's heart broke for him.

Red had gotten involved in playing bass guitar for a prison band made up of four other men shortly after they'd arrived from Springfield. When the men asked Luke to join, he'd declined, preferring to work on his own music.

Nevertheless, Luke was glad Red had found something to interest him and get him out of the depressions he tended to sink into.

Early in March 1977, Red came bursting into the cell with a big smile on his face. "Luke, you're not gonna believe this. Sonny and John have found a recording studio in Independence that has offered to bring their equipment in here and record a 45."

"Hell, Red, that's great. Who's behind it?"

"I don't know. Sonny told me that the studio is Cavern Sound and it's a small studio, but they're working with the warden on getting permission to come in."

"I'm sure Sonny's on cloud nine. Too bad there ain't a studio in here that we all could use."

"I don't think the warden would ever go for that, but it'd be nice. We could record a bunch of songs and start sending 'em out everywhere. They asked me to talk you into joining up with us. We need your help, Luke."

It had been a long time since Luke had seen Red excited about anything. "I'll help you guys any way I can. Ya'll know that."

"Hell, Luke, you know more about all of this than any of us. We need to get the press involved and you're damned good at that. Then once it's cut, we want to get it played on the radio and you're the only one of us that knows how to do that."

"I'll do what I can." Luke slapped his friend on the back. "This is fuckin' great news, hoss."

The next day, Luke made a list of newspapers in the area, using the prison library resource section. Then he moved on to the local television stations. This should catch someone's attention as being newsworthy. He carefully worded the letters and mailed one to each.

That evening, he and Red sat with Sonny Bridges and John Bradin (two of the men involved in the project) in the music room, discussing the prospect of the recording.

Sonny, a tall clean cut guy, with a voice equal to Vern Gosdin, was the lead singer. He was up for parole in a few months and making solid plans to continue in the entertainment business once he was released.

He leaned forward in his chair. "Luke, I need you to be the leader of this band. You know more about this shit than any of us. Ray's written a good song and now John's got this studio interested in us. We don't know what the hell we're doing."

John Bradin, a quiet spoken twenty-four-year-old kid from California, added. "Sonny's right, Luke. With you helping us and Mr. Nelms behind us too, maybe we can show the world that something good can come from behind these fuckin' walls."

Luke had always been a good judge of character and liked Sonny and John. "I don't have a whole lot of time to devote to this with the album project for Willie going on, but I'll do what I can. You're right, John. Something like this shows people on the outside that we can do something positive from in here. I've already contacted all of the local newspapers and TV stations. Somebody will want to pick up this story."

"Thanks, Luke." Sonny ran his hand through his dark wavy hair. "That's the sort of help we need. I'm no good at doing interviews. Hell, I get nervous just thinkin' about talking to a reporter."

"Well, I'll help all I can. I think we should meet with Mr. Nelms tomorrow."

The men sat talking for an hour or more, then shook hands and went their separate ways.

All of this talk of recording started wheels turning in Luke's mind. Maybe he could convince the warden to let him build a studio. He'd let the seed of the idea germinate and perhaps it would grow.

Within a week, Luke had a reply from a reporter with the Kansas City Star. He wanted to cover the story and would obtain permission from prison officials to come in for an interview with the men involved in the project.

When the article hit the Kansas City Star newspaper, it bore the title of *Inmates Shoot for Hit 45*.

Luke couldn't help but notice the hope that it gave a handful of inmates. The idea that they could do something worthwhile for the outside world to see created a spark of confidence.

Luke had been slightly disappointed at only one response to his many letters about the project, but six months later, a CBS television station decided to take the story farther and after going through all of the necessary red tape, came into the prison and filmed the band playing a song.

They told the men it would be aired on television within the next month.

The spark of hope re-ignited. By now over a dozen radio stations had started playing the record and things looked good for the recording.

***

Unbeknownst to Luke or any of the men, a reporter for Country Song Roundup music magazine had seen the news clip on CBS and contacted the prison requesting an interview with the men.

Judy Hedy arrived at Leavenworth on April 11, 1978. With Warden Day's permission, she interviewed Sonny, Luke and two other men.

Luke immediately liked this woman and knew she'd give them a fair shake. She wasn't bad to look at either.

She interviewed Sonny Bridges first, then Luke.

She turned on the tape recorder. "Luke Stone, what is your part in all of this?"

"I try and put the guys in here together the best I can. Like I tried to explain to the band, no vocalist sings better than the group that's backin' him and no group plays better than the vocalist frontin' them. So, we're just tryin' to make ol' Sonny sound as good as we can. I pick out the guys that are most advanced in music when we want to do somethin', but still we try and get other guys interested in what's goin' on too. I figure one guy can teach the next and I feel like I'm learnin' from them all. It's a lot different here than it was outside." Luke leaned back in his chair.

"Have you had any formal training in music?" Judy continued.

"Ah, no. Well, yes I did, in country music. I was about twelve and my uncle gave me a guitar. I was playin', or playin' at it, around the house quite a bit. My dad said, "Son, you like that guitar, don't you?" I said, "I sure do, Dad." He said, "I can see that and I like to see you enjoyin' yourself. Take it down there to the barn and you can go down and play it anytime you want to. Just get the damn thing out of the house." So that was my formal training. I got to sing to a lotta cows. A few years after that, I started playin' with the guys there in the clubs in Texas, that's where I'm from. Later on I had a publishing company and a recording studio."

Judy laughed. "So your first audience was cows, huh? What is your take on this project?"

"We're here, but we're here tryin' and that's the main thing to me. I spend my time tryin' to do somethin' constructive, playin', teachin', learnin'. That's what it's all about. Instead of wastin' time, I think we should do somethin' to help ourselves. If I'd have had this attitude before, I wouldn't be here today. I think prison has taught me one thing; to accept reality...To me, people waste too much of their time. You only have so much time and what you get accomplished between now and sundown, that's it for today. This year don't come back again."

Excerpt taken from interview published in Country Song Roundup Magazine, December 1978.

Of course, the guards never left the men alone with Judy, but by the end of the interview, she gave Luke her address and asked him to send her some of the songs he'd written.

Luke left the interview encouraged that maybe between this publicity and what he was doing with Willie Nelson, things would turn around for him.

More than anything, he wanted out from behind the bars. He wanted to take what he'd learned inside these walls to the outside world and have half a shot at making a life again.

When Luke arrived back at his cell that day after the interview, a letter from Darlina awaited. He read the words slowly, then let out an audible sigh. It had come as no surprise that she had left Will. But, with another baby, Luke could see a hard road ahead for her. She seemed to be growing and getting stronger in herself. He had no doubt she could do it, but life as a single mother with two babies was not going to be easy.

He hastily retrieved his writing tablet and pen and wrote her a long letter. He shared with her the excitement of the most recent turn of events with music and the publicity it brought. In closing, he decided to send one of the many sweet poems he'd written with her face steady in his mind. He would do what he could from where he was to encourage her, love her and offer advice if she asked. In some odd way, it almost felt as if he had her back again.

***

The months rolled by and soon, the hot stifling heat of another Kansas summer was replaced by bitterly cold winter.

He received a short letter from his daughter, Lexi, telling him that she was engaged to be married. Luke was stunned at this news. At the age of sixteen, she wasn't old enough to get married. He hoped that she wasn't already pregnant. How could her mother allow her to get married so young? Again he cursed the bars and walls that held him captive. He was trapped with only a pen and paper to talk to her with. He sat down and wrote.

He heard from his oldest son, Joseph, now and then. He'd tried his hand at bull riding and decided he didn't want to make a career out of it. In his last letter, he mentioned joining the Air Force. He seldom heard from the little boys other than through his mother who was stretched thin between helping Bobby and his family and trying to watch after his children. His kids were growing up without him. This wasn't what he'd planned.

Sending pieces of the artwork back and forth to Willie, he finally reached what he considered to be complete with his part of the project. There was nothing more to do other than to wait until Willie recorded the album.

Luke was glad he'd taken advantage of the opportunity to enroll in a Lay-Out and Design course along with another in Screen Process Printing offered through the education department back in January.

He'd learned more techniques that would be helpful with the album cover. Separating his art into layers and then over-laying them created screen-process-ready art.

That same month, Luke attended a meeting of the American Indian Movement in Leavenworth. He'd joined the American Indian Brotherhood while he was in Springfield, but had just recently become an official member of AIM.

He had many reasons for joining the organizations but mainly it was to honor his ancestral heritage.

He sat on a folding chair in a circle of men who had come together for the meeting in a private room next door to the recreation room.

The man in charge of the meeting, John Two Bears, held a makeshift peace pipe that he filled with tobacco and passed around the circle.

Luke accepted the pipe and sucked the smoke from it into his lungs, then passed it on.

John Two Bears stood in the middle of the circle. "Thank you my brothers for joining me today. We, the red man, have been oppressed and treated unjustly by the white man for many years and it continues now, even today. We have no way to fight back. They have destroyed our civilization..."

Luke listened as the man went on and on about the plight of the American Indian and how they were helpless against the force of government.

After a while, he slowly got to his feet. "I've been sitting here listening to you all talk about how you've been mistreated and how you are powerless to do anything about it." His eyes narrowed and voice sharpened. "What I see here in front me are sniveling belly-crawling cowards. Your ancestors would spit on you if they could see what you've become."

Grumbles came from the circle. Luke turned around to look into the eyes of each man. "My skin isn't brown like yours and my eyes are blue, but my grandfather was full-blood Cherokee Indian. My heart is Indian and my beliefs are of the old ways. I strive to walk upon the red road. I ask you, my Indian brothers, to take heart and become the men your ancestors were. John Two Bears is a direct descendent of Black Elk. That's a lineage to be proud of. Each of you have your own heritage to carry with you, head high and proud. That is all I have to say."

As Luke took his seat, a man across from him stood. "This man speaks the truth. Look what we've allowed ourselves to become. We stay drunk on crudely made hooch and we whine and complain when things don't go our way. I believe we can do better." He returned to his seat.

Several men nodded in agreement.

John Two Bears rose again. "This man, Luke Stone, has made a good point. If we can become better men, then perhaps the outside world won't look down their noses at us." Turning to the man to his left, he continued. "Gray Hawk, why are you in here?"

Gray Hawk hung his head. "I killed another man in a drunken stupor."

He proceeded around the circle. Almost every man replied they were locked up because of something they'd done while intoxicated.

Luke stood again. "That is exactly my point. But, now that you are here, you have the chance to study your ancestry and learn from your Fathers and Medicine Men. That is what I choose to do."

With that, he left the meeting.

As he walked back to his cell, he thought about the group and how their fathers, grandfathers and great grandfathers before them had trod upon the earth in a proud spirit way. He hoped they would think about the choices they could make now to honor that.

It became more apparent to him with each passing day that in some off-the-wall way, the prediction his grandmother had made before he was born would become truth, although not in the sense that she thought. She'd predicted he would be a boy, that he would be a preacher and have the gift of knowing. He'd never taken to religion and knew beyond a doubt he never would. But in his own way, he was turning into more of a teacher.

Once back in the cell, he strummed on his guitar and let his mind wander where it may. As always, his thoughts turned to Darlina.

She'd sent him pictures of the new baby and Lily and with the help of her parents, should now be settling into living in Shreveport.

His heart ached for the young girl. He wanted more than anything to help ease her burden. He knew things were tough even though she put up a good front. But, there was absolutely nothing he could do. She would have to find her own way. Thank God she was close to her parents and their relationship seemed to be repaired and solid. Funny how babies could do that.

He laid the guitar in its case and sat cross-legged on his bunk, eyes closed, communing with and giving thanks to the Great Spirit.

A lot of good things had come his way over the past year and he owed it all to his determination to think and act in a positive way.

He'd meant what he said to Judy Hedy in the interview, that if he'd only had this attitude on the outside, he wouldn't be locked away in a cage now.

He walked the right path of honor and of hope with a strong will to survive.

By God, he would get through this and one day, somehow, someway, he'd hold Darlina Flowers in his arms again. The spark of that hope burned as bright as any star in the sky.

"Looking over my shoulder at places I've been, hope to find somewhere that losers can win..."

Chapter 34

The two weeks Darlina spent at her Mom and Dad's house before moving to Shreveport flew by. The peace and serenity of the East Texas piney woods brought calm to her battered spirit. She couldn't remember the last time she'd slept so soundly. In the days that passed, her thoughts became clearer and her heart tranquil.

It seemed to Darlina that her mother flourished with babies in the house. She was amazed at how her parents were so willing to help out.

Being mid-August, Darlina's birthday was just a few days away.

When she walked into the kitchen on a bright sunshiny morning, her mother took Nicole from her arms. "Your daddy has gone to see about a car for you. He found one over in Henderson for four hundred dollars. Darlina, I don't have a clue what to feed you and Lily."

"Oh, Mama, Daddy didn't have to do that. Do you have any oatmeal?"

"I sure do. I'll fix you girls some."

"Why don't you take care of Nicole for me and I'll cook for me and Lily?" Darlina knew her mother wouldn't have health food in her kitchen, even though she was an excellent cook. Once she got to Shreveport, she could buy the kind of whole food they were accustomed to eating.

Her father walked in the door an hour later with a big grin on his face. "I found you a car, Darlina. Why don't you ride over with me and you can drive it back?"

Darlina jumped to her feet in excitement. It had been a long time since she'd had her own car. "Thank you, Daddy. When I get a job and get on my feet, I'll pay you back."

"Don't worry about it. I'm glad you're away from that idiot you married."

"Me too, Daddy."

Her mother rocked Nicole. "I knew something was wrong with that boy when we came to visit and he took us to the grocery store. The way he ran up and down the aisles with that grocery cart acting like a two-year-old embarrassed me. Go with your daddy to get the car. I'll watch these babies."

Darlina laughed. "Yes, Will could act pretty foolish. Thank you, Mama."

Darlina didn't know how she'd ever repay her parents for helping her like this. And they didn't even seem to mind. She hoped she could be that kind of parent for Lily and Nicole, although she vowed never to alienate her girls from her, no matter what. They would have the freedom to live however they chose without fear of being judged.

***

Nancy turned out to be an easy-going, loving woman who embraced Darlina and the girls into her home when they arrived at the first of September 1978.

Darlina knew she would need to find a job, but didn't know how she could while she still breastfed Nicole.

Nevertheless, she had to try.

Once they were settled, she seriously searched for work. She hoped for temporary work through Kelly Girls since she'd worked for them back in Austin.

On Nancy's next day off, Darlina dressed in her nicest clothes and meticulously applied her makeup, then drove to the nearest Kelly Girls office and signed up.

Before the week was over, she had a job assignment. Nancy introduced her to a neighbor who immediately offered to babysit. The construction company she'd been assigned to turned out to be only a few blocks away and Darlina could easily come on breaks and lunch to feed Nicole.

Things were coming together. She and the Lily slept on mats on the floor and Nicole slept in her baby crib in Nancy's spare bedroom. Life in a new place commenced.

The Premie community in Shreveport was small but active and they, like Nancy had done, embraced Darlina and the children.

Darlina's letters to Luke were filled with the new things she was doing. It wasn't easy being a single mommy, but she was managing with the help and support from her family and the Premies.

As 1979 rolled around, more changes loomed. Nancy received news that her job was transferring her to Washington, D.C.

Darlina looked at rent houses and apartments and decided she couldn't afford any of them on her meager earnings.

Alan, a local Premie, had taken a real interest in Lily and Nicole and often played with them in another room of the Premie house so Darlina could participate in satsang.

That evening, he brought them back into the main room after the meeting was over in time to hear Darlina voicing her concern about a place to live.

Alan handed Nicole to Darlina. "Why don't you think about moving in here? We have a spare room."

Darlina looked around at the other Premies who lived in the house. "How would ya'll feel about having children in the house?"

"They wouldn't bother me," Connor, the house-father, replied. "Does anyone have any objections?"

Everyone shook their heads.

Darlina sat both of her girls on her lap. "If no one has any objections, we could move in for a little while. At least until I can afford a place."

Alan hugged Darlina. "I'll help you move."

Nancy entered the room. "What are ya'll talking about?"

"About moving Darlina and the girls into this house with us." Connor stood. "Anyone want a cup of tea?"

"That's great. I was worried about what they'd do. I can tell you firsthand that they are no trouble. I'm going to miss them, and yes I would love a cup of tea. I'll help you." Nancy followed Connor into the kitchen.

Alan played with the girls and continued talking to Darlina.

Darlina liked the easy way these people got along with each other and that they were so willing to bring babies into the house. Maybe this would work out at least for a while. She breathed a sigh of relief.

Over the next few weeks, as she made plans to move, Darlina found herself spending a lot of time with Alan.

January the fourteenth, she and the girls moved into the Premie house on Kings Highway. She unpacked boxes and put their things away in a small chest of drawers her mom had bought for them at a garage sale. On that same trip, her parents also brought a twin-sized bed for Lily. Nicole still slept in her baby crib.

Alan knocked on the open door. "Can I come in?"

"Of course." Darlina folded Lily's clothes.

"Just wanted to see how things were going." Lily ran to him and he picked her up and twirled her around. "The girls seem happy."

Darlina smiled. "Yes, they do."

"What about you, Darlina?"

"What about me?" She walked to the crib and picked up Nicole who was holding onto the side, bouncing and gurgling.

"Are you happy?"

"Sure. It feels good to be here. What about you, Alan? Are you happy?"

"Yes, but I'll be happier once I tell you what's on my mind."

Darlina sat down on Lily's bed. "Okay. What's on your mind?"

"Well, I'm pretty sure you've noticed that I spend a lot of time with you and the girls."

"Yes and I appreciate it very much."

"I've got another reason. I think I'm falling in love with you."

Darlina gasped. "In love? You don't even know me."

"I know you enough to see that you're a loving mother and beautiful woman. You act like you don't see me looking at you when we're in satsang."

"I truly didn't think anything about it, Alan. Let's not get in any hurry. Me and the girls are living here now and we need to get to know each other before we jump off into anything."

"All right. What do you want to know about me?"

"I can't think of anything right now. Oh yeah, I've got one. When and how did you learn to play piano so well? I've always wanted to learn to play."

"My mom was a piano teacher. I'd love to show you how to play. There's a lot I want to know about you, but right now, Lily wants to play ball." Alan placed a hand on Darlina's shoulder. "Can we talk more later?"

"Of course. You two go play and I'll finish unpacking."

She watched as Lily skipped alongside Alan. He couldn't be more different from Will. He was nice looking with his tall slender build, dark hair, moustache and brown eyes. And the girls adored him. Maybe she should give him a chance.

With that thought, her feelings for Luke came flooding through her heart. How could she ever be involved with anyone in an honest way? After leaving Will, she'd vowed never to try again. It seemed useless.

Luke owned her heart – lock, stock and barrel.

She wasn't going to rush into anything. After all, she was still legally married to Will. For now, it felt good to have a friend.

Once she got settled, she made a phone call to Will. "Hello, Will, it's Darlina. I need to talk to you."

"How are the girls?" Will inquired.

"They're growing like little weeds. I wanted to let you know where we are and I sure could use a little help. I've moved into the Premie house in Shreveport and need to buy some things for the girls. I've been working off and on through Kelly Girls, but it doesn't pay much."

"I don't really have any money, Darlina. I'd like to see the girls, though."

Darlina was silent for a minute. How odd that he referred to them as "the" girls, instead of "my" girls. They may as well not have a father for all the concern he showed.

"Are you still there?" Will asked

"Yes I'm still here. Tell you what. Why don't you come for Lily's birthday next month?"

"To Shreveport?"

"Yes. She'll be three years old."

"I don't know. I'll see."

"Will, you need to make an effort to see your children. Lily asks about you and Nicole isn't even going to know who you are."

"And whose fault is that?" he snapped. "I didn't leave you."

"I know. It was my choice, but still they are your children. Just think about coming for her birthday."

"I'll think about it. Take care of yourself, Darlina."

"You too. Goodbye."

After she hung up, she sat staring at the phone. She'd never understand how a man could just forget his children even if he wasn't the one who left. She sighed. Maybe he'd come, or at least send Lily a present.

As spring, 1979, made its colorful debut, Darlina began to allow her thoughts to entertain a romantic relationship with Alan. They'd spent hours upon hours talking. Darlina had told him everything about Luke and how she'd not been able to let him go even though he was locked away in prison. She talked about Will and how that relationship started and ended. It was important to her for Alan to know she was still legally married. She also made plans to file for a divorce soon.

Alan listened quietly to everything she had to say. Every response he gave was supportive and accepting.

They'd shared a few kisses and Alan had held her in his arms.

She had to confess that the idea of being intimate with him excited her. She longed for that special touch and had for a very long time. Will had never filled the bill when it came to intimacy.

The deep loneliness inside her cried out for relief. She needed desperately to feel like a woman again.

***

Nervous about getting undressed in front of Alan, Darlina stood with her back to him in his bedroom. She'd regained her slender figure after being pregnant with Nicole, but had no confidence in herself as a woman anymore since her time with Will.

Alan sat on the side of his big double bed. "Come here, Darlina."

She turned and walked into his arms.

"Please don't be scared or nervous. I think you're beautiful and I won't ever put you down in any way for any reason."

She brushed the top of his head with her lips. "Thank you. I'm just a little out of practice at this."

"Me too, but we'll figure it out together." Alan slipped Darlina's blouse over her head and cupped her full, firm breasts.

She liked that Alan didn't get in any hurry. Again, she couldn't help comparing him to Will and the vast difference between them. She avoided comparing him to Luke because she already knew that every man would always come up short.

Slowly, they undressed each other and lay on the bed. Alan was more concerned about making sure that Darlina got what she needed than taking care of his own throbbing needs.

She relaxed and let the moments of passion carry her to wave after wave of release.

God how she'd needed to be loved like this.

She closed her eyes and let her thoughts drift to Luke. In some ways, Alan was much like him in the way that he approached making love.

Luke had always made sure Darlina was satisfied before he released his own needs. Alan did the same.

Maybe she'd found someone she could build a life with, a man who loved and accepted her children without question.

She was willing to give this relationship a fair try.

Tomorrow, she'd write to Luke and tell him about Alan. Since she'd left Will, their letters had been filled with raw expression of their needs and desires.

If she was going to give Alan a chance, she'd have put all those words of love once more under lock and key.

Luke would understand and he would encourage her to give this relationship a try. She also knew he would pull back just as he had before when she'd married Will.

God, why did Luke have to be taken away? Why did she have to be left to struggle with finding someone who could replace him? She didn't have any answers.

She let Alan take her to heights of pleasure and release and once they were both spent, she lay in his arms and allowed tears to escape from her eyelids.

"Why are you crying?" Alan stroked her hair.

"I don't know. It's just what I do." Darlina snuggled close beside him loving the feel of his arms around her.

Tomorrow she'd write Luke.

"...Others had a wanderlust to roam. Open skies, campfires, smoke of coal and powerful locomotives bound their soul."

Chapter 35

L uke had enjoyed being a part of the set-up crew for outside concerts that came to perform at Leavenworth. He'd helped with several shows but B.B. King topped them all. Luke immediately loved the old man. Not only was he a great artist, but a good man. He told Luke he'd been coming to the prison to perform for the inmates for a good many years, but didn't know how much longer he'd do it. It seemed that the guards had torn up some of his equipment looking for contraband and it was getting costly.

Lexi, Luke's only daughter, had surprised him again a few months back by telling him that she was pregnant. On November 8, 1978, she gave birth to a baby boy. Luke was now a grandfather. There was no way to measure all the things he'd missed out on over the years he'd spent behind bars. He asked her to send a snapshot of the baby and he'd paint a portrait of him.

Gray began to creep around the edges of his long brown hair that he kept pulled back in a pony tail. He watched time crawl by in this place where life meant only what you could make of it.

He lived for tiny moments of excitement and challenge. The craft shop in Leavenworth had a working kiln and he conquered the art of making ceramics and pottery. Never being satisfied with ordinary molds, he carved scenes into them or molded pieces together to make unique and one-of-a-kind objects. Most everything he made carried the American Indian theme.

He still continued doing beadwork and painting, but shipped his leather stamping tools home to his mom, since Leavenworth had no leather crafts program.

When 1979 rolled around, he thought about the file of artwork ready and waiting for Willie Nelson. He understood these things took time, but accidents happened inside the walls every day and he'd like to live to see the album completed and released with his name listed as the cover designer.

His correspondence list had grown tremendously due to his strong association with the Prisoner Visitation and Support Group in Pennsylvania. Bert and Honey Knopp along with Robert Horton headed the group and one of their primary functions was to provide outside communication for prisoners.

Luke and Red both began to receive letters from all over the country, after their names appeared in a Prisoner Support Group newsletter.

He'd never give up on the music. His friendship with Judy Hedy had grown and she now managed his music portfolio. He welcomed her help and soon, she was sending Luke's songs everywhere she could find an open door.

Being a personal friend of Janie Fricke, she pitched some of his songs to her.

In the latest letter Luke had received from her, she listed everything she'd found in her search through his BMI catalog and also through the U.S. Copyright Office. She'd done a lot of work and he was more than grateful.

Luke kept a constant hope that something would eventually strike a chord with someone.

Red accused him of being too driven and suggested that he relax more. Maybe he was right, but he knew if he ever wanted to accomplish anything against all of the odds, he had to keep his nose to the grindstone. Tirelessly he wrote and recorded songs on the small tape recorders he borrowed from the chapel.

He organized all of his poems and put them together in a binder and then drew sketches to go along with many of them. He titled the poetry book "Etchings In Stone." For the cover, he drew a man who resembled Johnny Cash sitting with his guitar behind bars.

There was never an idle moment for Luke Stone.

Spring raised her lovely head and once again, Luke enjoyed spending his daily allotted time outside in the fresh air and sunshine.

On April 1st, he returned from the yard and took the stairs to the third floor where the craft shop was housed, along with the music room. Today, he wanted to finish an intricate stein he was making. He'd carved scenes into the sides of the stein, then attached a horse with a warrior shield on one side and a spear on the other. He was carving the top into an Indian chief's profile in full head dress. He hoped to get it all fired without anything cracking. He'd found a delicate balance between leaving a piece in too long or taking it out too early. In books he'd checked out from the library, he learned that different types of clay required different firing temperatures and times. Sometimes a piece might stay in the kiln for two to three days.

He gently placed the finished stein into the kiln for the first firing. He wouldn't open the door for two days. Hopefully, it would stay intact.

That evening, back in the cell, he shuffled through his growing stack of mail. He sat smoking a pipe and reading one letter after the other. He spent most of his evenings between lockdown and lights-out answering each one. To make sure he didn't miss one, he put a red checkmark on the envelope once he'd replied.

In the stack of mail today, there was one from Darlina. Funny how he could sense it before he saw it. He slipped the letter out and read it.

My Dearest Luke...I've told you about Alan and what a good friend he has been to me and the girls...We have become involved. Last night I slept with him and I'm going to give this relationship a real try. Luke, I hope you will understand that I need someone to care for me and the girls...I wish it was you, more than anything in the world, but that can't be...I'll love you always, Darlina.

She'd filled pages with things about the girls and the most recent job assignment, but the words about the relationship struck Luke's heart like a man's fist. Of course he didn't blame her. She shouldn't have to be alone with two little babies. He hoped this Alan person was as good a man as she described him.

He would write and encourage her to enjoy having someone to help ease her burdens and take care of her physical needs. Once again, he truly wanted her to be happy and all he could offer was paper and words. She needed and deserved more than that.

His romance with Sue had ended when she married a man from Fort Stockton. But, there were plenty of other women who seemed to enjoy writing sexy hot letters and he enjoyed reading them. He knew that none of it meant a thing, but still it was a nice reprieve from the daily existence behind the walls.

The next day, Mr. Nelms stepped out into the hallway as Luke passed by the music room on the way to the craft shop. "Hey, Luke. You got a minute?"

"Sure." Luke turned and followed him into the music room. "What's on your mind, Mr. Nelms?"

"We've got an unusual show coming in a couple of weeks that I want to assign you to. It's an old man who is the king of the hobos. His name is Steam Train Maury Graham and he does motivational speaking and a short music show."

"A hobo, huh? Well, I'll be happy to help. Will he need a guitar player?"

"I'd like for you to meet with him before the show and see what he needs. He's never been here before, so I don't know what to expect."

"Sure, I'd be happy to. Should I meet him down in the auditorium or here?"

"The auditorium. It'll be an afternoon show."

"All right."

"Have ya'll heard anything else about Sonny's record deal?"

"Nah. A few radio stations played it, but as far as I know, nothing's really come of it. He's up for parole next month. He's hoping for a music career on the outside."

"Well, he's got a good voice. If he can stay straight and keep away from the dope, he might do okay." Mr. Nelms chuckled.

"That's for sure. Be down at the auditorium by three on Sunday."

"I will, sir. Thanks." Luke continued on his way to the craft shop.

***

Steam Train Maury had a jovial, easy-going way. The hobo stood around five foot eight inches tall, had a long white beard and hair and carried a walking stick. A red bandana hung out of the back pocket of his overalls and a well-worn floppy hat adorned his head.

He looked up as Luke walked in, carrying his guitar case. "Howdy young man. Are you the one who's going to help me with my show today?"

Luke extended his hand. "I'm Luke Stone, Sir. It's a pleasure to meet you. What do you have in mind for the show?"

"Well, mostly I tell lots of stories from the road and always try to encourage the fellas, then I play a jaw harp and do a little jig dancing. You play guitar?"

"Yessir, I do."

"Then I'd like you to play along with me."

"What songs do you do?"

"Mostly old folk songs like *Salty Dog, Keep on the Sunny Side, Railroad Bill, Casey Jones* and a few songs like that. Ever hear of any of those?"

"I've played all of 'em before. I'm sure I won't have any trouble following you."

"Thank you, son."

Luke asked the old man to tell him of his travels and two hours rolled by without either of them realizing it. It seemed they had a lot in common, although from two different worlds.

Accompanying him on his guitar came easy to Luke. Afterward, Luke and Red were allowed to visit with him for a while longer. Luke liked the way Steam Train walked out into the audience and shook hands with the inmates. He had a genuine interest in his fellow-man and told Luke and Red that his goal was to help folks see that life wasn't all bad.

By the time he left the prison, Luke and Steam Train had exchanged addresses. Luke felt as if he'd found a long lost brother. Steam Train gave Luke one of his signature red bandanas with a steam engine train drawn in one corner and smoke billowing out of the stack.

Back in the cell that night, he and Red talked about the show and Steam Train.

"You know, I guess we were sorta like hobos ourselves, Red. Runnin' up and down the roads playin' music, never settling down." Luke polished his guitar.

"I suppose we were at that. I sure did like the old man and he promised to write. He said he'd get his hobo brothers to write too."

"Yep, I do believe he's a good man and a man of his word. We'll be hearing from him."

***

Luke began to worry that he hadn't had any communication from Connie Nelson or Willie in a long while. He hoped they hadn't forgotten him.

Late in May, he received a new issue of Country Music Magazine. Halfway through it, he came across an interview with Willie. One paragraph caught his eye and gave him renewed hope.

There's also another concept album, a la The Red-Headed Stranger, that's been knocking around for a year or so called The Convict And The Rose. It had, at one point gotten as far as having an album cover commissioned for it before getting shunted to the back burner. I would still like to do that one. Waylon and I had even talked about co-producing it. That could be sometime in the future, I guess...

Excerpt taken from May 1979 issue of Country Music Magazine

Willie hadn't forgotten about it. He had put it on the back burner for some reason.

Luke had never been one to put all of his eggs in one basket and he couldn't sit around doing nothing while waiting on Willie Nelson to cut this album.

He kept Judy Hedy as busy as she wanted to be getting songs copyrighted for him and pitching them to artists and agents in Nashville whom she knew personally.

He mailed boxes of oil paintings, ceramics and beadwork home to his mom. He learned that if he insured them, anything that arrived broken could be turned into money for her.

With Darlina involved in a seemingly solid relationship, her letters came further apart. He sensed happiness in her that he hadn't seen in a long time. Maybe this man would take care of her and the babies in the way they needed.

With that thought, his heart constricted. That should be his job. He'd never stop trying to get out from behind these forty foot walls.

The prison library offered lots of resources and access to law books. He wasn't allowed to check them out and take them to his cell, like he could reading books, but anytime he had a chance, he sat at a long wooden table inside the library with law books spread open all around him, making notes of cases that were similar to his.

There had to be a way out. He needed to be home with his family and Darlina.

By the end of 1979, a plan formed solidly in Luke's mind. One November evening after count and lockdown, Luke put his paints away. He'd been struggling to get an elk's hind leg just right and in frustration, decided to hide it with shrubbery.

"Hey, Red, I've got this idea that keeps rollin' around in my head."

"Oh hell, I'm almost afraid to ask."

"What if I write a song good enough to get the warden's attention and try to convince him to let us build a recording studio in here?"

"I don't know, Luke. What are you thinking?"

"You and I both know that at least eighty percent of inmates are here because of either alcohol or drugs or both. What if I write a song about that?"

"I guess it'd be worth a shot. This new warden seems like an okay guy."

"Military Jerry is a fair man as far as I can see. I think it's time to approach him with this idea. From the bottle to the needle is all I've come up with so far." Luke carefully cleaned his paint brushes.

"Kinda like ol' Sonny's life story. He started out as a regular guy driving a truck, taking a little speed and drinking a few beers and wound up hooked on heroin, and that brought him here."

"Yeah, exactly. I wonder about him now and then and hope he's stayin' straight out there."

Luke had never tried to write a contrived song before. Every song he'd written had been inspirations or dreams.

Still, it was worth a shot. If he could talk the warden into giving him permission to put things together, he knew he could build a functional studio.

With Judy working on the outside for him, he needed a way to record decent demos.

That night as he performed his Indian ceremony, he asked the Great Spirit to intervene and give him the right words to touch the warden's heart.

As he'd grown accustomed to, with the ending of his prayers, he always asked for protection and guidance for Darlina and for his family.

His heart felt content about her relationship with Alan. She deserved a reprieve.

So did he, but his time hadn't come yet. Freedom was a goal he'd never let go of.

"All about you brightly glows, currents of warmth and sweet peace around you flows."

Chapter 36

D arlina enjoyed the Christmas holidays in a way that she hadn't in many years. She strung festive garland and lights over the doorway of the girls' bedroom in the Premie house. Lily, going on four years old, loved helping. Nicole, seventeen months old and quite the little toddler, played with stray pieces of the garland. Darlina had fun shopping for the girls with Alan and helped him select a red scarf to give to his mother.

Two days before the big day, they loaded the car and drove to Alexandria, Louisiana where Alan's mother lived, for a pre-Christmas visit. Then on Christmas Eve, they drove to Darlina's parents where they found the house packed and noisy. Christmas was always a big celebration.

With his easy nature, Alan had no trouble blending with her family. She was thankful no one raked him over the coals about being with her but felt sure he could handle himself if they did.

It turned out to be a jovial time with both of the children receiving many presents.

As always, Darlina's mom filled the tables with delicious smelling cakes and pies. She and Alan laughed about how they were glad cakes and pies didn't have meat in them and they could indulge. Knowing they'd be there a couple of days, Darlina had packed vegetarian food.

"Darlina, these babies need some meat. Look how skinny Lily is. She looks underfed." Darlina's mom wasn't shy about voicing her opinion.

"No, Mama, she's just fine. They don't need meat. They need healthy food."

"You can't make me believe that a little meat would hurt them or you," her mother fumed.

Darlina laughed. "It's all right, Mom. You're entitled to your opinion. I brought food for us. We'll be just fine."

She'd watched her mother form a deep bond with the two babies over the months they'd lived in Shreveport. The children, in turn, became very attached to their granny.

For a brief moment, she thought of Will and hoped that he wasn't spending Christmas alone. He'd mailed her a fifty dollar check and asked her to buy the girls something for Christmas from him. She was glad he at least did that much since he'd completely ignored both of their birthdays.

When she'd looked into the process of filing for divorce, she found the expense to be beyond her means because she lived in a different state. Maybe Will would eventually meet someone he wanted a relationship with and file.

She regretted that she hadn't sent Luke a Christmas card this year. She'd never missed wishing him Merry Christmas since they'd started communicating.

As her relationship with Alan flourished, her letters to Luke were fewer, further between and shorter. Mostly, she talked about the girls and the different things they were learning and doing. She should have sent him a Christmas card, though.

Maybe he got plenty from other people and wouldn't miss hers. He had shared with her that he corresponded with over fifty people. Surely most of those fifty people sent Christmas cards.

It had been easier weaning herself from Luke with Alan in her life. Alan truly cared for her and her children and showed this in every way.

Once the children were put to bed on Christmas Eve and the house grew quiet, Darlina and Alan sat outside on the porch of her parents' home huddled close with a blanket wrapped around them.

"Merry Christmas, Darlina." Alan turned her face toward his and kissed her.

"Merry Christmas, Alan," she whispered. "It's been a good one."

"The best. I've loved seeing you smile and laugh with your family. Do you realize how much you've changed since you first came to Shreveport?"

"Changed? How?"

"Well, you hardly ever smiled and always looked as if you carried the weight of the world on your shoulders."

"I did."

"And now?"

"And now, I have you to help carry my burdens and you do it so willingly. Thank you."

"No, thank you. You've given me far more than I've given you. Those two little girls asleep in the house are what I always dreamed of. Of course, I pictured my own children with dark hair instead of blonde." He laughed.

"You've been great with them."

"Do you think you'll ever be able to say I love you to me?"

She shifted nervously. "Maybe. But one thing I can promise you is that if I ever do say it, I will mean it."

"That's good enough." He stood and pulled Darlina to her feet. "It's getting cold out here. Let's go in."

"You know we can't sleep together in my parents' house, right?"

"Of course. I've already got the sofa staked out." He wrapped his arms tight around her and kissed her again.

They walked into the warmth of the home, arm in arm.

"Goodnight," Darlina said in a hushed voice.

"Goodnight." Alan took the blanket they'd shared, wrapped it around himself and plopped down on the sofa.

Darlina lay awake beside Lily that night for the longest time, thinking. She didn't use any form of birth control. The idea of taking the pill again didn't appeal to her because it was not natural or organic. She'd have to find some other way.

Her mind drifted back to a time so long ago when she'd sat in the car outside her sister's house with Luke and he'd expressed his worry about her possibly not taking birth control. That day he'd told her he didn't need or want any more children and she'd assured him she was on the pill.

What would life have been like, if she'd had his child? She quickly brushed that thought away.

She was foolish to even think about it. She'd been too young back then and it would have made everything more difficult. Now she was glad she'd taken precautions.

Alan, she'd discovered, was three years younger and he wanted a family more than anything. However, he seemed content with Lily and Nicole and had never mentioned a baby of his own, until tonight.

Her last thought before she closed her eyes was of Luke, lying alone in a cold cell. Tears came and she asked God to please watch over him and let him find some warmth from somewhere for Christmas. With these thoughts she felt a little guilty for the happiness that had come her way. She knew Luke was pleased for her, but it didn't ease his loneliness and isolation. Nothing would until he was freed.

Maybe someday, Luke...maybe someday.

***

1980 turned out to be a year of adventure for Darlina. She, Alan and the girls packed up their cars and moved to Tampa, Florida mid-year. Lily had already turned four years old and Nicole would soon be two.

Darlina's parents had been devastated again with her putting this great distance between them and the children they'd grown so attached to. She'd explained that there was more opportunity for them in Florida and that she and Alan had made some solid connections through Guru Maharaj Ji's festivals they'd attended there.

Once they arrived and settled into a two bedroom apartment, Darlina began to think about finding work, but Alan suggested that she enjoy staying home with the children. He assured her that he could make a living for them.

He came home from work one evening to find a very excited Darlina.

"Guess what I found today!" She twirled around from the stove with a wooden spoon in her hand.

"What did you find today?" Alan extracted Nicole's arms from around his leg and picked her up.

"I found a job that I can do from home."

"You did? That's wonderful." He put his free arm around Darlina's shoulders.

"What is it?"

"I am going to type addresses onto metal cards for a company that uses them for their mailing lists. They will pay me per piece, so what I make will depend on how fast I work."

Alan kissed her cheek. "That's very cool and very resourceful, Darlina."

"At least I'll feel like I'm contributing to the household a little more."

"You've contributed more than enough, but if it makes you happy, then I'm tickled pink." He put Nicole down. Both girls tugged on his hand begging him to come and play with them. He glanced back at Darlina and blew her a kiss.

She smiled and blew a kiss back. "Supper will be ready in fifteen minutes."

She loved the way he'd bonded so closely with the girls and they both obviously adored him. He never refused their requests to play dress-up, have a tea party or color with them.

The things Darlina loved the most about living in Florida were the abundance of fresh fruits and vegetables year-round and the fact that they could be at the beach in less than an hour.

Even with her light skin, Darlina had a healthy tan for the first time in her life. She loved taking the girls to play in the sand at the beach, hunt seashells and jump in the water. On the weekends, Alan could join them and they romped and played like the children themselves.

Life was good for Darlina...except for the distance between her and her family, especially her parents.

Shortly after they'd gotten settled in Florida, she sent Luke a short letter telling him that they had moved. She wanted to make sure he always had her address.

She received a prompt reply and a surprising message and request. It seemed that Luke had a friend in Orlando, Margaret Meadows. He insisted that Darlina go visit her, and provided the address and phone number.

She'd think about it. She couldn't imagine why Luke wanted her to go see this woman and thought back to the time when Sue had come to visit her at the farm, because Luke asked her to.

She didn't hide anything from Alan and that evening read the letter to him. "What do you make of this request?"

"It can't hurt. There must be some reason he wants you to meet her. I say do what your heart tells you to do."

"Thank you, Alan."

"For what?"

"For allowing me to tell you any and everything."

"My pleasure, my dear." He pulled her into his arms.

The next day, Darlina called Margaret and explained that she was a friend of Luke's living in Tampa and would like to come visit her.

It was settled that Darlina and the girls would go to Orlando the next week.

The drive from Tampa to Orlando was a little over an hour and both of the girls continually asked if they were there yet.

Darlina had taken care to look her best. She didn't know what to expect, but she'd not have a repeat of how Sue had made her feel.

To her surprise, Margaret turned out to be a much older woman with white hair. Surely Luke wasn't involved romantically with this woman. It wasn't his style.

As they talked, she showed Darlina all the work she was doing for Luke. She had typed volumes of his poems and compiled them along with the artwork in attractive binders.

She'd done the same with his songs.

Proudly, she showed Darlina a guitar that Luke had made in prison and sent for her son to play.

Luke's artwork adorned her walls. Margaret's eyes glowed when she spoke of Luke and how she was trying to help get him out of prison by writing letters to the parole board, senators, congressmen and even the warden.

A beaded necklace Luke had made hung around her neck and she showed Darlina a beautiful ceramic bowl with a buffalo head on top for a handle that Luke had also made for her.

The visit was warm and comfortable. By the time Darlina left to drive back to Tampa, she'd made a decision. She would stop writing Luke altogether. She was involved with Alan. He was obviously involved on some level with Margaret and it was time to let it be. She didn't know if she could just stop, but she had to try.

After several months of living in Florida, she began to feel the pull to return to Louisiana.

"Alan, I've been thinking." She lay contentedly in his arms one November night after the girls had been put to bed.

"Oh no. That usually means trouble."

She lightly punched his arm. "That's not nice. No, really, I've been thinking that maybe we need to go back to Louisiana. Florida is so far away from our families and I know my mom is grieving for the girls in a big way. What do you think?"

"I love living in Florida, but to tell the truth, I've been thinking the same thing. The last time I talked to my mother, she begged me to move back. Let's turn it over to the Universe and see where it leads us."

"Okay. Funny that we've been thinking the same thing. To me, that means the Universe has already spoken."

"You may be right. We'll see what the next few months bring. Darlina?"

"Yes."

"Have I told you lately how happy you and the girls make me?"

"Yes."

"Well, I'm telling you again."

She snuggled close beside him. Maybe she could build a life with this man. It seemed to be heading that way.

It had been almost a year since she'd quit writing to Luke. She even made it through a whole day now and then without thinking about him. Every time she realized that, she felt a pang of guilt, but was learning to put it away in a safe place along with the memories and love she had for him.

She knew it was time to go back home. She thought about the word, home. She really hadn't felt like she'd had one since Luke had taken her back Abilene that dreadful day so long ago. But now, Louisiana felt like home.

Christmas in Florida was different from any other Darlina had ever spent. The weather was in the 70s and they played outside most of the day. She and Alan had bought presents for the girls. Lily and Nicole had been thrilled with new dolls, purses, crayons, color books and new pajamas for both.

1981 rolled around with balmy weather and they spent the entire day at the beach. Darlina packed a picnic basket and they played until everyone was exhausted.

Still, Darlina felt the urge to go back to Shreveport. She didn't want the girls to spend another Christmas away from their granny and pawpaw.

They'd both enjoyed being a part of the Premie community in Tampa and made some very good friends in the process, but nevertheless, family trumped friends.

After satsang, driving home with the windows down and a warm breeze blowing, Darlina turned to look at Alan. "It's time for us to go back to Louisiana now."

"I know. We've put it off as long as we can. I have loved living here, though."

"Me too. But tonight when we were doing meditation, the message came through strong. It's time."

"Then we'll just do it. I'll turn in my two week notice on Monday and you can do the same with your job. It's okay. It's like vacation is over."

Darlina laughed. "It has kinda felt that way, hasn't it?"

"It has for me. I've loved every minute of it and it sure was nice to only have a short drive to Miami to see Guru Maharaj Ji."

"Yes, it was. Do you realize that the festival was the only time Will has seen his children since I left him?"

"Yeah, I can't understand that. Nicole didn't even know who he was. If Lily hadn't warmed up to him, Nicole wouldn't have even let him pick her up."

"I know. That's just weird. But, he did tell me he is in a relationship with someone, so I'm happy for him."

"We've been taught that our life path has a reason and season for everything that happens along it. We just have to trust that the Universe knows what's best for all of us."

"So true. It's so much easier when we let go of trying to control it."

Alan reached across and took her hand in his and they rode the rest of the way home listening to the two children chattering back and forth in the backseat.

Almost two weeks later, Darlina drove down the main street in Tampa on her way to turn in the typing machine along with the metal cards she'd completed and collect her pay.

Without thinking, she switched on the radio and dialed in a country music station.

Crystal Gayle sang *If You Ever Change Your Mind* followed by Anne Murray's *Can I Have This Dance*. Then John Denver's *Take Me Home Country Roads* rang out from the radio. The message was clear.

It was time to go back home.

"I was caught up in dreams, 'til dreaming caught up with me..."

Chapter 37

As fall arrived at Leavenworth Penitentiary, Luke received what he considered a real luxury. Because of his exemplary behavior, and good relations he'd established with the associate warden and guards, he was moved from cell block D to a one-man cell in block A.

To him, this represented a milestone. No more sharing the sink, the toilet or the space with anyone, not even Red. And, they had heating and cooling in cell block A.

He made short work of setting up his easel and paints. He then created a special place in one corner of the cell for his guitar. On a small table, he laid his bead loom and set the bead box along with his writing tablet beside it.

He used scotch tape to put up pictures of his family, some of the women he wrote to on a regular basis and last of all, a snapshot of Darlina and her two babies, on the walls.

Home sweet home. He stood in the middle of the 5' X 8' cell. It was a far cry from where he wanted to be, but better than where he had been.

Most of the inmates in cell block A were long-timers. They were interested only in doing their time the easiest way possible, which meant less homosexual activity, drugs or gambling. Luke fit right into that category.

He'd miss seeing Red every day, but it seemed that his friend had distanced himself over the past few months.

Red tended to sink into bouts of depression and Luke had no patience for it. He saw depression as a waste of precious and limited time.

In the months that followed Steam Train Maury's visit to the prison, Luke and Red both began to receive letters from hobos all over the United States and even one from Australia.

Hobo Bill Mainer, Hafey Zale, Mountain Dew, The Alabama Hobo, Horace Hampton, Reefer Charlie, Ole The Bo, Slow Freight Ben, Bud Filer, Don Howell and Lizzie Williams were a few who wrote to Luke and Red. Hobo Bill and his wife even came to visit.

Luke had occupied many hours of his time making beaded necklaces for them. He created pen and ink drawings of Steam Train and Hobo Bill and most of all, he loved doing it.

As the friendships and knowledge of the hobos grew, Luke penned songs about these men of the road. *Wheels of Steel, Come August In Britt, The Hobo King, Happy Hobo, Hoppin' John,* and *The Lady Hobo* were songs he couldn't wait to record and share.

He learned many things about the survival skills of these unique men and women.

Some of the hobos were highly educated and intelligent. They were honorable men and never asked for handouts without offering to work in exchange. They liked freedom to roam. It was in their blood, as they so stated in their letters. Often, when Luke read their letters, he could see himself sitting around a campfire with them, exchanging stories.

Even with the increasing correspondence from the hobos, it was a bleak year, more so than most.

With his declining health, Bobby and his family moved back to Texas. They returned to Coleman in order to be close to his mom. Luke's heart ached for the hardships his family faced. Dammit, he should be there to make things easier.

Darlina's letters had stopped. Luke missed the endearing words from her that he'd come to treasure. When Christmas passed with no word, he knew that she was trying to move on. He truly hoped that she'd found happiness this time.

He had no right to disturb her life if indeed, she had found what she needed. Nevertheless, when he closed his eyes at night to sleep, it was her sweet face he saw. The perfumed fragrance of her hair and silky smooth skin invaded his dreams. How foolish to keep wishing for something that could not be.

And yet, he did.

***

As 1981 made its way through the prison walls, Luke continued to craft the "Bottle To The Needle" song. It had to be spit-shined and polished before he would try the pitch.

He and Red talked to every musician who came into the music room on a regular basis about the idea of a recording studio. Luke could see a sparkle in their eyes at the prospect of having the means to record their music.

Finally, in April, Luke felt the song was ready. He and Red sat across from each other in the music room on the third floor playing and singing.

FROM THE BOTTLE TO THE NEEDLE

Living without Love is so hard to do
What good are memories when I need to touch you?
Sometimes tears won't wait for night to fall
Wish I could forget you
Have no memories to recall
From the bottle to the needle
The crutch became a master
Now I'm just a slave
Nothing to show for living
My life ain't nothing today
It's one way from the bottle to the needle
From the needle it's not too far on to the grave
I was caught up in dreams
'Til dreaming caught up with me
It's hard to know that's how it's gotta be
I kept on hoping one day you'd call
Just a fool's dreams,
Worse than no dreams at all

When Luke rang out the last chords of the song, the silence that followed was a stark contrast to the strong emotion in his voice.

"What do you think, Red?"

"I think we nailed it, hoss." Red leaned back in his chair and stretched his lanky legs out in front of him.

"I'm gonna talk to Marvin Hightower the first chance I get and see if he'll let us play it for him. He's a good dude for an associate warden." Luke polished his guitar with a scrap of t-shirt material.

"Well, we ain't going nowhere, so if he wants to hear it, we'll be available."

Luke grinned. "Reckon you're right, stud. I'll be damn sure to point that out."

When Luke arrived back at his cell that evening, mail call delivered another bundle of letters. He thumbed through them and lit his pipe.

Perhaps there would be a letter from Darlina, although he'd learned not to get his hopes up.

The last note he'd received from her had been before he'd asked her to visit Margaret. He truly hoped Darlina was happy. That was all he had ever wanted for her.

Margaret had glowingly written after Darlina's visit. She told Luke how much she'd enjoyed meeting Darlina and that she was beautiful. Luke acknowledged that he owed Margaret a lot, but he sent her a lot of things he'd made in exchange for her work.

She was lonely and had romantic ideas about him, but from the pictures he'd seen, she wasn't his type. Nevertheless, she was more than willing to help him. He never made any promises for the future. Hell, a man in his situation couldn't make many promises about anything.

***

It was late July of 1981 when Luke received a short letter from Connie Nelson. She apologized for being out of touch and informed him that Willie had been forced to abandon "The Convict And The Rose" project. She briefly explained that the IRS had started an investigation on Willie's tax returns and that he'd been advised by his attorneys not to have any association with a convict right now. She promised that if they ever resurrected the project, they would use his artwork.

Luke sat staring at the bars that made up the front of his cell after he finished reading the letter. Well, there was nothing he could do about it. He'd store the artwork away and maybe they'd eventually resurrect the project.

If they did, he'd have his part ready and waiting.

It neared September 1981 when Luke had the opportunity to pitch his song and idea.

"Mr. Hightower, I've written this song that I really want you to hear. You know how a large percent of the inmates are here either directly or indirectly because of drugs or alcohol?"

"Of course I do, Luke." Marvin Hightower was of slight build, with a receding hairline and warm green eyes. "It's a damned shame too."

"I've proven that the only way to make anything better in here is to be positive. I want a chance to put together a recording studio. I truly believe that it could be a straightforward program to help give prisoners confidence and something to be optimistic about."

Mr. Hightower rubbed his chin. "Do you have the song lyrics with you?"

"Right here in my pocket." Luke handed him a folded piece of paper.

Mr. Hightower pulled his glasses out of his shirt pocket and read the words. "Tell you what. I'll set up a time to hear the song and I'll see if I can get the warden to come along too."

"You just let me know. I'm here twenty-four-seven and I'll be glad to play it for you anytime." Luke extended his hand and Mr. Hightower shook it.

"You're all right, Stone. But, I don't understand why in the hell you don't cut that mess of long hair off. Don't you know you'd be hassled a lot less if you had a regular short haircut?"

"Reckon you're right, Sir, but I want to prove that not everyone who has long hair is a junkie. I never mind being piss-tested."

Mr. Hightower shook his head. "I'll be in touch."

"Thank you."

Luke couldn't wait to tell Red of their conversation. This could be something beneficial for the image of the whole prison.

Two weeks later, Luke and Red stood in front of microphones in the music room. The warden, associate wardens and the supervisor of the education and recreation department sat in chairs facing them. The men were gathered to hear the song and Luke's pitch.

Luke spoke into his microphone. "Thank you for giving me the opportunity to play my song for you. What I'm tryin' to do is get some sort of little recording studio set up in here. I write songs. Lots of guys in here write songs and we have no way to send 'em out. Nobody wants you to send 'em sheet music anymore. They all want some sort of demo cassette, no matter how poor the quality is. So what I propose and request is that you give me a room that I can set up a studio in. I had lots of experience recording music on the outside and I'd like to use that knowledge now in here. So, here we go. This song is called "From The Bottle To The Needle.""

Luke and Red strummed the chords and Luke lent his voice to the lyrics. He watched Warden O'Brien's face as he sang. He could normally read people pretty well, but he saw nothing in the man's expression that provided a clue as to his thoughts.

When the last notes rang out, Luke and Red quietly waited.

After a long minute, the warden put his hands together and started clapping. The other men looked at each other and followed suit.

Warden O'Brien got to his feet. "Stone, I'm going to take a chance on you. I'll designate an area for you to put your recording studio, but there are two things you need to know."

Luke stood eye to eye with the warden. "What's that, Sir?"

"The prison has no funds to appropriate to this project, so you are on your own as to how you put it together." He placed his hand on Luke's shoulder. "The second thing you need to know is that if you screw up, I'll come down hard on you."

Luke couldn't wipe the grin off of his face. "Thank you, Warden. You can trust me. You'll see. This will be good for the morale of the men and for the prison."

Warden O'Brien turned to the supervisor of education and recreation. "Paul, I want you to help this man anyway you can with this project."

Paul Witherspoon nodded.

Warden O'Brien left the room, as did most of the other men. Mr. Witherspoon and Marvin Hightower stayed behind.

"Mr. Stone, come up here tomorrow and meet with Mr. Nelms. He'll assist you in going through discarded equipment. I'll also let you know tomorrow what area the Warden designates for this project."

"Thank you, Sir. I appreciate it."

Luke couldn't wait to get started. There would be a lot of work to do, with very limited resources, but convicts could be very resourceful and by involving as many men as possible, he could make it happen.

He and Red talked non-stop as they meandered through the maze of hallways back to the cell blocks. Luke noted the sparkle in his eyes and hoped that this would bring him out of depression.

"We're gonna do this, hoss. I can't wait to see what I can start scrounging up." He slapped his old friend on the back. "See you tomorrow, stud."

Red waved over his shoulder as he turned toward his cell block.

Sleep would be of no interest to Luke Stone tonight. He got a new writing tablet and jotted down notes; things he didn't want to overlook or forget. He would make damn sure that this recording studio turned out to be something the men could take pride in. A showplace the warden would be proud to take anyone who toured the prison.

When he had several pages of notes, he laid the paper aside and closed his eyes.

Excitement coursed through his veins like rivers rushing to the sea. He couldn't wait for morning to arrive so he could get started.

As far as he knew, there had never been a studio put together behind walls.

This would make history.

"I need you with too great an affection. Still you need freedom, sometime of your own. That's why I'm walking, walking alone..."

Chapter 38

S pring in East Texas, presented a breathtaking sight, only two days after Darlina and the girls arrived back in Shreveport, Louisiana. The reunion between the two little girls and their granny and pawpaw brought tears and smiles at the same time. Darlina's mother held both of them on her lap, not daring to let them go.

"Granny has missed you girls terribly." She looked up at Darlina. "And you too, Darlina."

"I know, Mama. We've missed you too. But, we're back now and we aren't moving that far away ever again." She didn't miss the increasing gray strands of hair, the wrinkles and age spots on the backs of her hands.

"Lord, I hope not. Let me keep these babies for a few days while you get settled back in." She patted the children's backs.

"I was going to ask if they could stay here with you while I look for a job and a babysitter. It's time for me to find a good job that pays enough to get by on."

Darlina's mother raised her eyebrows. "Have you and Alan split up?"

"No. It's just time I started earning my way and taking care of my babies. He would have come with us today, but he's out looking for a job. He did ask me to tell you and Daddy hello."

"He's a nice young man, Darlina. You could do a lot worse."

Darlina laughed. "You mean I have done a lot worse?"

"Well, that too. Anyway, it's good to have you girls back home."

Before the end of the week, Darlina had a six-month job assignment through Kelly Girls at an oil refinery near the outskirts of Shreveport.

Alan found a job at a local supermarket and they settled back into living at the Premie house.

Now, to find a suitable babysitter. Darlina had never left her girls with anyone except family. She wanted to find someone who did babysitting in their home instead of a daycare center.

She read the classifieds and found an ad that looked promising. A middle-aged woman wanted four children to keep in her home. Darlina promptly called and set up a meeting with her.

The woman seemed genuinely warm and loving towards the children that were in her home and Darlina arranged to bring the girls on Monday for a trial run.

Darlina's position at the oil refinery, secretary to the maintenance department, seemed perfect for her. She had to be at work at 7 am, but got off at 3. That left a good part of the day to be with the girls.

During her first week on the job, she began to think that no one ever came into these offices. Other than the man training her, she didn't see another soul.

Finally, on Thursday afternoon, men filtered in. The quiet turned to chaos and from all of the talk, she learned there had been a major fire in a unit of the refinery and they'd been working around the clock.

Darlina finally had her feet on the ground. She enjoyed working again and learning new skills.

Finding the girls laughing and happy when she picked them up from the babysitter each day made her comfortable with that choice.

But as the weeks passed by, things changed between Darlina and Alan. She found herself looking at him differently. She'd never noticed how immature he acted at times and why had it never bothered her before that he was terribly thin?

She told herself maybe it was because of the men she now worked with every day. Alan hadn't changed, so it had to be her.

She thought of Luke and wondered how he was. If he tried to reach out to her, he wouldn't know where to find her. Perhaps she should write, but what would she say after almost a full year? She'd think about it.

Two months after starting the new job, Darlina overheard a conversation at the end of the hall.

"Hey, Corky. We're going to go get a drink after work. Wanna go?"

"Hell yeah, I wanna go," the shop foreman replied. "Where are you going?"

"There's a new bar over on Youree Drive. We thought we'd check out their happy hour."

"All right. Ya'll holler at me when you're ready to leave."

As Corky walked past Darlina's office, he stuck his head in. "You wanna go have a drink after work with us, kid?"

"I don't know, Corky. I need to go pick up my kids."

"Oh come on. How long's it been since you had a drink?"

"Too many years to count," she laughed.

"You don't have to stay long. Come on. My treat."

"Let me check with the babysitter and I'll let you know."

The thought of going to a bar made Darlina's stomach tie up in knots. She hadn't been out for a drink since before she'd left Abilene with Will. She might feel out of place, but it could be fun.

Being the only female in the maintenance office, the men took her under their wing and treated her like a little sister. It reminded her of the days in Abilene when she'd worked at the boiler factory.

She made a quick call to the babysitter and was told there would be no problem with her picking the girls up late.

She took a deep breath and walked into the hallway. "Okay, you guys, I'll go with you to happy hour, but I'm taking my car 'cause I have to go get my girls. Ya'll just tell me where you'll be and I'll meet you there."

One of the men wrote down an address and handed it to her. "Cool. We'll see you there."

Darlina parked her car at the front entrance of the bar, grabbed her purse and walked in.

The cigarette smoke, music blaring from the jukebox, glasses clinking behind the bar and the dim lights transported her back to a time when she'd accompanied Luke every night as he played music in bars much like this. Her heart thudded and her mouth went dry. In that moment, her body, mind and soul ached for Luke so strongly that she feared she might faint.

Her co-workers waved at her from a corner table. "Over here, Darlina."

She covered the short distance to them and they pulled out a chair for her.

"This is nice." Darlina's voice cracked.

"It's an okay place. They've only been open three months or so." What would you like to drink, Darlina?" her boss, Phil, asked.

She wracked her brain trying to remember what she used to drink so long ago.

"They've got kick-ass margaritas here," one of the men suggested.

"I'll have a margarita, then." She forced a smile.

Why did she feel so nervous? Did she feel guilty for being here, like she was doing something wrong? She tried to examine the feeling, but the cold frosty drink was soon in her hand and by the time she drank half of it, she relaxed.

Just as she finished and stood to leave, a man she'd never seen walked into the bar and immediately joined the group.

"What the hell are ya'll doing here?" he asked, shaking hands with each one.

"Wettin' our whistle. What are you doing here?" Phil slapped him on the back.

"Wait, wait, wait. Who is this young lady?"

"Oh sorry. This is our new secretary, Darlina, and this clown is one of our contractors, Doug."

Doug gallantly kissed the back of her hand. "Well well. So nice to meet you, Darlina. Where are you running off to?"

Shyly she answered. "I have to go pick up my children."

"Shit! Just my luck. I was hoping you'd run off to Mexico with me." He pulled an empty chair over from another table.

Darlina picked up her purse. "No such luck today, but it's nice to meet you, Doug. Thanks for the drink, guys. I'll see you tomorrow."

When she reached her car, she slid in and sat for a solid minute or two before starting the engine.

What had just happened in there? She'd found herself attracted to Doug with his dark good looks and easy flirtatious talk. What was wrong with her? She was in a relationship with Alan and Doug was probably married with a house full of kids.

Somehow, the thought of going back to the Premie house and Alan no longer appealed to her.

A familiar restlessness crept up inside. She was changing. She needed something more than satsang and organic living. She needed to be free to make her own choices. She needed to live her life for once without someone telling her what she should or shouldn't do.

Shaking off the mood, she drove to pick up her two rays of sunshine from the babysitter.

The next week, she received a petition for divorce in the mail from Will. She read it over carefully. It was obvious he'd drawn up the document himself. It did, however, state that he would pay her $100 per month in child support if she relinquished all rights to any of his personal possessions or property.

She signed it in front of a notary and put it back in the mail the next day. Just that easy, she was divorced from Will.

They spent another noisy but joyous Christmas at Darlina's parents' house. Alan didn't accompany them this holiday. Instead, he went to his mother's house.

Over the next few months, Darlina made solid plans to move out of the Premie house. She began spending every weekend looking at apartments.

She tried to put distance between her and Alan, but that wasn't easy living in the same house.

Finally in April she found an apartment she could afford in a fourplex building not far from Kings Highway.

Once she had the girls in bed that night, needing to clear the air between them, she went in search of Alan. She found him sitting outside on a picnic table and sat down beside him.

"Alan, I know you don't want to hear this, but I've found an apartment and we're moving. I put the deposit down and Mom and Dad are coming next weekend to help me."

Alan stared straight ahead. "I don't understand, Darlina. I thought we had something really special. What happened? Was it something I did?"

"Of course not. I've tried over and over to tell you that it has nothing to do with you at all. It's me. I've changed inside. I need independence. It's that simple."

"Are you writing to Luke again?"

"No. It has nothing to do with Luke either. I wish I could explain it in a way you could understand. I guess it goes all the way back to the way I was raised in the strict holy-roller religion. The feeling I have now is much like the one I had then. I needed to be free and live life in whatever way I chose and that is what I need now. I never intended to hurt you." She placed a hand on his arm. "Look at me, Alan."

"Why? So you can see my tears? So you can make me feel worse by pitying me?"

Darlina gasped. "Lord, no. Alan, you know me. I'm not that way at all."

Alan turned to look at her. "I don't think I ever really knew you." He stood and walked inside the house.

Darlina sat for the longest time struggling with her thoughts. Why did she feel so driven? Why couldn't she just be content to stay there with Alan? Finally, she stood and walked slowly back to the house. The truth was that she couldn't be content with this lifestyle anymore for whatever reason. If she'd forced herself to stay it would only have made things worse.

This was new to Darlina. When she'd left Will, he hadn't seemed to care all that much, but Alan was crushed. The only thing she could compare it to, was the devastation she'd felt when Luke had dumped her at her sister's house in Abilene.

The next weekend, her mom and dad came in their pickup with a load of furniture they'd collected from garage sales and to help them move.

Atlas Oil Refinery hired her as a permanent employee once her six-month contract with Kelly Girls ended. She was making more money than she'd made in her life and she liked her job.

When moving day came, Alan disappeared and Darlina didn't see him again until the following Saturday night at satsang.

They sat in the customary circle and Alan gave his testimony. Tears coursed down his face while he spoke and looked directly at Darlina.

"I've lost something that can't ever be replaced. I search inside of myself for the peace that comes from Guru Maharaj Ji and all I find is more pain. I need the help of my brothers and sisters." His bottom lip quivered.

Darlina felt the tears rushing from under her eyelids. What had she done? She would simply have to stop coming to satsang and remove herself from the Premie community. She couldn't stand watching Alan cry and seeing her only heightened his emotions.

She stood and fled into the adjoining room where a teenage girl played with her children. "Come on, Lily and Nicole. It's time for us to go."

Lily clamored. "But Mama you said we could play here."

"I know what I said, Lily, but we have to go to our apartment now." She didn't want either of the girls to see Alan crying. They wouldn't understand.

Lily balked. "No, Mama. I want to stay here."

She reached for Lily's hand, picked up Nicole and exited through the kitchen.

Her thoughts ran rampant. What kind of karma was she creating for herself? And why was she so driven? There was something in her that she couldn't explain and this time it had nothing to do with Luke, Alan or Will. She simply wanted to re-join the world and feel alive.

She couldn't wait to meander through stores and look at all the new clothes, makeup and perfume she'd deprived herself of for the past seven years. It reminded her of when she'd left home at the tender age of eighteen with the desire to try everything that had been forbidden by the church and her mother.

She'd call Alan in a few days and see if they could talk rationally. She needed to tell him how sorry she was for hurting him so much.

The neighbor directly above Darlina's apartment was a single mother with one little girl who was a year older than Lily. They'd hit it off when they first met and the children loved having a playmate.

Three weeks had passed since the incident at satsang. Darlina had talked to Alan on the phone but didn't feel like she'd made much progress getting through to him.

Anna Marie, Darlina's neighbor, knocked on her back door.

"Hi." Darlina opened the door. "Come in."

"Hey, what are you doing tomorrow night?"

"Nothing. Why?"

"There's a great band playing at a club over in Bossier City and I want you to go with me."

"I don't know, Anna Marie. Who would watch the girls?"

"We'll find someone. Please go with me. I don't want to go by myself."

"Let me think about it."

"Don't think too long, 'cause I'm going with or without you. Do you like country music?"

"I love country music."

"Then you have to go. This band's the best."

"All right. Let me see if I can find a babysitter."

"Ask if they'll keep Roxanne too and I'll pay for her."

"Okay. I'll let you know.

Darlina only knew one person she could ask to babysit, the woman who kept the girls during the week. She didn't know if Mrs. Gray would want to keep them plus Roxanne on a weekend, but she could ask. Just as she walked to the phone to make the call, it rang.

"Hello."

"Darlina, this is Alan. Are you busy?"

"Not really. I was just about to call the girls' babysitter to see if she could keep them tomorrow night."

"Where are you going?"

"My neighbor from upstairs asked me to go with her to hear a band in Bossier City and we need a babysitter."

"Why don't you let me keep them? That was the reason I was calling you. When will you be coming back to satsang?"

"I don't know, Alan. I would like to, but don't want to upset you any more than I already have."

"It won't upset me. I really need to see the girls."

"Then, why don't you come over and keep them Saturday night so I can go out with Anna Marie?"

"All right. I can do that."

"That'd be great. The girls will be so excited. Oh, and you'll have one extra little girl. Her name is Roxanne and she's a year older than Lily. Anna Marie and I would be more than happy to pay you."

"You don't have to pay me. I'll enjoy it. What time?"

"Around eight or so. Are you sure it's okay with you?"

"I'm sure. See you then."

The thought of going with Anna Marie to a nightclub to hear live music excited her. It had been years, and she'd missed it.

Of course, the idea of hearing a country band brought memories of Luke back around so strongly that it almost took her breath away.

If she lived to be a hundred years old, she'd never forget the intense sweet love they'd shared.

She'd tried with drugs, meditation and relationships, but they'd only worked temporarily. Luke was as much a part of her as the blood that coursed through her veins. Again, the tug came at her heart to contact him.

Saturday night found her both excited and nervous. She changed clothes several times before settling on a lavender blouse and blue jeans. In some crazy way, she felt as if she was getting dressed to go hear Luke play.

Alan arrived in a jovial mood to watch the girls and Darlina bounded up the stairs to Anna Marie's apartment.

"Come on, let's go. I'm ready." Darlina sang out.

She couldn't wait to hear the music and let the songs take her back to another day, a lifetime ago, when she was Luke Stone's woman.

"Not much to cling to, though in fond remembrance I find, they're all that's left of me...Those special memories of mine."

Chapter 39

With drive and determination equal to that of the marines storming ashore at Iwo Jima, Luke tackled creating the recording studio.

The day after he'd received the warden's blessing, Luke met with Mr. Nelms. They explored boxes and bins of discarded and broken equipment. They found several things worth fixing, including headphones.

The area designated to the project turned out to be a third floor corner area down a narrow hallway. It consisted of two rooms that had been used for storage for many years. The first order of business would be to empty them.

Luke solicited the help of every convict who'd played music with him or who showed any interest in the studio idea.

He found an old tube type recorder in the prison industries shop that hadn't worked in years and they willingly donated it. When he contacted the inmates in the machine shop about making a capstan for it, they readily agreed. Luke took it apart and cleaned every piece. When it was all said and done, the old machine worked almost as good as new.

Red helped Luke carry all of the broken equipment to the electronic shop to be repaired.

Mr. Nelms became instrumental in coordinating and working with supervisors in other departments. He shared Luke's excitement about the project.

By the time winter of 1981 rolled in with a vengeance, the rooms were finally emptied. Luke along with Red and two other inmates painted the walls and scrubbed every inch of the concrete floors. The supervisor of recreation and education advised Luke that he couldn't remove any of the doors or alter the structure of the rooms. Otherwise he was free to do whatever he chose.

All of the work had to be done after their daily jobs and before lockdown at night. One thing Luke had learned in prison was patience. If he kept going, one tiny step at a time, much like doing beadwork, it would all come together.

Once the repaired equipment came back, Luke carried it up to the main room that he envisioned as the recording area. He discovered that he could use transistor radios as amplifiers for the headphones. He put together bits and pieces from different types of electronics to make a homemade mixing board. With materials donated by prison industries, he built a console to house the mixing board.

Little by little, with the help of anyone he could enlist, it started to take shape.

Luke recruited one of the convicts who worked in the kitchen to ask his supervisor to donate all of the empty egg crates to the project. Gluing them onto the concrete block walls would make a great sound buffer.

The floor was another problem. The sound would bounce off the concrete without something to absorb it.

The answer to that issue came in January 1982. The carpet in the chapel was being torn out and replaced. Luke met with the chaplain and asked for the discarded carpet.

Luke found most everyone he approached willing to help.

When he heard that they were changing out the curtains on the auditorium stage, he and Mr. Nelms confiscated them. Luke took them to the clothing room and the inmates who repaired clothes cut and sewed them so they would cover the barred windows in the studio rooms.

The last and final touches were Luke's unique artwork skills. He painted music notes on the walls, camouflaged doors and painted concrete blocks different colors so that it looked like patterned tile.

Three other inmates, also artists, worked together to paint a large mural of Willie Nelson, Dolly Parton and Crystal Gayle on one wall.

The project took them close to three months to complete, but the artwork was impeccable.

Several associate wardens and guards came around out of curiosity to watch the progress. When they saw the dedication and perseverance Luke demonstrated, and how he was bringing the convicts in to work together, they began to show a level of respect.

One guard even came up on his day off and worked alongside Luke, gluing egg crates to the walls.

As the 1982 spring melted into summer, Luke felt that he was finally ready to put it all together and see if he could make a recording.

He stood in the middle of the main recording room and looked around. Excitement ran through him like an electrical current. The countless hours, weeks and months of hard work and dedication had paid off.

The door opened and Red strode in with a big grin on his face.

"We did it, Luke." He walked toward Luke and slapped him on the back.

"Damned sure did, hoss. I'm ready to try out this baby and see if we can make it work. Grab my guitar over there and I'll do a test run."

Red opened Luke's guitar case and picked up the Martin. It now had large pieces of turquoise and silver glued onto it that Luke had hand cut and soldered to fit. Even the pick guard was shiny silver.

Sitting at the console and mixing board, Luke threaded a spool of blank tape through the machine. He flipped on switches and plugged a microphone into the system. "Step up to the mic, Red, and let's see if we can hear through these head phones."

"Test one, two. Test one, two. Can you hear me, Luke?"

Luke nodded. "I can hear you. It's not real great, but I can hear. Play a few chords."

Red plugged the guitar into an amplifier that they'd brought up from the music room and strummed.

Luke fiddled with the knobs and slides until he could hear the guitar clearly. "This won't be anything we'll keep, but strum and sing a little of that last song we worked up, *Trouble Is*."

"Okay." Red stood closer to the microphone, played the opening licks and began to sing. "When first we met, I knew you were something special. Just for a start, you have that smile, one that tears me apart, your eyes promising all the while. Trouble is, do you feel the same too? Has a dream come true?"

Motioning for Red to continue singing, Luke made adjustments. He let the tape run until the song ended.

"Let's see what we got, stud."

Red pulled a chair over. Luke rewound the tape and flipped the control switch to play.

It started out somewhat garbled but by the end of the song, it leveled out and sounded decent.

A hint of tears glimmered in his eyes when he turned to his old friend. "By God, Red, we've got ourselves some sort of a recording studio."

Lighting a smoke for them both, Red leaned back. "I didn't see how in the hell you were gonna pull it off, but it came together."

"It's a bit of magic I've learned. If you're willing to work hard enough for something, you can bring it into existence. It all starts with a single thought."

"Shit, Luke, you're always talkin' over my head. I don't know what any of that means. All I know is that we have a recording studio and can start making some demos."

"Spread the word to anyone interested that I want the best players I can get to work with us on these recordings. If they'll help with my songs, I'll trade out some studio time for them and record theirs."

"Hell, it's almost like doing business on the outside."

"Almost, but not quite. It's time to head downstairs to our cages. Help me roll up these cables and put everything away."

Luke turned back for one last look, switched off the lights, and closed the door behind them.

Guitar case in hand, Luke and Red walked the length of the hallway to the stairs, then down three levels. At the bottom, they went their separate ways.

Luke Stone sat in his small cell that night, thinking about his accomplishments. Almost twelve years had slid by since the heavy doors and iron bars closed behind him, locking him away from the world.

Creating something worthwhile, something positive in a negative place, against all odds, had been his daily goal for many of those years.

He wondered where Darlina was and if she and the little girls were all right. She was trying to forget him, and in all honesty, he didn't blame her. After all, he'd encouraged her to do just that. Still, he couldn't help wishing for a way to share the excitement and gratification of his latest achievement. More than anything he wanted her to be proud of him. He'd worked hard to earn that.

Almost angrily, he pushed the thoughts away. No point in dwelling on empty wishes.

Turning his attention back to the recording studio, he looked through his belongings for the notebook he'd written media contact information in.

Now that the studio was completed, it was time to get some publicity.

The rest of the evening was spent composing letters. They would go out in tomorrow's mail.

Within a few weeks, he was contacted by Mr. Howard Goodman, a reporter from The Kansas City Times, requesting an interview.

Luke knew the red tape would take time, so he took Mr. Goodman's letter to the associate warden to properly respond to the request. He would wait.

His hobo friend, Steam Train Maury, would be coming to the prison in July to do a show and he couldn't wait to show off the studio.

With the main work of putting together the studio behind him, Luke now turned his energy and drive into recording as many songs as he could. He was ready to start mailing out cassette tapes.

He'd always told Red that if they could write something good enough, Nashville would break down the prison walls to get them out. Even though that was an exaggeration, he knew that if just one of his songs caught the attention of someone with influence, he certainly stood a better chance of gaining his freedom.

If hard work and perseverance paid off, he damned sure had something grand to look forward to.

He had a list of songs he felt were ready to record. He needed musicians and harmony singers. A lot of inmates professed to play music, but when it came right down to it, Luke had only found a small handful who could actually fill the bill. Out of that handful, there were two or three he felt could play well enough to use on recordings.

He listed the title of each song and beneath it the instrument arrangement he wanted. Next to that, he wrote each man's name that he knew for sure could play an instrument.

When he finally put his tablets of notes away for the night and lay on his bunk, he gave thanks to the Great Spirit for his generous blessings.

As much as he tried not to, his last thoughts of the day always turned to Darlina. He whispered prayers for protection of her and the babies. Maybe someday, he'd hear from her again. He counted the months since he'd last received a letter and it was now going on two years. A deep sadness covered him like a wet woolen blanket. Maybe she was gone for good. Wherever she was, he wished her well.

His heart would always belong to her, even if his body remained in a cage until he died.

"You're my special girl. Don't you know? Everyone knows. Been so long since I've held you, loved you long and slow..."

Chapter 40

Darlina had enjoyed going to the nightclub with Anna Marie. She'd danced with everyone who asked her and even though she was clumsy, it felt wonderful to try. She explained to each dancing partner that it had been a long time.

She'd always thought Luke Stone and The Rebel Rousers were the best band she'd ever heard. Listening to The Drifters in Bossier City that night re-confirmed her belief.

She drank too much, danced too much and flirted too much before the night ended. God, it felt great to be alive again.

Spring of 1982 softly courted the arrival of summer. Darlina had settled into living on her own with the two girls and enjoyed her freedom. Not just freedom from a relationship, but freedom from the restrictions that others had placed on her, as well as the ones she'd placed on herself.

No, she hadn't stopped doing meditation or even following the guru, but she had removed all of the limitations.

She'd gone with her co-workers to happy hour again and to her first crawfish boil, having given up the idea of being total vegetarian last Thanksgiving at her mom's house. She'd met Doug for coffee twice and loved the harmless flirting. She experimented with different eye shadow colors and perfumes. She was the proverbial bird out of a cage.

Going to garage sales with her mom on occasion proved to be fun. On one Saturday in May, she bought a stereo system along with a huge stack of record albums for twenty five dollars. She couldn't wait to get home and try it out.

Her love for music had never disappeared. She'd simply suppressed it. The only time she turned on the TV her mom had bought for them was to let the girls watch cartoons. The rest of the time, the stereo played one album after the other.

Lily was now in kindergarten, but it only lasted half a day, so the babysitter picked her up from school and kept her along with Nicole until Darlina got off work.

On a bright sunshiny day in June, Darlina left work on her way to pick up the girls. She rolled the windows down, enjoying the perfect weather, and switched on the radio.

The disc jockey announced a brand new release by Willie Nelson, and Darlina turned up the volume.

"Maybe I didn't love you quite as good as I could have...You were always on my mind, you were always on my mind..."

Darlina didn't know where they came from but tears flowed so fast and hard that she couldn't see the road. She pulled over and stopped the car.

Luke! This song was from Luke. She knew it. Her heart constricted in a way that almost strangled her and the tears wouldn't stop. She rested her forehead on the steering wheel and sobbed.

It was time to re-establish communication with him. Once she regained her composure, she looked for the nearest store and walked straight to the card section.

The perfect card stared back at her from the shelf. It had a beautiful serene scene on the outside with sun streaming through clouds, trees and flowers and it was blank on the inside.

When she returned to her car, she opened the card and wrote "You were always on my mind, Love Darlina."

There was no doubt in her mind that Luke had reached out to her through the forty foot walls and over the distance to touch her through Willie's song.

He needed her.

She didn't know if he'd respond to her card, but had to send it. As soon as she got back to the apartment with the girls, she addressed the envelope and put a stamp on it. Somehow, she'd allowed her world to be tilted off its axis for the past two years. Now was the chance to set it right again. The old yearning for Luke's arms around her swallowed her entire being.

A few days later, she opened the mailbox to find a letter from Luke.

"Hi, Princess, It was just great to hear from you. It has been so long and I've wondered and worried about you and the girls. No, I knew that you hadn't forgotten me, but I figured you were trying to. You can't write me off any more than I can you, this I'm sure of.

You must know that I've always loved you, but I couldn't show you in the ways I wanted. I'd done fell into a trap before I met you.

I've oft times thought that had I met you a year earlier, my whole life would have been different. You are good for me. You make me think and want to do good things. Your love for me gave me courage and confidence in a different sense than I'd ever known before.

It seems that I may be getting out soon now. I've got the National Prisoner's Rights Union attorneys on my case in Texas. If they can get the parole for me, then I can be out immediately.

More good news. Joyce is filing for a divorce, so I'll really be free when I do get out.

Honey, I hope that you will see me when I do get out. I'm not asking for any promises or anything except just to see you, rap with you, meet the girls and see them.

I think you'll agree that there is something between us that nothing will ever change. Life deals us certain things that last forever, even beyond life on this earth and what I feel for you will last beyond life and I am sure of this. What we did have is something that no one, not even death, will take from me...The Great Spirit has been extra generous to me.

You'll never know how much your loving letters always meant to me. I still hear your words in my mind and they soothe my ragged nerves and calm me many many nights when I'm drove up bad.

I would like to hear from you, about you, the kids and all...Sugar, let me know where you are, even if just a card now and then (thank you for the lovely card).

Willie's song, "Always On My Mind" was written by a friend of mine whose home is in Springfield, Missouri. His name is Wayne Carson.

Let me know if you'll be at this address for a while so I can send you some tapes of the songs I've recorded in here.

Please keep in touch...I miss you, baby, and I think of you most often. Love always, Luke"

Excerpt taken from actual letter

Tears ran unchecked down Darlina's cheeks. Nicole crawled up in her mother's lap. "Don't be sad, Mommy."

Lily sat quietly beside her mother.

Darlina brushed her tears away and hugged Nicole and Lily. "Come on, girls, let's go to the park and play for a while."

Her heart sang as she walked between the little girls, holding their hands. Luke still loved her even after all this time of not writing. His words echoed in her mind, "what I feel for you will last beyond this life."

She couldn't wait to get the children in bed that night and write a long letter in response. She had so much to tell him and how exciting that he might be getting out soon. Of course, she'd see him. There was no question in her mind.

The giggles of the girls matched the rejoicing in her heart as she pushed them on the swings and watched them play chase.

***

Darlina and Anna Marie had become close friends by now and it wasn't surprising when she popped into Darlina's apartment one Saturday afternoon and asked if she would keep Roxanne for her. Of course, Darlina didn't mind.

"But there's something else," Anna Marie added.

"What?"

"There's a lady I just met that's going riding with me and two guys on motorcycles today and she has a little boy. Would you mind keeping him too?"

"How old is he?"

"I don't know. He's close to Nicole's age, though."

Darlina laughed, "You crazy girl. Of course I'll keep him. Do you even know these guys?"

"Sure, I met 'em last night." She grinned at Darlina. "They'll be here around four o'clock. I'll bring Roxanne down."

"I'll be here. Hey, what's this lady's name?"

"Sally," she threw back over her shoulder.

"And the little boy?"

"Hell, I don't know. I bet he can tell you." With that, she was gone.

Darlina wasn't sure about some of Anna Marie's actions, but she liked her and Lily and Nicole enjoyed playing with Roxanne. She worried that her friend might take too many risks, but so far, she'd always came out okay.

At four o'clock, Darlina heard the roar of the Harleys and her heart skipped a beat. It had been a long time since she'd ridden on the back of one of the big motorcycles.

Before she could get the next thought out, Anna Marie rushed through the back door with Roxanne. "They're here."

"So I hear. You know, I used to ride a Harley. Remind me to tell you about it sometime. Is Sally here?"

Another knock came on the door. Darlina opened it to find a small built woman and little boy standing on her porch step. "Hi, I'm Sally and this is Fred. I couldn't believe it when Anna Marie gave me this address. I used to live here."

"Hi, I'm Darlina. Come on in." She opened the door wide.

Fred hesitated and Sally took his hand. "It's going to be all right, Fred. Mommy is going to go riding for a little bit and you're going to stay here with this nice lady and these girls. You'll have fun."

Fred had a sweet face and wide curious eyes. Darlina reached for his hand. "Hello, Fred. I'm Darlina. These are my girls, Lily and Nicole. This is Roxanne. How old are you?"

"Fhree."

"Well, I'll be. You're almost the same age as Nicole. She just turned four. You're gonna have fun playing, I promise."

"Thank you, for keeping him, Darlina."

"Come on, Sally. They're waiting," Anna Marie called from the doorway.

"Ya'll have fun and be careful." Darlina called out as they hurried off.

***

Darlina still occasionally attended satsang. She and Alan had been able to find an amicable but distant friendship. With her occasional excursions to the nightclubs with Anna Marie and sometimes Sally, her dancing skills improved.

Now that communication had been re-established with Luke, she held nothing back. She shared all of her passions, hopes, dreams and thoughts with him.

The year fairly flew by. Darlina, Sally and Anna Marie became inseparable. Between the three of them, one was almost always available to babysit, but when the three wanted to go out together, they found a babysitter.

Darlina most often reserved those times for when the girls were spending the weekend with their granny.

The bond between the three women and their children grew into a solid friendship.

As 1983 rolled around, Darlina began to think about moving out of the apartment. Her lease would soon be up for renewal and she wanted to find something closer to her job.

Anna Marie had the same idea and together the women spent weekends searching for houses.

Since the refinery employed so many people, Darlina put a notice on the company bulletin board that she was looking for a small house to rent.

Within a month, she had looked at three different houses, but none of them felt right. Either they were too run down, or too expensive, or in a bad neighborhood. She'd have to keep looking.

At the end of February 1983, she sat in her office working on the monthly report when an employee from the refinery stuck his head in her door.

"Hey, you got a minute?"

"Sure." Darlina moved the papers to one side.

"I saw your post on the bulletin board for a house. I live just a little ways from here. Me and my wife want to sell our house and get a bigger one. Would you interested in buying ours?"

"Wow, I don't know. I've never bought a house before, but I'd love to look at it."

"Let me show it to you after work today."

"Sure. That'd be great. I can't promise anything, but I'd love to look."

The first thing Darlina noticed when she pulled into the driveway behind the man, was a "For Rent" sign in front of the house next door. If this one didn't work out, she'd look at that one.

She followed the man into his house and fell in love with it immediately. It was small, only two bedrooms, but perfect for her and the children and appeared to be in good condition. And, it was only a few blocks from the refinery. Could she possibly qualify for a loan to buy it? She didn't know, but by the time she left, knew she would try.

The credit union at the refinery financed the house and in less than one month, she went from apartment-dweller to homeowner. Once she'd made the firm decision to buy that house, Anna Marie looked at the one next door and rented it. They would still be neighbors.

Darlina began to give a lot of serious thought about a way to get Luke paroled from prison. The recent attempt made by the attorneys with the National Prisoner's Rights Union had failed, so it was back to square one.

Luke had told her sometime back that he was eligible for parole from the feds and had been for a while, but that the Texas sentence still hung over his head. He described going from a federal prison to state as jumping from the frying pan right into the fire. So, he continued to turn down federal parole to keep from being transferred to Huntsville.

Darlina wrote letters to the parole board, state senators, representatives, prison activist groups and even to the governor's office, trying to find someone to help.

How could they not see that he'd accomplished so much since he'd been behind bars? Surely he'd earned his freedom after twelve years.

Each time she arrived home from work to find yet another package sitting on the porch, she thought back to the visit she'd had from Sue and the one she'd made to Margaret and how she'd been a little jealous of the gifts Luke had bestowed on them.

Now it was her turn. Her walls were covered with Luke's oil paintings. She wore beautiful beaded necklaces and had two ornate and uniquely magnificent leather purses. As more boxes arrived, she received cassette tapes of the music they recorded in the prison studio hidden inside intricately crafted ceramic bowls.

All she could think about was Luke's freedom. He belonged beside her and the girls where he dreamed of being.

If they could only find the right key that would unlock the doors of prison!

"Since skies were blue, I have loved you...Long before nights faded into day...Longer than tomorrows have been new."

Chapter 41

When Steam Train Maury Graham visited the prison in July, Luke anxiously waited for the opportunity to take him upstairs to the makeshift studio. Of course, they were accompanied by a guard, but Steam Train insisted on seeing it before he did his show.

The hobo stood in the middle of the recording room with Luke and slowly turned in a complete circle, taking everything in. "Pal, you sure did a fine job here. I ain't a professional musician by a long shot, but I can see the amount of work it took."

"Steam, it took months and months and lots of convicts helping, but now we're cranking out tapes and sending 'em all over the country."

"I want a copy of everything you've recorded before I leave here today."

"I'll make sure you do," Luke assured. "My old friend at Jolly Roger Radio has been playin' some of my songs on his show in Europe and Australia and he tells me he's gettin' a good response."

Steam Train placed his hand on Luke's shoulder. "You're a music man, Luke. Music is in you and this is a great outlet. I'm proud of you, my brother."

"I'm proud to show it to you. Hell, this has turned out to be the first place the warden brings people when they come in to tour the prison. He likes having something positive to show 'em. He's even brought Supreme Court Justices up here."

"I can understand why he would."

"I wish I had a four-track recorder instead of this little two. I could do so much more with the recordings. Don't get me wrong, though. I'm grateful for what I do have. The Great Spirit has blessed me."

"I'll tell you what. The head of Peavey Corporation is a good friend of mine. I'm going to be heading down to Meridian, Mississippi for the Jimmie Rodgers Festival before long. If you'd like, I'll see if Peavey might want to make a donation of equipment to you."

"Oh hell, Steam, that'd be wonderful. You know, the day you came in this prison and Mr. Nelms asked me to accompany you was a great day for me. I could never repay your kindness and the friendships I've formed because of you. I've got some pen and ink drawings I want to show you before we go back down."

Opening a cabinet beside the console, Luke removed a large manila envelope. As he slid the drawings out, Steam Train studied each one.

"Luke, these are some of the best depictions I've ever seen of Hobo Bill, Jimmie Rodgers and of me. I'm speechless."

"I have copies to send back with you. Because of my connection with Jimmie Rodgers' cousin, Anne Shine Landrum, the museum there in Meridian is going to display my pen and ink of him."

Steam Train brushed his eyes with the back of his hand and embraced Luke. "You've got so much talent, brother. It's a shame that you have to be locked away behind bars."

"I'm working on that, Steam. I've got a lot of folks on the outside helping me and if I can just get the parole from Texas, I'll be out of here. Like I've explained before, I'd be crazy to go from here to Huntsville."

"If there is anything I can do, you know without asking, I'd be glad to."

"I appreciate that. I'll give you addresses where you can write letters. I know my hobo brothers will all join in the effort as well."

"You can bet on it, pal."

Luke played his Martin guitar that day with Steam Train Maury Graham as the hobo did his show for the inmates. When Steam Train departed from the prison, he carried envelopes of drawings and recorded tapes with him, leaving Luke with hope for better equipment to work with.

Not long after that visit, Luke received a letter from the president of Peavey Corporation. It stated that he'd listened to Steam Train Maury's account of the recording studio project in Leavenworth and wanted to help. He went on to say that he would like to ship some scratched and dented equipment to him, if he could accept it.

Luke immediately carried the letter to Marvin Hightower.

"You can't receive the equipment personally, Luke, but if Peavey wants to donate it to the prison, we can damn sure accept it."

"That's good enough for me," Luke replied. "Do you want to answer his letter on behalf of the prison, or do you want me to respond back?"

"I'll answer it or better yet, I'll call him. If I were you, I'd certainly send him a thank you letter, though."

"Oh I will. Thank you, Marvin. You're a good man."

Marvin laughed. "Takes one to know one. I'll let you know the details of the shipment."

"Thanks."

Luke stepped lively down the hallway and up the stairs to his refuge. His heart beat in rhythm with his steps. He couldn't wait to see what Peavey would donate. Hell, anything had to be better than the homemade setup he had.

***

Luke's efforts with the recording studio began to pay off in a big way. The interview with Mr. Goodman, the reporter from the Kansas City Times, was still pending. Finally, by the first of September 1982, prison officials approved it.

The warden gave Mr. Goodman permission to conduct the interview inside the recording studio.

Luke found it easy to establish a rapport with Mr. Goodman and he talked in an easy relaxed way, explaining the arduous process he'd gone through to create this sanctuary of music inside the walls.

Mr. Goodman recorded the conversation, having to switch tapes twice before the interview ended.

"Thank you for meeting with me." Mr. Goodman extended his hand once as he stood to leave.

"Oh man, I appreciate you comin' out here to do this. It isn't easy getting access to come in here and I know you had to go through a shitload of red tape. Thank you for your interest and patience. I'll look forward to reading your article." Luke shook the man's hand.

September 18, 1982, the newspaper article appeared on the front page of the Kansas City Times.

JAILHOUSE SONGWRITER LIVES AN OUTLAW BALLAD...

...Today, Convict No. 87047-132, Stone plays music as his refuge and rehabilitation. He writes songs and records them in a makeshift studio deep inside the gray federal penitentiary. "We have more equipment than any joint I know of anywhere," Stone said. Here surrounded by sound-cushioning egg cartons tacked to the walls, the 47-year-old Stone works the controls of a sound board fashioned from old radio parts while other convicts sing his compositions and play guitars. Stone would prefer to do the singing, but he says he's the only one who knows the recording equipment.

The songs are put on tape. The tapes go out to friends around the country. He writes about love and memories and sunsets and rail-roads. Freedom, really:

"I ain't thinking about tomorrow,
Today I'll ramble without care,
Travel alone free of sorrow,
Riding on wheels of steel..."

"I've been an outlaw and a rebel all my life," Stone said. He describes himself as a hell-raiser who never did anybody any harm...In Leavenworth, it took several years of requests and good behavior until authorities permitted him to do recordings. He says he caught their attention with an anti-drug composition he called "From The Bottle To The Needle." Put together from scavenged parts, the studio is now used by many prisoners. The music has been an outlet that has helped him lose the hostility that put him in prison. Stone said, "And here we are; we started with nothing and we built a recording studio. And sooner or later someone in here's going to write a song that someone's gonna record. That will be a success story."

"I want to prove that if someone has enough ambition ¬¬¬— and does what he can with what he has — he can pull himself up."

Taken from actual newspaper article printed in The Kansas City Times, September 18, 1982

Luke read the newspaper article over three times before he laid it down. It was good. It got the message across.

He cut and pasted the article so that he could make copies to send out to everyone on his correspondence list.

Two months later, Marvin Hightower called Luke down to his office. "I received notification that a truck from Peavey Corporation left Meridian, Mississippi heading this way today. They will make delivery tomorrow."

Luke didn't try to hide his excitement. "That's great, man."

"We'll have to process it all in and examine it for contraband. You know the drill."

"Of course."

"Once that's done, the crew will bring it up to the third floor. I'll notify you when that happens."

"Can't wait. Thank you again for everything, sir."

"My pleasure. Merry Christmas, Luke."

"No shit, man. This is truly Christmas for me."

When the truckload of equipment arrived, Luke exuberantly took inventory of everything. He had a four-track recorder, Peavey speakers, headphones, microphones, cables, rhythm, electric and bass guitars, keyboard, amplifiers and a modern new mixing board.

Upon examination, he could barely find a scratch or dent on any of it.

He made short work of unhooking the old homemade equipment, said his farewells to it, and neatly stored it in the room adjoining the studio. Maybe years from now someone would find a need for it again.

When time came to return to his cell for count, he hated to leave the studio. He had only half of the new equipment hooked up.

But, patience was one thing he'd learned completely. Tomorrow would be another chance to work on it.

***

Luke Stone hardly remembered the angry, bitter, rebellious man who had arrived on a cold December day at Leavenworth Penitentiary thirteen years ago.

His latest expression of art, the pen and ink drawings, attracted a lot of attention from other inmates and staff. He'd discovered how to use a dot technique. Each depiction consisted of hundreds of tiny dots. The sketch that sat on his easel, this cold gray evening early in 1983, was a striking likeness of Merle Haggard. He almost had it finished. His friend, Hobo Bill, had promised to hand carry the drawing to the singing star.

He'd felt Red drawing farther away from him for some time. He still came up to the studio to play guitar or bass and sing Luke's songs while Luke recorded them, but there was no spark in his eyes.

Something weighed heavy on his old friend, but if he refused to tell Luke, there was nothing he could do. So Luke tried to keep him busy singing and playing music. Maybe, eventually, he'd share what burdened him. Luke instinctively knew it was more than just being in prison.

He cherished the warm and open letters he now received regularly from Darlina. He couldn't begin to express how appreciative he was of the woman she'd become.

Buying a house was no small feat. Being a single mom, and taking good care of her children was not a walk in the park either and he understood all of that. His heart swelled with pride. She'd valiantly joined in the effort to get him paroled from prison.

He never tired of hearing her say that she couldn't wait for him to be free, to see him and to make love to him.

He enjoyed reading about her escapades with her two friends, Anna Marie and Sally, although he worried about the women going out to the nightclubs. He knew firsthand the kinds of monsters that lurked around every corner looking for victims. He always warned Darlina not to make herself a target.

More than anything, he worried about them bringing strangers to their homes and exposing the children to possible danger.

If they could only get a small glimpse into the world that he existed in; where he was forced to rub elbows with men who'd preyed on unsuspecting women and innocent children. The horrible acts some of them had committed were almost unspeakable and nauseated Luke. He didn't know what he'd do if someone harmed any of his girls.

So, over and over again, he stressed to Darlina to be cautious and not so trusting of everyone. He could only hope that she listened and paid attention.

He knew that she was enjoying going out and partying with her friends and was happy for her to live again. But, there was a fine line and he wasn't sure that she understood that. He prayed for her safety.

But most of all, he loved the easy way he could be totally sexual with her in his letters again, and the enthusiastic way that she responded with her own passions.

He assured her that every time he relieved himself, it was her face he saw, it was her soft sensuous body he imagined.

More than anything, he knew that they would be completely compatible in every way if only he could gain his freedom and join her.

One night, as spring morphed into 1983's blazing hot summer, he asked her to marry him.

She was divorced from Will. He was divorced from Joyce and so they were both free except for the walls and bars that held him. He didn't know what she would say, but he'd keep asking until she said yes.

She'd always told him her ultimate dream was to be Mrs. Luke Stone. If he could get out of this cage, he would make that dream and every other one she had, come true.

"So, Darlina, I'm on one knee begging you to say you'll marry me once I'm free from this cage..." were the words he formed on the paper.

He knew she wasn't ready to say "yes" just yet, but had every confidence that she would and when she did, it would be for real. He couldn't wait for that day.

He closed his eyes and let his imagination take him into the future where he stood with Darlina in front of a preacher vowing to love and cherish her forever. He was reminded of a vivid dream he'd had so long ago shortly after he'd been locked away. The dream was the same scene as he now imagined.

Her blue eyes would gaze into his and speak her love louder than any words that came from her mouth. Once he slipped a ring on her finger, he'd kiss her long and sweet. After the festivities, he'd carry her to bed and take his time exploring every curve of her sensuous body, satisfying her every desire and lastly satisfying his own need.

He opened his eyes and sighed. "Patience, Luke Stone. Patience."

"I've never loved so completely, been taken so sweetly, or thrilled so when another touched me."

Chapter 42

D arlina Flowers moved through her days with a spark of hope in her heart. When she'd received Luke's letter asking her to marry him, she sank into the nearest chair and gripped the letter as though it might disappear. Her hand trembled violently and she had trouble reading the words Luke had written from his heart.

It wasn't that she hadn't expected it, but not while he was still in prison. How could she say yes to an empty dream that promised only more loving words written on paper? No, it wasn't time to answer that question, although the thought of marrying Luke filled her with joy and fear simultaneously.

How could she be sure that she could satisfy Luke's every need? She never wanted to go through the agony of him turning to someone else.

The memory of the night he'd spent with the go-go dancer, DeeDee, in their home, was burned forever in her mind. She'd never repeat a scene like that again for Luke or anyone else.

So, she answered him back and shared all these thoughts and fears. She told him the timing was all wrong. She wrote honestly that she couldn't base her entire future on a dream that may or may not come true. She had to think of her children as well as herself.

With all of that said, she assured him that there was no one else waiting in the wings to take his place in her life. No one ever had and nor ever would.

Her heart belonged only to Luke.

The year rolled on. Luke had been turned down again for the Texas parole. As discouraging as it was, they had to keep trying.

Lily was now about to go into the second grade and Nicole into kindergarten. Darlina couldn't believe how quickly her babies were growing up. The neighborhood they'd moved into consisted mostly of families. An elderly retired couple lived next door and of course, Anna Marie and Roxanne on the other side. The girls made friends with other children on the block and most of the time, they congregated at Darlina's house. She didn't mind because she'd rather have a backyard full of children and know where her girls were and what they were doing.

Sally and Fred became a constant in their lives. Fred and Nicole interacted more like siblings. They loved to play together but occasionally they'd fuss. Nicole loved to rub in the fact that she was older than Fred and it always made him cry. He didn't want her to be older.

October of 1983 delivered a blow to Darlina that she hadn't seen coming. She'd just arrived home from work with the girls in tow when the phone rang.

"Hello." She sat her purse down.

"Darlina, this is Norma. Daddy has had a heart attack and is in the Jacksonville hospital. We're leaving Houston heading that way. Mom asked me to call everyone."

"Oh no!" Her heart sank. From the way her sister's voice cracked she knew it was serious. "How bad is it?"

"I don't know, but Mom wants all of us there."

"All right. I'll make a few phone calls and get on the road. Thank you for calling. See you there."

She knew her mom and dad were getting up in years, but they were too young to die. Surely he would be okay. She flew around the house gathering clothes and things for the girls.

Her mind raced. She needed to call someone at work and let them know she wouldn't be there tomorrow. She'd have to notify the girls' school. She simply couldn't imagine her daddy sick. He'd always been strong. But a heart attack was nothing to take lightly.

In less than an hour, she and the girls were on the road to Jacksonville.

After two days, seeing firsthand the seriousness of the situation, Darlina called Anna Marie and asked her to pick up the girls and take them back to Shreveport. They didn't need to sit in the hospital for hours on end and she desperately needed to be there with her family. Her daddy fought for his life, but the doctors weren't giving much hope.

In a few short days, Darlina's father passed from this life. The grief that overwhelmed her heart was foreign to her. It went deeper than anything she'd ever felt, even losing Luke to prison. Death was permanent. She'd never see her daddy again, or hear his voice and the funny way he pronounced certain words. In that instant, she realized just how much she loved him and wished for one more chance to tell him.

She joined with the rest of her family in rallying around their mother and promised to come back every weekend that she could and bring the girls to keep her company.

As 1984 came with promise and hope, Darlina and Luke were now able to talk on the phone once a month. She assured him that the expense of the collect calls wasn't going to break her. They needed those conversations.

Letters were wonderful but one-sided and they always had so much to share. Before long, the girls were clamoring to talk too, so Darlina let each of them take a turn.

Efforts doubled to obtain a parole from Texas. Luke had explained over and over how he would continue to turn down federal parole because they'd ship him straight to Huntsville. It made no sense to keep him locked up as they made solid plans for their future.

Luke had stopped asking Darlina to marry him, telling her that when she was ready, she could ask him.

Finally, Darlina made up her mind that she needed to go to Kansas and see Luke. She felt that was the only way she could settle her mind with the doubts and fears she constantly dredged up when she thought about marrying him. It took her back to the time she'd hitchhiked to Springfield to see Luke after Will had asked her to marry him. She needed some answers.

She and Lily left Shreveport on June 27th and headed north to see Luke. Nicole was angry and hurt that she got left behind, but when Sally offered to keep her so that she could play with Fred, she stopped arguing. It would make the trip easier for Darlina.

Lily was now eight years old and all grown up. Darlina played the radio and they sang songs and talked about the countryside. It was a far cry from the haphazardly planned hitchhike so long ago.

Luke had sent Darlina the name and phone number of a guard that he'd become very good friends with and instructed her to call when she arrived in Leavenworth. It took her and Lily all day to travel the 575 miles. Darlina stopped often to stretch her legs and let Lily get some exercise.

Even though the summer days were long, it was nearing dark when they finally arrived. Darlina stopped at two motels before she found one suitable for them that she could afford.

Once they were settled in their room, she called Jerry Cox just as Luke had instructed. Darlina could no more still her pounding heart than she could stop breathing. To be so close to Luke and the anticipation of seeing him tomorrow put her emotions into a tizzy. Everything from being rapturous joy to gripping fear and anxiety rippled through her.

Once she'd made the call to Mr. Cox, he insisted that he and his wife come to pick her and Lily up and take them to dinner.

Jerry and Linda Cox turned out to be two genuine caring and warm people. Jerry loved Luke like a brother and explained to Darlina that this was a very rare thing in his profession. He'd been trained to avoid relationships with inmates, but Luke had earned his respect and trust over the years.

She smiled when they told her of how Linda had packed Jerry an extra large lunch box during the holidays so that he could share some homemade goodies with Luke. Darlina felt completely comfortable to leave Lily with Linda the next day so that she could make the first visit to Luke alone.

June 28th dawned bright, full of sunshine and expectancy.

Darlina brushed her hair until it shone, meticulously applied her makeup and donned a soft colorful summer dress.

Once she'd dropped Lily off at the address Linda Cox had provided, she turned her car in the direction of Leavenworth Penitentiary.

The massive imposing gray walls and towers made her heart lurch. She stopped at the entrance guard tower.

"State your name and business," a gruff voice demanded.

"My name is Darlina Flowers and I am here to visit inmate, Luke Stone."

"Do you have any firearms or contraband of any kind?"

"No sir." Her voice sounded strange to her ears.

"Just a minute while I check the visitor's log."

Darlina tapped her fingernails on the steering wheel and dared a long look around. She could not begin to imagine being locked away in this cold forbidding place that resembled an 1800s fortress.

"Pull on through." The man startled her. "You'll find visitor's parking on your left."

"Thank you."

She drove slowly into the parking lot, checked herself in the rear-view mirror and got out. Luke had advised her to only carry a small purse and to remove anything that could be considered a weapon, including nail clippers. She clutched her small handbag and trudged up the long imposing steps to the front entrance.

It took almost an hour to go through the rigorous security check, including being patted down by a female guard. Darlina's legs wobbled as a guard led her to the large visiting room and told her to have a seat.

No matter how hard she tried to sit still, she couldn't stop biting her fingernails or fidgeting with her hands on her lap. Finally the door opened and Luke strode in.

She jumped to her feet and flew across the room toward him.

Remembering the rules, they only allowed themselves a short and quick embrace, but in that few seconds, Darlina breathed in his scent, took note of the ripples in his arms that went around her so easily, and the feel of his body pressing against hers.

"My princess! You're more beautiful than I remembered." Luke held her at arm's length.

"Luke, I want to stay in your arms and for you to never let me go."

"Me too, sugar. Believe me, I want that too. Let's sit over here as far away from the guard's desk as possible." Luke took her hand and led her to two chairs at the end of a long row. "My God, baby, I can't believe you're here."

"It was a long trip, but one I had to make. I needed to see you."

"Not as bad as I needed to see you, sweetheart. You are a sight for these ol' sore eyes. God, I just want to sit you on my lap and pet you and kiss you until we melt into each other."

Darlina smiled up at him, eyes wet with tears. "Baby, I've missed you so much. I've tried to live without you and it's been almost impossible. I love you."

Luke let out a long slow breath. "I love you, Darlina, more than I can ever say. I want to show you how much I love you for the rest of our lives. No, I'm not fixing to ask you to marry me. I told you that when you were ready, you could ask me." He grinned the crooked smile that Darlina remembered so well.

"I know, honey. I know. I really appreciate your friends, Jerry and Linda helping us out. Lily is spending the day with Linda. Tomorrow, I'll bring her in to see you. I gave Jerry an envelope to deliver to you. Such nice folks."

"They are both jewels. Jerry's helped me a lot in getting music tapes out and he'll bring me the envelope. I can't wait to see what my angel put in it. Did he tell you that Linda sent out a feast for Jerry to share with me last Christmas?"

"Yes, and Linda was carrying the purse you made for her. Luke, we've got to get you out of here. I've written letters everywhere I can think of and so have a lot of other people. I don't know what it's going to take."

"Me neither, honey, but when the time is right, the doors will swing open for me. I live and breathe for that day."

"How's Red doing? You mentioned he was having some problems."

"Yeah, he's going through some sort of weird shit, but he won't talk to me about it, so there's not much I can do for him. None of this is what I want to talk about, Darlina. I want to talk about how beautiful your sweet face is and your body is perfect and begging for your man to love it. Did you do what I asked?"

"Yes."

"Turn yourself toward me and put your back to the guard."

Darlina glanced around and then did as he asked. He leaned forward slightly, lifted her dress and slid his hand unnoticed under it. She gasped as he found her hot wetness.

Luke trembled. "Try to look as though we are deep in conversation. Keep talking to me."

Breathlessly, she continued talking. "I need you so badly, Luke. You've gotta know that. I want so much to feel you inside of me, making love long and slow the way you used to."

Panting, Luke whispered. "Maybe you better talk about something else so I don't lose complete control. Tell me about your job and the girls and Anna Marie and Sally."

Forced words came hoarsely. "The girls are growing," she sucked air in sharply, "so fast. I love Anna Marie and Sally. We have a lot of fun together and other than going out to the nightclubs, anything else we do, we always take all the kids along with us."

"God, you feel good, baby. So hot and ready, just like I've dreamed of. I've gotta stop or I'm gonna be walkin' around with wet underwear." Glancing at the guard, he removed his shaking hand and brought his fingers up to his mouth. "You taste just like I remember. Honey, I don't know how to convince you that I don't need any other woman but you. I understand how that might be a hard thing to wrap your pretty little head around given my past history, but I know that you have exactly what I need."

Smoothing her dress, she leaned back against her chair and brushed a tear away that escaped. "I want to believe that, Luke, with all my heart."

"You can, sweetheart. You know me well enough to know that when I make a promise, I keep it and I promise that is true."

Luke and Darlina sat with their heads and shoulders close together and talked about everything each of them could think of. By one o'clock in the afternoon, Darlina's stomach growled and she purchased peanut butter crackers and sodas out of the vending machines for her and Luke.

A comfortable easy peace filled her as she sat beside Luke munching on crackers.

Knowing that visiting hours ended at 3 pm, they didn't waste any time in silence. The conversation never lagged and too soon, they had to say their goodbyes, with the promise of another visit tomorrow.

The next day, Lily and Darlina sat with Luke. Lily didn't hesitate to crawl up in his lap and call him Daddy. Luke grinned a wide smile and smoothed her blonde hair as he sat her on the chair between him and Darlina.

Looking over her head at Darlina, tears misted his eyes. "I've screwed up a lot in this life. My own kids have suffered greatly for it, but I swear to you that if I get a second chance at a family, I will give it one hundred percent. These little girls will never be without a daddy again in their lives. All I need is a chance."

Darlina kissed Lily on her cheek and leaned in toward Luke. "Luke Stone, will you marry me?"

Luke jumped up from his chair, and kneeled in front of her.

"Stone!" The guard's voice sliced through the air. "Back in your seat."

Luke sat down. Taking Darlina's small hand in his own large one, he whispered. "Thank you, sweetheart. Thank you. You'll see. This is a decision I promise that you won't ever regret."

"I know." Darlina whispered back through tears.

"Mommy, why are you and Daddy crying?" Lily screwed up her face.

"Because we're so filled up with happiness that some of it has to run out, sweetheart."

Both she and Luke laughed. The visit ended too soon and Darlina and Lily left the penitentiary, turned south and drove until darkness came. They spent the night in a quaint little cabin in the Ozark Mountains of Arkansas. After Lily had gone to sleep, Darlina sat at a hand hewn table in the soft glow of the lamp and wrote from her heart.

Checked into a Motel in Leavenworth, Kansas
Drove all that way, had to have some answers
You see, there was this man I'd loved for a long long time
He'd written me long letters; said he wanted to be mine
I brought my daughter with me to the Penitentiary today
We surveyed the gray building with nothing to say
Our reunion inside was a celebration
Really it was worthy of publication
And that is why I sit here now
To relate to you our solemn vow
There we sat that 28th day of June
In the stark prison visiting room

We spoke of Love and Truth and Freedom
Our dreams took shape as we boldly portrayed 'em
We had woven a spell
Long before he had ever seen that cell
So, I guess you've figured out by now
Exactly what was that solemn vow
Yes, we swore to live as mates
A lifetime or more with no restraints
I am at peace and so very content
To return home with full intent
To plan and work and prepare
For my man to come and take his chair
At the head of our table
For as long as he is able
And we will be
His family
To the ultimate degree.

She leaned back and closed her weary eyes. The only thing left to do was to somehow get Luke free from the walls and bars.

How could he be so confident that when the time was right, it would happen? She wasn't so sure, but renewed her determination to do everything in her power.

The entire two-day visit replayed in her mind. She loved the feel of his hand under her dress and the scent of his hot breath on her face. She groaned with want and need.

A need that only Luke Stone could fill.

"She wrote beautiful cherished lines. "I want you, I need you, you are the sun that shines." On one page alone, she wrote, "I love you" seven times..."

Chapter 43

L uke walked on air back to his cell. Nothing could wipe the smile off his face, not even the guard who made him bend over while he probed for contraband after he left the visiting room.

Darlina had asked him to marry her and he got to meet a beautiful blonde-haired blue-eyed little girl who'd called him daddy today.

He thought about how Darlina had looked at him with pure undeniable lust in her eyes. He'd told her that when lights went out tonight, he would relieve himself over and over again thinking of her. And he would.

She was more beautiful, more desirable than he remembered. There were still traces of the little girl he'd fallen in love with so long ago, but mostly they'd faded. There was no doubt she was all woman and totally capable of taking care of her man. He puffed his chest out. And that man was him.

He had to break free from this damnable place! But how? He'd followed every lead, exhausted every resource that he could find. Nevertheless, there had to be a way.

With a love as strong as he and Darlina shared, surely the Great Spirit would intervene.

***

Over the next many months, an article appeared in Time magazine, which included Luke, along with an article in the Syracuse New York

Sentinel about the recording studio. A reporter, Michael Kroll, had taken on the challenge of writing about the horrors of prison. He'd questioned Luke extensively and used many of Luke's words to form his writing.

The world needed to know the truth about life inside prison and Luke was certain that the Great Spirit chose Michael Kroll to tell it.

***

In the fall of 1984, Luke walked down the hallway on his way to the stairs that led to the third floor.

His old friend, Red, had suddenly and without explanation, taken voluntary lockup. Luke hadn't seen him in several weeks and worried about him.

Just as he rounded a corner, he came face to face with Red. A guard walked on each side of him.

"Hey, hoss. Everything okay?"

"Hi, Luke. Oh yeah, everything's good. They're fixing to take me over to Kansas City to do more surgery on my eyes. I'll see you when I get back."

"Red, is there anything you need me to take care of?" Luke narrowed his eyes.

"No, not a thing. Hey, I'll talk to you when I get back from Kansas City."

"You take care, man." Luke stood and watched until Red and the two guards were out of sight.

Something was wrong and Luke knew it. Red hadn't acted right since they'd transferred a batch Florida prisoners in to Leavenworth after a riot at Tallahassee.

He'd asked around to see if anyone knew what Red's mysterious behavior was all about, but no one volunteered anything. If one of the Florida prisoners had threatened Red, Luke would eventually find out and take care of it.

He sought out his friend, Jerry Cox. "Do you think you might be able to find out what's going on with Red? I saw him today and he said they were taking him to Kansas City for some kind of eye surgery. Somethin' ain't right. He's acted weird since the Florida prisoners shipped in."

"I don't know, Luke. I can look into it, but convicts don't talk about things like that to guards."

"I'm worried about him. He's been so depressed, then he went and took lockup and now this."

"I'll let you know if I hear anything, but I wouldn't get my hopes up. How's Darlina and Lily?"

Luke grinned. "They're good. They just need their ol' man out there to take care of 'em. I'm going to get out of here, Jerry. You watch me."

Jerry slapped Luke on the back. "I'm betting on it, Luke." He turned to go. "I'll holler at you if I find out anything about Red."

"Thank you hoss."

That was all he could do. If anyone could get to the bottom of it, Jerry could.

***

The months passed and Luke had the haunting feeling that he'd never see Red again.

With Christmas right around the corner, he crafted gifts for his girls. He knew exactly what he wanted to send Darlina.

He fingered the silver and turquoise cross he'd worn around his neck for many years. It was time to transfer the magic it held to her. He knew she would be able to feel its power when she put it on. The necklace had been his constant companion for the past ten years or more and held more of his DNA than any other possession he had.

The ceramic candle lamps he'd made for the girls with their names carved into the molds backward sat ready to go into the kiln. When they lit the lamps, their names would display on the wall. He painted a Unicorn for Lily and a little Indian girl holding a God's Eye for Nicole.

A ceramic bowl with an intricately carved antelope on top of the lid would be another gift for Darlina. He considered stringing the bead loom and including a choker or some earrings for her, but decided the silver cross necklace would be the crowning touch of her Christmas gifts.

While he worked, he pictured her pretty face. He imagined her opening the box and how her eyes would shine when she touched each piece, made with love from his hands and heart.

Once he had everything finished and packed for shipment, he removed the silver and turquoise cross from around his neck and placed it in a leather pouch along with a note to Darlina. This would be her engagement ring. The cross held a strong magic that only he knew of and Darlina would be the recipient of it.

She'd become instrumental in helping him get things he made mailed to people on the outside. They, in turn, sent payment for them to her.

Helping his new little family in this way brought him great satisfaction.

The hours crawled by between their monthly phone calls. He'd begun addressing letters to Mrs. Darlina Stone.

It was past time to be out of this godforsaken prison. They were both ready to begin their lives together as husband and wife.

This instant couldn't be soon enough for Luke.

He occupied himself with art, music, the recordings and letters. Now wasn't the time to let negativity creep in. Not when the goal of freedom loomed closer than ever before.

Christmas didn't seem quite so gloomy to Luke this year. Nothing had changed inside prison, but something big had changed inside of him. He now had reason to celebrate.

The longing to be with his girls grew more intense with each passing day. He needed all three of them to love and depend on him and would make damned sure they always had everything they desired.

He was the luckiest man alive. Dreaming of the things they would do together filled his thoughts. He'd have all sorts of projects to involve the little girls in and then at night, he'd have his big girl to give all of his love to.

They say that life is the stuff dreams are made of, but to Luke, dreams were what he banked the rest of his life on.

Not only his life, but Darlina's, Lily's and Nicole's. They would get his very best.

All he needed was a chance to prove it. He could hear a quiet voice whisper in the wind, "Soon. Very soon."

"If you grow weary while waiting for me, remember to dream of what can be..."

Chapter 44

F ive days before Christmas 1984, Darlina arrived home from work to find a large box sitting on her front porch.

She hurriedly unlocked the door and tossed her purse inside. Luke's Christmas gifts lay inside the box and Darlina's eyes misted over as she thought of the love he would show through the things he'd made for them. The girls clamored around her.

"Mama, I want to see what Daddy sent me." Lily tore at the tape on the box.

"Me too." Nicole pushed her sister over to get a better look.

"Girls, settle down. Let's get it inside the house first, then we'll get it open. I want to see what Daddy sent as much as you do."

The girls ooohed and ahhhhed over the lamps and oil paintings Luke had made for them. Darlina felt her heart swell with love for the thoughtfulness Luke had put into making each gift. And he did it all with such limited resources. He never ceased to amaze her with his artistic talents and the way he seemed to know exactly what Nicole and Lily would love.

Once Darlina had opened and emptied the box, she found candles to go in the girls' lamps. From her tool drawer, she got nails and hung the oil paintings on their bedroom wall.

She placed the large ceramic tureen in the center of a table and admired the intricate artwork that graced it. The detail of the antelope perched on top of the lid made him look as if he could leap off. The handles resembled horns.

When she reached inside the bowl to remove the packing paper, her fingers found something else. She'd learned long ago not to throw any packing away out of the boxes Luke sent without carefully going through it. He always tucked little things amidst the packing.

The small black leather pouch she pulled from the wadded paper had something hard inside. When she opened it, a silver and turquoise cross necklace tumbled out. She cradled it in the palm of her hand then brought it to her lips and she gently kissed it. A lump formed in her throat and she swallowed hard. Warmth spread throughout her body starting in the center of her heart. She knew how important this necklace was to Luke.

But he'd sent it to her. She peeked inside to see a small folded piece of paper.

Carefully, she pulled it out and unfolded it.

"Merry Christmas, my dearest darling Princess. This is very old and very Indian. It has been around my neck for over ten years. It has not been off even to shower. I've lain sick, hurting, depressed and angry with it on, but in the last year, I've dreamed the most wonderful dreams with it on. Those dreams, plans, thoughts and hopes are all for us four. I couldn't make or even buy anything that would have the "magic," the power and essence of my love and devotion to you, as much as this gift. You will feel me in touching it or looking at it and you'll feel me and my love for you as it hangs around your beautiful neck and rests upon your loving bosom. This is the strongest token of my "magic" and only in person could it be stronger. It is time that I give it to the one I love most and who I will give my magic to. Yes, it is worn from my fingers' caresses and tarnished from my sweat, but it's filled with hundreds of hours of "medicine" (prayers) for the one who will wear it – you. Wear it in confidence. We will soon be together to share our strengths, my love. Yours Forever, Your Husband, Luke"

Darlina held the note in her trembling hand and read the words again. She gently closed her fingers around the cross and pictured Luke removing this token of trust and love from his neck. A silent tear escaped and emotions rippled through the very core of her being.

She couldn't wait for their phone call on Saturday, to tell him how much this gift touched her and assure him she'd always respect the magic it held. The cross warmed the palm of her hand as she slipped the chain over her head. She felt the very essence of Luke with her. If she closed her eyes and concentrated, she could smell his scent. Her heart filled with unbridled love.

***

New Year's Eve came and went quietly. No parties, no drinking or dancing. Anna Marie and Roxanne had moved to Midland with a job offer. Sally had married a man Darlina didn't much care for. So as 1985 arrived, Darlina and her two daughters watched the ball drop on TV and drank grape juice out of wine glasses.

Darlina missed her two girlfriends, but she understood that life had its own way of unfolding for each person.

She immersed herself in Luke. There were times when she wrote daily letters. She had so much to say. So many plans and dreams to lay out and Luke did the same.

***

Lily and Nicole made friends with a new little girl who moved in two blocks over. Heather was in Nicole's class at school and they quickly bonded. Heather's flashing brown eyes, freckles on her nose and long curly dark locks contrasted with Lily and Nicole's blue eyes and blond hair, but the girls hit it off.

The little girl spent a good deal of time playing at Darlina's house. It seemed that she never wanted to go home.

One afternoon, Heather's mother knocked on Darlina's door.

"Come on in. Heather is playing with the girls in their bedroom. Can I get you a glass of tea or something?" Darlina held the door open.

"Oh, I can't stay. I just need to get Heather."

"She and the girls sure do play well together. Nicole wants to know if Heather can spend the night on Saturday. Oh goodness me, I didn't even introduce myself. I'm Darlina."

The woman blinked and chewed on her bottom lip. "I'm Jackie. I really can't stay. My husband is waiting on us."

"No problem. I'll get Heather."

Something about Jackie reminded Darlina of a scared rabbit. She was small, shy and nervous as if she expected something to jump out and grab her any minute.

In seconds, Darlina returned with Heather in tow, her girls following.

"Come on, Heather. Daddy is waiting on us. We have to go."

"Mama, can I spend the night with Nicole and Lily on Saturday?"

"I don't know, Heather. We'll have to ask your daddy."

"Jackie, please come by sometime when you can visit. I miss my girlfriends and would love to have someone to talk to."

"Maybe. I'll have to ask my husband."

"Okay. Ya'll take care and let me know if Heather can spend the night Saturday." After a second thought, she scribbled on a piece of paper. "Here's my phone number."

"Thank you. I'll let you know. Come on, Heather." Impatience showed in her voice.

"Bye, Heather," Nicole threw her arms around her friend's neck.

Lily and Nicole stood on the porch and waved until they were out of sight.

***

A month later, near the end of March, Jackie Silverfarb came to visit Darlina. Her husband escorted her to the door. He towered over Jackie and weighed well over three hundred pounds.

"I'll be back to get you in an hour," he said gruffly.

Heather scooted around both parents, looking for her friends.

"Okay." Jackie darted inside.

"Heather, the girls are in the backyard. Go on out and join them. Have a seat, Jackie," Darlina invited.

Once Darlina poured a glass of tea for them and Kool-Aid for the children, she and Jackie sat at the dining table and talked. Well, Darlina talked. Jackie mostly listened, occasionally taking a sip of her tea. She asked Darlina about the beautiful paintings on the walls and the ceramics displayed around the room.

Her interest opened the door for Darlina to tell Jackie about Luke. The hour flew by and both women jumped when a knock rattled the door.

Darlina answered it to find Jackie's husband standing on the porch.

He ignored Darlina, stuck his head in and bellowed. "Come on Jackie. The hour's up. Where's Heather?"

Darlina quickly responded. "She's outside with my girls. I'll get her. Won't you come in, Mr. Silverfarb?"

"Name's Roger and we need to get going."

Darlina did not miss the way Jackie's demeanor changed instantly as she shrank back into the shy little rabbit.

Darlina returned with Heather holding her hand. "Thank you for letting Jackie visit. I really enjoyed talking to her. I hope she can come back again soon "Bye, Jackie. Bye, Heather. See you soon."

Darlina pondered over this family. Something wasn't right, but who was she to judge? She shrugged it off and decided she had plenty on her own plate.

The letters between her and Luke flowed fast and furious. Both opened up totally and they planned every tiny detail of their lives together to the point that the detail began to take a life of its own.

The determination to find a way to gain his freedom grew inside each of them with every day that passed.

Someone had to have the answer, the solution, the magic key to open the door of prison. If only she or Luke could find them.

***

A few weeks after Jackie's visit, Darlina noticed that she hadn't seen hide nor hair of Heather. She asked Nicole if Heather had been at school and she said yes. She couldn't shake the feeling that something was wrong.

Finally, she gave in, picked up the phone and called the Silverfarb house.

Roger answered. "Hello."

"Roger, this is Darlina. I was wondering if Heather could come and play with the girls this afternoon and I'd love to visit with Jackie again."

"Heather's busy and Jackie's not here."

"Oh. Okay. Has Jackie gone on a trip?"

He snorted. "Yeah a trip to the hospital."

"Oh no. Is she okay? What hospital?"

"She just went off her rocker again. She's at Willis Knighton on the psych ward if you wanna go see her."

"Oh yes, I surely do. Is Heather okay? Do you need any help with her? I'd be happy to take her for a few days."

"No. Me and Heather are managing just fine."

"When can she come visit the girls again?"

"I don't know."

"Okay. Roger, please, if you need my help in any way, call me."

"We'll be fine. Thanks."

With that, he hung up. Darlina sat stunned. Jackie was in a psychiatric ward. She would take the girls to Sally's house and go visit her this evening.

At first, when Darlina arrived at the hospital, she wasn't sure Jackie recognized her, but by the time she left, the woman had come around. Darlina told her emphatically that if she could do anything for her, to please call. Jackie asked her to check on Heather and Darlina promised she would.

***

The next time Darlina had a chance to visit alone with Jackie, it was mid-April. Her heart went out to the tiny frightened woman.

As they'd done the last time Jackie visited, Darlina talked endlessly about Luke and told Jackie about how she was searching everywhere for a way to get him out of prison so they could start their lives together.

Jackie sat quietly listening, then dropped a bombshell on Darlina.

"I have a friend in Austin. She's dating a lawyer who used to be on the Texas Parole Board. I could call and ask if her boyfriend might be able to help."

"Oh my God, Jackie." She jumped off her chair and hugged the woman. "That would be an amazing answer to prayer. Do you have her number with you? You can use my phone to call."

"No, it's at home. I promise I'll call her this evening though, and let you know what she says."

The ray of hope burning inside Darlina went from a flashlight to a high powered spotlight. Maybe this was the answer she and Luke had been searching for. And who could have dreamed that it would come through this frightened wisp of a woman? She couldn't wait to hear from Jackie later that evening.

True to her word, she called Darlina at 8 o'clock.

"Tammy said she was sure her boyfriend could help. I wrote down all of his information. His name is Herman Goffe."

Darlina wrote furiously as Jackie read off his address and phone number. She wouldn't waste time with a letter. She'd call Mr. Goffe first thing in the morning.

She wrote the most hopeful and positive letter to Luke that night. Something inside her said that this was what they'd waited so long to find.

Mr. Goffe turned out to be very cordial. He listened attentively to Darlina as she told him the whole story of Luke's arrest and conviction and the length of time he'd been in prison. She explained that Luke had been an exemplary inmate and listed his accomplishments from the past fourteen years.

She answered every question Mr. Goffe asked. Finally, he told her he was sure he could help.

In conclusion, Mr. Goffe informed her that it would cost two thousand dollars to get Luke out. He would take a payment of one thousand in advance and the other thousand once Luke was freed.

Darlina didn't hesitate. She assured him that she'd have a thousand dollar check in the mail to him within the next few days.

When she hung up the phone, she found herself in a daze. It all came down to money. Luke had always told her that you can get only as much justice in America as you can afford. It looked as if he was right.

Where on earth would she find a thousand dollars? She made just enough money from her job to pay the bills and take care of the children. She never had any surplus.

All day, she tossed the money issue around in her mind. She went down the entire list of family and friends and couldn't come up with a single soul who would loan her a thousand dollars. Her car was paid for, but it was only worth $800, so borrowing against it wasn't an option.

What to do?

While walking down the hallway at work, the solution hit her like a bolt of lightning. She could borrow a thousand dollars against the equity she had in her house. Her feet wouldn't move fast enough to carry her to the other side of the complex and into the credit union office.

When she left, she held a thousand dollar check in her hand. As soon as her workday ended, she made a beeline for the bank, deposited it and then wrote a short letter to Mr. Goffe and enclosed a thousand dollar check made out to him.

Luke was finally coming home. There was not a doubt in her mind.

That night after the children had been tucked in their beds, Darlina's pen raced furiously across the paper. She couldn't write fast enough to tell Luke every detail.

Her heart raced and she struggled to keep the tears at bay. Concentrating on the words she wrote, it almost felt as if she moved through a dream or a fantasy that she'd imagined a thousand times.

In a short time, she would be Mrs. Luke Stone. Her heart's deepest desire realized.

They had a lot of planning to do and she understood that even though Mr. Goffe promised a parole, there would still be hoops to jump through.

It didn't matter. They'd persevered and now they would be together through all eternity.

No doubt lingered in her mind. Soon, she'd be lying in Luke's arms every night, satisfying him in every way. She remembered the feel of his hand under her dress when she'd visited him last summer. She longed for Luke to fill and complete her.

When she'd finished the letter, as an afterthought, she applied lipstick and sealed it with a kiss.

She touched the silver cross around her neck and closed her eyes. "It's time for you to come home, my husband."

"I dreamed I was out of prison last night...You were a picture of loveliness in my sight. For hours we kissed, as I held you tight..."

Chapter 45

L uke never doubted that he would eventually be freed from prison. Darlina had finally found someone with the means to make it a reality.

Until the parole papers were placed in his hands, it wasn't a done deal, but this was closer than he'd ever gotten, although many lawyers had tried over the years.

He knew of the sacrifice Darlina made to come up with the money for Mr. Goffe and it only made him love her more. He resolved to make sure she never regretted it for an instant.

The sweet smells of spring, the melody of the birds and the brilliance of the blue sky lifted his spirits and put a song of hope in his heart.

He was going home. He didn't know the day or even the month, but he knew the Great Spirit had heard his thousands of prayers for freedom and answered.

He gazed around his small cell and mentally took inventory of his possessions. How could a man accumulate so much, even in prison? He made plans to bring in boxes and pack everything he didn't need on a daily basis. He would ship it to his mother's address for safekeeping until he could reclaim it.

Luke had done enough research during his time of incarceration to know that he'd need a solid job to show to the parole board before the release would come.

Thinking about Darlina and her little house in Shreveport, he prayed for answers. He didn't know anyone there except Darlina. How could he have a promise of a job from someone he'd never met? On the other hand, he hated for Darlina to have to uproot the children from a life they'd settled comfortably into to join him elsewhere.

He wrote letters that day to his mom, brother and to Darlina. His nephew, Gary, had opened a sign constructing business in Coleman. Perhaps his brother's son could provide a solid job offer that the parole board would accept.

The urgency to get all of his ducks in a row grew.

Luke gave a lot of thought to the recording studio on the third floor. In many ways, it seemed like his baby and as he had done his own children many years ago, he would have to leave it.

He had to find someone who was interested enough in it to learn how to use and respect the equipment.

Sitting in front of the console and mixing board, he looked around the room, taking in every detail. This room reflected many hours of his blood, sweat and tears. He ran through the list of men who had been through the doors and used the facility to record their music. Who could he trust to carry it on when he was gone?

It almost seemed like an answer to prayer when the door swung open and Russell McIntyre ambled in. "Hello, Luke, what's up, man?"

"Hey, Russell. Good to see you. Got a new song to record?"

"Nah, nothing ready yet. Just thought I'd drop in and visit."

"Russell, I'm gonna get my parole very soon. I wanna teach somebody how to operate of this equipment before I go. Are you interested?"

"I don't know. I've never done anything like that. I just sing and play."

"I can teach you. It's not all that hard. A lot of it is common sense."

"I'd love to learn. It just might give me a new skill I could use once I get out of this shit hole."

Luke and Russell sat for hours as Luke went over every detail from how the equipment had to be connected to what each dial, slide and knob did.

Russell took notes and when it came time for the men to go to their cells for count, Luke felt they'd made some good headway.

Over the next several weeks, Luke dedicated a good deal of time to teaching Russell and letting him practice using the set-up. He felt fairly confident the man could successfully make a basic recording.

He hoped Russell would stick with it and carry on long after Luke was gone.

Many years ago Luke had learned that holding on to anything in prison was fruitless. Yet, it sliced him to the quick to think that the studio might go unused, or even worse, be dismantled when he was no longer there to tend it.

And there was not a doubt anywhere in his mind that he'd be leaving soon.

The days dragged by even slower than usual as Luke waited for his walking papers. Mr. Goffe had explained in his direct contact with Luke that these things take time and nothing happens overnight in the penal system.

So, Luke moved forward with the process of sending things to his mother. When the confirmation came from his nephew of a job offer, he broke the news to Darlina. As much as he hated to put more burdens on her, he desperately needed her to agree to leave Shreveport and join him in Coleman, Texas.

To his surprise, she didn't hesitate. She assured him she'd put her house on the market, quit her job and move to Coleman to get a household set up before he came home.

Tears of joy filled his eyes when she mailed him pictures of the wedding dresses she'd found on sale for the girls and the ivory lace gown she'd found for herself as well. He loved all three of his girls so much it hurt.

How could one man be so lucky? The way she jumped in with both feet without a minute's hesitation only cemented the proof of her love for him.

Their life together was about to start on a real level of daily living and not just in dreams and on paper.

***

Finally, the day they'd both waited patiently for arrived. Luke walked down the corridor leading to the room where he'd been summoned

Jan Sikes

for a meeting on the 28th day of June, 1985. He felt confident this would be about his release.

Hopes high, chin up and shoulders straight, he walked into the room.

The parole committee, made up of three men and one woman, sat behind a long wooden table and looked up when he entered.

"Mr. Stone, please have a seat." A man with horn-rimmed glasses urged.

Luke sat facing the group.

A woman, dressed in a navy tailored suit, spoke next. "Mr. Stone, we have some news for you that is going to make you very happy. We've received the paperwork from the Texas Penal System, granting you parole from the State of Texas in absentia."

Luke sucked his breath in audibly.

Another man with kind eyes sitting to the right of the woman offered. "This parole in absentia is a new thing and you are the thirty-seventh prisoner to be released under the new rule."

Luke had failed to notice the warden sitting at the very end of the table, but when he stood, Luke thought he saw a look of triumph on the warden's face. "Luke Stone, you've been an exemplary inmate in this penitentiary under my administration and it is with great pleasure that I give you these release papers."

Luke stood and strode toward the warden. "Sir, you have no idea how happy this makes me. I just want to say that I appreciate you, Mr. O'brien. You've always played fair with me." He shook the man's extended hand.

Mr. O'Brien gave Luke a stack of papers. "We need your signature on the first two pages. The rest are your copies to keep."

Tears filled Luke's eyes and he fought to keep his voice strong. He turned to the group seated at the table. "Thank you from the bottom of my heart. I've got a family waiting on me and I can easily make a promise to you here today that you'll never see my face again in any penitentiary."

They smiled at Luke. "You're done here, Mr. Stone. All the details are in the papers. We wish you the very best for your future."

Luke walked from the room, his heart beating fast. He all but ran back to his cell so that he could read over all the papers.

He was going home at last...home to Darlina and two little girls that needed a daddy...home to his aging mother and brother...home to his own children who were now grown with children of their own.

When he looked in the mirror, age showed in his face, graying hair and stooped shoulders. He was a far cry from the vital young man who'd played music all over the country, living a dream and doing what he loved. The years hadn't been kind to Luke Stone.

But, he had a strong back and willing hands so had no doubt he could carve out a whole new life for himself. Especially with a princess and two little girls who believed in him and loved him in spite of faults and imperfections.

***

On August 15, 1985, Luke walked through the massive doors and down the forty-two long steps he'd clumsily climbed almost fifteen years ago. He stopped at the gate and looked back at the forbidding forty foot walls and iron bars that had held him captive. Triumphantly, he acknowledged that they hadn't been able to keep him from his well-earned freedom.

He took a deep breath of air, of liberty into his lungs and with the back of his hand swiped at a tear that escaped.

He turned at the sound of someone calling his name.

Some members of the Sicilian family waited for him just outside the gates of the penitentiary in a limo. They drove him to an apartment in Kansas City, where they offered him anything he wanted to celebrate his release. He turned down women, drink and drugs, but gladly filled his belly with a t-bone steak the size of the plate it sat on.

With a short styled haircut and civilian clothes, he hardly resembled the convict that had been locked in a cage for years.

He gave most sincere and deep thanks to the Great Spirit.

It was time to go home. He couldn't wait to hold Darlina in his arms.

He vowed to never let her go.

Not even in death would they be separated. He'd never been so sure of anything in his entire life. Together they'd beat the odds.

The constant North Star of their undying love had carried them over insurmountable obstacles.

He'd survived sickness, heartbreak, loss, solitude and deprivation. He'd witnessed murders, beatings, rapes, junkies stabbing their arms over and over again with a straight pen, homosexuals openly engaged in sexual activity, men sinking deep into depression to finally end their own lives and others getting their jollies in every perverse behavior possible.

And in the midst of all of the negativity, he'd found a way to be positive, creative and productive. He'd instilled hope in others.

He was leaving prison flat broke with nothing but willingness and a promise to work hard for his family. Even though it wouldn't be easy, he embraced the challenge.

His heart beat strong and true for Darlina Flowers, as strong and true as hers did for him.

Nothing would ever separate them again. He'd make sure of that.

August 16, 1985, Luke Stone left Kansas City on a Greyhound bus bound for Texas and the woman who held his heart. The sweet victory of freedom renewed his battered spirit.

THE END

~About the Author~

Jan Sikes started writing when she was a young girl, around the age of eight. Her first writing was a gospel song. She had an uncle whom she loved dearly, but he was an alcoholic and his drinking caused such family discord that at times, resulted in him being banished from their home. So, she wrote a song about Uncle Luke finding Jesus. That is her first memory of feeling the passion deep down to her toes for writing.

The stories she writes (so far) are true stories about the journey of two people moving through adversity in order to grow and learn to become better humans. She believes with all her heart there is something that is worthy of sharing in these stories. Bits and pieces of wisdom, hard-learned lessons and above and beyond all, love…True love that you read about in fiction stories and yet this is truth. The old saying that *truth is stranger than fiction* fits the stories that she shares through her writing.

She is passionate about her writing projects and is driven to tell a story with the hope that it might touch someone's heart or life in a positive way.

She also releases a music cd of original songs along with each book that fits the time period of the story. Why? Because the stories revolve and evolve around a passion for music.

She is widowed, lives in North Texas, attends music festivals and has four incredible grandchildren.

www.jansikes.com

www.ingramcontent.com/pod-product-compliance
Lightning Source LLC
Chambersburg PA
CBHW060153260626
47160CB00001B/245